Pamela Deakin graduated from London University and enjoyed a successful advertising career in London during the booming 1960s. In 1967 she moved permanently to live in Ibiza where she and a partner produced the first foreign language newspapers on the island. In 2009 she was awarded the MBE for her cancer charity work.

Dedication

In memory of Jack, who shared his wife with a computer, and Mashe, who first thought it possible.
To Barbara and Nigel, who provided much needed encouragement.
To Jonathan, Libi, Theo, future grandchildren and all my family and friends for making my life wonderful.

Pamela Deakin

THE POWER OF LOVE

AUSTIN MACAULEY
PUBLISHERS LTD.

A CIP catalogue record for this title is available from the British Library.

ISBN 978 184963 962 0

www.austinmacauley.com

First Published (2014)
Austin Macauley Publishers Ltd.
25 Canada Square
Canary Wharf
London
E14 5LB

Printed and bound in Great Britain

Acknowledgments

I would like to thank all the kind people and institutions who helped in the preparation of this novel, and in particular for their invaluable assistance:

The Imperial War Museum, The British Museum and Bosky – both the man and the yacht - for help and inspiration.

Love so Amazing

Hymn by Isaac Watts

*The course of true love never did
run smooth.*

A Midsummer Night's Dream,
William Shakespeare

*It's love, it's love that makes the
world go round.*

Chansons National de France 4

Prologue

Ibiza, Spain. 3.11 a.m. Tuesday July 20th 1967

The growl of a powerful sportscar broke the black and silver silence of the hot still Mediterranean night. The gleaming vehicle streaked like a phantom down the long straight highway which stretched some ten miles from the east coast of the island to the west – a legacy from Roman invaders who had made Ibiza a strategic crossroads in their vast empire.

A pale crescent moon hovered low in the heavens, but a million stars, shimmering and glittering against the black velvet of the sky, radiated almost as much light as a full moon.

The driver of the open car, a lean young man with thick blond hair and a neatly-trimmed beard, sat alert but confident at the wheel of the Lotus. Well-acquainted with this narrow road – one of the few asphalt highways on the island and the main link between the two island centres, Ibiza Town and San Antonio Abad – he knew the chances of meeting an oncoming vehicle at that early hour of the morning were a thousand to one against. But he kept a wary eye open for any farm-cart which might pull out from the numerous tracks at the side. Although imaginative and fearless in his driving, he hated to be unduly reckless.

Exhilarated by the surge of the engine and the smooth response of the powerful car, he glanced at the girl at his side and smiled. Her sun-streaked hair streamed in the wind; her face glowed, her eyes gleamed with excitement. The magic of the night had obviously infected them both. Knowing their closeness of thought and mood, he felt sure she shared his own euphoria, relishing like him every new sensation – the radiant night-sky, the deserted road, the rush of hot air and the thrill of speed, as intoxicating as a fine wine.

The girl sensed his glance, placed her hand affectionately on his knee. She stared up again at the glittering night sky. Breathtaking, she thought, quite breathtaking! So many stars – so bright and clear, she could almost reach out and touch them. A sudden awesome feeling of splendid isolation enveloped her, as if the two of them were completely alone in the world, speeding towards some unknown destiny.

She turned eagerly to the young man, shouted above the roar of the engine and the fierce rush of air.

"Darling, there's not a soul about. Let's try to beat the six-minute record!" Ibiza's fast young set had already established a six-minute record for the fifteen kilometre stretch between the two town centres, but it was always open to challenge.

He grinned back at her, his teeth reflecting luminous white in the darkness.

"What about the timing?"

"I've already set my stop-watch at the starting point – it's become a habit!" She gave him a mischievous sidelong glance.

His foot was already to the floor, but the car, seeming to find some extra source of energy from their youthful excitement or the sparkling night air, sped at well over a hundred miles an hour down the gleaming stretch of road.

"Don't forget the bend at San Rafael!" yelled the girl, referring to the only curve on the otherwise straight highway.

"Don't worry, I know exactly the speed I can take that one."

The car flashed on, slowed marginally as it approached the sharp bend. Nearly round, the driver put his foot to the floor again, accelerating smoothly out of the turn.

A sharp explosive crack resounded like rifleshot through the still night air, swiftly followed by a fierce hiss. The car slewed wildly across the road. White-faced but deadly calm, the young man fought to regain control.

"A front wheel blowout!" he yelled to the girl. "Hold tight!"

He tried frantically to rectify the steering – breaking hard would only aggravate the skid. The car continued to lunge to the left. Despite the heat of the night, he felt suddenly ice-cold. His stomach churned wildly. The girl sat still as a statue, completely mesmerised by the speed of events, too terrified to utter a sound. Her sun-tanned face blanched with fear.

The car careered wildly down the road, bounced along a dry-stone wall. The slim dark shadow of a telegraph pole loomed suddenly in front of the bonnet. The girl managed a fierce squeeze of her companion's hand before everything went black.

Her scream pierced even the harsh strident sound of shattering metal and breaking glass. Its ghastly echo continued to reverberate through the still, starlit Ibiza night.

Then ... silence once again.

PART ONE

CATHERINE

She is not fair to outward view
As many maidens be;
Her loveliness I never knew
Until she smiled on me.
Oh! then I saw her eye was bright,
A well of love, a spring of light.

Hartley Coleridge

But to see her was to love her,
Love but her, and love for ever.

Robert Burns

Chapter 1

Ashfield, Hampshire, England. November 1924

"I'm very sorry, sir," said the doctor. His tone was non-committal, but his words had a devastating effect on the tall man with a military bearing who stood before him. "I'm afraid there were complications. The child survived only a few moments. I couldn't save her."

Charles Harvey reeled backwards in shock. Fear seized him. He felt it gnawing at his stomach like an animal. He hadn't known this kind of terrifying apprehension since his days in those dreadful French trenches. He was almost too frightened to ask the inevitable question.

"What ... what about my wife?" he stammered eventually, his sensitive grey eyes begging reassurance. "What about Denise?"

This time the doctor spoke more gently.

"Colonel Harvey ... I think you should go to your wife. She may not last very long ..."

Charles had already passed him. Long strides took him swiftly to his wife's side. The usually light, airy room was in semi-darkness and an evil, cloying smell stifled him. He knelt by Denise's bedside, searched for her hand. She looked very frail, completely spent; all colour had left her almost translucent skin. Yet her violet eyes, now dark and sunken, still reflected a fierce desire to live. They burned not only with fever, but with an inner determination.

"Denise, my love," Charles whispered. "Don´t worry – everything is going to be fine." How empty and trite the words sounded. Just when he so desperately needed the right words, they eluded him. He felt her hand tremble and her eyes searched his; they were feverish, but flashed suddenly with a strange ferocity.

"Charles ..." He leant close, but could scarcely hear her hushed words. Paradoxically, her faint French accent seemed more apparent. "Charles ... I love you. You – you know that, always. Remember, *mon cheri* ... always."

He nodded, unable to speak, realised he was holding his breath.

She closed her eyes, then suddenly opened them wide.

"Charles ... Catherine! Please look after Catherine." She smiled. For one brief moment it was almost the Denise he had always known. Then her violet eyes dulled. The feeble trembling of her hand faded away. He knew he had lost her.

The midwife sensed the moment and moved to his side. He heard the starched rustle of her uniform, smelt a sharp antiseptic odour mingle with the sweeter smell of death.

"Come along, sir – I'm afraid there is nothing more you can do." She added, gently, "She was a lovely lady, sir, and very beautiful. I'm so sorry."

Charles staggered out of the room in disbelieving despair. Sorry – everyone was sorry, but what had gone wrong? Surely it was all some terrible dream; but deep in his soul he knew it was only too real. How could he ever live without his adored Denise? He could, with reluctance, accept the loss of the yet-unknown baby who had just entered the world, only to leave it again with such ugly haste; but he was in no way prepared for the loss of his beloved wife.

* * * * *

Colonel Charles Harvey, a man of comfortable means, had been born into the gentry and a world war had accelerated his army promotions. True to his background, no expense had been spared during his wife's two pregnancies and confinements, which had been organised for his part with military efficiency and logistical precision. His wife had given birth in comfortable, well-equipped surroundings, with a capable nurse and fine doctor in attendance. Charles had expected everything this time to go without a hitch, as it had three years ago, when his first child, Catherine, was born. He had not bargained for the vagaries of nature, which at times confound the skills and expectations of man.

His wife's death left Charles distraught, practically demented. Never an extremely demonstrative man, he was, beneath a stern military veneer, sensitive and highly-emotional. He had adored his fascinating French wife. Since the moment he had set eyes on Denise Fortier during the war, in her native France, there had been no other person in Charles Harvey's world. His life had revolved around this petite Parisienne, a slip of a girl whom he found at times demure, at times utterly dazzling.

Denise Fortier had been orphaned as a child, but her delicate appearance belied a tenacity and strength of character which had come to the fore in the dark war years. An excellent scholar, her knowledge of languages had led her into the field of interpretation and liaison. It was in this role that Charles had met her. Charles's parents strongly disapproved of the match.

"A girl of no background, and French to boot!"

But Charles had made up his mind. He married Denise at the first opportunity and, disregarding the resulting family schism, never looked back From that day, his life had centred around his career and his wife; but most of all his adored young wife. Her death broke him.

* * * * * * *

Two weeks after Denise's death, Rawlings the butler slipped silently into Charles's study. His master sat slumped in a winged armchair. The deep-orange flames of a friendly fire leapt in the grate, reflecting brightly off the gleaming brass ornaments of the warm richly furnished room. A strong aroma of leather, cigars and wax-polish hung comfortably in the air. The panelled walls, soft furnishings and polished floors were all in shades of brown; yet the study never seemed oppressive, only essentially masculine. It was Charles's favourite room where he normally worked, read or enjoyed a relaxing cigar. But not any longer. He now sat gazing morosely in front of him, taking no pleasure from his surroundings, his eyes dull and vacant. His long, solid body, normally taut and straight even in moments of relaxation, slumped awkwardly in the chair, adding years and pounds to his appearance. His normally neat brown hair and immaculate moustache had grown ragged and unkempt.

Rawlings stepped silently across the deep carpet.

"Is there anything I can get you, sir?"

Charles stirred but continued to stare into the distance.

"No ... no thank you, Rawlings."

The butler noticed that even Charles's deep voice had lost its former resonance. Before his mistress died, Rawlings would never dare to venture into the master's study, unless he had been called. But now he knew Charles would never ring for him – just sit alone for hours in heavy, oppressive silence. From time to time, Rawlings made it his business to look into the study. On occasions, he even went so far as to pour Charles a whisky-and-soda without being asked. Not that this was much help – the drink was invariably left, untouched, on the table.

Mrs. Philips, the cook, complained continually that the master was scarcely eating.

"He has the appetite of a sparrow. It's just not right, Mr. Rawlings. I can understand the poor man mourning. But this just isn't natural – him taking it so hard. And the poor little girl, never a word to his daughter, and her suffering just as much as him. If he's not careful, he'll end up in the same place as his wife!"

That evening Rawlings studied the colonel intently. Could Mrs. Philips be right? Was it possible for someone to die of a broken heart? Stuff and nonsense, he would have said, before the mistress passed away. But now, before his eyes, this lion of a man was just wasting away, and him, someone he respected, a real gentleman who was much more to him than an employer.

Colonel Harvey and his lady had always treated him with fairness and kindness – an appreciative word here, a gift for his children there. Mind you they knew a good worker when they saw one; but all the same, he knew he had had a good run for his money in this household. Besides, it irked him to see a good man run to waste. Then there was that daughter of his; only three years old and no mother, and as things stood at the moment, no father either.

Rawlings decided it was time to act. He coughed his habitual discreet cough.

"Excuse me sir, I hope I'm not intruding ..."

Charles looked at him, absently. The colonel's face was bland, his eyes expressionless. Even sadness seemed to be strangely missing from his empty gaze.

"Well, sir, – if you'll pardon me, sir, – I know it's not my business, but it's about Miss Catherine, sir."

"Catherine?" Charles looked puzzled. Rawlings could see his master desperately trying to pull his thoughts together, to return to the everyday world. "What's the matter, Rawlings? Is Catherine ill?"

"Not ill, sir, at least, not in the way you mean, but she's sorely upset, keeps sobbing in her room. The nurse says she refuses to believe her mother's dead. She badly needs you to talk to her, sir. She needs some kind of comfort, you see. She's really just a babe. I think you should speak with her, sir ... if you don't mind me saying so."

Rawlings drew a deep breath. It had been a long speech for him, especially to his employer, and he had never been good with words. Had he gone too far? Had Charles understood what he was trying to say?

Colonel Harvey was silent. Then with a long sigh he raised himself from the armchair. He straightened his back.

"Thank you, Rawlings," he said very slowly. "Would you go now."

"Certainly, sir. I hope I haven't spoken out of place." He slipped quietly from the room.

Tears started to trickle down Charles's face. He hadn't cried since he had been a small boy, but it was a cleansing, cool relief. Then guilt washed over him. He realised he had been so wrapped up in his own desolation he had quite forgotten his little girl; he had even ignored Denise's last request to look after Catherine. Charles's innate self-discipline started to reassert itself. Impatiently he combed his fingers through his thick brown hair. How was he to organize the future care of his daughter? His grey eyes narrowed with concentration. What could he do with Cathy? She obviously needed a woman's care, but not that infernal, cold-fish nurse. He himself had neither the ability nor the inclination to look after a three-year-old. What Cathy needed was life among a real family, not in this shell of a home with no Denise. But where? Estranged from his parents since his marriage to Denise, Charles had only one other living relative – his sister, Annie. The lives of both of his brothers had been wiped out in that horrific slaughter of a generation which people had called the Great War. Annie, a brittle, high-spirited and egocentric girl and her equally self-indulgent young husband, epitomised the younger generation of the frenetic twenties. Charles could envision no help from that quarter as far as his young daughter was concerned. His sister and brother-in-law were far too involved in their own social whirl and frenzied pleasure-seeking.

Then he remembered Nanny Hoskins. Of course! That was the answer. Nanny Hoskins had been Charles's own nanny. Employed by his parents, who had themselves been raised in stern Victorian households, Nanny Hoskins had played out the part of a gruff disciplinarian. She had known what was expected of her. But her kindly soul and affectionate nature couldn't be denied. All the children in her care had adored 'Old Hosky' and Charles still had a very soft spot in his heart for his former nanny.

* * * * * *

So it was Nanny Hoskins who came to his rescue – just as she had done so many times before, in his more tender and vulnerable boyhood. 'Hosky' was delighted to take on this new charge; to abandon her lonely retirement. Though greyer, plumper and less agile than in the years of Charles's youth, she was still the same old Hosky he remembered – as warm and dependable as ever. Cathy took to her almost immediately and Charles felt a great weight lifted from him.

But he still could not come to terms with his bereavement. He treated his young daughter with kindliness and gentleness – he was sensitive enough to appreciate that she, too, had lost the person most dear to her. But he could never feel really close to Cathy, nor show her the deep, warm affection he had felt for

Denise. That part of his character had been cut out, as if by the same surgeon's knife which had failed to save his young wife's life.

Within a year of Denise's death, Charles was offered a posting abroad. With a strange hunger and yearning for he knew not what, he readily accepted. He desperately wanted to flee the scene of his loss, his inconsolable loneliness.

Guiltily he had to admit to himself that there was another more unworthy reason. He had caught himself staring at Cathy, resenting the fact that she favoured himself in looks, rather than her mother. Cathy had little of Denise's delicate and petite style of beauty. She was a robust child, dark like her mother, but with broader features; thick straight hair framed her face, in contrast to Denise's fine, gentle curls. His daughter's firm, straight nose bore no resemblance to the finely-chiselled, slightly upturned nose of her mother. Most of all, Cathy's grey-blue eyes lacked the violet, velvet depths of those of his beloved wife.

Charles knew he was behaving irrationally, expecting Cathy to develop into a carbon copy of her mother. It was unreasonable and completely unfair to his daughter. He had to learn to love and accept her for herself, not as a substitute for his wife. He hoped that an enforced period of separation would enable his emotions to become reconciled with reality.

So he fled to India. Cathy would not see him again for another three years.

Chapter 2

Ashfield, Hampshire, England. September 1934

Cathy Harvey sighed as she laid back on the velvet stretch of lawn. Anxiety and uncertainty about her future had roused the butterflies in her stomach again. Nervously she fingered the grass. It was that fresh lush shade of green which can normally be found only in England and in springtime; but September had arrived and though the afternoon felt pleasantly warm, she sensed in the freshening breeze the cooler air of fast-approaching Autumn. It matched and kindled her own mood of apprehension.

How quickly the summer always passes, she thought to herself. She had reached the great age of thirteen and tomorrow would start her first term at boarding school. She had avoided thinking about it as long as possible. But now her new future loomed alarmingly near. It was impossible to force her fears and misgivings once more into the background.

If only there were someone she could talk to and confide her innermost thoughts. Hosky was a dear – really wonderful. Cathy adored her kindly old nanny. But she longed for company of her own age-group, a member of her own family, someone she could laugh and play with, chat to in bed and exchange girlish confidences. How wonderful it would be to have a sister!

Catherine Harvey had always wanted a sister. She should have had a younger sister, just three years her junior, but the birth of that child had proved to be a double tragedy for Cathy. She lost not only her longed-for sister, but her beloved mother. It left an emotional void in her young life. Memories of her mother, though often vague and without form, were nevertheless heart-wrenching.

Cathy had been too young to remember the delicate features of her mother's face, but she vividly recalled the warm sensations she associated with her. She had been cocooned with love during her infant years, perhaps – she thought – because her mother had been an orphan herself deprived of parental love. Denise had lavished affection on her daughter and Cathy's first three years of life had been almost idyllic.

She could still recall her mother's delicate perfume; her soft, sensitive hands; the low voice which had crooned to her in musical French during their more intimate moments. Her father had spoken proudly of his wife's excellent command of English, her charming French accent. But alone with her baby, her mother had often allowed herself the luxury of her native tongue. Perhaps that was why Cathy found French such an easy, comforting language.

She wished her father would speak to her more often about her mother, but on the rare occasions she saw him and when the subject was raised, a strange dead look would come over his face; his eyes would darken and Cathy would hastily change the subject. She hated to see her father sink into that black mood of melancholy which cut him off from her completely. Just occasionally, his face would light up with memory. Then he would talk about her mother with love and animation. But the mood wouldn't last long. Cathy had become adept at leading him quickly to another topic – before the black mood returned.

She stirred, restlessly, in the cool grass. Turning onto her stomach, she impatiently shook back her dark hair, cupped her hands beneath her chin. Her grey-blue eyes scanned the soothing country scene. Ironically enough, her anxiety and melancholy mood were in complete contrast to the tranquil setting.

She adored the countryside and had wanted to relish these last moments at home. She lay quite still, listening to the musical sounds of nature itself: the breeze whispering in the large oaks, the hum of insects, the liquid lilt of the birds. In the distance, beyond the lawn, stretched the daisy-strewn meadow and sprawling paddock. Amber, her pony, now getting on in years, still showed signs of friskiness as he gambolled in the lush pasture. A tender smile lit Cathy's face. Amber had been a gift from her father for her sixth birthday.

"Cathy dear, it's teatime!"

She looked over her shoulder to see the plump form of Hosky trudging slowly across the lawn in her direction. Her old nanny puffed and panted as she came nearer, but her lined face was split in a wide smile. Cathy knew Hosky was desperately trying to disguise her own anguish at their forthcoming separation. She felt a sudden rush of love for the warm-hearted old lady, who had tried so hard to fill the gap in her life.

"Come along, dear. I've made some lovely fresh scones and there's home-made strawberry jam and cream to go with them."

"I'm sorry, Hosky, I just don't feel very hungry, my tummy's all knotted inside."

Hosky's pale eyes softened.

"You'll soon feel better with some good food inside you."

Typical Hosky! A hot glass of milk, a good meal or a warm bath were the always the answer to every problem. Did she really understand what leaving Ashfield meant to Cathy?

"I can't help it, Hosky. I shall miss all this so very, very much. What happens if the school turns out to be absolutely dreadful and all the girls complete ogres?"

"It's a wonderful school, my dear. You visited Pinewood yourself. You know how lovely the grounds are, and the headmistress seemed delightful. I'm sure all the new girls will be feeling as shy and lonely as you, so it should be easy to make lots of nice friends."

"Hosky, you're such a comfort! What shall I do without you?" Cathy's sniff was verging on a sob, when Hosky delved into her ample apron pocket and withdrew a bulky letter, bearing familiar foreign stamps.

She beamed at Cathy.

"Perhaps this will help you feel better."

Cathy's face immediately lit up.

"It's from father, isn't it?" She could scarcely stop herself snatching the envelope from Hosky's hands. She pressed the letter to her lips and sped off across the lawn to the house, to the seclusion of her own room. It was her habit to read her father's letters from India all alone, relishing every piece of news, each little comment. She would carry the letter around with her for the next few days, frequently pulling it out to read all over again.

"My dearest Cathy," the letter began. *"I am hoping that this will reach you before you start your new life at school. I shall be thinking of you, my dear, and beg you not to be too worried about your new future. You are academically bright enough to fare well in your studies. I have always received excellent reports from your governesses, and trust this will continue in your new academic life.*
"Be diligent and attentive, my dearest; work hard at your studies and enjoy the new opportunities for happiness and friendship which your school will provide.
"I am sorry I cannot be there with you, to support you at this important cross-roads in your life, but I have every confidence in my daughter's good sense and strength of character. I am sure that you will make the best of your opportunities, and always carry your family name with pride and responsibility."

The letter continued with news about her father's recent activities, but most of the narrative was in the form of anecdotes which, as always, were full of interest and local colour. When writing about his beloved India, her father's normally rather stilted prose waxed eloquent and dramatic. Cathy could almost smell the exotic scents, taste the strange flavours. His colourful images brought him closer to her than any endearments ever could. She could let her imagination run riot and fantasise that she was out there with him.

She needed to feel his presence in spirit, if not in fact. Since Charles's posting to India, Cathy had seen little of her father. He had been home on leave just three times, but those precious days spent with him had been the highlights of her childhood experience. Together they had visited London: its beautiful parks, zoos, enthralling museums and picture galleries, its royal pageantry. During his last visit, her father had taken her to see the ballet, *Swan Lake*. And on a later occasion they had both exulted at the glorious melodies of Bizet's *Carmen* at the Royal Opera House in Covent Garden. Cathy had been overwhelmed, not only by the music, but by the spectacular settings and costumes and the breath-taking grandeur of the opera house itself.

At first, her father had been reserved with her, somewhat ill-at-ease; but as they spent more time together and as Cathy grew older, he came to understand her better. She sensed a change in the relationship between them. He seemed more relaxed in her company, laughed more readily. They started to share 'secrets' with each other.

"Cathy, my little one, remember ... this is our secret," her father would say, and Cathy would nod her head emphatically, giggling with the fun of it all. It was wonderful to share something with her tall, handsome father, a secret which only they knew about. It was usually some silly or poignant little moment, like the time Cathy had stood by and watched while her father rescued a little bird. The fledgling had fallen from its nest. His strong hands had gently caressed the tiny creature, before he had climbed the old oak tree and gently deposited it back in its nest. Had he known that Cathy adored birds?

Another time, they had been crossing the stepping-stones on the meadow stream. Her father had overbalanced and ended up with two wet feet and both boots full of water. Cathy had dissolved into laughter. Her father joined in and they giggled about it the rest of the day, making sidelong, knowing glances in the direction of Nanny Hoskins. Hosky became more suspicious every minute. But it was THEIR secret, something Cathy could hug to herself and relish in lonely moments.

She took a toffee from her bedside drawer, chewed it slowly, relishing the reading of the letter, wanting to make it last as long as possible. It was a lovely long letter this time. She drew her knees up to her chest, eagerly scanned the next flimsy page. When she reached the final paragraphs, her heart began to pound.

"Now, dear daughter, here is the best news of all. In three months I shall be back in England. We shall be able to celebrate Christmas together and all your school holidays. Cathy dear, one day I may be able to explain why I have spent so much of my life away from you. I know this must not continue. I have realised, very tardily, that my place is with you. You have been alone too long. I know I have failed both you and your mother in not fully accepting my responsibilities as far as you are concerned. More important, I love you and miss you very much.

"I have two more years to serve in India, but then I shall be coming back to live in England permanently. I am afraid our life-style will have to change somewhat; during my absences, my investments have not been going so well. As you know, the world depression has left few people unscathed, and my pride will not allow me to claim my share of what remains of the family inheritance. You are aware that, through an accident of birth, my parents despised your wonderful mother and disowned me, their only remaining son. Nevertheless, don't worry, dear Cathy, we shall be able to live quite comfortably.

"Before my final return, my solicitors will organise the sale of the Hampshire estate and the purchase of a comfortable flat in London. I know you love the countryside, but you have always enjoyed our visits to the city. I am sure we can have a wonderful life together – until, of course, some handsome young man scoops you up! Then I can look forward to a brood of wonderful grandchildren to keep me busy in my old age!

"Good luck, Cathy, my darling Cathy. God bless you. I shall be with you soon.

"Your loving father."

Cathy's heart sang. Just a few months and her father would be home. More important, in two years they would be together for ever, with no more tearful partings. She felt so happy, she thought she must burst. All her fears for the future disappeared, like a mist evaporating in the warmth of the rising sun. Now she could face the prospect of her new life at school with hope and optimism. How wonderful it was to be alive!

She clasped the letter to her and scampered downstairs to the dining room and to Hosky. She couldn't wait to tell her the great news.

* * * * * * *

That night, she was so excited and happy she couldn't sleep. Feeling suddenly ravenously hungry, she stole from her bedroom to fetch some milk and biscuits from the downstairs kitchen. Passing Hosky's bedroom, she could hear faint sounds from the other side of the stout, panelled door.

Whatever was happening? Was Hosky ill? She put her ear to the door. Sobs, she realised; Hosky was crying! Cathy remembered the number of times she had sobbed herself to sleep, only to be suddenly aware of the warm, comforting presence of her devoted nanny.

She knocked softly on the door and slipped into the bedroom. The plump form huddled beneath the blankets, seemed suddenly more frail and very vulnerable. With a shock, Cathy realised that now their positions were reversed. Hosky needed her comfort, her strength. She had relied on Hosky so long and taken her presence for granted. She hadn't stopped to imagine how her nanny must be feeling now her young protégée was going off to school, knowing Charles would be returning soon to take over the care of his daughter.

How awful it must be, Cathy thought, to be old and lonely. She herself had known loneliness, but always there had been a hope for the future and, of course, the reassuring presence of Hosky. Cathy vowed, there and then, that she would always take care of her old nanny; that her loving companion would always be a part of their family, even when her father returned.

"Hosky," she whispered in the darkness. "It's me, Cathy. Please don't cry. I'll never leave you alone. Your home is always here with us."

Elizabeth Hoskins looked up at her through her tears. For the first time, Cathy saw her as she really was – not her warm, dependable protector, but a sixty-eight-year-old spinster, about to be left alone.

"Hosky ..."

"Cathy, my dear, don't worry about me. I'm being a stupid old lady. I'm sad because I'm losing you ... because I shall miss you so very, very much. But I'm also crying because I'm happy."

Cathy frowned in puzzlement.

"Yes, my dearest." Hosky smiled her gentle smile. In the dim light, her lined face suddenly looked far younger. "I'm happy because I think your dear father has found himself at last. I'm sure you both have a wonderful, bright future ahead of you." She brushed the tears from her tired eyes. "Aren't I a silly old thing! Fancy crying about such a lovely prospect."

Cathy felt the prickle of tears in her own eyes.

"No, Hosky, you're an absolute dear, and I shall always love you." She kissed her gently on the cheek. "Come along, no more tears. Everything from now on is going to be absolutely splendid!" She hugged her tightly.

"I know, my dear. You'll love your new school and soon your father will be home for the holidays. Then you can plan your new life together. Everything will be perfect."

But even as she hugged the child she adored, Hosky managed to keep her slightly arthritic fingers firmly crossed.

Chapter 3

London, England. April 1940

A dark-haired young girl, smartly dressed in the dark-blue uniform of the recently-formed Women's Auxiliary Air Force, strode with a light but purposeful step along a footpath in St James's Park.

Spring had arrived, she thought, but the day though fine felt chill. She stared around her as she walked, her face flushed by the gentle exercise. Her gaze fell on some young children frolicking in the grass and a smile lit up Cathy's blue-grey eyes, disguising for a moment the sadness which lingered in their depths. She loved lunchtime in St James's. Despite the usual bustle of the city during that hour of the day, an aura of calm and leisure prevailed in the popular West End park. It was a favourite place of escape for city dwellers and workers living in the tense, confused atmosphere of scepticism and expectancy induced by the 'phoney war'. She feared the nation would soon be involved in a bitter battle for its very survival, but in the meantime St James's seemed unchanged and at peace with the world. Mothers and nannies wheeled babies in prams, old people strolled along, sniffing the fresh air, office workers sat on park benches munching sandwiches or lazed on coats stretched across the slightly-damp grass.

Leslie Bourne spotted her from across the park, saw how she drew appreciative glances from other passers-by. Yet he had to admit she wasn't outstandingly beautiful. Catherine was of average height and build, in fact a little on the plump side. But, he thought to himself, she carried herself well. Her body was well-proportioned, with good breasts and hips and a neat waist. Beneath the smart peaked WAAF cap, her thick, dark-brown hair was rolled in the fashion of the day. As she drew nearer, he tried to analyse her appearance dispassionately. Her broad even features were unremarkable, but good cheek bones, clear frank eyes, and a sensitive, disarming smile gave her instant appeal.

She waved as she spotted him and her whole face lit up. He realised the most striking aspect of Cathy Harvey was the aura that surrounded her; a natural cheerfulness and vivacity shone through like a breath of fresh air. She radiated good humour and a pure joy of living, unusual amid the cynicism dominating these tense, artificial times. He had watched her many times without her knowing; observed how her unassuming manner enabled her to communicate at any level. She had an intuitive knack of instantly sympathising with other people's feelings and moods. As a friend had remarked to him: 'A few minutes in Cathy's company are a tonic for anyone!'

He would have loved to jump up, run over to meet her, but instinctively knew she wasn't yet ready for such an obvious display of emotion.

Leslie had known her since she was fifteen and he twenty; but he was finding it difficult to convert their long-standing, easy friendship into a more romantic type of relationship. He adored Cathy, had been in love with her for as long as he could remember, but he sensed that the warmth and fondness she felt for him had not as yet matured into anything beyond sisterly affection.

"Leslie, you've beaten me to it again!" She laughed as she bounced down on the seat beside him. "One day I'm determined I shall get here first."

He smiled tolerantly. Punctuality wasn't one of Cathy's strong points. But he knew she really looked forward to their regular lunchtime meetings when she had a forty-eight hour leave from work. He also knew why. He was a link with her past: a consistent, enduring factor in her, at times, topsy-turvy world.

"I feel so safe and secure when I'm with you, Leslie," she had told him one day. "You're so down-to-earth, so dependable and practical about everything, and such a good friend."

A good friend! That was true. He would always be there for Cathy to lean on, as he had been in the past. He wished he were a more handsome, swashbuckling kind of fellow, who could sweep her off her feet. He was only too aware of his lean, narrow face and long, gangling frame. He found his lofty height an embarrassment rather than an asset, and stooped slightly, as if to bring himself down to the level of normal mankind.

"You're looking in great form, Cath. Here, have one of my sandwiches. I've got far too many and it's your favourite – cheese with lots of pickle." He tried to sound nonchalant and light-hearted, not too adoring. "How's everything at Flight Ops?"

"Tremendous, but exhausting – we're really snowed under."

He smiled at her WAAF slang. Phrases like 'snowed under', 'cheesed off' and 'cadging' had started to litter Cathy's previously immaculate English. Then he noticed the traces of strain on her face, the sadness in her eyes, but just as quickly, she was smiling once again. She helped herself to one of his sandwiches, then withdrew her own lunch-pack from her leather shoulder bag.

"Sorry, Leslie, I really don't feel up to talking much. Tell me about your week."

He did, appreciating again her understated sympathy and understanding. He could always talk easily to Cathy and found it really helped. Working in a hush-hush section of military intelligence, he was unable to discuss in detail his workaday problems with anyone outside the department. Cathy never probed too far, but seemed able to glean from his general chatter when he was particularly worried or depressed. Somehow she seemed to sense his mood and cheer him in an almost imperceptible way. All he knew was that after an hour in her company, his batteries were recharged, his spirits reanimated.

"I thought tonight we might go to a concert at the Albert Hall," he ventured. "Perhaps finish off with a good hot curry at the Taj Mahal."

"That would be super! You're making me feel hungry again. Oh Leslie, just look at those pigeons stealing that chap's sandwich. I can't believe how cheeky they can be. I've a sparrow at the flat and every morning he comes tapping with his beak on my window. He won't give up until I provide him with some breakfast!"

"He recognises you for the softie you are. These birds aren't stupid, you know." He saw a shadow flit swiftly across her face – there one moment, gone the next. "What's troubling you, Cath?" he asked more softly. "You're not your usual self."

"Oh, it's just the 'phoney war', I think. The future seems so uncertain, and I hate not being able to plan ahead. Heaven knows what we shall all be doing this time next year." She stared at him with troubled eyes. "Do you really believe this war will soon be over, Leslie? I have nightmares that we shall all end up as just another part of Nazi Germany."

It was a common fear at the time, but Leslie knew that in Cathy's case it was probably worse. Her childhood, with its tragic moments, had left her especially vulnerable. She longed more than most young people for stability and security, not in the economic sense, but the mental security of knowing what she could expect of her future. The loss of her mother when she was a child, her father's absences abroad and his tragic death had left her apprehensive of what further surprises fate might have in store for her. Knowing so well her feelings in this respect, it amazed him that she remained so apparently cheerful and optimistic. He was sure nobody else, other than Hosky of course, was aware of Cathy's innate feelings of insecurity.

"Are you sure it's just the war, Cathy? You don't normally let it get you down." He saw her melt a little at the softness of his tone, his obvious sympathy. Tears shone in her blue-grey eyes.

"Leslie, I'm so sorry. I shouldn't always burden you with my problems and silly sentimentality. But ... do you remember what day it is today?"

He did, and inwardly cursed his insensitivity and fickle memory. It was the anniversary of her father's death and, incidentally, the start of their own deep friendship.

He and his family had lived in Ashfield, the same village as Cathy. During his vacations from university, Leslie would often come across her at the village store when she was home on holiday from boarding school, or see her cycling or riding her pony along the country lanes. He had discovered she was only fifteen, but had been impressed by her maturity, her cheerful smile and kind words for everyone with whom she came into contact.

He remembered the first day they had really started talking. In his usual clumsy way, he had quite literally bumped into her in the village shop, nearly knocking her off her feet. Blushing and inwardly cursing himself, he stammered his apologies, but Cathy's wide smile and twinkling eyes immediately made him forget his embarrassment – he was always shy with girls. Soon they were laughing together like old friends.

Then there had been the day he had seen her cantering wildly along the lane outside his house. Normally Cathy rode the narrow country roads at a sedate trot. He had waved as usual, but she sailed passed him without a glance. But not before he had seen her haggard, tear-streaked face. He jumped astride his cycle and followed her to the meadow behind her house. He could still remember the sound of her sobs as he stole up to her. She had flung herself from her pony and was lying, face down, on the damp grass, her head in her hands. Amber stood untethered by her side, looking bemused, occasionally bending his chestnut head to nuzzle the shoulder of his mistress.

Her sobs seemed to wrack her whole body. For a moment he thought she would choke. He had never before seen anybody so convulsed in tears, her whole body heaving and trembling. He realised it was a very private moment for Cathy, but he found it impossible to leave her alone in such distressing personal agony.

He knelt by her side, lifted her face as tenderly as possible. Between convulsive sobs, the words came tumbling out in a torrent.

"It's my father ... in India ... they told me at the Post Office there was a telegram." She spoke the words with difficulty, her normal low, warm voice grown harsh and strangled. "I was so excited ... you see I thought it would contain the exact date of Father's arrival in England, but ... when I opened it ... it was just to say that he had been taken very ill and ... died quite suddenly." Her voice broke completely and it seemed an age before she continued. "Oh Leslie, I wasn't even there when he died. Now I shall never, never see him again ..."

She had paused a moment, then suddenly all the pent-up words came tumbling out. She told him all about her mother's death and her own lonely childhood. He learned of her adoration of her father, of Charles's growing love for his daughter, of his plans to return to live with her in England. She told him of her exciting life at boarding school, of the new friends she had made, and how her life had taken on a completely new meaning with the knowledge that her father would soon be back home with her.

Then that day, out of the blue and within weeks of his proposed return to England, had come the terrible news that he had suddenly been taken ill with some rare tropical disease, dying only a few days later.

The irony and tragedy of the situation hadn't been lost on Leslie. He realised Cathy's whole world had collapsed around her. How could so much misfortune befall such a delightful, innocent young girl? He reflected on his own straightforward life to date. That day he determined to put the world to rights – at least as far as Catherine Harvey was concerned.

Now exactly three years later in his delight at seeing her again he had forgotten the tragedy of that day. He felt Cathy's hand reaching for his own, gently rousing him from his memories. Her voice was scarcely more than a whisper.

"Leslie, why is life so cruel? All those wasted years when I scarcely saw my father, never got to know him as well as I should. And then for him to die – just when he was to come back to England."

He squeezed her hand affectionately – it was best to let her talk. She had obviously spent far too many years bottling up her feelings.

"If it hadn't been for you that day, and all the help you gave me, just being there and listening to me ... well, I don't know what I should have done. Somehow it was so much easier pouring out my troubles to someone who was practically a stranger. Poor old Hosky was so upset herself with the news – it just made it worse trying to talk to her."

"Cathy, my dear, please try not to dwell on it too much. I know it was absolutely dreadful, but you have to put the past behind you. You're a bright, attractive young lady – with your whole life ahead of you." He bit back his next words, stopped himself from adding that he would love her to spend that life with him.

"You're right, of course, Leslie. You always are. I know I dwell on my father too much, much more than my mother. You see, I never knew her as a real person, only as a vague, warm, comfortable memory. That makes it so different." She stared up at him, concern clouding her eyes. "Leslie, you don't believe I could be one of those women with a 'father complex', do you?" She dropped her eyes, nervously fingered her hair, then fidgeted with the paper bag which had held her sandwiches.

Leslie chuckled. One of the things he loved most about Cathy was her refreshing innocence, her utter lack of guile.

"Now don't start all that Freudian nonsense with me," he told her. "You're a perfectly healthy young woman – as normal as anyone I know. In fact – if you want to know – I think your personal tragedies have made you a much nicer, more sympathetic person."

"Leslie, you're a treasure." She gave a wide grin. "But also a great flatterer! I have a frightful temper, and as for the 'attractive' bit – I'm much too fat and very plain. And don't think I'm fishing for compliments!"

"Cath, you know I never lie. I'm far from being one of those suave, smooth talkers." He spoke softly, seriously, and saw a hint of alarm widen her eyes. She had been expecting a more light-hearted, flippant reply. Oh hell, I've done it again, he thought.

Cathy fumbled again with the paper bag, then crumpled it up, deposited it in the bin by the side of the park bench. She caught hold of his hand.

"Come on, Leslie. I think a good walk will send my shadows away."

Leslie ambled by her side, trying to adjust his long strides and loping gait to Cathy's neat, quick steps. He found himself wondering once again how long he could refrain from revealing his true feelings to this girl. She had become such a vital part of his life.

He was becoming more and more frustrated by the fact that the only physical contact he had with Cathy was the occasional swift, affectionate hug. Each meeting was increasingly difficult for him; he wanted to take her in his arms, tell her how much he loved her. He knew she was devoted to him, but he sensed her withdrawal whenever he departed from the role of the 'good, old friend'.

Yet, as far as he knew, Cathy had no other boyfriends, and never had had – other than very casual relationships. Was she perhaps right, that she did have a father fixation? Was she subconsciously searching for an older man, or was she still sexually and emotionally immature? Perhaps he should be more bold in his approaches; after all, despite her friendly nature, Cathy was rather shy with men. She had had little experience of the opposite sex during her tender eighteen years of life.

He decided that in future he would at least try the bolder approach. He only hoped it wouldn't frighten her away. He couldn't face the prospect of life without Cathy. Shuddering inwardly at the thought, he grasped her determinedly by the hand and they ran, laughing, towards the park gates.

Chapter 4

"Hi, Cath, you're late," called Vanessa from the kitchen as Cathy let herself into the flat.

"Hello, Nessie," she said, distractedly, her mind still on Leslie.

Her flat-mate glided into the living room. She looked radiant.

"You haven't been teasing poor old Leslie again, have you?"

Cathy blushed. She knew Vanessa was only joking, but despite her fondness for Leslie, Cathy was starting to realize that she might be leading him on. She preferred to leave Nessie's question unanswered.

"Did you have a good lunch?"

"Absolutely splendid!" said Nessie, with a gleaming smile.

"You look like the cat who's just swallowed the cream."

"I feel like it. I've just met the most fabulous young man!"

"Again?"

"Now don't spoil it, Cath. This one's absolutely super. I've invited him to the flat for supper, on our next leave. Why don't you invite Leslie and we'll make it a foursome?"

Cathy smiled. She was used to Vanessa's ravings about each new man she met. Nessie was extremely popular with the male sex. Her sheer animal magnetism and striking good looks would always assure her of all the male companionship she wanted; but she did tend to flit from one man to the other. Very few could hold her attention for long.

"So what's his name – this new Mr Wonderful?" she said, teasing. "You'd better put me in the picture before I slip up again." It was a joke between them that Nessie was supposed to write the name of her current flame on the grocery list hanging in the kitchen, or on the bed-post at their billet. That way Cathy avoided mixing up Nessie's constant flow of male companions and kept abreast of the current attraction.

"Oh, but this one's really special," enthused Vanessa. His name's James Proctor, but of course everyone knows him as Jimmy. He's a pilot and devastatingly good-looking – a real charmer. I even suspect he may be somewhat intelligent, which makes a change!"

"Oh Nessie, you're incorrigible."

"Yes, but at least there's never a dull moment when I'm around."

"That's true," grinned Cathy. "The flat hasn't been the same since you walked in. But I have to admit it – I like the change!" And she did.

When her father died so prematurely in 1937, he had left her, his only child, emotionally bereft but financially comfortably off. Cathy inherited a delightful London flat in a gracious Georgian mansion, situated in the pleasant and socially-recognised borough of South Kensington. He also left her an adequate income, which would have enabled her to lead a comfortable existence for the rest of her life, without the necessity to work.

But Cathy certainly wasn't the type to accept a life of idleness, especially in a time of war. She had joined the WAAF and was later posted to Fighter

Command Headquarters at Bentley Priory in Stanmore, Middlesex. Despite the pressures and strain of her work, she discovered a tremendous sense of satisfaction in the responsibilities and demands of the job. She also enjoyed the warm atmosphere of camaraderie which prevailed in the WAAF, making it so easy to make new friends.

Nessie was her closest girlfriend. Tall and red-headed, she went under the rather pretentious title of Vanessa Forbes-Smith. An exotic, superbly-sculptured female, she was as vivacious as a litter of puppies, as witty as Noel Coward in his hey-day, and at times as cutting in her bright sharply-honed remarks as a diamond edge.

When Cathy first met Nessie soon after joining the WAAF, she had been intrigued and amused, but on first impressions had decided that 'Volatile Vanessa' – as some of their less-kindly female colleagues had nicknamed her – was fun but superficial: plenty of froth, but very little substance. She admired her striking good looks and ready wit, but winced at the sometimes cruel edge of her clever tongue.

Then something between the two of them seemed to click – perhaps the very difference in their characters. Vanessa for some reason immediately accepted Cathy in her own right, grew to respect her and rarely used her as a sounding board for her caustic comments. Cathy in turn realised there was a sharp intelligence behind Vanessa's sardonic wit, as well as a competent, conscientious member of the WAAF.

Above all, she discovered a kinder, more thoughtful person beneath the slick exterior – when she chose to show it! Nessie spoke her mind without reservation. She wouldn't suffer fools or frauds; but having accepted a person as her equal – or superior – she then proved to be not only a delightful and amusing companion, but a warm, dependable friend. Perhaps, Cathy thought, this was partly due to the fact that on the few occasions she herself had suffered the sharp edge of Nessie's tongue, she had firmly but quietly replied in kind – much to Nessie's delight as well as chagrin.

It wasn't long before Cathy asked Vanessa to share her London flat with her during their leaves from Bentley Priory. The girls enjoyed a forty-eight-hour pass every month and a week's leave four times a year. Cathy had made it a free invitation – she knew Nessie was not terribly well-off – but to her credit, Nessie had insisted on sharing some of the costs. The partnership worked well. The previously lonely flat soon buzzed with conversation, rang with laughter. It became a focal point for other girls from their billet, for pre-war friends and, of course, a multitude of boyfriends. Their leisure hours were short but fun-packed.

"Tell me more about this chap, Jim," said Cathy.

"Jimmy," corrected Nessie.

"Well, Jimmy then. What does he look like? Tall, dark and handsome, I suppose?"

"Handsome, yes, but actually he's fair-haired, and really sexy!" Nessie's crimson mouth hardened a little. "He's obviously got quite a way with the women."

"You're a fine one to talk! Perhaps you've met your match at last."

"Cath, dear, haven't you learned? I'll never meet my match. If I did I'd shoot him on sight."

"If you shot him on sight, how would you know he was your match?"

"Don't quibble – you know what I mean. At any rate, he's most awfully charming – very softly spoken, but with a devil-may-care attitude to everything. I'm sure he takes nothing very seriously, so that suits me down to the ground."

"He's probably got to be like that if he's pilot," said Cathy, more seriously.

"Now don't go looking for the soft touch as usual, Cath. You've got to learn that most people have a hard streak. They're not all like you – soft as putty."

"I am not soft as putty," Cathy said, indignantly.

"No, I know you're not. You're really quite tough in your own way, thank goodness. But you do always expect the best from everyone, your best at any rate. I just hope you're not going to be badly disillusioned one day."

"I believe you get from people what you expect from them," said Cathy firmly.

"It depends on the person – take my word for it. But knowing you, Cath, you'll still see people through rose-tinted glasses and believe what you want to believe. Only experience will change that." Her eyes started to sparkle once again. "Now, what about next month's leave?"

"Isn't it a full week this time?"

"Yes it is. As I said before, I've asked Jimmy to supper on the Saturday night. Would you like to invite lovely lanky Leslie?"

Cathy hesitated.

"Well, actually I'm going out with Leslie tonight. I don't think it would be a good idea to have another tête-à-tête with him so soon, even though you two love-birds will be present."

"I think you're right, Cath. I'm afraid Leslie's very much in love with you. I gather you don't feel the same. Have you thought what you're going to do about it?"

"No, Nessie, I'm so muddled." She sat down on an upright chair, her ankles neatly crossed. She felt rather prim sitting like that, but could never bring herself to cross her legs. Hosky had always impressed on her that it was 'unladylike'. "You see, I'm so awfully fond of Leslie, I would hate to lose him. I enjoy his company, and he's always so dependable – always there when I need him. But I don't love him in a physical, sexual way. He's more like a wonderful, protective brother."

"Cath, you're using him as a prop. In the end it won't be fair to either of you. Be realistic, tell him exactly how you feel."

"Do you really think he's in love with me? After all we've been good friends for so long."

"Don't kid yourself, Cath. In any case I think you're right about the supper foursome. Wait a minute. Isn't your birthday around then? Why don't we make it a party, then there can be no misunderstandings."

Cathy's eyes lit up.

"Yes, that would be fun. We haven't had a properly organised party for ages. What about fancy dress?"

"Now don't get carried away. There just isn't the time to arrange a 'do' like that, to organise costumes and so on. Let's keep it simple."

"OK Food first. Something hot and tasty that we can prepare in advance. But promise you won't tell anyone it's my birthday."

As they started to discuss all the details, Cathy's delight grew. She adored parties. As a child it had been the one way she had met other children. As an adult she still felt the same excitement and anticipation. She loved the noisy gregariousness of the party scene, found it stimulating – yet at the same time comforting – to be surrounded by so many happy laughing faces. Then there was the fun of preparation. For a moment she forgot about her father, forgot about her situation with Leslie. She was so looking forward to their next leave!

* * * * * * *

It was raining hard when Cathy and Leslie reached the Indian restaurant later that night, but for her it had been a perfect evening. The concert had been enthralling. Mozart's 'Eine kleine Nachtmusik' had been the main item on the programme, and Mozart was her favourite composer. She loved the neat precision of his classical style; it was so fulfilling, so satisfying.

Cathy had never been able to come to terms with Beethoven, and the strong emotional appeal of the Russian composers frightened her in a way she couldn't explain. They seemed to open her very soul and leave it bare. She preferred the security of Mozart. Hours of childhood practice at the piano had made her familiar with all his work. Listening to Mozart was like returning to an old friend. How clever and thoughtful of Leslie to pick just the right music for her!

Their favourite Indian restaurant was the Taj Mahal in Glendower Place, not far from her flat. They were dripping wet by the time they arrived, especially Leslie; as usual in the rain, it had taken him ages to find a taxi. As he opened the restaurant door for her, she gazed fondly at the gangling young man feeling a strong surge of affection for him. His short-cropped hair was plastered down by the rain, but his deep-set brown eyes were attentive and reassuring.

He gave her a wide smile as she passed in front of him to enter the restaurant. His long thin aesthetic face was strong-boned and ageless. He didn't seem to have changed one iota since she had first met him. She could imagine him looking just the same in fifteen years time. Dear, dependable Leslie!

The cosy somewhat stuffy warmth of the Taj Mahal was in complete contrast to the damp cold outside, rich with the pungent aroma of curry spices. Cathy always loved these first magic moments when she entered an Indian restaurant. Her father had first introduced her to Indian food and ever since then, the enticing smells set her taste buds instantly twitching.

"Mmm ... blissful!" she said. "I could almost feed on the smell itself."

"Not you," replied Leslie. "Any minute now you'll start to salivate like a dog. Let's get some food inside you."

The waiter, recognising them both, led them to a reserved table for two in a quieter corner. Cathy gazed around at the familiar fading decor. The imitation red velvet around the walls was looking worn. Rather tawdry attempts had been made to reconstruct the opulence of an exotic East. Vague, repetitive strains of

Indian music reverberated faintly in the background. Was it genuine Indian music, Cathy wondered? However, the table-cloths were starched a crisp white and completely spotless; the service, as usual, couldn't be faulted. No wonder the Taj Mahal, renowned for its cheap prices and excellent value, was always busy.

Leslie ordered their usual favourites: rich Rogan josh, prawn curry, spicy Tarka dhal, plenty of pilau rice, crispy pappadums and light fluffy puris. And of course, their favourite chutneys and hot lime pickle.

They ate ravenously for the first few minutes, then chatted, in a desultory fashion between mouthfuls of food, about the history book Leslie was writing in his limited spare time. He had graduated from Oxford with a first in History and had been involved in research until the war had prompted his move to Military Intelligence. Both he and Cathy shared a common passion for the subject.

It was as they were enjoying their coffee that Leslie abruptly changed the subject. He coughed nervously, covered her hand on the table with his own long fingers.

"Cathy, I've been wanting to speak to you about this for some time now, but I didn't think you were quite ready. But now I have to tell you." His brown eyes met hers.

She stared at him, half-mesmerised, willing him not to utter the words she feared might follow.

"Cath, I might as well put it straight to you. I love you very much. I would do anything for you." He squeezed her hand and continued, hastily. "Please don't be alarmed. I know you're still very young ... and I think you look on me only as a friend. But I wanted you to know. I believe with time... knowing how I feel, you may grow to love me. Of one thing I'm sure – you need me."

The last few sentences were rather gabbled. Like a child, Cathy thought, reciting a much-rehearsed poem; but her heart swelled with tenderness for Leslie. His cheeks were flushed, but he sat upright, more proud and determined than she had ever seen him. She smiled an encouraging smile.

"You don't have to say anything at the moment," Leslie continued, more confident now. "I don't want to rush you. Just think about it. You have all the time in the world." He gave her a warm smile. "But I meant what I said about you needing me. I don't believe all this anaemic poppycock about loving without needing. Need is a vital ingredient of love."

"Yes, Leslie," she said simply. She had never known him so commanding. It made her feel unusually safe and secure – as if someone had placed a warm comforting blanket around her. How restful and reassuring it was to be loved and wanted. All her worries seemed suddenly less important.

They left the restaurant, hand in hand. She felt content inside, but suddenly very tired. Too much food and too much emotion, she thought.

"I won't come in," said Leslie in a gruff voice, as they arrived back at her flat. "We're both very tired." He leant forward to kiss her, and for the first time he kissed her properly – not just the usual peck on the cheek.

Cathy hadn't known what to expect. It was her first real kiss. She was surprised at how firm his lips felt, yet soft and sensual at the same time. His arms were strong around her and his lean body beneath her fingers was harder, more substantial than it looked. The world didn't turn over for her as she had read it might in some of her favourite historical romances. But the kiss was very sweet and she felt safe in his arms. Was this, she thought, the way love began?

Chapter 5

The party was in full swing.

Cathy glanced happily across the room to Nessie. Her flat mate gave her a conspiratory wink. They both knew it was going well. Above the rhythmic strains of Glen Miller, she could hear the social chatter. Lively and staccato, it had not as yet degenerated to that raucous stage where everybody talks and nobody listens. Several couples had already started dancing. A fragrant culinary odour filtered discreetly from the direction of the kitchen where a delicious boeuf bourguignon simmered gently on the hob.

Cathy had to admit that Nessie excelled at organising a party. Her flatmate had happily left the actual mechanics of food, drink and music in Cathy's capable hands though helping wherever possible, but when it came to compiling the guest list, Nessie came into her own. She had the knack of judging exactly the right party mix. The result was a perfect blend of contrasting personalities, an electric and stimulating atmosphere, but somehow the conflict of egos never degenerated to acrimony.

"It's easy," she told Cathy. "Start from a base of good close friends whom you know get on together, then add plenty of exciting new personalities. Give them plenty to eat and drink, lots of good music, and you can't fail."

She was right. Her wide range of acquaintances made it much easier.

Cathy gazed around her at the lively crowd – some service people, of course, but also actors, artists, dancers, writers, business executives, secretaries, several friends up from the country and some of Cathy's old school friends, She was glad to see that Leslie had as requested brought some of his close friends from Military Intelligence: the 'spies' Nessie loudly christened them when they arrived, causing embarrassed blushes and shuffles from the young men concerned.

She spotted Leslie, his light-brown hair smoothed down, his long form propped against the back of an arm-chair. He gave her a friendly wave and she smiled warmly back. She was glad to see him chatting happily with some of the girls from her Ops Room. He seemed to be mixing well. She had noticed a new self-confidence about him since that night at the Indian restaurant.

Then Nessie caught her eye again. She was indicating her watch and smiling, knowingly. Cathy realised Jimmy was due at any moment. He and several pilot friends had been unable to get away from their base at Duxford any earlier.

She decided she had better check on the food and get the rice underway. With difficulty she pushed her way past a very blonde girl talking animatedly to a rather plump balding young man who was immaculately and conservatively dressed. The girl looked decidedly Bohemian, her style of dress flamboyant, slightly outrageous – the result Cathy was sure of a studied attempt to look dishevelled and, above all, striking. What an odd combination, she thought with delight.

It was something she adored about parties – the unlikely matches that were stimulated, the intriguing snatches of conversation. It was like throwing a random selection of chemicals into a large bowl and watching the reaction: lots of bubble and sizzle, and sometimes a flame or two!

She was suddenly aware of a stir at the front door. Jimmy and his friends had arrived at last. She saw Nessie hurry over, but with the crush of people, she was unable to see who had come in.

Her flat-mate called to her. She edged through the crowd towards the door. Nessie's eyes were shining.

"Cath, I'd like you to meet Jimmy Proctor. Jimmy, this is Cathy Harvey".

Cathy caught her breath as she looked into penetrating tawny eyes. They seemed to look right through her, to read every thought in her mind.

"Hello, Cathy. So you're Nessie's flat-mate. I've heard a lot about you."

He spoke softly, his voice deep and cultured, every word perfectly enunciated.

She couldn't stop staring at him, knew instinctively that the eyes of every other female in the room were also on Jimmy. He was tall, lean and broad-shouldered with sleek dark-blond hair, his perfect teeth framed by a sensual mouth, now curved in a sardonic smile. Youthful regular features gave an overall impression of boyishness, yet she was paradoxically aware of the overwhelming sexuality which emanated from his body. She wanted to reach out and touch him. Nessie had been right. He was certainly handsome and charismatic – and he knew it!

She suddenly felt nervous and uncertain of herself, at a loss for words. He was obviously aware of her discomfort and the twinkle in his eyes seemed more mocking than friendly.

Embarrassed, she ran her fingers nervously through her hair.

"Nessie's told me a lot about you, too," she said lamely, adding hurriedly, "Can I get you a drink?" Anything, she thought, to get away from those eyes. He was visually undressing her! She suddenly regretted she didn't have Nessie's superb figure, felt uncomfortably aware of her own rather plump ankles, her nondescript hair compared to Nessie's vibrant auburn mane. Why hadn't she bought herself a new frock for the party?

She looked across to her flatmate for moral support but Nessie was laughing with Jimmy's friends. She tried to lower her gaze, but found she couldn't take her eyes from him. It seemed an age before he replied, but probably in that never-never land it was only a few seconds.

"Thank you, Cathy. I'd love a gin and tonic." Again that deep liquid voice which sent shivers down her spine. The teasing smile had changed to a youthful grin, but she noticed signs of strain around those worldly, compelling eyes. He took her firmly by the arm. "Let me help you. I know all my friends' favourite tipples."

He propelled her easily across the room, seeming to know instinctively where to find the drinks cabinet. Yet despite his confident exterior, even as she trembled slightly beneath the touch of his long lean fingers, she sensed a strange nervous current, a certain tautness and anxiety beneath his nonchalant exterior. Her own embarrassment quickly disappeared. She began to feel more at ease.

"Isn't it dreadful being a pilot?" she asked softly.

"Dreadful?" For an instant his tone was sharp, but then he gave his easy smile. "Of course not. Hasn't anyone ever told you how exciting it is up there in the blue. Man and machine against the elements and all that ... The thrill of battle!" Something in his voice told her he didn't mean a word of it.

"It sounds very glamorous, but if were you I'd be terrified!"

He studied her shrewdly, seemed not quite sure how to reply, but then quickly shrugged his shoulders.

"Ah, yes, but I'm a man and you're a woman." The soft smooth voice suddenly became brittle. It's a man's instinct to be the adventurer, the hunter."

"Yes. I suppose so. But you can't really mean you're enjoying this dreadful war?"

He laughed, but there was no real joy in it. He gave her one more hard look before his face relaxed in a warm grin which this time she knew was genuine.

"I'll be frank with you," he confided. "Since I left training school I've been on several patrols but so far I haven't even spotted the enemy! I think you and the rest of the 'beauty chorus' down at Command Headquarters stand as much chance of being hit as I do."

"Not since March. They've stuck us underground in a concrete basement. We're quite safe – not like the girls in the Ops Rooms of the Fighter Stations!"

"I'm glad you're safe," he said quietly, then grinned wickedly. "But I'm still trusting you not to tell the other girls my secret. Spoils the hero image, you know." He gave an exaggerated wink.

She laughed, her memories flying back to her father.

"I've always loved secrets and I never tell."

He was suddenly serious.

"No, I don't believe you do ... " He touched her lightly on the cheek.

She felt herself blushing again.

"I must go and check on the food. I was just on my way when you arrived."

She left him organising the drinks and fled in the direction of the kitchen and its enticing smells. She felt his eyes still on her and was relieved to close the kitchen door behind her. She leant back against it, feeling quite giddy, then drew a deep breath. What was the matter with her? Her whole body tingled with an excitement she had never experienced before. She must pull herself together before she spoke to him again – before she made a complete fool of herself.

She busied herself with the food, checked everything was ready for serving. At last, feeling more in control, she went back into the living room.

The noise level had already risen a few decibels. Thank goodness for well-built walls, she thought, otherwise the neighbours would be complaining! She spotted Leslie nearby, but as she moved towards him, couldn't stop her eyes darting around the rest of the room. There was no sign of Nessie, nor of Jimmy. Her heart sank. Had they already left the party?

"Right, you noisy rabble. Can we have some hush, please?" It was Nessie's commanding voice, and it had the required effect. She glided in from the hallway.

"I have an important announcement to make." She paused for effect. "I've just discovered it's Simon's birthday today. She pulled a tall, swarthy man to his feet. "Now, don't be shy, Simon. You know you've been waiting all night to get your hands on me. Now's your chance. Are you a simple Simon or a sagacious Simon? At least show me you can dance."

Everyone hooted and shouted and some started chanting 'Happy Birthday To You', but it was all very off-key and ended in peals of laughter. Simon, covered in confusion, was trying to keep pace with Nessie's wild gyrations. Cathy spotted Jimmy surrounded by a bevy of girls, laughing and clapping in time to the music.

Within seconds Simon's confusion had changed to elation. Encouraged by the applause and attention, by Nessie's fluid movements, he was soon having the time of his life.

Leslie appeared at her side.

"She certainly has a way with people, doesn't she?"

"She's fantastic!" Cathy agreed, laughing. "It's her vitality, I think. It's completely contagious."

Minutes later, Simon sank into a chair, exhausted by his efforts. Nessie grabbed Jimmy. He whirled her around a couple of times, then gave her a quick hug. She whispered something in his ear. He escorted her, laughing, in the direction of Cathy and Leslie. Cathy felt her heart start to pound.

"How's the food, Cath?" asked Nessie. "Can I do anything?"

"No, it's all just about ready. Could you help serve?"

"Help? That's my job. You've done plenty already. Just go and enjoy yourself. Jimmy here will give me a hand."

Cathy gave her a grateful smile, trying desperately not to look at Jimmy.

"Thanks, Nessie. I might even get Leslie to dance with me."

"If he doesn't, I'd love the pleasure," volunteered Jimmy.

"Oh no you don't," warned Nessie. "No shirking from my workers! – And that means you!"

But Cathy had already dragged Leslie into the throng of dancers.

"You should have told me before you wanted to dance," said Leslie, surprised by her haste.

She laughed nervously.

"I didn't have the time before."

The music had changed to a slow romantic foxtrot. Leslie's arms were strong about her, but Cathy felt strangely ill at ease.

* * * * * * *

The party came slowly to a close. Only a few die-hards and close friends were still chatting in the relaxed atmosphere of the living room. Cathy and Nessie retreated to the bedroom to repair their make-up.

"It must be wonderful to be gorgeous-looking like you." Cathy gazed miserably into the mirror.

"What a load of twaddle, Cath. What's the matter with you? I never heard you mooning about your looks before."

"Perhaps I never realised before just how plain I am – although I know my father never thought I could compare with my mother. He didn't say as much, but I could tell. In any case, I only had to look at her pictures."

"But Cath, you're very attractive."

"Attractive, maybe – most girls are attractive – but not stunning, not ravishing." She sighed into the mirror.

"Cath, what on earth have you been drinking? Not too much gin, I hope!"

"I'm not depressed, Nessie, just realistic."

"Now, Cathy Harvey, just listen to me. OK so you're not absolutely ravishing, but you have something much more important." She paused. "I don't know how to explain it – you're just a lovely person inside. That's why everyone likes you."

Cathy was embarrassed but deeply touched.

"It's sweet of you to say that, Nessie. But you're wrong – look how everyone flocks about you. You're dynamic!"

Nessie laughed.

"Wrong again. It's a simple case of moths around a candle. But what happens when the flame snuffs out?" She threw her arms in the air to demonstrate the point. "When it comes to it, Cath, I've plenty of acquaintances, but you're my only real friend."

Cathy was silent.

"But take you," continued Nessie in full swing. "People really like you. I mean that, Cath. So cheer up!"

"I'll try. I don't know what's the matter with me. Just tired, I suppose." She brightened suddenly. "The party was a great success, wasn't it?"

"And still is," laughed Nessie. "Don't forget we've still got the hardcore of our guests littering the living room."

"Yes, I suppose we'd better get back to them, before they take root. I just couldn't face that pompous Hugh chap at breakfast time."

"Don't worry. Jimmy's superb at diplomatically disposing of unwanted bodies. You do approve of him don't you, Cath?"

Cathy looked down, confused.

"He's wonderful, Nessie." she whispered. She looked up with what she hoped was a bright smile.

Nessie smiled happily back, turned and swept gaily from the room.

Where does she get the energy from, mused Cathy. No wonder Jimmy's besotted by her. She followed more slowly in her friend's wake.

"Congratulations, Cathy." It was Leslie. "The party was great. My 'spy' friends, as Nessie would call them, had to leave. They asked me to thank you both. It must have taken a lot of hard work."

"Oh, Nessie was the dynamo that set the whole thing alight."

"But she couldn't have done it without you as her anchor. Gosh, we are mixing our metaphors, but you know what I mean ..."

Cathy giggled.

"You're probably right. I'm the big fat anchor and Nessie's the bright flame."

"What a silly thing to say. Are you feeling all right?

"Yes, fine thank you, just a little tired."

"You sit right here and relax. I'll go and make appropriate noises – see if I can get rid of the residue so you and Nessie can get some sleep. Have you been on late shifts?"

"Yes, unfortunately."

Leslie loped away and was soon chatting quietly to a group in the far corner. She saw them nod their heads in agreement and start to move. Good old Leslie!

Her eyes roved to the other side of the room. Nessie had her hand possessively on Jimmy's arm. Cathy felt a sharp stab of jealousy. What was the matter with her? Nessie was her closest friend. Guiltily she recalled their recent conversation. How could she feel jealous of a person who had just been so nice to her – who had told her she was a lovely person? She didn't feel very lovely at the moment. And why this sudden envy? She had never felt jealous of Nessie before.

It was Jimmy, of course. How perfectly stupid to be so affected by her best friend's boyfriend. As Nessie had said, he was a typical lady-killer. It had only taken a couple of seconds for Cathy to fall for his smooth charm. Worse still, he was Nessie's beau. What a cad she was – if women could be cads – fancying Nessie's boyfriend!

And what about Leslie? She was being completely disloyal to him, too. She must pull herself together, or her nice safe future with Leslie would be jeopardised. It was just as well Nessie was so stunning. Jimmy would never look at her while Nessie was around.

She closed her eyes, desperately trying to eliminate him from her thoughts. Yes, she decided. No more stupidity from now on. She opened her eyes.

Jimmy was standing right in front of her!

"Do you realise you've just nodded off when your most important guests are dying for your company?" His tone was light-hearted, but his eyes were coolly determined.

Flustered, she leapt up from her chair.

He was immediately apologetic.

" I'm sorry. I didn't mean to startle you. But I would like the chance to talk to my hostess – before the party finally breaks up." He smiled disarmingly.

She felt cornered and looked anxiously about her. Where had Leslie gone, just when she needed him?

Eventually she managed a nervous reply.

"What did you want to talk about?" After his own soft tones, her voice seemed strangely harsh. She had wanted to be coolly polite, not childishly petulant.

"What are you frightened of, Cathy?" he asked gently.

"Nothing – nothing at all. I'm just rather tired ..." Golly, she was starting to sound like gramophone record with the needle stuck.

He took her hand, raised it gently to his lips, his eyes never leaving hers.

"In that case, my charming hostess, I won't keep you from your beauty sleep. Sweet dreams!"

He gave her hand a final squeeze.

"You know I shall be back."

"But … Nessie …"

He was gone. She saw him put his arm around Nessie, give her a light peck on the cheek. Then he and his friends disappeared through the door. She felt suddenly very empty.

Well, that seems to be everyone," said Leslie, reappearing by her side. "I'd better get moving myself. Thanks again, Cathy. It was a lovely party. Don't forget we're going to the cinema on Monday." He kissed her tenderly.

"No, no … I won't," she said, distractedly.

"You look all in. Off to bed with you!"

"Goodnight, Leslie." It was a whisper. She turned on her heels and fled to her bedroom. She couldn't face Nessie at that moment.

She thought she wouldn't sleep — her mind was in turmoil. Yet within minutes, she felt her eyelids grow heavy and soon fell blissfully unconscious. But her sleep was fitful, disturbed by a flurry of dreams. Awakening suddenly at five in the morning, she broke her dream. The man filling her vision – the man she was kissing and caressing with a passion she had never known before, whose sensitive fingers were exploring all the secret parts of her body – was Jimmy Proctor!

Chapter 6

The telephone shrilled loudly. She came out of a heavy sleep, reaching mistakenly for the alarm clock. Darn it! It was the phone. She stumbled quickly to the hall. Checking her watch, she saw it was past midnight. Who could be calling at that hour?

And where was Nessie? Then she remembered. Nessie had gone to the theatre with some friends. Cathy had declined the invitation. It was the night after the party and before this leave she had worked some demanding shifts. Preparations for the party, and her emotional reactions the night before, had left her exhausted and out of sorts. She had hoped to get a good night's rest. Curse the phone!

It rang, more insistently.

"Kensington 2595." Her voice was still fuzzy with sleep.

"Hello, is that you, Cathy?"

"Yes." Her voice wavered. She immediately recognised the voice on the other end of the line.

"It's Jimmy."

"Yes, I know. I'm afraid Nessie's not here at the moment. She shouldn't be long."

"I rang to speak to you – not Nessie."

"Oh ..."

"Cathy ... Are you still there?"

"Yes ..." She couldn't think what else to say.

"Listen, I haven't got much time and it's a rotten line. Can I see you tomorrow night?"

"No." She sounded like an automaton. She must say something more than yes and no. "I'm going out." She remembered Leslie was taking her to the cinema.

"Well, what about lunchtime?"

"Look Jimmy, I'm afraid I can't." Had she really managed to refuse him?

"What do you mean – 'can't'? You mean 'won't'? What's the matter, Cathy?"

"I just don't think it would be a good idea."

"What's happened to the friendly, sympathetic girl I met last night?"

She didn't answer. The line fell silent. She twitched nervously at her hair, at a loss for words.

"What's the matter, Cathy? Are you worried about Nessie?"

"Partly."

"Cathy, you don't understand. Nessie and I are only friends. I've hardly known her any time. That doesn't mean I can't take you out."

"It's not as easy as that, Jimmy. I'm sorry ..."

"Cathy, don't be silly."

"I'm sorry, Jimmy. I have to call off now."

"Cathy!"

"Goodbye, Jimmy."

With a heavy sigh, she replaced the receiver. She found she was shivering, yet it wasn't cold. Fastening the tie on her dressing gown she headed for the kitchen. Now she was awake, she might as well make a cup of tea.

She heard Nessie's key in the lock.

"You're not still up, Cath? I thought you wanted an early night."

Nessie's eyes were bright, her cheeks flushed.

"Oh, the phone woke me." Cathy quickly changed the subject. "How was the show? You look as though you've enjoyed yourself."

"It was great fun – I wish you'd come. Who was phoning at this time of night – Leslie?"

Cathy was cornered. Damnation! Why had she mentioned the telephone? She was obviously still in a stupor – sleepy, and shocked by Jimmy's call.

"I'm making some tea. Would you like a cup?"

"It was Jimmy, wasn't it?"

Cathy nearly dropped the saucer she had just picked up.

"I ... I told him you were out, should be back soon." She busied herself with the teacups. "Did you say yes to tea?"

"He wanted to speak to you, didn't he?"

"Well, when you weren't here, he did ask if I was free tomorrow. I think he was feeling lonely. I told him I was tied up." She tried to sound casual, but her hand holding the tea-pot was shaking. It was the truth, as far as it went. She hated to lie, yet was determined not to hurt Nessie. Let her think it was a spontaneous suggestion by Jimmy – because Nessie hadn't been there.

"Cathy, look at me." Nessie's voice was stern, but as Cathy raised her eyes to meet her gaze, her flat-mate gave a warm smile. "I'm not blind, you know, nor stupid. I saw the looks Jimmy was giving you at the party, especially just before he left in such a hurry. Had you given him the push?"

Nessie never minced her words, and there was no point in denying it. She was too bright. It would be an insult to her intelligence.

"I'm sorry, Nessie. I didn't try to encourage him. But you were always surrounded by other people. In any case, I've told him I'm not interested."

"But you are, aren't you?" Nessie's voice was soft but determined. "Look, Cathy, I'm no fool. I know you didn't make a special play for Jimmy. I also know there's no point in trying to hold on to a man when he's more interested in somebody else. Besides, you know me – it doesn't bother me that much. Jimmy's a super boy, but there's plenty more fish in the sea ..."

"Do you really mean that?"

"Yes, but let me continue. You're different from me. I can tell you've been really smitten by him. Why else did you rush off to bed last night? Ever since then, you've not been your usual self – all moody and strange. I'm just not affected that way. In a way I wish I could be ..."

Her voice trailed away. She pushed a thick lock of auburn hair from her eyes.

"So have you got the message? Grab him if you can, and good luck to you!"

"Nessie, you're wonderful!" There were tears in Cathy's eyes – tears of happiness for herself, and relief that she wasn't hurting Nessie. "Now you're not just saying that to be nice to me?"

"Don't be silly, Cath. I always say exactly what I mean – you know that."

Cathy hugged her with joy. Then her face dropped.

"But I've just rung off, refused to speak to him ..."

"I wouldn't worry about that," laughed Nessie. "From what I know of Jimmy, that will only make him the more eager." Her smile changed to a frown. "Take it easy, won't you, Cath. He's certainly interested in you, but he is something of a lady-killer and ... I wouldn't like you to be hurt."

Cathy flopped into a chair.

"Don't worry. I'll try to keep myself in hand. I only wish I knew what he sees in me. Oh no ..." She sat up with a start. "Nessie, what am I going to do about Leslie?"

"Nothing," said Nessie promptly. "Tell him the truth – if he asks. But say you want to remain friends. You do, don't you?"

"Of course I do. I'm awfully fond of him."

"I know you are. If Jimmy's worth anything, he'll understand that. Now, whatever happened to that tea you were offering me?" Her emerald-green eyes twinkled.

"Goodness me, it's nearly cold! I'll make some more. Nessie, you're really tremendous. I'm so lucky to have a friend like you!"

Nessie actually blushed, a rare occurrence for her.

Cathy hadn't meant to embarrass her, but she meant every word. There couldn't be many people with friends as generous and unselfish as Nessie. Her tiredness suddenly disappeared. Confident their friendship was as close as ever, reassured by Nessie's comments about Jimmy, she felt gloriously happy.

She floated into the kitchen, brought back some fresh hot tea for the two of them, then settled back on the sofa, her legs tucked beneath her.

"Nessie, I'm so confused, yet so excited. I've never felt this way about any man. Tell me all you know about Jimmy." Her eyes sparkled with anticipation.

"In all truth, Cathy, I don't know very much. In some ways Jimmy's a strange one. He doesn't talk much about himself – doesn't like to discuss his background. As far as his private life's concerned, he keeps himself very much to himself. He's great company, of course, utterly charming and often very witty. But I don't think he's a deep person."

"How strange," murmured Cathy. In some respects Nessie was right, she thought. But she had sensed something else in Jimmy. He was holding something back, an important part of himself – which he wouldn't reveal to anyone else. She didn't share Nessie's opinion that he lacked depth. Beneath the casual veneer, Jimmy seemed like a giant spring, just waiting to uncoil. She had felt his inner tension. It intrigued, yet in a strange way, frightened her

"I do know his father died in the Gallipoli campaign," Nessie continued. "But he's very reticent about his mother – just says they don't get on, that they hardly ever see, even speak to one another."

"There's definitely something mysterious about him," said Cathy.

Nessie laughed. "That's just you being your usual romantic self. Be careful, Cathy. For all his charm, Jimmy could be a very selfish person. He's not another Leslie, you know."

"Yes, I know that. But I'm sure he's a fine person at heart." She cupped her face in her hands. "What a fool I am, Nessie. I have a warm secure relationship with Leslie, and now I'm throwing it all away for a date with a man who just isn't my type at all. He's certainly not the dependable, stay-at-home, reliable husband type!"

"You can say that again!"

"In fact, he's the opposite to the sort of man I thought I would fall for," continued Cathy. "And a fighter pilot is an extremely risky proposition for a girl looking for a stable relationship!"

"Don't worry about that. Jimmy's definitely the survivor type."

"But what on earth does he see in me?" Cathy moaned. "From what you said before, he normally goes for smart sophisticated lady-friends."

"That's true," mused Nessie. "And they're often older than he is. Many have been married."

"Oh, Nessie! You make him sound a real cad," cried Cathy.

"Don't let that worry you. After all, we are at war. Fighter pilots take their lives in their hands every time they go into the air. I've heard Jimmy's one of the bravest and most devil-may-care. Most of them want to grab their pleasures wherever and whenever they can."

"Of course – how naive I am. It must be a terrible strain for him. Oh, Nessie, do you really think he'll telephone again?"

"Of course he will. I think you've really got under his skin. Jimmy doesn't normally have to chase girls. I haven't seen him so smitten before."

"If I knew why, it would be a help."

"Don't worry, Cath. Just be your normal self. That's obviously what he likes, so don't change the formula."

"I couldn't if I tried." She giggled nervously.

"My advice is to take each day as it comes. Don't get too involved – until you're sure it's right."

"I think I'm already involved, and I hardly know the man." Cathy looked despondent, but there was still a gleam in her eyes.

"Poor Cathy. You have got it bad. Still, it isn't going to help just sitting around here talking about it. We both need our beauty sleep."

"You're right," laughed Cathy. "This was supposed to be my early night, and it's nearly one o'clock in the morning."

"Well, we can both sleep in this morning. I intend to do just that. Just one thing, Cath. I meant to ask you before, but we were so busy with the preparations. Then I was reminded by Simon's birthday celebration at the party. Why didn't you want anyone to know about your own birthday?"

Cathy hesitated.

"It's silly, really. I love parties, but I always get over sentimental when it's my birthday. It brings back too many memories of my father. If anyone had mentioned it at the party, I'd probably have burst into tears!"

Nessie nodded and smiled.

"Typical Cathy Harvey! Good night, Cath dear, and sweet dreams!"

She gave her an affectionate hug and they both wandered off to their rooms.

Cathy normally read before going to sleep, but tonight she felt too confused and aroused to even pick up her book. She relaxed her head on the pillow, wanting to savour the moment – to sort out her thoughts about Jimmy. Was he really interested in her or was it just another of his flash-in-the-pan impulses? What sort of man was she getting involved with? And how would dear Leslie take her sudden change of heart?

Eventually, tiredness got the better of her. As she fell asleep there was just one thought in her mind. Please let Jimmy ring again!

He did ring – the next morning.

* * * * * *

Three weeks later they were married.

Chapter 7

On May 10th, a week after the party, Hitler without any formal declaration of war invaded both Holland and Belgium. The 'phoney war' was over. The balloon had gone up at last!

Yet the pattern of operations at Duxford, Jimmy's fighter station some forty miles north of London, stayed much the same – practice flying and convoy patrols. But both he and Cathy knew that any day now, he could be involved in direct action, perhaps posted elsewhere. They decided to get married right away.

The wedding, held on May 24th, was a quiet affair at Cathy's parish church, St Peter's in Cranley Gardens, South Kensington. Jimmy managed to get a two-day pass and Cathy's request for a few days' extra leave was sympathetically granted. They invited only a few guests – Hosky, Jimmy's mother, and some close friends – and kept the ceremony as simple as possible.

Hosky was delighted to come up for the wedding. Soon after Cathy joined the WAAF, her old nanny had moved from Cathy's South Kensington flat to a tiny cottage in the Hampshire countryside, near Ashfield. Cathy's work at Fighter Command Headquarters involved all hours, and she could only return home on monthly leaves. Hosky had managed to convince Cathy she was quite capable of looking after herself and would prefer to move to the country.

"I'm an old lady now, Cathy, and I often have a yearning to get back to village life. London isn't for me when you're not around, my dear. As long as you promise to visit me in Ashfield whenever possible, I'm sure it will be the best for both of us. After all, you have a busy life in the WAAF. You can't come rushing back to see an old lady all the time."

"But Hosky ..." pleaded Cathy.

"Now be a good girl and do as I tell you," said Hosky, with a knowing smile. It was the phrase she had so often used when Cathy was a child. Cathy knew when she was beaten. With reluctance, she had agreed.

At the wedding, Hosky was in tears. She had met Jimmy just once before, when the two of them had visited her at the cottage. She was instantly charmed and captivated by Cathy's new young man, thrilled by the fact they were both obviously very much in love.

"Cathy, darling!" She gazed adoringly at Cathy as she stood, radiant but slightly bewildered, in her simple but elegant bridal outfit. "You look beautiful. I'm so happy for you both. But I do wish it could have been a full white wedding, with all the trimmings." Tears came to her eyes. "That's what your father – and your mother – would have wanted. These dreadful wars ruin everything!"

"Don't worry, Hosky," laughed Cathy. "The war will soon be over. Then we'll have another ceremony – just for you!"

Two other people cried at the wedding. Strangely enough, one was Nessie – although she took great pains to disguise the fact. Cathy saw the glint of tears in Nessie's green eyes as they hugged each other just before the ceremony. Cathy had never known her friend anything but dry-eyed before. Tears and Nessie just didn't seem to go together.

Cathy herself was the third to succumb – she was unable to hold back a tiny sob when Jimmy took her firmly in his arms and kissed her at the end of the service.

Jimmy's closest friend, Simon Carstairs, was best man. Cathy couldn't stop grinning, when she remembered how he had danced so wildly with Nessie at their fateful party. 'Are you a simple Simon or a sagacious Simon?', Nessie had teased. Had it been only three weeks ago that Cathy's life had changed so radically? She never imagined on the night of the party that, within a month, she would be a married woman – Mrs James Proctor!

Nessie, of course, was chief bridesmaid. She was a tower of strength during the morning before the wedding when a frantically joyful Cathy was reduced to a bundle of nerves. Fortunately, once she reached the church, Cathy relaxed. The dream became reality and she was determined to enjoy and treasure every moment of the day.

She sailed through the ceremony, radiant with joy. Never before had she felt so ecstatically happy. The tension and excitement of wartime intensified rather than diminished her euphoria. The significance of the day took on new dimensions. She sensed that everybody at the wedding was in a state of greater awareness. The atmosphere was electric.

Was it the imminence of invasion, of Hitler's threat to England itself, that made each minute more precious? It seemed that every little gesture and sensation assumed a vital significance in this new world, where each individual had suddenly become acutely aware of his or her own vulnerability.

Only one thing marred the perfection of the day. That was the presence of Jimmy's mother, Rowena Proctor.

Jimmy hadn't wanted his mother to come at all.

"It's such short notice, Cath, and for such a simple ceremony it hardly seems worth her coming all the way down from Scotland – especially as she hasn't been so fit lately. In any case, we've never been close. I'd prefer she didn't come."

But Cathy, with her strong sentiments regarding family ties, could never accept this.

"She's the only close family either of us have, Jimmy!" she cried. "How can you ignore your own mother?" Cathy had a hot temper when it was roused – fortunately a rare occurrence. She hoped he would understand her strong feelings about families. He did. Unable to resist Cathy's pleadings, he had reluctantly agreed.

Mrs. Rowena Proctor arrived late at the church. A slim striking woman with hair and eyes of steely grey, she had a proud, almost arrogant bearing; but what frightened Cathy most was the fiery wildness which would suddenly flash in Rowena's otherwise ice-cold eyes.

Despite Cathy's heartfelt attempts to be friendly, Rowena Proctor remained coolly polite to her, hardly seeming to acknowledge Cathy's existence as her son's new bride. She ignored the other guests, but twice Cathy caught her mother-in-law staring fiercely at her son. She couldn't fathom whether love – or could it possibly be hatred? – lay behind the sinister gaze. She shivered and looked away. Within minutes of the end of the marriage ceremony, Jimmy's elegant but hostile mother gave them a stern nod, turned her back and was gone. Cathy couldn't prevent a faint sigh of relief. Jimmy squeezed her hand. She could feel his tension melt slowly away.

The reception was held in a private room at the Dorchester Hotel. Amid laughter, enthusiastic well-wishing and the inevitable ribald comments from Jimmy's pilot friends, the wedding guests left with reasonable promptness. They knew Cathy and Jimmy had limited time together. For their briefest of honeymoons, the couple had elected to stay on at the Dorchester. It seemed pointless to waste any of their precious two days together travelling elsewhere.

Leslie was the last guest to leave. He had been shattered when Cathy told him she was to marry Jimmy. Was she absolutely certain of her feelings, he had asked? Eventually she had managed to convince him. A few days later, he visited her to wish her every happiness, to tell her he would always love her, always be her friend. Cathy had wept.

Before leaving them at the Dorchester, Leslie shook Jimmy warmly by the hand, and gave Cathy a fierce hug.

"If you ever need anything, remember I shall always be there." He turned quickly and loped away.

"Leslie's a helluva man, Cathy," said Jimmy, gruffly. "Any regrets?"

"Darling, don't be silly. How could you possibly think ..?" She nestled her head against his chest.

He gave a faint groan, clasped her head in his hands, then reluctantly pulled away from her.

"Come on Cath, or I shall rape you – right here in public."

He grabbed her hand and they ran laughing together to their suite. But the moment he put the key in the lock, she felt suddenly apprehensive. Their whirlwind relationship and wedding had left her with no time to contemplate what would come after. Her stomach contracted as, with a start, she realised she hardly knew Jimmy. During their brief courtship, their total time spent together amounted to little more than a few stolen hours when her leave and shifts and Jimmy's few spare hours from flying had coincided. Yet, in another way, she felt she knew him better than anyone else in the world.

Physically their relationship had never gone beyond passionate kisses and embraces. She knew Jimmy was an experienced man of the world, yet paradoxically enough, he had always treated her with gentleness and restraint, almost with reverence – as if the sexual act would shatter their perfect harmony. What if he should be disappointed with her? She was completely inexperienced and untutored as far as sex was concerned. She had been highly aroused by the electric currents between them, yet ironically enough these strange new feelings made her even more aware that she was totally out of her depth – childishly naive about male-female relationships.

Jimmy must have sensed her change of mood, her growing embarrassment. With a touch of theatrical drama he opened the door of the suite, whisked her into his strong arms, and with great aplomb, carried her across the threshold.

Her tension dissolved with her laughter.

"Jimmy, you're an idiot. Now put me down before you drop me." Her apprehension and embarrassment had already disappeared.

"Not likely, young lady." He deepened his voice, playing to perfection the role of wicked seducer. "Aha! Now I have you in my power. At last I can have my evil way with you!"

With Cathy still in his arms, hysterical with laughter, he lunged towards the bedroom. In one swift movement, he flung her dramatically onto the bed, leapt on top of her, his lean body and long muscular legs pinning her so firmly down she could scarcely move.

"Help, help," squealed Cathy, joining in the charade. "I am but a poor virgin."

"Yes, I know that." His voice changed, became hushed and gentle again. "That's one of the reasons I love you so. You are the most truly innocent person I have ever met; yet you have the understanding of a wise old lady."

"But I'm only nineteen," she whined, still playing her part. Then she realised his tawny eyes were serious.

His hands were already stroking her body. She shivered uncontrollably; but it was a shiver of delight, not of apprehension. Jimmy used her body as if it were a delicate musical instrument. His touch was gentle, yet electric. He was sensing, gently exploiting every stage of her growing arousal and excitement. With infinite care he led her through each fiery moment of mounting sensation.

Before she realised it, they were both naked. His fingers and mouth worked with a skill she had never dreamed possible. She could sense his own growing need. She knew, intuitively, that he was restraining his own fierce desire, wanting her to share and relish every moment with him.

She wanted his caresses to go on forever, found she was wantonly crying out for more. All her inhibitions shattered in glorious moments of self-revelation. She desperately wanted him inside her, found she was demanding, moaning, pleading.

Just when she could bear it no longer, he thrust into her. She felt no pain, only a glorious sensation of oneness, of complete fulfilment. Her whole body was afire, every nerve tingling. With every movement and thrust her ecstasy spiralled, came to a crescendo. She was riding on a high unbreaking wave of exquisite physical delight.

She climaxed several seconds ahead of him. The last thing she remembered was murmuring over and over: "I love you. Oh, Jimmy, how I love you!"

"Yes, I know, Mrs. Proctor, and I love you," whispered Jimmy, hoarsely.

Gloriously happy, physically and emotionally spent, they both fell instantly asleep.

* * * * * * * *

Cathy was the first to awake the following morning. She lay on her back, blissfully content, noticed her hand was still in Jimmy's. They must have slept hand in hand all night, like two young children. She couldn't believe how natural and easy it had all been. Nor could she believe the depths of her own sensuality. She had discovered not only a wonderful new aspect of Jimmy, but a whole world of new sensations, new feelings. She was dizzily in love for the very first time.

She turned her head, looked fondly at Jimmy. He appeared even younger in sleep – his dark-blond hair tousled and boyish, the lines of strain scarcely visible on his face. He looked serenely peaceful, but intensely vulnerable. Her heart twisted in her chest. She knew she would do anything to protect him from pain or harm of any kind.

He stirred beside her, opened his eyes and smiled.

"What a wonderful way to wake up – with you beside me." He leaned over, covered her face and breasts with kisses.

She moaned softly, started to explore his body in the dim, dawn light which filtered into the bedroom. The excitement of the previous night was with her again.

He responded instantly to her touch and they made easy, gentle, unhurried love, content to explore every inch of each other's bodies, intent on giving as much pleasure as possible.

"Will it always be like this?" she murmured, praying it would be. "I'm not beautiful and sophisticated like your previous girl-friends."

"Don't be silly, Cathy," he said sharply. "You are the most beautiful person I have ever known. Don't you understand? You offer so much more than any of those women. I've been waiting for you all my life. With you I can be myself at last."

He started to caress her again and she felt her passion return.

Much later, he lay back on the pillow, a cigarette in his hand. He inhaled deeply and a smile crinkled his face.

"Cathy, my love, you never cease to amaze me. I thought I had married a shy demure young lady, and I discover instead that my wife is a raving sex maniac! Mind you, I'm not complaining. In fact ..." He took her in his arms ... "It's absolutely marvellous!"

She grinned, happily.

"I don't know what's come over me. To think that only a couple of years ago, I didn't know whether you made love on top of the sheets or underneath them."

Jimmy guffawed loudly and stroked her hair.

"Cathy, you're adorable!"

"I mean it," she gurgled. "At school, in the dorms, we all used to discuss what it would be like. We were terrified we wouldn't know what to do when the time came. The most baffling question was whether you made love on top of the sheets, or inside the bed. We spent hours trying to figure that one out! The whole sexual act seemed so absurd and ridiculous."

"I suppose it is, when you come to think about it." He looked at her quizzically. "After all, if a little man came down from Mars and studied our mating romps, he'd probably decide we were all complete maniacs." He gazed into her eyes and winked wickedly. "Aren't you glad we're not Martians?"

"I certainly am," sighed Cathy and snuggled up to him.

* * * * * * *

The honeymoon flew by. Cathy knew that whatever happened in the future, she would never forget those blissful two days together, nor regret her decision to marry Jimmy. Before the wedding she had harboured certain doubts. She had never been quite sure what Jimmy found so irresistible about her. She feared he might suddenly tire of her, discover it had been some silly passing whim. For Cathy, this was the most powerful threat to their relationship. She desperately wanted an utterly secure as well as loving relationship. She couldn't bear to suddenly lose another loved one.

From the beginning he hardly seemed the right type for her. Nor did the fact that that he was a fighter pilot help. What sort of chance did he have to survive this dreadful war? Entrusting her love to him had been a major step for her, one that went against the very grain of her character and emotions.

But after the honeymoon, she no longer doubted his love. She was sublimely sure their relationship would last for ever – as long as nothing happened to Jimmy ...

* * * * * * *

The war, however, was taking a more ominous turn.

A few days after the wedding, a series of setbacks led to the evacuation of Dunkirk. Her husband's squadron moved to Hornchurch, a fighter base twelve miles east of London. From there they patrolled the evacuation. Jimmy was in daily contact with German fighter planes. Her worries about his flying couldn't be brushed away as easily as her fears about the depth of his attachment to her.

She tried to convince herself his fellow pilots were right – her husband was invincible.

"He leads a charmed life," Simon Carstairs had told her one day. "His devil-may-care attitude seems to create a protective shield around him. In any case, Cath, he's our lucky mascot. Nothing can happen to Jimmy!" She hadn't realised just how superstitious airmen could be!

Another thing bothered her – Jimmy's own attitude to his invincibility. For all his light-hearted banter and apparent unconcern for his personal safety, she still sensed anxiety beneath the surface. She had felt it from the moment they first met. At times she thought it was the normal tension of being a fighter pilot. But since she had got to know him better, she was convinced that beneath the careless veneer, Jimmy was as concerned as the rest about the dangers involved.

Yet nobody else seemed to sense this mental vulnerability. Perhaps, after all, she was imagining it.

After the honeymoon, life went back to the normal wartime routine. Cathy was grateful when Jimmy insisted Nessie should still share the flat with them.

"Look Cathy, it makes sense," he told her. "You and I will have little enough time together. The tempo of the war and my patrols are hotting up now. I don't want you spending your leaves alone when I'm away ... And when I do manage to get home, the flat's big enough for the three of us. Nessie's good for you. She'll stop you worrying too much! Mind you, after the war," he added, a twinkle in his eye, "we'll be moving to a cottage in the country – big enough to start a family!"

Cathy was more than happy to agree and hugged him for his understanding. She knew only Nessie could see her through the dark hours of worry for Jimmy's safety. Even then she sorely underestimated just how much she was going to need the help and support of her friend.

Chapter 8

London, England. November 1940

The day had started like any other, except the weather was unexpectedly fine for that time of year. Cathy now dreaded these clear sunny days. She preferred overcast rainy weather when the visibility and flying conditions were too bad for the pilots to carry out any patrols or special missions. Then at least she knew Jimmy was safe on the ground.

But today she felt alive with anticipation. Hastening along the Old Brompton Road, she couldn't prevent the occasional skip in her step. The birds, seemingly inspired by the unexpected good weather, twittered joyfully from the bare branches of the trees lining the road. Life was good! She had seven days of leave and Jimmy was due home on a two-day pass. They would have a whole weekend together – a period of calm and relaxation for them both. Jimmy would be able to get the rest he so desperately needed.

During the unremitting days and nights of the Battle of Britain, she had been increasingly aware of his fatigue and tension. He tried not to show it – at least with everybody but Cathy. She was glad he could relax in her company, but it pained her to see how much the stress affected him.

She understood all too well the physical demands of flying a fighter plane, but knew the mental strain was even greater – a pilot's reactions had to be continually razor sharp. Day after day Jimmy and the rest of the squadron grabbed what rest they could; but then would come the strident demand to scramble after only a few hours of sleep. During the height of the Battle of Britain, Jimmy flew up to seven or eight times a day, sometimes dropping asleep, exhausted, by the side of his aircraft, knowing the next call to scramble might come at any time.

During the critical months of the Battle of Britain, Fighter Command lost more than a thousand aircraft and worse still, over five hundred pilots. She knew these brave young men and their surviving colleagues had saved Britain from Hitler. But the sheer physical and mental exhaustion, the constant danger, the death of fellow pilots, had left an indelible mark on her husband.

Even with Cathy, he found it difficult to catch up on sleep. They would make love desperately. Afterwards he would fall instantly into a comatose state; but his rest was fitful and unsatisfying. He dreamed and wrestled all night. Sometimes when the nightmares were too horrific, Cathy would waken him from his nocturnal terrors; nurse him like a child.

His whole squadron was exhausted and on edge, but Jimmy – newly promoted to flight commander – suffered the additional stress of keeping morale to an optimum, of maintaining his own devil-may-care image which seemed so important to both him and his comrades. He lived on a knife-edge.

Thank goodness those awful summer months were over. Hitler, thwarted in his attempt to destroy Britain's fighter force, had now turned his wrath on the country's civilian population. Cathy's reaction to the ferocious night-time bombing raids had been one of relief. It meant Jimmy would be under less pressure. Oblivious to any danger to herself in London, the focus of Hitler's fury, she thanked God that Spitfires and Hurricanes could hardly be expected to play blind man's buff against the German night-bombers. As yet the fighter planes had no radar, though it was rumoured at headquarters that it wouldn't be long before this was rectified. Occasionally the fighters went up and roamed the skies, but they rarely found the German bombers.

Unfortunately the lull didn't last long. The decision was soon made to take the fight to the enemy camp. Currently Jimmy was taking part in offensives over France, escorting British bombers. Now he had flak to contend with, as well as enemy fighters. More recently he'd been sent on what he called 'rhubarb' missions. He refused to go into details about these on the telephone, saying he would tell her more when he saw her at the weekend – at least as much as he was allowed to divulge.

Entering the flat, she heard the shrill ring of the telephone. Perhaps it was Jimmy! He normally called the moment he returned from a patrol. He would know she was dying for news of his arrival time on Saturday. What he didn't know was that this leave was going to be extra special. Cathy had wonderful news for him!

She raced to the phone, breathlessly raised the receiver.

"Kensington 2595."

"Is that you, Cathy?"

Her heart sank. It wasn't Jimmy.

"Yes, who's calling?" She realized the disappointment must show in her voice.

"It's me, Simon."

"Oh, hello Simon. Sorry – I didn't recognise your voice with all the crackle on the line." Her tone had softened. She was fond of Simon Carstairs, Jimmy's best man at the wedding and his closest friend. "I was expecting Jimmy to ring. Have you a message from him?"

There was moment of silence.

"Simon, are you still there?"

"Yes, Cathy." His voice sounded strained. She was seized by a sense of foreboding.

"Something ... something's happened to him, hasn't it?" she stammered.

"Yes, I'm afraid so. Cathy, I'm sorry."

Her mind seemed to go blank. She sank into the chair by the phone, vaguely heard Simon's voice above the interference on the line.

"We were in a dog fight over France. His plane was shot down. But don't worry – I think he's OK, I was flying close to him. There was quite a *melée*, but I'm sure I saw him parachute out. I think he made it, so try not to worry. I wanted to speak to you myself – before you heard the news officially."

She found she couldn't speak. Surely this wasn't really happening to her – like her worst nightmare come true – just when she had started to believe Jimmy was indestructible. He had escaped the terrible slaughter of the Battle of Britain – she had thought the worst was over.

Cathy did you hear me? I think Jimmy's OK"

"Yes, yes ... thank you, Simon." Her mind was still a blank, no longer registering, refusing to accept the terrible news. But she knew Simon wouldn't lie to her. It was true. Jimmy had been shot down. She began to sob into the phone.

"Listen, Cathy. You must pull yourself together. Jimmy's going to be all right. I'm sure."

All right? What was he saying? She came out of the mist of shock.

"Simon, what do you mean?"

"I told you before – he managed to bale out!"

"You mean he's alive!" Oh God! In the shock of hearing Jimmy had been shot down, her paralysed mind had missed the rest of Simon's words.

"Yes. I think there's a really good chance. With luck he may be picked up by the Resistance. If not, the worst that can happen is that he'll spend the rest of the war in a prison-of-war camp."

"The ... the Germans ... they won't shoot him, will they?"

"I don't think so. Most of our chaps seem to turn up in the camps. And you know old Jimmy – he's a real survivor!"

She wanted to shout at him: Yes that's what you all told me before, but he has been shot down. He may even now be lying dead in France. Instead she said: "Thank you, Simon for ringing. Sorry I broke down."

"Don't worry about that, old girl. Is Nessie in?"

"No. No, she's not back yet."

"Well, make yourself a nice cup of tea and go to bed until Nessie gets there. You've had a frightful shock."

"Yes, Simon."

"I'm afraid I must shoot off now. Take care of yourself, Cathy and don't worry. I know in my bones Jimmy is fine. I'll let you know any news I get."

"Thanks, Simon. Goodbye." Her voice was a dull monotone. She still couldn't believe what had happened.

"Now chin up, old girl, and off to bed with you. 'Bye for now."

The phone went dead.

She tried to take a hold of herself. Perhaps Simon was right. Jimmy was alive. She certainly didn't feel as if she'd lost him. Surely, if he were dead, she would know inside? Or was that just wishful thinking? No, she too could feel it in her bones. Jimmy had to be alive. Now more than ever. He had to be – he was her life and she was expecting his child!

* * * * * * *

The official news came the following day – Jimmy's aircraft had 'failed to return'. But by this time, Cathy's natural resilience had reasserted itself. She was convinced Jimmy was alive. At home with Nessie, she waited with painful eagerness for news of her husband. Her thoughts were constantly with him, willing him to be alive and well. In the Ops Room she worked like an automaton, existing in a kind of vacuum – in a cocoon of hope.

Nessie didn't share Cathy's optimism, her belief that Jimmy was still alive. She was convinced her friend would soon have to come face-to-face with the reality of his death. The shock, when it came, would be all the greater after this cruel period of eager, but wasted hope. If only the news – one way or the other – would come soon. She hated to think of Cathy, lost in a wilderness of uncertainty. So many service wives lived through this mental purgatory, never knowing if their loved ones were dead or alive – waiting, always waiting.

Thank goodness Cathy had confided to her about her pregnancy. The night Simon rang with the news about Jimmy, Nessie had returned to the flat to find a distraught Cathy. In broken, breathless sentences Cathy explained all she knew. Then between sobs she confided she was pregnant.

"I wanted Jimmy to be the first to know." Tears streamed down Cathy's face. "I was so excited when I found out, but I wanted to be absolutely sure. And Jimmy seemed so exhausted and tense, I thought it better to wait a while – not cause him any more worries on my behalf." She wiped her eyes and looked up at her. "Oh, Nessie, I thought this leave would be the perfect time to tell him; the worst seemed to be over and the flying pressures less. He – he seemed almost like his old self last time on the phone." She broke down again.

"Don't talk any more, Cath – it's only upsetting you."

"I'm sorry, Nessie – it's just that I was so happy, so looking forward to seeing Jimmy and telling him the news. I knew he would be as thrilled as I am. You see, we always talked about having a large family – when the war was over, of course."

Her eyes behind the tears suddenly lit up. "That's why he's got to be alive – the baby ... it's a kind of good omen!"

Nessie wasn't convinced, but she felt happy and relieved that Cathy was pregnant. If something had happened to Jimmy, a baby would be the finest form of consolation. It would stop Cathy dwelling too long on her loss. She desperately needed someone of her own to love. If Jimmy were dead, the next best thing for her would be his child.

In the meantime she had to see Cathy through this period of crisis. So when her friend had no appetite, Nessie made sure she ate something, even 'cadged' nutritious little snacks for her from the canteen cooks. Though outdoor activities had never been her forte, she insisted they take walks in the fresh air. She even managed to get Cathy practising those new-fangled exercises which were supposed to ease the process of childbirth.

"Cath, you must think of your baby, yours and Jimmy's. You want him to be strong and healthy, don't you? – so you must look after yourself."

Cathy responded well. Nessie, proud of her efforts, was pleased to see that dreaming about her baby had given Cathy a new sense of purpose, made her think beyond Jimmy.

* * * * * * *

Then the letter arrived. They were in the billet at Bentley Priory. Fortunately the rest of the girls had gone ahead into the canteen.

"Shall I open it for you, Cath?" asked Nessie, hesitantly.

Cathy shook her head nervously, her face as white as alabaster. She sat down, crossed her ankles as she always did. For a few seconds she simply gazed at the letter. Nessie didn't know what to do to help her. She felt helpless, as if watching a scene in a play. With trembling, fumbling fingers Cathy opened the envelope, slowly unfolded the slim sheet of paper inside and started to read.

"Nessie! He's been found by the Resistance!" For a moment her blue-grey eyes were shining, but almost instantly her expression changed. Her face clouded and seemed to crumple up. "Oh no, no!" She gave an agonised wail, threw the letter down and flung herself on the bed, beating the pillow with her fists.

Nessie hastily bent down and retrieved the sheet of paper. Her own fingers shook uncontrollably.

The letter explained in a few simple words that Jimmy had been picked up by the Resistance. Unfortunately, in the course of an attempted escape to England, he had been shot by the Germans. A few personal effects would be returned to Cathy.

Nessie was stunned. Jimmy had survived the plane crash; he had reached the Resistance, only to be killed in the course of escape. The cruelty of fate once again! She tossed her auburn curls, her green eyes fierce and angry like those of a tigress determined to protect its cubs. Poor, poor Cathy! She would be absolutely devastated. She had really believed Jimmy was alive, that he would be coming back to her.

She glanced across at her friend's distraught figure on the bed. Should I comfort her now, she thought, or leave her alone for a while to get over the worst of her grief? Best to leave her a few minutes, she eventually decided.

She walked slowly to the telephone, made one short call to Hosky, Cathy's old nanny, another to Leslie Bourne. Then with a sigh, she headed back to Cathy. She opened the door and tiptoed across the room. Cathy lay prone on the bed, her face buried in the pillow; her whole body was heaving, but she made no sound. Nessie put her arm round Cathy's shoulders, and slowly stroked her hair
...

Chapter 9

Cathy's youth had been marked by tragedy, but no period of her life had seemed as black as the winter of 1940-41. The only silver lining was the baby, alive and kicking inside her. She couldn't wait for the Spring – for late April when the baby was due. She was sure her child would be a boy; never even considered the possibility of a girl. The baby for her would be a replacement Jimmy. She was convinced he would look like Jimmy, be like his father in every respect.

At work she managed to disguise her pregnancy for some time. Fortunately during the early months she put on little weight. Although entitled to six month's leave before the baby's birth, she preferred to continue working as long as possible, taking solace from the lively companionship, finding her demanding duties at Fighter Command Headquarters occupied her mind, prevented her from dwelling constantly on Jimmy. She eventually stopped working just before Christmas.

After the bustle of the Ops Room, time hung heavily on her hands. Nessie was fantastic. She tried to encourage Cathy to go out more, to join in the Christmas party-round; but the parties which she had previously adored, were now painful reminders of Jimmy and their first meeting. Cathy noticed Nessie didn't go out as much as before. She often spent her leaves at the flat, despite Cathy's remonstrations.

"Nessie, please don't feel you have to stay in and nursemaid me. I'm perfectly capable of looking after myself. You've told me yourself – having a baby is a completely natural thing! I'm perfectly happy here on my own – doing my exercises, reading, listening to that glorious Mozart record you bought me."

Nessie would smile and plead tiredness; insist she too enjoyed an evening at home. But Cathy knew she must be itching to be back in the swing. Whatever was said, they were both aware that Nessie was more concerned for Cathy's mental and emotional welfare than her own physical well-being. The bonds of friendship, already so strong between the two girls, took on another dimension. As far as Cathy was concerned, her flatmate became the sister she had always wanted. Unable to express her feelings in words, Nessie quietly demonstrated the strength of her friendship in everything she did for her.

Cathy was thrilled by one new development in her flatmate's life. Early in the New Year, Nessie brought Simon Carstairs home to the flat. The relationship between the two seemed warm and easy, Nessie's caustic comments less in evidence. Simon wasn't her flatmate's usual type – although he had certainly blossomed and grown in confidence since he had been with Nessie. Cathy caught the occasional affectionate glances between the two of them. She crossed her fingers, hoping that at last Nessie had discovered a deeper, more enduring relationship.

* * * * * * *

The winter days passed quickly. One evening in late February, Leslie visited her. It wasn't a surprise visit. Since Jimmy's death, and at Nessie's instigation, Leslie had often called to see her when she was on leave, and more frequently since she had stopped working. Sometimes they took a ride into the country – visited Hosky or Leslie's father down at Ashfield. Despite the numbed state of her emotions, she started to enjoy these days they spent together. Her friendship with Leslie was easy and comfortable. It required no effort on her part. They discussed history, music, animals, the countryside. It took her mind off memories of Jimmy.

Instead of the flowers which Leslie invariably brought for her, he arrived this time with a covered wicker basket.

"How are you feeling, mother-to-be?" he asked, patting her gently on the tummy. "I've a present for you."

He handed her the basket. Cathy was immediately intrigued. She heard a furious 'meow', and the basket seemed to come alive in her hands.

"Oh, Leslie, it's a cat!"

"Ten out of ten!" he teased. "A kitten, to be more precise. Don't you want to look at him? "

Cathy set the basket on the carpet, eagerly unbuckled the straps. The tiny kitten inside hissed viciously, leapt from the basket and scampered into hiding beneath a sofa. All she had seen was a scurry of black fur. Cathy laughed and scrambled to find him.

"He's a little wild at the moment," explained Leslie, "one of a litter from Coombe's farm. I picked him specially for you – he was the only totally black cat in the whole bunch. I know you love cats, and he'll bring you lots of good luck."

Cathy already had the kitten in her arms. "He's beautiful, Leslie. I can still smell the countryside on his fur – mmm ... wonderful – thyme and rosemary!" The kitten scrambled to her shoulder, nestled in the fold of her neck. "Have you just got back from Ashfield?" She remembered Coombe's Farm was quite close to Leslie's family home, not so far from her father's former estate.

"Yes. I've driven straight up. I needed to speak to you." His face became serious. "Cathy, dear, I'm afraid I have some bad news. Would you like to sit down?"

Cathy stiffened, then perched warily on the edge of the sofa. Leslie joined her. She was still stroking the kitten, but he knew it was a purely automatic gesture. He found himself twitching nervously at his tie. Cathy watched him, intently studying the pattern of the material.

He coughed, swallowed hard. It was difficult to find the right words. He decided to be as direct as possible. Gently, he took hold of her hand.

"Cathy, dearest ... I'm afraid Hosky has had a heart attack." Before she could interrupt him, he continued quickly: "It all happened very fast. She suffered no pain. Would you like to hear the details?"

"You mean she's dead." Cathy's voice was strangely quiet, resigned – as if the news came as no surprise. She bent her head over the kitten, stroked it more vigorously. "Yes, Leslie, I'd like to know what happened."

"Apparently Mrs Potter from the village was with her at the time. Hosky complained of feeling a little unwell, so her friend went into the kitchen to make a pot of tea. She heard a thud, rushed back into the living room. Hosky had collapsed. Her head was resting on the dining table. She was already dead, Cathy, but according to Mrs Potter, it looked as if she had simply fallen asleep. She insists Hosky didn't suffer in any way.

"At any rate, as you know my father was Hosky's doctor. He and Mrs Potter discussed it, thought it better you heard the news from me rather than over the telephone. So I came here straight away."

"But not until you'd picked up the kitten – something to soften the blow," whispered Cathy. "Oh, Leslie! Poor, dear Hosky!" She buried her head in her hands. The kitten, in a huff at being disturbed, moved onto Leslie's lap.

"Thank you for coming to tell me, Leslie, and for bringing the kitten. That was very kind ..." Her voice broke.

"Cathy, I know it's a dreadful time for this to have happened. So soon after ... Well, I know how attached you were to Hosky. But if it's any consolation to you, she had a very happy life with your family. And you know how content she was when she retired to the cottage in Ashfield. You have nothing to reproach yourself for. She had a good life ... and died the best way possible."

Cathy, her face white and strained, didn't answer. But he was relieved to see she remained relatively calm. She seemed to have taken the news quite well. Knowing Cathy, the succession of tragedies had probably deadened her reactions.

Leslie was terrified for both her and the baby; frightened how the unexpected news of Hosky's death would affect her. In her condition you could never tell. Cathy was already suffering the worst kind of bereavement. He longed to comfort her, to see her happy and light-hearted again. Just a few moments ago, with the kitten, she had really come alive, had seemed more like her old self.

"Cath, I know it's not the right time. I'm never any good at this kind of thing, and I know it's only a few months since Jimmy died. But with the baby and everything ... Well, what I'm trying to say is that I still want to marry you. You know I'd treat the baby as my own ... I just want you to know I'll be waiting."

"Leslie! You're my dearest friend. But please put marriage out of your mind. Can't you see, I'm bad luck for anyone who loves me? In any case, you deserve something better than a second-hand woman. It wouldn't be right." He could see the tears in her troubled eyes.

"Cathy, to me you will never be second-hand. You've always been – and always will be – the only woman for me. Forget about it now, but as I told you before, I'll always be here."

She squeezed his hand. Her voice was thick with emotion.

"You'd better tell me about the funeral arrangements." She rested her head on his shoulders. The tears started to slide slowly down her pale cheeks.

* * * * * * *

61

Cathy's baby was born on April 28th, the day before her own birthday. Right up until the time of the birth, she had kept fairly trim. If anything, apart from her relatively small bump in front and swelling breasts, her figure had become more trim, her face slimmer, showing her good bone structure to better advantage. Paradoxically, despite her state of pregnancy, she took on a more delicate appearance.

Nessie teased her.

"You look more glamorous every day. I'm sure you're carrying a rabbit, not a child – your tummy's just not big enough!"

Cathy had laughed, but inside she felt a flicker of worry. Her doctor had assured her all was well; but she had nagging memories of the ill-fated birth of her sister, and what had happened to her own mother. Nobody had expected any complications on that occasion either.

"Don't worry," the gynaecologist confirmed. "You're probably not carrying much water with the baby."

When her pains started, it was Leslie who took her to the hospital. She moved into a private ward with one other girl, Sue – a down-to-earth, robustly cheerful blonde, plump, with chipmunk cheeks. Soon after Cathy's arrival, and before she had the opportunity to get undressed and into bed, Sue's husband came to visit.

He leant across his wife's bed, gave her some bright yellow daffodils and a self-conscious kiss.

Turning to Cathy, he asked politely: "When did your baby arrive?"

"He hasn't, as yet," she replied, with a wan smile.

"Oh, I'm terribly sorry. It's just that you don't look at all fat – not like my wife here before the event!"

"Yes, it's awful, isn't it," agreed Cathy.

"I wouldn't worry about that," laughed Sue. "I had a friend who was just the same, but her baby bounced in at a hefty nine pounds. I only wish I'd stayed that slim. I looked like a mountain before Denise made her appearance."

Cathy was comforted by her words.

"Denise – is that your daughter's name? How lovely! That was my mother's name – she was French."

"You don't look at all French," said Sue.

Cathy laughed, trying to imagine the prototype of a French girl.

"I took after my father. The only thing I inherited from my mother was a certain flair for the language." She suddenly fell silent, remembering how, for fun, she and Jimmy had often spoken together in French. Jimmy's French had been excellent. He had spent several years of his childhood in France.

Sue and her husband seemed not to notice her preoccupation.

"What are you going to call your baby?"

"James," said Cathy firmly.

"But what if it's a girl?"

"He won't be. Oooouch! I'd better get undressed." She gave a nervous laugh. "He's definitely on the way!"

She was wrong! The baby was on the way, but it was a girl and, as it turned out, weighed a healthy seven-and-three-quarter pounds. The delivery went without incident. From the instant her baby was born, when she slithered like an eel from her protesting body, Cathy experienced fleeting moments of utter euphoria. She felt she could have run a mile, scaled a mountain. She chatted non-stop to the surgeon while he handled the few necessary stitches, and couldn't wait to see Nessie and Leslie.

At first she couldn't believe she had a daughter – not the son she had longed for. But taking the tiny infant in her arms, it suddenly didn't matter anymore. All her plans for Jimmy's son went out of the window. Jimmy's daughter, for all her femininity, looked just like him and Cathy was captivated. The baby had Jimmy's tawny eyes and fair complexion. Delicate wisps of blonde hair dusted her head. Cathy was enthralled by her new daughter.

Nessie and Leslie arrived shortly after she returned to her room from the delivery ward. Sue and her husband had already left with their baby. Her two friends peeped tentatively round the door, obviously expecting to find her asleep, but Cathy was lying wide-awake – proud and blissful – her baby nestled in her arms.

"Oh Cathy, she's beautiful!" enthused Nessie, rushing into the room. She touched the baby's perfect fingers and toes in wonderment. "It's a miracle! I still can't really believe it. But how are you feeling – you look wonderful!"

"Absolutely ecstatic!" laughed Cathy. "I couldn't have had a better birthday present!"

"Congratulations, Cathy! You both look marvellous." Leslie's face was one huge smile. He sat on the bed and studied the baby intently. "She looks just like Jimmy."

Cathy stared at him, searchingly. For all that Leslie had said before the birth, she couldn't help wondering how he would take the reality of the baby, especially a child which resembled Jimmy so strongly. She need not have worried. Leslie's face was devoid of any expression but genuine pleasure. There was no edge to his voice. If anything, she could see pride and awe in his eyes, as if the baby, despite her appearance, were his own.

Cathy smiled happily.

"Yes, she does, doesn't she?"

"So what are we going to call her?" asked Nessie, briskly. Cathy was delighted that her flat-mate already considered herself a joint owner of this wonderful new addition to their 'family'.

"Samantha," said Cathy determinedly. "And you, of course, must be her godmother."

"It's a pretty name," said Leslie. "Unusual. What made you think of it?"

"I don't really know. I'd only thought as far as 'James' – as you know. But 'Samantha' came to me just now and it seems to suit her so well."

"Samantha it is then," said Nessie. "But it's a bit of a mouthful. I shall always call her Sam!"

"You would," said Cathy with a grin, "and I expect we'll all end up doing the same."

"Must rush now," said Leslie standing up. "I'm officially still at work. I'll be back tomorrow, and we'll celebrate both your birthdays! Take it easy, Cath.

You'll need plenty of rest now." He bent his long frame and kissed her tenderly, then planted another quick kiss on the baby's head.

"Goodnight, Samantha. Goodnight, Cathy. Sleep well."

When he had gone, Nessie took Cathy's hand.

"Are you really OK, Cath?" she asked, anxiously. "No regrets about motherhood?"

"Just one," sighed Cathy. "I wish Jimmy could have seen his baby."

CHAPTER 10

Cathy's whole outlook on life changed after Samantha's birth. She still mourned Jimmy, missed him at times with a wrenching intensity; but her days with the baby were so full of love, activity, fun and friendship, she scarcely had time to dwell on the tragic past. She was determined to provide her daughter with all the love and affection she herself had enjoyed as a small child – with one difference. She vowed Samantha would never be left alone to suffer her own later deprivations.

The flat became a lively family centre. Nessie, who doted on Samantha, spent a whole seven-day leave helping Cathy when she came out of hospital. Leslie, too, virtually lived at the flat. Whenever he had any free time, he would call round. Simon Carstairs also took to dropping in more frequently, especially when Nessie was on leave! Nessie was obviously the main attraction, but for Simon, a man still caught up in the horrors of war, an innocent baby and the pattern of everyday family life at the flat, seemed to reassure and soothe him.

Samantha's life was so full of doting adults, Cathy's feared her daughter might be spoiled by so much loving attention. But Samantha thrived on the affection. She was an easy child. Right from the start she slept well, hardly ever cried. Enjoying a good six to seven hours of solid sleep each night, Cathy began to doubt all the stories she had heard about screaming babies, sleepless nights. She breast-fed her baby, so if her daughter did wake in the night, she would simply lift her into her own bed and feed her. Samantha would soon fall fast asleep again.

Even the black kitten Leslie had given her loved the baby, despite Cathy's fears that he might be jealous. Christened Sable because of his colour, he was a very possessive animal as far as Cathy was concerned. He adored to drape himself around her shoulders where he would stay perched, wherever she went.

"He's twice as good as a fur stole," declared Nessie. "He fits better, and you could never lose him."

When the baby first arrived at the flat, Sable, intrigued and fascinated by this new addition to the family, would try to climb into her cot. But Cathy wouldn't allow it, fearing he might, with misplaced affection, settle on the baby's face and suffocate her. Sable soon learned the cot was out of bounds. But if Samantha started to cry, the cat was always the first to hear the sound. He would run to Cathy's side meowing loudly, as if to warn her the baby needed attention.

"Just wait until Sam is old enough to play with Sable," Nessie exclaimed. "I shall be upstaged in my favourite's affections by a wretched cat!" Although no animal lover herself, Nessie had been unable to resist Sable. But she still made a joke of not liking cats.

However idyllic her new life in the South Kensington flat, Cathy couldn't escape the reality of war. The most upsetting factor was the incessant bombing raids. Fortunately for her and Samantha, most of the bombers headed for London's East End and docklands. But some bombs did fall on their side of

London, including one which landed at Buckingham Palace. Although concerned for her baby, Cathy felt no real fear. But she found the continual air-raid warnings, the black-out, the food shortages and rationing and all the other problems of living in war-time London, irritating and trying. The progress of the war itself was another continual concern.

However, like the majority of Londoners, she refused to be demoralized. Hitler's bombing raids made them all the more determined to resist his attacks – his savage incursions into their lives. Since Jimmy's death, Cathy hated the Germans with a vengeance. She would have done anything possible to help in their defeat. If it weren't for Samantha she would have been back in the WAAF. However bad the war news, she was stubbornly convinced that Hitler would eventually be defeated.

One evening in late May Leslie called at the flat, a huge teddy bear filling his arms.

"For Samantha," he explained.

"I didn't think it was for me," laughed Cathy. Sable as usual was curled across her shoulders.

"Knowing you, I wouldn't be so sure. I've seen that panda you keep by your pillow."

Cathy blushed, remembering the day so many years ago when her father had given her the fluffy toy she had kept close to her ever since.

She stroked the huge bear.

"He's gorgeous, Leslie. Where did you find him?"

"Discovered him in the attic down at Ashfield," he said airily.

"He's yours!" laughed Cathy. "And you talk about my panda!"

"At least it's more than twenty years since he's been on my bed!" said Leslie indignantly. He carried the bear over to Samantha's cot, where the baby lay fast asleep.

"He's far too big for the cot," laughed Cathy. "He'll smother her!"

Leslie grinned, planted a kiss on Samantha's cheek and with great ceremony sat the huge teddy bear by the side of the cot.

Sable gave a furious meow and launched himself on the bear, hissing and spitting, until finally convinced his foe was a harmless, inanimate object.

Cathy and Leslie both collapsed on the sofa, crying with laughter.

"Leslie – you're so good for my soul!" said Cathy wiping the tears from her eyes.

"And you're good for mine," he said, more seriously.

Her heart warmed to him. They fell to chatting about Samantha's latest activities but inevitably the conversation reverted, as always, to the progress of the war. News on the war front wasn't good, but Leslie was convinced that if the Americans could be won over to the struggle, the tide could soon be turned.

Watching him explaining in his habitually calm but forthright manner, Cathy was filled with tenderness for him. Over the last months, she had grown to appreciate his qualities more than ever. She had, in fact, already made up her mind to marry Leslie. It only remained to tell him. She didn't feel the same fierce heady love she had felt for Jimmy; but she did feel infinitely content and secure with him. Leslie had to be right for her. There was no doubting the depth of his affection for both herself and Samantha. He was a perfect companion and he would make a wonderful father for her baby, providing them with the family unity she had always craved. She couldn't really ask for more.

"That bomb which fell in Basil Street the other day was a bit too close for comfort," Leslie was saying.

But Cathy's attention had drifted to the open window; it was still quite light now the long summer evenings had set in. She liked to savour the soft colours of the sunset, before yielding again to the drab darkness of the blackout.

"What was that, Leslie? Sorry I was suddenly miles away, day-dreaming about those wonderful summer evenings at Ashford, before the war. They seem a life-time away."

"Don't worry, Cath. This mess of a war may take some time to sort out. But we shall do it. Then we can get back to real living once again."

"Can it ever be quite the same again?" mused Cathy.

"Quite honestly, no. Wars seem to create watersheds in history, the way the last war did. Nothing will be quite the same, even if we do manage to squash Hitler, restore all the countries he's grabbed. That doesn't mean it will all necessarily turn out for the worse. Some good may come out of this awful upheaval. As they say, 'It's an ill wind ...'"

"Have you thought what you'll do after it's all over?"

He smiled. "I can't stop thinking about it. I'm really not the type for this cloak-and-dagger stuff, you know. I'm far happier in the ivory towers of the academic world. Research and lecturing are what I plan to get back to. How about you, Cath? Have you any thoughts?"

His lean, strong face looked unusually boyish in the soft evening light, but his eyes were as penetrating as ever.

Cathy took a deep breath.

"I was wondering if there might be a place for me – as the wife of a future Oxford don?"

Leslie was silent. The tick of the carriage clock on her mantelpiece sounded unusually loud. She could hear a young child crying on the pavement outside.

"Do you really mean that, Cathy – or am I dreaming?" His voice was a whisper.

She nodded and edged closer to him.

He put his head in his hands, then slowly raised his eyes to meet hers again. "You know, I've imagined and dreamed of you saying something like that countless times. Now it's happened ... I just can't believe it ... Do you mean it – do you really want to marry me, Cath?" His grey eyes searched hers for reassurance.

"Yes, my darling – if you're still prepared to have me!" She smiled softly. "I know it's not been the easiest of courtships."

He suddenly came alive, pulled her to her feet, grabbed her in his arms. Together they danced and gambolled round the room like a couple of children, half-laughing, half-crying."

"Just wait till I tell Samantha," cried Leslie.

Cathy chuckled. "I've already told her. After all, I needed to get her approval."

"And did she approve, or will I need to bribe her with an even bigger cuddly toy?"

"Oh, she approved all right," laughed Cathy. "She gave a huge burp, then that enigmatic smile she always bestows just before she messes her nappy."

"That's settled then. What I'd do for a bottle of champagne!"

"Strange you should say that. I just happen to have one in the refrigerator – at great cost I should add. A bottle of Dom Perignon!"

"You actually thought I'd accept your proposal?" said Leslie, in mock severity. He hugged her again. Cathy had never seen him so light-hearted – it was so unlike Leslie to banter with her.

"Now, young lady, come and sit beside me and I'll tell you what I've planned for tomorrow." He became more serious. "Cath, as you know, I'm free this weekend. Would you come down to Ashfield with me to see my father?"

"But Leslie ..."

"I already had it planned – before you dropped your bombshell. Now it seems even more appropriate. After all he will be your father-in-law and he's only seen you a few times since you were a young girl. I do nothing but talk about you. The old boy gruffly suggested the other week that it was about time I brought you down to visit him again."

"But I was going to do some shopping in the morning. Sam's growing so quickly, I need some new clothes for her. And I thought I'd paint the kitchen this weekend – it's desperately in need of a spring-clean."

"No problem. We can pick up some stuff for Sam on the way down. I'll give you a hand with the kitchen another day. I was going to keep it a secret, but I'd better tell you – my elder brother, Paul, has just arrived back on leave from the Navy. I'm dying for you to meet him."

He was so proud and enthusiastic, Cathy couldn't refuse him. Besides, she knew she would enjoy a couple of days in the country. And it would be fun to meet Leslie's brother. She already had a soft spot for his father, but had hardly seen him since Hosky died. And it would certainly do the baby good to get some fresh country air.

"OK, Leslie, tomorrow it is. What time?"

"I'll pick you up at nine-thirty. We'll stop off in Kensington High Street to get some things for Sam. I want her to look smart as paint for her new uncle and Grandpa." He gave a wide grin. Cathy smiled back, but realised her eyes were moist with tears.

* * * * * * *

The weekend at Ashfield was a great success. Leslie's father obviously doted on both his sons. A tall lean balding man with a gruff manner and sardonic wit, he had been a widower for three years. But his work as a GP with a thriving country practice kept him well occupied. He seemed genuinely pleased to see Cathy again, and a wide smile lit his stern features when Leslie told him they were getting married.

"I was beginning to think these two young men of mine would never settle down," he growled, with a sidelong wink at Cathy. "I know it's war-time and all that, but in my young days, that wouldn't have put us off! Leslie's always doted on you, my dear. And Paul here had plenty of time before the war – even if he was in the Navy."

"But I was never lucky enough to find a girl like Cathy," laughed Paul. "Otherwise I might have thought twice about becoming a family man."

Cathy went crimson. She'd instinctively taken to Paul. He looked a lot like Leslie in features and build, but was far more worldly and extrovert, and always laughing. He lacked Leslie's quiet sensitivity, but she knew she would have no problems getting on with this wonderful new family of hers. Neither Paul nor Leslie's father seemed to resent the fact she had been married before, and Sam as usual was the centre of attention.

The day flew past – a family day full of fun and affection. Cathy hadn't felt so happy since the birth of Samantha. She was thrilled to be so easily accepted as a part of Leslie's family.

Unfortunately their weekend stay was cut short. The news bulletin the following morning mentioned South Kensington as one of the areas damaged during the previous night's air-raid. When she heard, Cathy couldn't stop worrying. It wasn't the flat so much, she explained to Leslie, as poor Sable, who had been left with her neighbour, Mrs Dauncey, who lived above. He would be completely terrified – as would Mrs Dauncey – if any bombs had dropped nearby. They decided to leave after breakfast and motored straight up to London.

It was soon after eleven o'clock when they reached South Kensington. As the car swung out of Queensgate into her avenue, Cathy let out a gasp of horror. She couldn't believe the scene which met her eyes. The building containing her home was no longer there – a huge crater gaped deep and wide in its place! Miraculously enough, the neighbouring house to the left was still standing, practically intact. The entrance to the mews, on the other side of the wiped-out building, was littered with concrete and debris. Smoke still rose from the crater and hung heavily in the air.

She stared across at Leslie in stunned silence. He hesitated for a moment, then quickly recovering from the initial shock, swung the car as close as possible to the scene of devastation. Leaving Samantha fast asleep in her carry cot, they both leapt out and ran towards the police cordon.

"Cathy – you're sure Nessie didn't come up on leave this weekend?" demanded Leslie.

"Quite sure. She didn't have another forty-eight-hour leave for two weeks. I only spoke to her a few days ago ... But Leslie – poor Mrs. Dauncey...and Sable!"

Pushing their way through the crowd of onlookers, Leslie grabbed hold of the nearest policeman, explained Cathy's flat had been one of those in the bombed-out building. The bobby, nodding sympathetically, directed them through the police cordon.

They spotted a neighbour standing dazed outside the next-door building. He waved them over. Cathy, cold and trembling from shock, was happy to leave the questions and talking to Leslie.

Her neighbour looked drawn and tired. He shook his head in apparent disbelief. "It was a heavy explosive ..." he explained, in little more than whisper,

" ...just before one in the morning. You wouldn't have believed the noise and the blast. My wife and I are lucky to be alive!"

"How many casualties?" asked Leslie tersely.

"Three dead in your building, as far as we can tell – everyone who was in the house at the time ... it was a direct hit. A few light injuries in neighbouring houses. All of Queensgate was cordoned off at one time, to help the firemen and ambulances."

"My upstairs neighbour ... Mrs Dauncey ..." Cathy managed to stammer. "Was she among the people who died?"

"I'm afraid so – and Mr and Mrs Pollard in the downstairs flat."

"Oh no," moaned Cathy. "Mary Dauncey was such a lovely old lady. I never knew the Pollards very well – they only moved in a couple of weeks ago. The flat had been empty since Mr and Mrs Wells moved to the country."

"You don't know how lucky you were young lady – not being here last night. My wife saw you and your young man leaving yesterday with the baby. We were pretty sure you didn't return last night. You'd better give your details to the police – they've just finished digging out the last of the bodies. They're still trying to check on missing people."

"We'll do that right away," said Leslie gruffly, visibly shaken himself by the scene of devastation. He took Cathy firmly by the hand.

Cathy was dying to ask if anybody had seen her cat, but it seemed too trite and silly a question to ask when three people had just died so tragically.

They gave their details to the police and went back to the car to check on Samantha in her carry cot. At a loss to know what to do next, Cathy slumped down on the pavement beside the car.

Tears started to stream down her face.

"Oh, Leslie – my lovely home ... dear old Mrs Dauncey and the Pollards ... and poor, poor Sable!"

"Cathy! Think how lucky we've been!" said Leslie fiercely. "It could have been ten times worse. Both you and Sam might have been killed! Thank God you weren't there! It could have been the two of you – buried under all that rubble."

He shuddered and pulled her into his arms, held her tightly for several seconds, then started to stroke her hair.

"I'm sorry about poor Sable," he said more gently.

She looked up at him in horror as the full realisation finally sank into her numbed mind.

"Oh God, Leslie, you're right! If it hadn't been for you, both Sam and I would have been in there!" She turned and stared in horror at the gaping crater, the ugly piles of rubble. "If you hadn't persuaded me to go down to the country ..." A shiver went through her body at the thought of what might have happened.

"Listen, Cathy – believe me and trust me. This is going to be the last of your bad luck. From now on, you're with me and everything is going to be all right." He turned her face firmly towards his, then grasped her hands so tightly she flinched. "I promise you, Cath. I'm looking after you from now on. Nothing bad will ever happen to you again." His grey eyes searched hers. "Can you believe what I'm saying?"

At that moment, a fluffy black object launched itself onto Cathy's shoulders, draped itself with obvious relief around her neck.

"Sable, oh Sable!" Overwhelmed, she grasped the cat by his paws, turned to Leslie with glowing eyes. "I can't believe it – he's alive... oh, Leslie ... after all that's happened! I just can't believe it. He doesn't even seem to be hurt."

Leslie gently extricated the cat from Cathy's neck and shoulders, examined him carefully. Sable was trembling with shock, covered in dust and cement, but otherwise appeared none the worse for wear. They both hugged and kissed the bewildered animal.

Cathy turned to Leslie. Tears streamed down her cheeks, but her face was wreathed with smiles.

"Going back to your last question, Leslie," she said, happily. "Yes, I do believe you. I know you'll look after me and I'm sure that from now on, everything will get better and better!"

PART TWO

JAMES

His flight was madness: when our actions do not,
Our fears do make us traitors.

William Shakespeare

The shackles of an old love straighten'd him,
His honour rooted in dishonour stood,
And faith unfaithful kept him falsely true.

Tennyson

CHAPTER 11

Normandy, France November 1940

Everybody said Jimmy Proctor was born lucky, but in late November his luck ran out – as he always knew it would.

He spotted them as they came diving out of the clouds – at least half a dozen Messerschmitt 109s.

"Bandits at five o'clock above!" he yelled to Simon. "Climb, climb!" Wheeling sharply, he headed for the layer of cloud above. Simon followed, but so did the Messerschmitts. Jimmy could hear the pounding of his heart above the sound of the Hurricane's engines. He felt the familiar tightening in his chest, the gnawing at his stomach. Despite the countless hours he'd now spent in air combat, he could never rid himself of the incessant fear.

His stomach churned wildly as the fighter clawed its way up through the swirling clouds. Damn these 'rhubarb missions', he thought. Chances were you'd end up a sitting duck. They'd been the latest brainwave of some of the big wigs at group HQ – a new way of striking at the enemy, they called it. Why had he volunteered? He knew the answer to that one – to prove his non-existent bravery once again! Would he never learn?

The idea behind the 'rhubarb missions' was simple enough. Whenever there was a deep layer of cloud hanging low over the land, pairs of fighters would dart off across the Channel to shoot at anything German on the ground or in the air. Should the going get tough, the fighters were supposed to climb and hide in the cloud. It sounded simple enough – until everything went wrong!

Today had been a perfect day for such a mission with a deep layer of cloud at nine hundred feet. He and Simon had set off together across the Channel, had just reached the French coast when they'd spotted a German battalion in a field near Le Touquet. They had been successfully strafing when they were 'bounced' by the 109s.

They needed height. He and Simon were hopelessly outnumbered. By the time they came out of the cloud, they must have the advantage of sun and height to stand an earthly. At eighteen thousand feet his Hurricane cleared the cloud layer; he carried on climbing and wheeled round to come out of the sun. Below and just emerging from the cloud, he spotted Simon, with three of the 109s hard on his heels.

He picked the middle Messerschmitt and plunged downwards. A hundred yards from the enemy plane, he aimed and gave a three-second burst. He saw flame spurt from the side of the 109. Suddenly the whole plane was a single fire-ball. He wheeled violently to the left, banking steeply. One of the fighters broke away with him.

Again he spun round on his wing tip. The mounting 'g' forced the blood from his brain, clouded his vision. He eased the pressure on the stick and as his sight improved saw the flash of bullets. He felt a sickening shudder, heard a crashing explosion as cannon shells slammed into his machine. He knew he'd been hit but his mind went suddenly numb, refusing to accept the reality. The Hurricane no longer responded to the controls. It lurched, then started to fall. Soon it was diving in a deep spiral.

Wild panic flooded through him dispelling the numbness in his brain, bringing him viciously back to reality. This is it, he thought, his mind and body awash with fear. I've finally bought it. Then pure animal instinct for survival came to his rescue.

"Christ! I MUST get out!"

That choice seemed even worse than his present predicament. How tempting to just give in, to leave behind all the nerve-wracking traumas; never again to feel the numbing fear, the pressures of keeping up a brave front. Then he remembered – Cathy!

"Damn it!" he yelled to himself. "Get out – before it's too late." He knew he wouldn't stand a chance once his air-speed increased – he must be doing 400 mph already!

Panic still gripped him, but with wildly fumbling hands he managed to wrench off his helmet and mask. Desperately trying to think clearly, he yanked the rubber ball above his head. The hood ripped away and he was suddenly surrounded by a hell of shrieking noise. He levered himself out and thrust with his legs. The wind tore and clawed at him, sucked him up and away. The noise and buffeting suddenly stopped – he was falling, free and silent.

He felt a wave of relief flood through his body, then panic again. Christ, the parachute! He felt for the D-ring, grasped it hard. There was a crack like a rifle shot as the parachute opened, then blissfully he was floating. The sensation was so pleasant, so timeless and effortless that everything seemed unreal. Was he already dead? Could this be some strange kind of heaven?

Cloud swirled around him, but as he fell clear of it, he came quickly to his senses. He could see for miles. Immediately below him were strips of green grass and neat corn-fields. Several peasant figures stood close by a cottage gate. He could see them gazing up at him as he fell. God, I've actually made it, he thought. Just when I thought it was all over. Lucky Jimmy again – or was he? He didn't know whether to feel relief or sadness. One thing he did know – he couldn't go through this again, he wasn't ever going back. But what about Cathy shouted his heart and his conscience?

The ground suddenly rose to meet him, much too fast. Christ! I've misjudged it, he thought with horror. He was going to land in a tree. He tried desperately to spill air, to slip sideways. He lost control and all too suddenly the ground rose up before him, hit him, hard as iron. Everything went cold and grey as he slipped into a soft cotton-wool cloud of unconsciousness.

* * * * * * *

James Proctor's friends had every good reason to say Jimmy was born lucky. A clever and attractive child born to doting wealthy parents, he grew up, as was to be expected, a handsome and capable young man with a more-than-comfortable income.

Jimmy often wondered if this so-called 'luck' hadn't been the source of all his problems. Nobody could believe that a young man, who appeared to have every natural and financial advantage, could be anything but happy and secure. Jimmy wasn't. But he felt bound to live up to everyone's expectations. Charming and intelligent, with undeniable sex appeal, he endeavoured to keep up the somewhat sardonic front of the experienced man-about-town with a whole world of dazzling opportunities at his fingertips.

But psychologically he couldn't live up to these intellectual and physical perfections. The root of his trouble was raw fear – he knew he was a coward at heart. He tried to fight it, but the demon never left his side. It gnawed at his stomach whenever he was under any physical or even mental pressure, became a raging monster when he was in real danger.

He had tried to work out when the devil fear started to take over his life. Born in Scotland in 1915, he had never known his naval father, Commander John Proctor, who died in action in 1917. His mother, Rowena, smothered him with love and affection, the more so following the death of her adored husband.

As Jimmy grew older this lavish affection changed to excessive possessiveness and domination. He found her overwhelming love frightening rather than reassuring. It made him nervous and apprehensive. His mother, recognising his exceptional physical and mental gifts, demanded excellence in all he did. This had made it even worse.

As a child, with an understanding tutor and later at prep school, he found life relatively easy. He excelled at his lessons and did just as well on the sportsfield. Although never brawny for his age, his well-proportioned body and perfect co-ordination ensured him success at every kind of sport from rugger to sailing. He had an easy charm and manner with both his superiors and contemporaries, never lacking friends. Despite his obvious gifts, his unassuming personality rarely roused envy or resentment.

Jimmy won a scholarship to Harrow. It was there he first came face to face with his fear. Prior to this, he had experienced occasional moments when a strange unexplicable terror had gripped him: finding himself out of his depth in water, though he was a superb swimmer; climbing steep mountain paths in his native highlands; show-jumping on his favourite pony. An excellent young rider with an unusual affinity for the animals he rode, his unreasonable fear of falling led him to give up hunting and jumping. There was so much else he preferred to do, he told his mother – much to Rowena's chagrin.

These moments of terror had worried him, but he eventually dismissed them as quite normal for a young boy. After all, he thought, everyone was frightened of something. He never discussed his fears with his mother – knowing her reaction would be one of complete disbelief if not disgust. Jimmy to her was the perfect child. To suggest otherwise would have shattered her every illusion. So he kept up the brave front, remained silent.

He would always remember that day of revelation during his first term at Harrow. Jimmy had walked into the quad one sunny morning on his way to a Latin class. His attention was drawn to a small group in one corner of the otherwise deserted area. Three large lads surrounded a much younger boy. He immediately recognised the smaller boy – Henry Forsythe Minor, a classmate of his.

About to call to his friend that he would be late for class, he suddenly noticed the menacing posture of the older boys. Two of them were burly lads he vaguely recognised from their activities on the rugger field. The other was a relatively small but wiry boy with freckles, a narrow mean face and plastered-down, sandy-coloured hair. His thin lips were smiling at Forsythe Minor, a cruel twisted smile, his eyes full of menace. He reminded Jimmy of a weasel eyeing its prey. Instinctively he knew that this boy, despite his smaller build, was in charge of the situation.

Weasel Face glanced meaningly at the darker of his companions who nodded, suddenly moved in closer, punched Henry Forsythe low in the stomach. The young boy screamed, doubling over with pain.

"That'll teach you to do as you're told," hissed Weasel Face, his voice low and harsh.

Forsythe Minor had already straightened up.

"I've done all I'm prepared to do," he said, defiantly. "You can't make me do any more. I know the rules of fagging. In any case what you want me to do isn't right. You're all sick!" He raised his head high, but his tiny frame trembled.

This time it was Weasel Face himself who cuffed him round the ears. The blow brought tears to Henry's eyes, but still he stood firm.

"I ... I shall do what I have to – nothing more," he stammered bravely.

Both of the bigger youths moved in, started punching the fragile figure.

Jimmy stood mesmerised, watching in horror as his friend was beaten up. He was incapable of moving – as if his legs were glued to the ground. He wanted to shout to the bullies to stop, to run to Henry's aid, but instead he shook with terror. The demon fear was back, tearing at his stomach.

He knew he wouldn't stand a chance in a fight with the three bigger boys, but his conscience insisted he should at least run and get help, perhaps report the bullies to someone in authority.

The burly youths dragged Forsythe Minor to his feet again. Jimmy could see his friend's face, all crumpled with tears, pain and fright. He felt himself trembling at the horror of the situation; could sense cold sweat oozing from his pores. He must help Henry. Oh God, why wouldn't his limbs respond?

Forsythe Minor stared appealingly at his tormentors. From the corner of his eye he must have spotted Jimmy. He turned suddenly, looked beseechingly at his class-mate. Jimmy's heart sank. The other boys followed Henry's gaze and spotting Jimmy, stared at him long and hard, their expressions fierce yet apprehensive. Weasel Face stayed cool, his top lip raised in a malicious sneer.

Jimmy ran – as fast as his legs could carry him. But he didn't fetch help. His agile mind easily justified his lack of action: it would only make it worse for Henry in the future. If the bullies were reported and punished, they would find some other way of getting back at Forsythe Minor. But deep down he knew the truth. It wasn't only Henry he was concerned about but himself; he had vicariously suffered every one of the blows Henry had borne so bravely; he feared if he reported the youths, they would get back at him as well, not just Henry. He couldn't bear the thought of what he might suffer at their hands.

"You did see what was happening, didn't you, Proctor?" appealed Forsythe Minor, when he finally caught up with Jimmy. "I want to report them. Will you come with me as a witness? I'm too afraid to do it on my own. They wouldn't believe the last boy who informed on them ... said he had a grudge – it was his word against the three of them."

"I ... I really don't think that's such a good idea," stammered Jimmy. "They'll only try to get back at you again. Don't worry – they won't touch you any more, now they know I've seen them." He hated himself as he said it, wished he had the courage of young Henry. He knew he would never have stood up to the three youths. The thought of it made him feel sick inside. An insistent little voice inside his head told him to report the bullying, the evil intentions of the three youths. Other small boys might be at risk. His stomach churned. He couldn't bring himself to do it.

Forsythe Minor gave him a long, strange look.

"I thought you were my friend, Proctor."

Jimmy's heart sank. He felt ashamed and sickened.

"I'm sorry, Henry," he said, weakly. "But I think it's for the best."

His friendship with Henry Forsythe was never the same after that day. But at least Jimmy came face to face with his fear. Thoroughly shamed by his dreadful act of cowardice, he vowed he would never let his terror get the better of him again. Whatever it cost him, however he must suffer, he was determined he would never act the coward again. His fear and cowardice would remain his own terrible secret, never to be revealed to any other human being.

From that day on, only one other person ever realised that Jimmy was anything but the fearless, devil-may-care character he endeavoured constantly to portray.

That person was Cathy.

His mother was another matter!

Chapter 12

Aberdeen, Scotland. August 1934

"No, Mother I've made up my mind – I'm going into the Air Force."

"James, you know that's absolutely impossible!" Rowena's voice was hard, the tone commanding. She stood proud and straight. Jimmy had to admit that despite her slim form, his mother in one of her arrogant moods made an imposing figure.

"It's not impossible, Mother. In fact I've already been accepted for a training course at Cranwell.

"But we've always planned you would go on to Oxford when you left Harrow."

"*You've* always planned, Mother," said Jimmy quietly. "I don't recall my own part in that decision."

"Don't be silly, darling. It's always been an understanding between us. In any case, you know I only have your welfare at heart. I just don't understand the attraction of all this flying nonsense."

She smoothed her already immaculate hair and sat down gracefully by Jimmy's side. Rowena was now well into middle-age, but her figure remained as trim as ever. She was dressed in a classic dove-grey suit, a contrasting blue silk scarf draped casually around her slender neck. Rowena's intuitive dress-sense and natural style added to the aura of easy elegance always surrounding her. Grudgingly, Jimmy had to admit his mother was still a stylish, striking woman. 'A real classy dame', a young American classmate of his had commented, one Speech Day at Harrow. If only she would marry again, thought Jimmy, perhaps then she would loosen her attempted stranglehold on his life.

Rowena moved closer to his side. Jimmy sensed a softening in her manner. He knew what that meant. Since he had grown older, more independent, his mother could no longer rely on her authoritative approach. When this failed she would try gentle persuasion, followed eventually by tears and pleadings. It had become a familiar pattern – one that Jimmy dreaded. He loved his mother, but found her over-protection and attempts to dominate his life completely suffocating.

"I'm sorry, mother, but my mind's made up."

"Now, darling, let's discuss this sensibly." She spoke softly, but her grey eyes remained hard and determined. She placed a slender hand on Jimmy's knee. "You have great academic talent and with a double first from Oxford your future would be secure. Your grandfather was an extremely successful ambassador. With your talents and flair for languages, I'm sure you could follow an equally accomplished diplomatic career."

"Mother, please don't exaggerate. My French is pretty good simply because of the years we spent in France when I was a youngster. In any case, I'm just not interested in all that diplomatic scene. Half the problems in Europe now including those upstarts, Hitler and Mussolini, could be solved if the diplomats sorted themselves out – stopped chin-wagging. At least I shall have some excitement flying."

"But darling, flying's so dangerous," pleaded Rowena.

Jimmy felt the old familiar fear surge through him.

"What nonsense, Mother! It's no more dangerous than driving that sports car of yours." How could he ever explain to his mother. It was because flying had an edge of danger that he had to do it. He couldn't admit it, but deep down he would love to settle for the fascinating diplomatic life his grandfather had enjoyed – his agile brain and winning manner well-suited him for the profession. But he still had to prove himself, not take the easy way out; he had to overcome the fear demon before he could enjoy any inner peace. He was hoping flying would exorcise his terror in much the same way that continual handling of snakes can overcome a person's fear of reptiles!

Rowena clasped his arm. Her eyes began to fill with tears.

"James, darling, you're all I have left in the world. My only wish is for you to be safe and secure in a fine career. I couldn't bear the thought of you up in the sky all the time in one of those dreadful machines. And what future is there for you in the RAF? It's not as if you were wanting to go into the Navy like your father ... and that was bad enough ..." Her voice broke.

James put his arm around her.

"Please don't upset yourself, Mother. The RAF is a jolly good outfit; lots of my friends are joining up. The Air Force may not have the reputation of the 'Senior Service', but I bet that in any future flare-up, the RAF will become more important than the rest of the armed forces!"

"Oh, don't start talking about wars, James. I could never go through another. Let's hope it won't come to that. Please, darling, please reconsider your decision. Tell me now you'll give up all this flying nonsense." Carefully she dabbed her tears dry, her mascara remaining miraculously intact. Finally she gave him a tremulous, winning smile.

Jimmy felt his patience slip away.

"Mother, I've already told you. I'm very sorry, but I've made up my mind!"

Rowena's eyes flashed, her words tumbling out harsh and fast.

"How can you do this to me, James? You know all I've had to suffer, all I've done for you. How can you be so utterly heartless and ungrateful!" She stood up and glared at him, her face white with anger. "I'm warning you, James. I shall never forgive you if you go ahead with this ridiculous career!"

"It is not a ridiculous career!" retorted Jimmy heatedly. "It's as honourable as any other, if not more so. Mother, you have to realise I'm no longer a child. I love you dearly, but I must organise my life as I see fit."

"James, I repeat that if you continue with this ridiculous idea, I shall never forgive you. If you want to make a complete mess of your life, I want no part of it."

"That's your choice, Mother, but I'm sure in time you'll understand what I am doing and why."

"I'm afraid you underestimate the strength of my feelings, James. Don't think you can take advantage of my love for you. I'm amazed by your utter selfishness and arrogance, your complete disregard for my feelings. You're not the son I once knew."

She turned and swept regally from the room. Jimmy sighed. He hated these scenes, regretted upsetting her. But what else could he do? She would come round with time; best to leave her to her own devices until she calmed down.

Unfortunately, Rowena never really calmed down. If anything she became more implacable. With the passing of the years, her relationship with her son went from bad to worse.

* * * * * * *

If it hadn't been for the flying, Jimmy would have thoroughly enjoyed his days at Cranwell! There was plenty of discipline, but unlike school the flight cadets were treated as adults. They could smoke and drink within moderation and as cadets stay out until midnight. He and most of his friends had motorbikes and they had great fun visiting local pubs and dances. The girls came flocking to Jimmy's side. For the first time he became fully aware of his powerful attraction for the opposite sex.

Best of all there was plenty of opportunity for the sports he adored. He played rugger, hockey and cricket and excelled at them all. In the classroom he found the theory side of flying – engines, weapons and communications – equally fascinating and easy to absorb.

Flying was another matter. Paradoxically he had a natural aptitude which the instructors soon spotted, but unfortunately his talent at flying didn't diminish the fear in the pit of his stomach every time he took off. He listened with envy when friends described their time spent in the air as thrilling, exhilarating. Eventually his fear did grow less; it shrank to a dull gnawing in his stomach, like a tiresome ulcer which he had learned to live with.

To his friends and instructors he was breezy and fearless; never once did he fail to keep up his devil-may-care image. At times he didn't know which was worse – the burden of his fears, or the pressures of keeping up a brave front. One thing was certain: with his natural aptitude he was sure he would be accepted as a fighter pilot.

Once his mother realised he had no intention of giving up his flying career, their relationship deteriorated even further. Alone in Scotland, Rowena sometimes refused to accept his telephone calls. Jimmy was convinced she was becoming mentally unbalanced. On the occasions she did agree to speak to him, she would sometimes plead hysterically with him to give up flying; at other times she would act cool and detached, as if he were a stranger.

Her doctor confirmed his worse fears.

"I'm afraid your mother has been slightly unbalanced ever since the death of your father," he told Jimmy. "For a long time she refused to accept the reality of his death. You became a replacement for him. Now she believes she's lost you as well. She finds it difficult to reconcile herself with the facts, so she retreats into disbelief. Unfortunately, talking to you forces her to face the truth."

"But there's no reason why she should lose me – why we can't remain friends," said Jimmy, disconsolately. "She simply refuses to accept my decision to fly."

The doctor looked at him, nodded his head in sympathy.

"She refuses because she doesn't want you to fly; she fears for your safety – that she might lose you completely just as she lost your father. By shutting you out of her life, she shuts out the possibility that something might happen to you. It sounds illogical, but to her tortured mind it's the only possible way out."

Jimmy may have lacked the outward expression of a mother's love, but he certainly made up for it with the weight of affection he received from a multitude of girlfriends. But he never became more than mildly attached to any of them. This aura of unattainability, together with his good looks and disarming charm, made him even more magnetic to the female sex. With the passing of time he found the fawning young girls ingenuous and uninspiring. He moved on to older women, some of them married.

His friends teased him.

"Not only do you dice with death in the air; you're also running as many risks in your mistresses' bedrooms!" one told him. "Any day now an irate husband will chop you up in little pieces!"

Jimmy would only wink and grin.

After receiving his commission from Cranwell, he was posted to Kenley. His reputation for skill and bravado in the air had grown. He was already becoming something of a legend amongst his fellow pilots. He and his new friend, Simon Carstairs – a cool, fearless young pilot – were chosen as the aerobatic team for that year's Hendon pageant. Their brilliant synchronised flying brought the highest accolades from press and public alike. For Jimmy the show had been ten minutes of living hell, even though he was becoming more confident of his flying skills. But when he read the extravagant words of praise for his performance in the *The Times*, he felt the happiest he'd been for years. The fear was still there, but muted.

Yet as the international situation worsened, the inner terror grew again – like a foul grey worm insinuating its way into his very entrails.

* * * * * * *

In 1939 the threat of war became reality. On September 1st Hitler invaded Poland. Two days later, Chamberlain announced that Britain was now at war with Germany.

Jimmy and Simon were posted to Duxford; but life continued much as usual throughout the 'phoney war' with convoy patrols and practice flying. News of the activities of the RAF squadrons stationed in France, of their dog-fights with the Luftwaffe, filtered through to Jimmy's fighter station. Many of his fellow pilots started to complain about the lack of action at Duxford. They feared the war would all be over before they had a chance to get at the enemy.

But the demon terror was back again with Jimmy. His confidence in his own flying skills was now outweighed by his dread of air combat. There was a big difference between executing pretty tricks in mid-air, and being shot at by another trained fighter intent on killing his adversary. He knew that in combat the luck factor was vital. The most skilful of pilots wouldn't stand a chance against the vagaries of hard metal bullets. Sick at heart, he joined in the impatient complaints with the others, giving every impression he was dying to get at the enemy.

"Just wait until Jimmy comes up against the Huns," joked Simon, "he'll soon sort them out."

Jimmy thumped his friend on the shoulder, grinned his agreement. But he dreaded anyone looking at him more closely, lest his eyes betray the haunting fear within.

In March 1940 the air war in France, which had been quiet over the winter months, flared up anew. Still Jimmy's squadron were stuck with the eternal convoys. Even he was becoming bored with training and patrols. The fear and anticipation of action seemed worse than the reality. Like most of his squadron, he now wished they could get on with it.

Then he met Cathy Harvey. His whole life changed in one swift instant of time. He'd never forget that moment.

* * * * * * *

Nessie had been particularly eager to introduce them. She'd often mentioned her flatmate. He knew Cathy Harvey was one of the few women Nessie really respected. At the party Nessie had led him straight over to meet her.

'Cathy, I'd like you to meet Jimmy Proctor. Jimmy, this is Cathy Harvey.'

He looked into candid blue-grey eyes and immediately sensed a strange empathy he'd never felt before. The girl was obviously shy and a little nervous – goodness knows what Nessie had been telling her about him! Her full lips trembled slightly as they shook hands, but her fingers were cool, firm, capable. He gazed at her from top to toe, amused by her obvious embarrassment at his candid appraisal. She had an aura of wholesomeness and innocence he found instantly appealing. In recent months he had grown cynical about his lady friends. Nessie had been a welcome relief from previous companions. At least she had spark and wit, despite her sometimes acid tongue. There was never a dull moment with Nessie.

But this girl was something different. Not obviously sexy, but attractive in a frank, disarming way. Chatting to her as they prepared the drinks, he felt strangely protective. At the same time he was enchanted and impressed by her sensitivity. She seemed to read through him, to understand his innermost fear without condemnation. For one crazy moment he felt he could have told this girl everything, revealed his innermost soul, his every fear. Yet he'd only known her a few brief minutes.

He remembered her soft, searching question: 'Isn't it dreadful being a pilot?' She didn't see him as the others did – as a steely, glamorous superman. Her eyes reflected total understanding of his terror. Yet he'd still felt forced to play his eternal role as the brash warrior. At least he'd been able to joke with her about his 'hero' image.

Leaving the party, he knew he had to see her again. For some strange reason she was a kindred spirit. He'd been annoyed at Cathy's later coolness. She was probably the first woman not to fall instantly captive to his charm. It was only later he realised her initial resistance was due to her loyalty to Nessie. Once again she soared in his estimation.

Their whirlwind courtship had taken far too long for Jimmy. All he knew was that being with Cathy was like coming home after years of absence. Always sensitive to his own short-comings, he had questioned his inner motives. Was his sudden infatuation in any way due to his estrangement from Rowena? Cathy did offer the warmth, comfort and protection of a mother figure – yet it wasn't just that. She also had the child-like appeal of innocence, which brought out his deepest protective instincts. More importantly – she was his *alter ego*, the only person who instinctively understood his every need and emotion. It was a kind of liberation. He didn't need to express his fears – Cathy already knew and understood.

He had planned to explain it all to her one day – the whole story from the very beginning.

But now, as he made hard vicious contact with the unyielding French soil, he realised he would never have the opportunity.

Chapter 13

Normandy, France November 1940

Drifting back into consciousness, Jimmy could hear their voices, hushed but excited. Why the dickens were they speaking French? Probably the chaps in the billet – up to their silly pranks again. But he didn't recognise the vocal inflections and why was his head pounding so? It was ages since he'd suffered such a dreadful hangover – not since he'd met Cathy ...

Cathy! Suddenly the haze cleared and memory flooded back. The dog fight! He'd been hit – but he obviously hadn't bought it! He'd baled out. He couldn't remember landing. Of course – the tree ... had he missed the tree? It didn't matter – he was still alive.

Panic seized him. Alive, yes ... but in one piece? He tried to feel his hands, his legs. Don't be silly, he told himself. They say you can still sense those – even when they're cut off! Right now he couldn't feel anything – except the dreadful throbbing in his head. He groaned.

"He opens the eyes," whispered one of the figures hovering above him. Jimmy recognised the regional French accent. Of course! He'd baled out over Normandy, but goodness knows where. In his hasty retreat into the clouds, the wheeling battle – he'd lost all track of his bearings.

Someone pressed water to his cracked lips – he suddenly realised how dry his mouth and throat were.

"Everything eez good ... not to worry." It was a deep gruff voice, its stilted English thickly accented.

"Je ... je parle ... francais ..." Jimmy managed to tell them, his mouth still thick and furry.

"Bon, bon, beaucoup mieux," came the gruff voice – in nasal French this time. "Much better if we speak in French – my English is ten year's rusty!"

"Where am I?" asked Jimmy in French, too frightened to ask if he was still in one piece.

"In a farmhouse near Caen. There is nothing to worry about. You are safe for the moment and unhurt – just a few cuts and bruises. You will feel a little dazed – you have been unconscious for nearly half an hour."

"Thank you for your help," sighed Jimmy, relief flooding through his body.

"We have to move you quickly – the Germans will be searching for you. Fortunately we have their confidence – they think we are collaborators!" He spat fiercely onto the stone floor. "But we can take no chances – we must take you to the barn. There we have a hidden cellar."

They moved him, quickly and quietly. The throbbing in his head lessened, but he became aware of a new sensation – as if his skull were encompassed in a white fluffy cloud. All sounds was muffled, his vision faint and blurred. He felt totally disorientated. His head started to spin, but it wasn't a part of him.

Everything seemed confused. If only he could think straight. Cathy! Where was Cathy ...? He drifted again into unconsciousness.

* * * * * * *

The next time he awoke his head was still fuzzy, but he felt more like his old self. A young girl stood by his side, smiling archly. She had long and tousled black hair, large slanting green eyes and a young gamine face. He smiled back, trying to marshal his thoughts as he studied her. She couldn't have been more than fifteen years old, yet he was aware of the swelling contours of a mature female body against the crisp white of her blouse, the course folds of the skirt. She held a steaming bowl in her hands. Jimmy smelt a fantastic aroma and realised he was absolutely starving.

"How is the hero airman feeling?" asked the girl. Her voice, low and husky, had a marked Parisian accent. The words were teasing, the smile warm and flirtatious. "If you are well enough, I have some hot soup." She watched him, catlike.

"Couldn't feel better," grinned Jimmy, raising himself from the rough mattress. His head started to pound again, but the smell of the food was far too enticing for him to admit it. He tried desperately not to wince as he moved.

The girl must have seen the flash of pain in his eyes.

"I think you may have a little ... what do you call it ..? The concussion? My uncle, he thinks so."

"I think your uncle's right, but nothing's going to stop me enjoying that soup."

The girl laughed, her green eyes crinkling at the corners, her white teeth flashing.

"What is your name, Englishman?"

"James ... James Proctor, but my friends all call my Jimmy."

"Then I shall call you James," said the girl, perversely. "It is a very nice name, why change it? I do not like nicknames. My name is Monique."

"Enchanted to make your acquaintance, Monique," said Jimmy.

She giggled and carefully passed the soup.

"I have been watching you while you sleep – you are very nice." Nestling down by his side like a young kitten, she watched in fascination while he ate, occasionally giving a sly mischievous smile of encouragement, her eye-lashes fluttering.

Little minx thought Jimmy! Practising all her woman's wiles on a poor, helpless airman – I bet she gives her boy-friend a bad time.

"I am from Paris, but my father was killed at the beginning of the war," she confided. "My mother died when I was a little girl. I lived with my father and his lady-friend. Now he is dead, I stay with my uncle. It is much nicer – I did not like my father's whore!" She tossed her dark curls and smiled brilliantly at Jimmy, then laughed out loud at his shocked expression.

Before he knew it, Jimmy had joined in her laughter. The girl had brought him back to reality. Fear left the pit of his stomach. He started to relish the delicious, piping hot vegetable soup. Even with the shortages of wartime, the French hadn't lost their culinary skills.

Monique's expression turned more serious.

"My uncle, he says I must tell you he will come to see you soon. At the moment he has many urgent arrangements to make ... to organise your escape. He must act fast before the Boche catch up with you."

"Organise my escape ...?" repeated Jimmy, lamely.

"Yes. You have been very fortunate to land near here. My uncle is a member of the Maquis – the Resistance, you know. He is a very brave man – he and his friends have helped many airmen. Soon you will be back in England." She took the empty bowl. "Now I must go or my aunt will wonder why I take so long. Soon I shall be back."

She gave a jaunty wink and with a flash of slim ankles and calves leapt to her feet, ran swiftly up a stone staircase in the corner of the cellar. Before disappearing from sight, she blew an exaggerated kiss. He heard the clunk of a trapdoor closing, muffled sounds from above; then he was alone.

Return to England, she had said. His heart pounded as the words sank in. He knew there was no possibility of going back, no way he could live another minute with the terror of combat flying.

But what about Cathy? He could see her so clearly in his mind's eye – every feature of her adored face, every inch of her vibrant, responsive body. He thought of her warmth and sensitivity, her shining spirit, her utter trust and dependence on him. Oh God! How could he leave Cathy alone, allow her to think he was dead? Could he ever face life again without her? Cathy deserved something better than a feeble, fear-ridden coward. Why did he suffer this terrible flaw?

Guilt and emptiness hit him with the impact of a heavy blow. He fell back on the hard mattress, sobbed like a child, the warm tears coursing freely down his dirt-streaked, handsome features.

* * * * * * *

He must have dropped back to sleep again, but he had no idea for how long; he had lost all track of time since baling out. He gazed at his watch. It had stopped, the face badly cracked, obviously by his heavy landing. He was relieved to find his head no longer throbbed whenever he moved; only a dull ache remained.

Then panic seized him. He had to make some rapid decisions – before his rescuers returned! Monique had said they wouldn't be long. In his heart he'd already accepted he couldn't go back to England, yet that was just what the Resistance were endeavouring to organise for him. His presence here was a terrible threat to them. They would automatically assume he was dying to get back to 'Blighty', to join the fray once again. 'Hero-airman', Monique had called him. If she only knew!

He thought wryly of the irony of the situation: the Resistance bravely risking not only their own lives, but those of their families, not to mention the horrors of torture – all for the skin of a man too frightened to continue taking part in this murderous war, however necessary and honourable the cause.

How could he confound the plans of the Resistance? Two factors were to his advantage – a fluent command of the French language and first-hand knowledge of the country's geography. Jimmy had his mother to thank for that – for that vital period of his youth spent in France. After his father's death, Rowena had insisted all their holidays should be spent in France, where she and Jimmy's father had previously enjoyed so many happy vacations.

As a young child, Jimmy absorbed the language, the geography, the culture and customs of France with the greed of a dry sponge dipped in water. Only children can learn so rapidly, so easily. He played with local youngsters, devoured the delightful food. French became almost as natural to him as his own native language – no trace of an English accent marred his speech.

His love of the language had been shared by Cathy. He and his half-French wife had loved to chat together in the lyrical language. Cathy wasn't as fluent as Jimmy, but it soon became their special means of communicating when alone – even in company, if they wanted to pass on a confidential comment. Most of their English acquaintances would have been hard-pressed to follow Jimmy and Cathy's rapid, colloquial French.

He thought hard. OK. He was sure he could live secretly in France, be accepted as a Frenchman. He had no papers, of course, but the Resistance could surely help in that respect. He made a swift and logical decision – to use the resources of the Resistance, then disappear before progressing too far along the rescue-chain to England. He would need to escape not only the Germans, but the Resistance, and make that escape look like an accident – as if he'd perished in his freedom flight to England. Whatever happened, the Resistance and the British authorities had to believe he was dead. It must never come to light that he had actually deserted.

Desertion! The very thought of it made him go cold all over. He started to tremble violently, not caring for his own sake, but for Cathy. He couldn't bear the thought of her knowing, not only that he had deserted England and the Air Force during a time of war, but even worse – that he had abandoned her.

Cathy, Cathy, my love, I have to do this! Can you ever forgive me? It was a cry from the heart; but ironically enough, deep within him, he knew he could be sure of one thing – Cathy would always forgive him. But could he ever forgive himself?

He heard the creak of the trap-door opening. They were back. No more time to plan – he would have to trust to his wits. The fact his own life now meant so little to him gave him an audacity he'd previously never known.

He grinned jauntily as the two men approached.

"Ah, monsieur Rip Van Winkle, he has awoken," said the older man with the gruff voice and Normandy accent. He had the dark and swarthy build of a peasant, but his bright blue eyes flashed alert and intelligent. They glittered now with tolerant humour, like a parent with a mischievous but loveable child. "We visited you some time ago, but you were in a deep sleep."

"Thank you, my friends, for the risks you are taking," said Jimmy in impeccable French. "I'm sorry to put you all in so much danger." He rose shakily to his feet. "Please tell me your plans. Now I'm fully recovered, I can move on as soon as you wish."

"I am afraid we had to abandon our plans to move you on quickly," explained the older man. "The Boche were too close. That is why we left you to your slumbers." He gave a sudden, loud guffaw.

"What time is it?" asked Jimmy. "My watch is broken."

"It is Thursday evening, a little past eight o'clock," said the younger man. He spoke more rapidly than the other and fidgeted nervously. "You have slept nearly thirty hours."

Jimmy gave a start. He hadn't realised he'd slept so long. He tried to match the older man's ebullient mood.

"No wonder I'm so ravenously hungry!" He gave a conspiratory wink. "Please congratulate your wife on the magnificent soup, but I have to admit I'm starving again. I'm sorry! How ungrateful I sound!" He staggered towards them, feeling stiff and bruised, offered his hand in formal greeting.

"I am happy to see you are fully recovered from your inauspicious landing in France," said the older man, with a grin. "I am Pierre – at least that is how you shall know me. This is my son, Jean-Paul." Ignoring the proffered handshake, he embraced Jimmy in an all-encompassing bear-hug.

Jimmy could feel the restrained strength in the man's steely arms.

"My name is James Proctor," he told them.

"My family are pleased to help one of our brave allies," declared Pierre, as if quoting from a speech. "As you will see, many of us in France fully understand we still have our part to play against the Boche. We may not be able to battle as a traditional army, but we can still fight!" He stood tall and proud, seeming to increase in stature as he spoke. His son coughed, slightly embarrassed.

"My father is right. France has been defeated, but only temporarily. You can be assured most of us will continue fighting."

Jimmy's face blanched white with shame.

"I know," he said, quietly. "The British people are well aware of the brave work of the French Resistance – your courage is already becoming legendary."

Pierre relaxed, his honour vindicated. He smiled his infectious smile.

"Tell me where you learned your excellent French, my friend. I have never before met an Englishman who could get his tongue so cleverly round our language. You even roll your 'Rs' to perfection!" He turned to his son. "Mr Proctor could pass as a Frenchman any day, don't you think Jean-Paul? Without the uniform, of course!" He laughed loudly, enjoying his own little witticism.

Jimmy grinned, found himself being drawn irresistibly to the swarthy Frenchman with his infectious bonhomie.

"I visited France for many years as a young boy," he told them. "My family has always loved your country."

"Mais oui, that would explain it. Young cubs learn fast. We are fortunate – it makes it easier for us and for you. I spent a little time in your country before the war, but I am afraid I was too old to absorb more than a few words of your difficult language." He put his broad arm round Jimmy's shoulder. "You will be pleased to hear that food is on its way. Then we shall be moving on. But eat first and enjoy some warm French hospitality!"

There was a clatter of dishes as Monique descended the cellar stairs. Her cat-eyes raked Jimmy, her hips swaying provocatively from side to side as she approached.

"You have already met my niece, Monique, I believe," said Pierre with a wicked grin. He gave her a playful slap on her shapely behind.

"You are a wicked man, mon oncle." She gave the older man the benefit of her flashing smile, but her green eyes focused slyly on Jimmy.

"My niece is very young but, like all females, she is a tease," explained Pierre. "Do you have a woman back in England, my friend?"

"Yes ... yes, I have a wife. Her name is Cathy. Her mother was also French."

Monique pouted prettily.

"How lucky she is, your wife, to have such a brave handsome husband. Is she very beautiful?"

There was a brief moment of silence.

"Yes," replied Jimmy, softly, "very beautiful." His hazel eyes glistened in the dim cellar light. Embarrassed he brushed a nervous hand through his hair. "That food smells terrific! May I eat while you tell me your plans?"

Pierre grinned widely.

"Mais oui! My wife would be insulted if her food did not come first! When you are fully satisfied, we shall discuss your escape."

CHAPTER 14

Pierre and Jimmy left the farm at midnight. There should have been a full moon, but dark clouds and a steady drizzle ensured a black night, full of eerie gloom. At least, explained Pierre, the murky shadows would shield them from the Boche patrols.

They trudged mile after mile over flat muddy farmlands, through dank, dripping woods. Pierre had insisted they avoid any form of mechanised transport in case of road blocks or other checks. Seeming to know every inch of the countryside despite the pitch darkness, he never faltered but moved surely, gracefully for such a heavy man. Jimmy was surprised at the Frenchman's fitness – he found himself starting to puff when Pierre was still breathing easily.

He had no idea where they were going. Pierre had refused to give him any indication of their destination, or their next contact in the chain of escape.

"The less you know, my friend, the better. We trust you, but the Boche have terrible ways of making even the bravest men talk. The names we have given you are code-names – it is safer that way. Perhaps one day, after the war, you will return to France and we can renew our acquaintanceship in much happier circumstances."

Jimmy nodded in the darkness. He was glad he knew no compromising details about these courageous men, just in case ...

"When it is necessary," continued Pierre in a low whisper, "you will be told all you need to know to finalise your escape. Then you are on your own. It will be up to you. In the meantime, should you be picked up by the Boche, you must never let them guess you have been in contact with the Resistance. If captured as a lone airman in flight, you have a good chance of reaching a prisoner-of-war camp. So for the time being you must continue to wear your uniform." He grinned and thumped Jimmy on the shoulder. "Be careful, my friend. Should they discover you have been in touch with us, everything will be done to prise information from you. If there is any possible danger we must separate until the hazard is past. That way the risks are reduced."

Jimmy winced and shivered in the damp night, but not from the cold. Pierre had already given him vivid descriptions of Gestapo torture techniques.

"How will I get back to England?" he enquired, nervously.

"All I can tell you is that it will be by sea. You will eventually be given clothes and papers to show you are a fisherman. Fortunately your excellent French should fool even the most observant of our German occupiers." He spat into the undergrowth and strode ahead more vigorously.

Jimmy silently cursed the efficiency of the Resistance. He didn't dare try to escape until he had been provided with both civilian clothes and a new identity; but now it seemed there would then be little time or opportunity to effect an escape before he was whisked back home again. He certainly didn't fancy an icy swim in the English Channel!

The drizzle had stopped, but the sky was still heavily overcast when they reached a small apparently disused farmhouse. Pierre placed a finger to his pursed lips. The two of them stood silently in the darkness. When a full three minutes had passed without sound, the Frenchman gave two high-pitched whistles. Within seconds a dark figure appeared behind them. Jimmy gave a start. The man seemed to materialise from nowhere, without the slightest sound.

"C'est toi, Michel?"

"Mais oui. You are right on time. I have just arrived myself. The Gestapo apes made a comprehensive spot-check in the village tonight. It caused many problems for our people. The Germans grow more suspicious every day."

Pierre spat again. Jimmy was growing accustomed to this reaction of disgust from the Frenchman, whenever the enemy were mentioned.

"After this package has been despatched, you must lie low for a while," muttered Pierre. "We must not compromise the network."

Jimmy shuffled uneasily in the darkness. He felt guilty enough, knowing his own future intentions. It didn't help to be continually reminded of the many lives being put at risk to help his escape.

Pierre turned his attention to Jimmy.

"My friend, here we must part. Michel will take good care of you. I wish you good luck and bon voyage. Fight bravely! We in France will be thinking about you. I hope we shall meet again one day."

Jimmy swallowed hard and returned Pierre's iron embrace.

"I hope so, too, Pierre."

The Frenchman pressed a small hard object into the palm of his hand.

"It is a good-luck gift from Monique. She was very impressed with you. My niece is a little minx," he added, gruffly, "but a good brave girl at heart. Farewell, Jimmy."

He turned abruptly, strode quickly away into the shadows.

Jimmy looked down at the tiny solid object in his hand. In the darkness he could just make out its form – a gold replica of St. Christopher, the patron saint of travellers. Feeling strangely moved, he slipped it quickly into his pocket.

Michel nodded to Jimmy, then moved briskly ahead.

"Come, we have two more hours of walking before we can rest. We must not delay."

The rain began to fall again more heavily.

Michel led him into a small village. Leaving the relative safety of the countryside, his guide became visibly more nervous. They moved silently along the wet streets, using every possible cover. Half way up a short but steep hill, they passed a church, then turned into a narrow alley. The rain began to pour down. Within seconds both he and Michel were soaked to the skin. Yet his companion seemed more cheerful in the torrential rain.

"The Boche like their comfort," he explained, "the fouler the night, the less our risk of being spotted and apprehended."

Drawing level with one impoverished building, Jimmy saw a door suddenly whisk open. He started like a frightened rabbit. Michel grabbed fiercely at his arm, pulled him inside. Removing his sodden hat, the Frenchman gave a deep sigh of relief.

"We are home!"

A plump woman with neatly-rolled, shoulder-length hair bustled around them. She removed Jimmy's flying jacket, thrust a towel into his hands.

"You will both die of the cold. Michel take the gentleman upstairs. I have hot water ready for the tub. You must bathe now, while you have the opportunity. Be quick."

By the time he had bathed and changed into the dry clothes provided by Michel, Jimmy felt decidedly more comfortable. The trousers and heavy-knit fisherman's jumper were on the large size for his lean form, but it was wonderful to feel clean and warm again. Michel showed him into a small cramped kitchen. Their wet clothes were already steaming by the side of a bright fire. A delicious aroma of herb-garnished stew filled the tiny room. Jimmy immediately felt at home.

"Welcome," said Michel's wife with a shy smile. "I'm afraid we must speak quietly. This is a small house and I do not want to wake the children. Please sit down." She served them huge plates full of the sizzling aromatic stew, then tactfully withdrew from the room.

"You have a wonderful wife, Michel. Please thank her for her kindness and hospitality."

Michel smiled broadly. He was a man of few words but he obviously doted on his ripely-endowed but demure young wife.

"Thank you. She is a marvellous woman and very brave. I think it is even harder for Resistance wives than it is for us. At least we are involved in action. So many nights they must just wait and pray, always fearing that special knock on the door. Sometimes their husbands never return from a mission ..."

Jimmy nodded, sympathetically, and they finished their meal in companionable silence.

When Jimmy's plate was wiped clean, Michel coughed apologetically.

"I'm afraid you must leave us soon. Normally you would spend a couple of days here, but it has become too dangerous. We have decided to move you on this morning – as soon as it is light. You will travel hidden in my baker's van as far as the port."

"What about papers?" asked Jimmy, anxiously.

"One of my colleagues will be here soon. It has all been organised. Your identity papers will show you are a fisherman. You will be delivered as near as possible to the harbour."

There was a knock at the door. Jimmy froze as he saw Michel's face blanch. Three more knocks came in swift succession. Michel let out a sigh of relief, moved cat-like to the door.

A voice from the other side whispered a few words, inaudible to Jimmy. Michel strode across to the kitchen table. He opened a small drawer, pulled out a tattered map.

"We shall be moving soon. There is a place for you to hide, here in this warehouse." He pointed to a building in the port area. "You cannot board the boat until evening. The most dangerous time will be your journey in the van. Should you be discovered ... The Gestapo know an airman landed by parachute – they are searching for you. We must be careful."

Jimmy nodded in silent agreement. Strangely enough, for the first time in his life, he felt no fear.

* * * * * * *

Two hours later he was in the back of the baker's van, hidden beneath a warm mountain of French loaves and pastries. The mouth-watering aroma of freshly-baked bread filled his nostrils. He felt strangely calm and nerveless, even knowing the minutes ahead would be critical. If the van were stopped and searched, their lives would all be forfeit; he was no longer in uniform so could be shot as a spy; Michel's and the baker's covers would be blown. He tried not to think about it, concentrated instead on the plan of escape slowly forming in his mind.

They had transferred him to the van just before dawn. Though the rain had stopped the air was damp and chill, but once inside the vehicle, he was comforted by the warmth and wholesomeness of his hiding place, despite the imminent danger. He had been told that – all being well – the journey in the van would take some twelve minutes. Their destination was a warehouse near the quay. Once safely installed inside, he was to wait through the day until one hour after darkness.

Then he should make his move – they told him – to the fishing boat, *Marie-Claire*, moored close by. The boat had been searched that same night. Hopefully, she would not be subjected to further scrutiny before leaving port. In any case, he would be deposited in a relatively safe if stench-ridden hiding place aboard the craft.

Jimmy had already decided the only possible opportunity for escape would be during that first hour of darkness – before he was due to board the fishing boat. He would need to move swiftly and without trace to evade both the Germans and the Resistance. He still had to work out how to cover his tracks, how to make his rescuers believe he had been captured, perhaps killed.

The van slowed twice during the short journey, but then picked up speed and continued on its way. He wished he could look at the new watch Michel had given him – the twelve minute journey seemed an eternity. But he dared not move lest he disturb his fragilely constructed hidey-hole. He took a deep breath to calm his nerves. They must be nearly at the warehouse by now.

Quite suddenly the vehicle came to a complete halt. Jimmy held his breath, tried to remain motionless beneath the protective layer of crusty loaves, waiting for the code-sign to indicate they had arrived at the warehouse. His own heartbeat sounded like peals of thunder – he was sure the mound of bread above him must be heaving from the pounding in his chest. Muffled voices sounded outside – but no reassuring knocks. After what seemed an eternity, the van-door was suddenly wrenched open.

Jimmy lay paralysed, willing his heart to stop beating. There was a furtive movement amongst the loaves and baskets of pâtisserie above him. He held his breath but his body still trembled uncontrollably. Abruptly the door closed. The van moved off again.

He let out a long sigh of relief, took three very deep breaths to renew his oxygen level – in case they stopped again. They did, but this time as Jimmy broke out in a fresh sweat, there came two sharp knocks on the van door – the signal for their safe arrival at the warehouse.

He scrambled through the pile of fresh loaves. Michel quickly took his arm and they crept stealthily into a large damply-cold building, stacked to its high ceiling with bales and boxes of all shapes and sizes. The Frenchman pushed him roughly along the aisles of packing cases, anxious to get away before the van was discovered outside the warehouse. Eventually they stopped by the side of some tall crates. Michel heaved one aside, revealing a hollow space behind. The tiny area was completely surrounded by large packing cases. Unless a determined effort were made to move every item in the warehouse, it was unlikely the hidey-hole would ever be discovered.

"I hope you were not too worried when we stopped," said Michel in a low voice. "It was one of the regular patrollers. He often stops us to get a free supply of fresh croissants. That's typical of our German occupiers." He gave a bitter smile. "It is cramped in here, but you should be safe enough until after dark when you can board the boat. But please do not move until the arranged time – the quay is a very dangerous area, continually patrolled by the Boche." He handed Jimmy a cardboard carton. "There is food and drink inside. Good luck. I wish you a safe journey home."

"Thank you for everything, Michel. Take good care of yourself." The two men shook hands warmly before the man from the Maquis slipped swiftly back into the aisle, replacing the packing case behind him.

Jimmy heard his soft footfall along the passage. Alone again, he studied his watch. He had more than twelve hours to wait before he could attempt his escape. Making himself as comfortable as possible in the cramped quarters, he settled down to wait.

He had fallen into a state of drowsiness, when a faint noise at the other end of the warehouse suddenly alerted him. Instinctively he checked his watch. Only an hour left before he could make his move. The noise came again. Footsteps and they were coming closer! He stiffened with apprehension. How ironical to be taken by the Germans at this stage.

The footsteps came closer – purposeful and determined. Whoever it was knew exactly where he was going, and for what reason. Yet Michel had told him he would be completely undisturbed. The warehouse was not be used until the following day. Now the footsteps were close-by, only a few yards away. They stopped – just the other side of the packing case concealing Jimmy. There was a shuffling sound and the large empty crate was eased aside. Jimmy held his breath.

An unkempt figure in a thick sweater and fisherman's trousers stood in front of him, a wide almost evil grin on his weathered face.

"Don't worry," he hissed. "You are quite safe, but there is a change of plan. The Germans have been searching all the boats again. The captain decided you must delay boarding a further hour beyond the scheduled time. We will let you know any further change of plan." He grinned wolfishly and without waiting for Jimmy to reply, turned rapidly, pushed the crate back into position and disappeared.

Jimmy cursed under his breath. The last thing he wanted was anyone returning to the warehouse, perhaps just at the moment he chose to make his escape. But there was no alternative. He would have to take the chance. At least if there was no further change of plan, he had an extra hour to escape before his absence on the boat was noticed.

The next hour seemed an eternity. He continually studied his watch, became increasingly nervous, frequently imagining he could hear noises in the warehouse. Each time they came to nothing. Must be rats, he decided. Relief surged through him when his watch-hands finally reached the allotted time. The suspense of waiting had got to him.

He rose to his feet, stretched and massaged his limbs as best he could in the confined space, then listened intently for a full minute before easing the packing case aside. Once in the aisle, he replaced the crate in its former position, walked quickly but stealthily along the dark passage. Reaching the side door, he saw as expected, that it was secured from the inside. He took the key, carefully locked the door behind him, then hid the key beneath a large stone near the door as instructed.

The night was cold and clear but, thank God, black as ink with no hint of a moon. He ran swiftly down a narrow road – away from the quayside. Negotiating a maze of alleyways, he arrived at a small deserted square.

A harsh, guttural cry pierced the silence. God! A German soldier – on the other side of the square! A second furious shout echoed in his ears. He couldn't understand the words, but the meaning was clear – a command to stop!

He turned on his heels, fled in the opposite direction.

Two shots rang out, shattering the peace of the night. The sound reverberated like thunder round the concrete buildings, before finally dying away. Christ! It must have awakened the whole town!

His legs were already pounding the pavement with renewed strength, the adrenaline starting to course through his body. He had to get away fast, before the guard followed or summoned help. Thank God, he had memorised the town plan!

He covered a further half mile before deciding it was safe to pause a moment. His breath came in short gasps, the stitch in his side now a searing pain. Only fear had kept him running. He listened intently for sounds of pursuit; but all he could hear was the loud thumping of his own heart.

He couldn't believe he had got away with it. What a piece of luck! The shots must have been audible aboard the *Marie-Claire*. They would assume he'd been killed. The complicated schemes he'd been hatching to cover his escape were no longer necessary. But would his luck hold out? There was still a long way to go.

He headed south, moving more carefully now, his eyes alert, his stride purposeful. Soon he was in open countryside. To the left he spotted the main highway leading from the town and headed towards it. Keeping to the limited cover at the side of the road, he scrambled along, taking advantage of his second wind. He decided to travel all night, then hide up during the day. Once he was far enough south he could make use of his new identity.

Headlights suddenly pierced the road ahead of him. Ducking for cover, he saw two German jeeps rush by heading towards the town – probably searching for him.

His head started to throb again. Grief and remorse swamped his soul. He had made his play! Now there was no turning back and his prospects were bleak. If he made it – against the odds – he would have to start a whole new life of deceit, this time without Cathy! Sick at heart, he set off again scrambling along the grassy verge. His future had never seemed bleaker.

Chapter 15

New York, U.S.A. November 1950

"If you're sure there's nothing else you need, Mr. Pritchard, I'll be going. I've a special date tonight!"

James Proctor gave a slight start. Even after five years his new name could still take him by surprise, especially when in a distracted mood, as he was that day.

His tall, svelte secretary gave him a bright smile, showing her even white teeth to perfection. Her face was flushed with youth and eagerness. Tracey was the perfect private secretary – neat, unobtrusively efficient, and able with one flash of her dazzling smile to protect him from any unwanted demands on his attention. Whoever said blondes were dumb had never come across Tracey.

"Yes, you get along, Tracey. You've already stayed far too long."

"Oh, that's OK, Mr. Pritchard. I've cleared up the presentation room as best I can." Concern showed in her clear blue eyes. "You're looking tired. Don't you think you should be getting home too? I wouldn't worry too much about the new account. I'm sure it's in the bag."

"Thanks, Tracey. I hope you're right. Enjoy your date."

"I will. Goodnight." She swept out of the room, leaving behind fragrant traces of her perfume.

Jimmy walked slowly across the room to the huge picture windows, which took up a whole side of his sumptuous office. He stood motionless, gazing out across the Manhattan skyline. It was a cold clear night with no moon – hauntingly similar to that night exactly ten years ago when he'd fled the Resistance. The date, heavily imprinted on his memory, had been a turning point in his life – a poignant anniversary, but one he was unable to share with any other person.

Loneliness flooded through him, more acute than the usual dull ache of his solitary existence in this bustling city. He spent most of his life surrounded with people, but that didn't help his essential isolation. For the thousandth time he regretted the decision he had made during those dramatic days in France – a decision which had cut him off from his home country, his friends and, most of all, from Cathy.

As the years went by the remembrance of his terror grew dim. Had it been as bad as he thought? Why had he lacked the strength to return and face the music? Would it have been so impossible to confront his fear, to participate again in the turmoil of that fierce battle of the skies?

He had accepted years ago that his mental state when he eluded the Resistance had probably been far from normal. Months of fatigue and stress during the Battle of Britain, and his own struggle with his suffocating terror, had obviously affected his mental stability. When he landed in France, he must have been close to a nervous breakdown. His subsequent concussion hadn't helped.

For the rest of his life he would pay for those few moments of overwrought desperation when he had made an irrevocable decision. He tried to comfort himself with the thought that in similar circumstances, other men might have done exactly the same. But he knew the majority had done just the opposite – they had returned to fight again!

He was a failure. Yet materially he'd become extremely successful – already a wealthy and powerful man in his field. He gazed at the glittering lights of the Manhattan skyscrapers. Their brittle almost garish brilliance seemed to reflect his own current life-style as joint-owner and managing director of one of the most successful advertising agencies in New York.

The year 1940 seemed so far away – a different world entirely. Was it really only ten years ago? His life, in a country fighting for its very existence during the Battle of Britain, was a far cry from the current affluent, almost frivolous life-style of New York where most people's only concern was making a fast buck. Tension, aggression, and frantic haste all played their part in this frenetic city, just as they had in war-time Britain. But here it was just a game of dollars and cents, not a battle involving the lives of thousands of young men.

The telephone shrilled loudly on his desk. Damn it! No Tracey to fend off the call. Lost in his memories, he felt tempted to let it ring, but eventually like one of Pavlov's dogs, couldn't resist its summons. With a deep sigh he lifted the receiver.

"Jimmy. We've got it, we've landed the account!" It was Pete Brady, his partner and the creative director of the agency. "Crispy Flakes is ours!"

Jimmy's face lit up. Crispy Flakes – the new cereal account for which they, along with two other top agencies, had just made an expensive presentation. They'd won it! Their first million dollar account! Now they were really in the big time – the top ten!

"Are you sure, Pete? I thought we weren't being notified until Monday."

"You bet!" Pete's voice was breathless and excited. "I've just had the tip-off from their ad. manager, Tom Scilone. The account's definitely ours, Jim. Of course, it's strictly under wraps – until the official announcement on Monday."

"My lips are sealed. Thank goodness Scilone happens to be an old college chum of yours." Jimmy grinned into the 'phone.

"It certainly helps. Tom's a great pal. But as you know all too well, Jimmy, we won this account fair and square. Ours was definitely the most original and powerful presentation – thanks to you. The others didn't stand a chance. The board of Crispy Flakes were over the moon with the new ideas we put forward for the product. 'Revolutionary Concepts' they called them!"

"Hell! It was a team effort, Pete. Everyone should be congratulated, especially you on the creative side." Jimmy knew he was lucky to have Pete Brady as a partner. Pete's prolific creative talents, plus his numerous contacts in the ad world, served as a perfect complement to Jimmy's liaison skills in the media, marketing and client field. "The whole staff worked like slaves to win this account," he insisted. "Poor Tracey's only just finished clearing up all the presentation debris."

"That girl's a gem! Don't let her get away, Jimmy. Brains as well as beauty, you know, not to mention her dedication to you and the company. Best thing you could do is marry her!"

"No danger of that, she's already madly in love with someone else. That's why I hired her. I'm fed up with secretaries who get emotionally involved with their bosses. It ruins their efficiency!"

"You're a tough nut, Jimmy. I don't know how you have so much success with women, except, of course, that you're charming, handsome, powerful and dripping with money!"

"You're wrong, laughed Jimmy. "It's the English accent that does it. No American – male or female – can resist that."

It was true. Jimmy knew one of the main reasons for his success had been his cultured English accent. In the brash harsh world of commercial New York, Jimmy's refined and softly spoken manner plus his boyish charm soon had many a hard-bitten businessman, not to mention the ladies, eating out of his hand.

"Yep, a touch of class is what they call it," agreed Pete. "Well how about a celebration? I've got a date, but I can soon break that. I think we two bachelors should go out and get drunk tonight."

"Sounds a great idea. Where shall we meet? Our local on the Avenue?"

"Why not, for a start at least. See you in half-an-hour."

The line went dead. Jimmy settled into his massive leather armchair – an outrageously comfortable contraption he found difficult to leave.

So he was to celebrate tonight's fateful anniversary after all. He wondered what Pete Brady would think, if he knew the whole story – if Jimmy were to tell him what had happened on this same day ten years ago.

He knew most of his staff looked on him with a kind of awe and reverence. His success in the States had been swift, even by American standards. His laid-back style kept them all guessing. It fascinated their clients, many of whom were convinced he was at least a member of the British aristocracy.

It had all happened so easily. Jimmy had never considered himself a potentially successful businessman. For deep-rooted reasons, flying had been his life. He had always taken for granted his easy way with people, his popularity with men and women alike, never realising he might be able to capitalise on this instinctive talent – for his own financial benefit.

Having eluded capture in France, he had eventually found his way to the delightful Mediterranean port town of Sete, famous for its oysters and mussels. Still using his assumed French identity, he was drawn into the restaurant business, eventually branching out on his own, with a small but cosy bistro specialising in sea-food. People had to eat, even in wartime. Later he involved himself with the ever-widening distribution of molluscs and shellfish throughout occupied France. Ironically enough, he even joined the local Underground movement, feeling it was the least he could do in the circumstances.

For some strange reason his fear seemed to have dissolved, as if purged by the very act of desertion. The real reason, he told himself, was that he didn't really care much any more whether he lived or died. He accepted increasingly dangerous missions for the Resistance.

When the war ended in 1945, he decided to move to the United States – partly because America seemed a land of opportunity, partly out of homesickness and a desire to return to his native language; but most of all to distance himself from England. With the war over, he knew the temptation to return to his native land would be too strong and could only lead to disaster. He was a deserter. Even if he were able to take up a new identity, he could never disrupt Cathy's life again. She was probably happily married to someone else by now.

His contacts in the Resistance once again provided him with a new identity. He became James Pritchard, as close an approximation to his real identity as he dared.

The shrill call of the telephone again broke into his thoughts. He glanced at his watch. God, it was almost half-past. He'd be late for Pete. Fortunately the bar was only fifty yards from his office block on Madison Avenue. Half-reluctantly, he aroused himself from his reverie and, with more difficulty, from his armchair. Ignoring the phone, he strode quickly out of his office.

* * * * * * *

Pete Brady was already there when Jimmy arrived, his powerful body perched precariously on a red-velvet bar stool. In front of him towered a large gin-and-tonic, brimming with ice and lemon. He beamed at Jimmy as he approached the bar.

"Your usual, Jim?" His blue eyes twinkled in his good-natured face.

"Please." He perched on the stool next to Pete, feeling strangely tired and depressed, despite the celebratory occasion. He tried to pull himself together, not wanting to spoil the evening for his partner. Big new accounts were the highlight of an adman's life!

It was then he saw her. Cathy! – standing at the other end of the bar, chatting to a tall slim man. He could see only the back of her head and shoulders; but he immediately recognised the way she held her head, the quick impatient shake of her soft dark curls. The hairstyle was different of course, but the gestures were the same.

The girl half-turned towards him.

But it wasn't Cathy! This girl had a narrower face. Her lips and eyes had none of the warmth and mobility of Cathy. Oh God! How could he be so stupid! He was almost certain that Cathy had died during the war. But the glass shook in his hand and he found he'd broken into a sweat. The girl's likeness, her similar mannerisms had been uncanny – taken him completely by surprise. He could never reconcile himself to the fact that Cathy was dead.

"What the hell's the matter, Jim?" Pete grasped his arm. You've gone white as a sheet. Are you feeling all right?"

"It's ... it's nothing."

"Nothing! You'd better put that glass down before you break it! You look as if someone's just walked over your grave!"

Jimmy managed a wry smile.

"They almost have." He took a deep gulp from his gin-and-tonic. "I'm sorry Pete – that girl over there ... from the back ... just for a moment she looked like my wife, Cathy." Jimmy felt safe telling Peter this part of the truth. He had told his closest friends in America that his main reason for coming to the States was the death of his English wife, during the London Blitz. America was his new beginning.

It had been a tremendous shock for Jimmy, finding out about Cathy. Soon after settling in New York, he'd decided to make some sort of contact with his wife. Telephoning their London flat, he prayed Cathy would answer. He had no intention of speaking to her, only wanted to listen to her voice once more, assure himself she was well.

His hands had trembled as he held the receiver, waited impatiently for the operator to connect him.

"I'm sorry, sir, there's no reply from your number in England. In fact the line seems to be disconnected."

Jimmy's heart sank.

"Could you check it out please operator – it's most important."

"Certainly, sir. I'll call you right back."

When she did call back, it was to inform him the number had been disconnected. Perhaps, she suggested helpfully, the building had been damaged during the war. That was often the case with unobtainable European numbers.

Jimmy was distraught. He tried Hosky's number, only to be told Miss Hoskins had died years ago and they – the new owners of the cottage knew nothing about a Mrs James Proctor.

A letter to Kensington Townhall confirmed his worst fears – the flat in Elvaston Place had been destroyed by bombing and three residents killed. Oh God, thought Jimmy, that was both Cathy and Nessie and old Mrs Dauncey, who had the flat above. The ground floor flat had been unoccupied since the Wells family moved to the country. Jimmy was devastated by the news.

Without revealing his own identity, he tried to make contact with his mother's solicitor, only to discover Rowena herself had died of a stroke, just before the end of the war. Her mental and physical condition, they told him, deteriorated rapidly after the death of her son, James. She had died in a special clinic.

Jimmy was overcome with shame and remorse. Whatever his mother's shortcomings, she had always loved him. He had betrayed her, as well as Cathy.

He tried to check further with the official records at Somerset House, but these were incomplete for that period, due to war damage. Perhaps it was just as well. Now he could never interfere in Cathy's life again, even if by some strange chance she were still alive.

His commonsense insisted she was dead, yet at least in his dreams he could imagine her alive somewhere. Damn that girl in the bar – raising his crazy hopes! She had looked so like Cathy from behind.

Pete's hand on his arm brought him back to the present.

"I'm sorry Jim, I didn't realise. It must have been quite a shock."

"That's OK, Pete." Jimmy could see a hint of puzzlement in Pete's deepset eyes. His colleague was obviously surprised Jimmy should be so visibly upset by a reminder of a wife who had died some ten years before. In New York Jimmy normally showed little emotion or strong feeling in his dealings with women. Even at work he was he was coolly competent, rarely aroused. He realised Pete must be quite taken aback by this unexpected betrayal of his feelings.

He took another deep gulp of his drink. How could he ever explain to anybody that never a day passed when he didn't think of Cathy; that on numerous nights he would awake in a cold sweat following some terrible nightmare in which Cathy – buried alive beneath tons of concrete – was calling, calling to him for help. Her face always haunted him. She was never far from his thoughts. Unconsciously, every other woman he met he had compared, unfavourably, with Cathy. When he discovered his wife had died, Jimmy's own life lost all real meaning.

"Cheer up, Jim. This is a night for celebration. Here's to Crispy Flakes!" Pete held his freshly-filled glass high in the air.

Jimmy raised his own, crackling with fresh ice.

"Of course! To Crispy Flakes! And many more million-dollar accounts to come!"

If he couldn't be happy, he thought, he could at least be rich! He thumped Pete on the shoulder and settled down to a hard night's drinking.

Chapter 16

New York, U.S.A. March 1953

"Frank, would you give us a brief run-down on the media schedule for the autumn campaign?" said Jimmy, nodding to Frank Browne, his media director. He glanced down at the notes he had jotted on the pad in front of him. The letters 'TV' were ringed in red. He intended to recommend substantial television coverage for the launch of their latest account – a new range of cosmetics under the brand name, 'Pretty Girl'. But he would let Frank present his suggestions first. He liked to give his young talented staff plenty of opportunity to submit their own ideas before he disclosed any of his own.

The great attraction of the advertising business, even for him as owner-chairman, was the absence of rank-pulling or seniority preference. Every employee in this vibrant young industry was judged by their talents and results alone. Any idea would be accepted – even if it came from the cleaning-lady! – as long it was fresh, persuasive and stood a good chance of success. The advertising business revolved around ideas, and Jimmy's enthusiastic young staff were brimming with them.

"If you look at our recommended schedules," Frank began briskly, "you'll see that the launch will start with a saturation campaign in women's magazines, with simultaneous coverage on billboards and TV. The campaign will continue right through till Christmas, to capitalise on the gift market. The magazines with the best net coverage and cost-per-thousand are listed on page three. As you know our target group is C1 and C2 women in the 16-24 age group.

He shuffled some papers and took a sip of water.

"In our proposed schedules we've drawn on some recent in-depth research into reading patterns, advertising recall and so on. We've also weighted those magazines which have a more trendy racy editorial style – these would seem more in keeping with the Pretty Girl range of cosmetics as far as atmosphere is concerned.

He turned and pointed to a chart on the blackboard next to him.

"As you can see, the billboard and TV campaigns are fairly self-explanatory. We're proposing long sixty-second television spots at the beginning of the campaign, interspersed with short fifteen-sec. reminders to increase frequency. Then we shall go into thirty-second spots until Christmas." He looked around enquiringly. "Any questions before Janey goes into the details?"

Jimmy spoke softly.

"Just one thing, Frank. Do you think the proportion of the budget recommended for television is adequate? I feel the immediacy and impact of the TV medium is vital for a new launch."

"I agree, Jimmy. It's just finances. Television is so expensive now. It's already taking a hefty chunk of the budget. If we use more TV, our magazine and billboard campaign will be seriously depleted."

"What about cancelling the billboards until the launch is over?" suggested Jimmy. "We can use them later as a product reminder, when the new range has been established. Once the consumer is fully aware of the new product we can reduce the amount spent on television."

There was a moment of silence, followed by a faint hum of conversation.

"Our strongest competitors are strongly into billboards," said Cliff Curtis from the Merchandising Department.

"I'm aware of that, Cliff, but our closest rivals are already well-established in the market. 'Pretty Girl' has to break into a highly competitive field. In the first weeks of the campaign we must hit those young girls with everything we've got. They've got to have 'Pretty Girl' so imprinted on their minds, they can't resist trying the product. Nothing can match TV for impact and immediacy." Jimmy looked around the table, encouraging more comments.

"We won't have the creative and marketing advantages of colour in the TV spots." This remark came from Ken Jakes, Jimmy's new Creative Director, who had replaced Pete Brady, Jimmy's former partner. Two years earlier, Pete had married Pat Lyons, a talented girl from the copy department. Only months later Pat had discovered she was suffering from multiple sclerosis. She and Pete had moved to southern California to make the most of the few good years left to Pat. Jimmy sorely missed his partner; but he had to admit that Ken, the new creative man, was red-hot at his job.

Jimmy now figured as overall owner and director of Pritchard and Brady, having bought out Pete's share. But he'd refused to alter the name of the agency. His friendship and loyalty to Pete were an important factor in his life. Visiting the couple whenever possible, he marvelled at the warm happy relationship they enjoyed together, despite their problems.

"That's true," agreed Jimmy, returning to Ken Jakes' question. "TV at present does lack the advantages of colour. Once the networks get the colour problems sorted out, it will be an incredibly powerful medium. But I still feel we can stress the young appeal of the product on TV, emphasising the relative cheapness of the 'Pretty Girl' range. It will enable women who previously couldn't afford a variety of cosmetics to change shades and colours according to their clothes or mood.

"We can still use magazines to show the wide range of exciting and unusual colours in the range," continued Jimmy, "and emphasise the youthful trendy qualities of the product. As you know, our research has shown that – apart from the expensive end of the market – it's the 16-24 age group which spends and experiments the most with cosmetics."

"There is one other important factor, Jimmy," said Frank Browne with a frown. "The intrinsic authority of women's magazines for beauty products. It's difficult to evaluate in financial terms, but it's always been recognised and our most recent research reinforces these findings. Women will certainly see the TV advertising, but will it have the same authority as their favourite magazines? They read magazines for serious beauty advice, as well as entertainment."

"I fully agree, Frank," said Jimmy softly. "That's why I've haven't suggested reducing the magazine coverage, only the billboards. I consider use of both magazines and TV to be vital, each reinforcing and complementing the other. But I do feel we should spend more of the budget on TV. The medium is so popular now, you need to make a good showing to stand out from the rest. I also believe women are coming to accept the authority of TV. for beauty products. Look at the amount now being spent on television by the beauty-soap manufacturers."

The discussion continued for several more minutes before the product team came to agreement with Jimmy's suggestion. He would have been perfectly happy for the decision to go the other way, had their research and opinions shown a better alternative. Jimmy encouraged his staff to disagree with him whenever they saw fit and the agency was the better for the amalgam of their various talents.

As the conference moved on to finer media details, Jimmy glanced down at the recommended magazines Frank had already passed round for their perusal. His attention was drawn to the front cover of one well-known magazine specialising in news stories and gossip relating to royalty and show-biz stars. A raven-haired beauty stared out from the page. Her slanting green eyes, fringed with long dark lashes, shone with the brilliance of emeralds; her lips were full and glossy. The girl's smile was tantalising and provocative. She had an unusual style of beauty and an obvious sexual magnetism.

But it wasn't her stunning looks which attracted Jimmy's attention. There was something familiar about the girl – yet her identity eluded him. Jimmy was acquainted with many beautiful females. They abounded in his type of business; but this girl was different. He still couldn't place her, yet he felt a strange stirring inside.

He turned to the photo-credits and captions inside the front page. The name he saw took his breath away: "Top French filmstar, Monique Vergnory, currently visiting New York. Story and exclusive interview on Page 12."

Of course, the French girl – that minx, Monique! It had to be!

His memory rushed back twelve years to the day he landed in France, to the cellar beneath the barn, to the flirtatious slip of a girl who had served him soup, then sent him her lucky talisman. He felt instinctively for the St Christopher which he now wore on a gold chain around his neck, a nostalgic reminder of his years in France. He gazed back at the front cover. There was no mistaking the slanting cat eyes, the sly kittenish appeal in the flashing provocative smile. So the teenage minx had become a famous star, he thought. But there was no mistaking her identity.

He skipped quickly to the interview pages. According to the magazine, Monique was staying at the Waldorf Hotel. Jimmy felt an unusual excitement and a strong sense of nostalgia. Someone from his past was here in New York – a link with his previous existence; someone who had known him as a young man, before his irreversible act of betrayal.

He forced himself to concentrate on the meeting at hand.

"I think we you should book 'bleed' for the double page spreads," Ken Jakes was saying, referring to magazine pages whose contents 'bled' into the margins rather than carrying a white border. "I know it's more expensive, but it will give the creative team far more scope. What do you think, Jimmy?"

Jimmy tried desperately to concentrate on the discussion, but during the rest of the campaign meeting his mind was in turmoil. Did he dare confront his past? If he tried to make contact with Monique, would she even remember him? It could prove embarrassing.

Yet something inside him seemed to compel him to action. He resolved to telephone her that evening, come what may. He suddenly felt more alive than he had for years!

* * * * * * *

"Could I speak to Mademoiselle Vergnory, please?" Jimmy's fingers were crossed. He had managed to get through on Monique's hotel extension line, but he had a feeling he would get no further.

"Who is that speaking," said a male voice with a marked French accent.

"This is James Proctor." Jimmy had decided to risk using his correct name. He was sure he would have enough difficulties getting through to Monique, without the additional problem of an unknown identity. "I'm a very old friend of hers." It sounded corny, he knew. Monique was probably pestered by hundreds of men using the same line. 'Old friend' was also a considerable exaggeration. He couldn't really describe himself as such. But how else could he explain their relationship?

"I'm afraid the mademoiselle is taking no further calls this evening – she has an important appointment shortly. I will make a note you telephoned. Would you care to leave a number to return your call?"

"No, it's important I speak to her tonight." After so much anticipation, he realised he would never sleep if he didn't manage to get through to Monique that evening.

"I'm sorry, sir, that is quite impossible." The voice now held a trace of irritability. He sensed the Frenchman was about to hang up.

"Tell her it's James ... the English airman," he said in desperation. "The one she gave her St Christopher to ... she helped to save my life."

Something in his voice or words must have got through to the man at the other end of the line. There was a moment's silence.

"Just one moment, sir. I'll see if Mademoiselle Vergnory can call you back later. Mr James, you said?"

"Yes, James ... James Proctor," he said eagerly, remembering how Monique had refused to call him Jimmy. There was silence once again.

Minutes passed. Jimmy was about to give up. He'd probably been cut off – perhaps on purpose. But suddenly he heard a low, breathless voice on the line.

"James ... is that really you?" She spoke in French, obviously still not certain his call was genuine. "I thought you were dead."

"I'm very much alive, Monique. Gosh, I thought I'd never get through to you. Who's the watchdog?"

Her voice was husky but excited.

"I am so sorry, James, but I was in the bath when you called. In any case Henri has to be very careful. You would never believe some of the crank calls I receive, plus the usual pestering busybodies I have no desire to speak to. But you – what are you doing here in America? I thought you were shot by the Germans."

For a moment panic gripped him. Of course, that was what he had wanted them to believe. Monique was bound to know he had never made his rendezvous aboard the *Marie Claire*.

"Oh ... it's a long story. We'll talk about it when I see you. I am going to see you, aren't I?"

"Of course, James," she murmured, her voice a seductive purr. "What time will you pick me up?"

"Your watchdog said you had an 'important appointment' tonight – or was that just to put me off?"

"As it happens, Henri was telling the truth. But no matter. I would certainly not give up seeing my first love for a boring old film agent." She laughed throatily into the phone.

Jimmy felt his excitement mount with her every word.

"The same flirtatious minx I met back in 1940. You haven't changed an iota, Monique."

"I mean it, James. I was really quite smitten by you. Fifteen is a very impressionable age, you know – even though I only knew you a few hours."

Jimmy laughed. "Impressionable, maybe, but certainly not innocent! Mind you, I have to admit the circumstances were rather dramatic. But you knew me a matter of minutes, not a few hours."

"Oh, but it was a few hours! You seem to forget – I spent ages by your side while you were asleep." Her voice suddenly changed. "How is your beautiful wife?"

His voice went cold. "I'm ... I'm afraid she's dead. Our flat was bombed during the Blitz ..."

He heard her gasp. The line went silent for several moments.

"James, I'm sorry. I know you loved her very much."

Silence again. The spell was broken. He didn't know what to say next.

"James? James, are you still there?"

"Yes." He spoke abruptly. "I'll pick you up in half an hour."

He rang off, not even waiting for her reply. Damn it, he thought. Why did she have to mention Cathy? But of course, it was only natural. Monique would automatically assume Cathy was still alive. It was his fault for being so jumpy, so sensitive as far as she was concerned. Cathy herself would have hated to think her death would affect him so. He had to learn to live with her memory – without this excessive grief and bitterness.

Not bothering to call his butler, he collected his overcoat himself from the hall cupboard. Within seconds he was on his way to the elevator.

Chapter 17

Monique hugged him in unabashed delight the moment he walked into her hotel suite. He was touched and flattered to realise how thrilled she was to see him again.

"James, you look marvellous – more handsome than ever, and quite distinguished! Ah ... but now you smile, I see you still have your little-boy appeal. You cannot imagine how happy I am to see you again – I was so sure you were dead."

Jimmy gently released himself from her enthusiastic embrace, held her at arms' distance and slowly studied her all over.

In many respects Monique looked just the same, yet maturity had given her a beauty and voluptuousness she had lacked as a young girl. The tousled unruly hair he remembered from that time in France was now perfectly groomed – as sleek and shiny as polished ebony.

Her figure had also blossomed. Large firm breasts and curvaceous hips were accentuated by an unbelievably slim waist. She resembled a ripe heavily-corseted beauty from the nineteenth century, but Jimmy could see Monique's tiny waist owed nothing to artificial aids.

Her cat-eyes gleamed more vivid and brilliant than ever – the magazine photograph hadn't lied. Her expression, still arch and teasing, hadn't lost that hint of the devilish gamine.

She quivered slightly under his serious scrutiny.

"Well, James, do you find me attractive? I am no longer the little girl you knew twelve years ago." Unashamedly, she fluttered her long, black lashes.

"You weren't so little, even then," laughed Jimmy. "Seriously, Monique, you look stunning. But I suppose everyone tells you that."

Her voice lost its teasing quality.

"That is true. But I only concern myself with the opinions of a few people. You, James, are very much one of those. After all – you are my hero-airman!" She looked down in mock innocence, then gave another dazzling smile.

Jimmy lowered his eyes.

"Monique, do you mind? I'd rather not talk about those days in France. Just tell me one thing. How are your uncle and your cousin? And what about Michel?"

"My uncle is well, as lively and good-humoured as ever. My cousin is married and now lives in Rouen. I am afraid Cédric - the man you knew as Michel – was captured and killed about a year after you left." Her voice softened. "I'm sorry, James. I understand you do not wish to talk about those dreadful days. You must have suffered a great deal. Perhaps later, when we know each other a little better ..."

He smiled, catching hold of her hand.

"Will we have time to know each other better – now you're an important and busy film actress? The magazine said your visit here was only a short one."

"Not now I have found you again! Shall we eat? I am starving. Over supper I shall tell you all about it."

* * * * * * *

They dined in a little French restaurant Jimmy knew well. He liked it, not only for its excellent food, but for the superb unobtrusive service.

Monique, still in an excited bubbling mood, explained between enthusiastic mouthfuls of food how she had returned to Paris at the end of the war, determined to make her name in the magical world of the cinema.

"My uncle thought I was a fool. He warned me I would be wasting my time, that the only thing the wicked men in the film business would be interested in was my body." Her green eyes twinkled with mischief. "He was right. But I am a forceful and persistent lady. And I think my physical attributes helped just a little." She flashed another brilliant smile. "Apparently I am also very photogenic as far as the cinema cameras are concerned."

"I can see that," agreed Jimmy with a grin. He was already intensely excited by the physical presence of Monique, more than he had been for years with any woman, however attractive. His contact with the opposite sex in France and America had been little more than ritualistic mating, involving little real passion and no deep emotion. Monique was different – beautiful, with an animal magnetism which he found difficult to resist; he felt himself come alive in her company.

"Where did you learn your magnificent English?"

"I have you to thank for that, James. I was so impressed by you I decided I must visit England some day – to see if there were more men like you! I studied hard during the war years and later, in Paris, I had an English lover. That is the best way to learn, you know?" She raised her eyebrows quizzically, but Jimmy refused to show any reaction.

"I still have not been to your country, but my knowledge of English has helped much in my career. I am here now to see my new American agent. He is trying to organise a Hollywood contract for me."

"My, my! So my little Monique is to become a world star."

Monique gave a small pout.

"I am surprised you have not heard of me before. I am already very famous in Europe."

"I'm sure you are, Monique. You mustn't take any notice of an old man like me. I rarely watch films or read gossip magazines – except to study the ads. In the past, none of my accounts were of the type to appear in film magazines. And don't forget, I never knew your surname, or even if Monique was your real christian name. The photo was the give-away."

Mollified, she gave him a warm smile, placed her slim hand over his on the table.

"Now you must tell me about yourself. You are obviously very successful. How did you get into advertising?"

They chatted for hours, only leaving the restaurant when Jimmy realised the staff were hovering embarrassedly in a corner unwilling to insist they should leave, even though it was long past closing-time.

Despite the cold night air they decided to walk back to Monique's hotel, the warmth of their companionship insulating them against the icy temperatures. Their faces flushed with the exercise, they arrived laughing at the huge glass entrance to the tall skyscraper. Monique clasped Jimmy by the hand, led him towards the revolving doors.

"You will stay with me tonight, James?" she said, her eyes large and imploring.

"I seem to remember one occasion when you lay patiently by my side for hours – looked after me when I was in need of care and attention. It would be most ungentlemanly to refuse the same favours to such a caring lady." His hazel eyes twinkled at her, but his heart had started to pound. He could feel his desire growing every second but tried to remain as calm as his teasing words suggested.

She smiled her relief, then looked at him more archly.

"I hope my attentions will be better rewarded this time."

"You can be sure of that," said Jimmy softly, hardly able to restrain himself from grabbing hold of her on the spot.

They stared longingly at each other. He saw his own desire reflected in Monique's cat-eyes. They turned and hurried towards the elevator. The air seemed charged with electricity. As the automatic doors closed behind them, they fell into each other's arms.

Even as they raced together to Monique's suite, while she fumbled in her excitement to unlock the door, he couldn't refrain from touching her, from exploring her exquisite body. Once inside the room, they tore at each other's clothes in a feverish haste. Monique was trembling with excitement.

"Oh James, James. I never thought I would see you again ..."

He groaned as her felt her nipples harden beneath his touch. Never since Cathy had he felt this intensity of desire.

Their love-making was fierce and frenetic. Monique often took the initiative, demanding more and more of Jimmy. He met her needs with ease, his desire rekindled by hers, by the skilful probings of her experienced fingers and lips. He discovered Monique had no inhibitions. She used every part of her body to give and receive pleasure. Making love to this vibrant Frenchwoman was like playing an exquisite concerto on a finely-tuned instrument.

At last, exhausted by their love-making, they lay motionless together. The last thing he remembered was softly stroking her silky black hair. Within seconds he had drifted into a deep dreamless sleep.

* * * * * * *

During the following week they spent every evening together. He realised Monique had fallen helplessly in love with him. It was almost inevitable. He believed her when she insisted her feelings for him in France had been more than a girlhood crush. Jimmy had been a hero figure, a focus for the frustrations of a young girl growing up in war-torn France. It was a natural development for her to fall madly in love with her former idol.

For Jimmy it was different. He was extremely fond of Monique, adored being with her – found her company lively and stimulating. Not only incredibly beautiful, she was exciting and passionate. Sexually he couldn't have asked for more. Yet she still hadn't penetrated his inner self in the way his young wife had done. He tried desperately not to compare the two of them. They were totally different women – Monique so worldly, so outrageously seductive; Cathy so innocent, yet with a depth of passion her guileless eyes never betrayed.

He had also noticed a strong streak of selfishness in Monique. It rarely showed itself in her relationship with Jimmy – she was so devoted to pleasing him. But he became aware of it in various small ways in her dealings with other people.

He knew Monique expected more from their liaison than a romantic fling in New York. Although not in love with her, he had to admit he would miss her terribly when she returned to France or moved on to Hollywood.

One evening, as he settled down to catch up with some office work, the telephone rang. He was expecting a call from Monique, to decide where they would eat that night. He lifted the receiver, excited by the thought of seeing her soon.

"James, darling, I have wonderful news! The Paramount contract is mine!"

"That's marvellous, Monique. Congratulations!"

"Oh, James, I am so happy. It will make it so much easier for us."

"Yes, I wasn't looking forward to you being whisked back to France."

"I shall have to go back for a short while – just to sort out my affairs." She giggled. "My financial affairs, I mean, not my men friends."

"Monique, you're English is far too good – even if you do cheat with words of French origin!"

"But you know I am only joking, don't you James? There will be nobody else – now I have you. I shall be back in New York within a month. I have to be in Hollywood by the beginning of May."

"That won't leave us much time together, before you head for the West Coast."

"No." Monique's husky voice had lost its bouncy enthusiasm. "Jimmy, I wondered ..."

He was startled by her use of the diminutive of his name. From that first moment in France, she had perversely insisted on calling him James. Not that he minded in the slightest. But to resort to calling him Jimmy she must be up to one of her woman's tricks – probably wanted to wheedle a special going-away present.

"What were you wondering, Monique?"

"Do you love me, Jimmy?"

The sudden question took him completely by surprise.

"What a strange time to ask such a silly question. You know how much I care for you. Don't you remember last night?"

"Of course I do. How could I ever forget? But do you love me – really love me, I mean?" She paused. "Enough to marry me?"

He was taken further aback. He had never considered marriage with Monique, with anyone in fact – except Cathy when it had seemed the obvious, the only thing to do.

"Monique, you've taken me a little by surprise. Can we talk about it tonight?"

"Of course, James." He could hear the disappointment in her voice. "When shall I see you?"

"I'll pick you up at eight."

* * * * * * *

The evening hadn't gone well. Monique had been pensive and serious, not her usually vivacious self. She had sensed almost immediately that he wasn't ready to commit himself – at least not as far as marriage was concerned.

She wore a particularly attractive ensemble in flame red. He had to admit she looked quite stunning, the colour setting off her dark sultry beauty to perfection. As they walked through the restaurant everybody had turned to admire her. She held herself regally, as if playing a part in some stage drama.

As the evening advanced she became more depressed. When dessert arrived she stared miserably at her plate laden with pavlova. Normally she would have polished it off in seconds, but tonight she only picked at the exotic fruits and fluffy meringue.

"Cheer up, Monique. Tonight is a night for celebration. You're acceptance by Hollywood must be the most important step in your career."

"I know James, but I so desperately wanted to go there as your wife. It would not affect your work," she added quickly. "I know you cannot leave New York except perhaps for short breaks. We would be apart for long periods but at least, if we were married, I should feel settled. Knowing you will be waiting for me would make it all worthwhile." She looked at him, pleading, her green eyes glistening with unshed tears.

He began to consider a life without Monique, remembered his sterile existence before she arrived on the scene. He had enjoyed his work but there had been very little else in his life. Did he really want to go back to that? Monique had hinted that if she went to Hollywood without his commitment she would probably end up with another man. It wasn't a threat. She was the kind of woman who needed a man in her life.

They lingered over their coffee, neither of them quite sure what to say next. Monique looked across at him, almost coyly.

"James, have you never wanted a child of your own? After all you are a wealthy man. What will happen to your fortune, to all you have achieved, when you die? Have you never wanted a son?"

He sipped the last of his coffee, toyed with the golden liquid in his brandy glass, swishing it slowly against the sparkling balloon-shaped crystal. Monique was right. She wasn't the first person to raise the question of a family. When Pete Brady had married he'd become a complete convert to matrimony and had constantly tried to persuade Jimmy that he, too, should settle down and have some kids. Jimmy had always liked children; he would have liked a family one day. But marriage to Monique ...?

"James, you cannot mourn Cathy for ever, you know."

He looked up in surprise. It was the first time Monique had mentioned Cathy since the evening of their first meeting. He was astonished by her perception – her penetrating words struck at the roots of his reluctance.

He took a long sip of his brandy, slowly stirred the fresh coffee which had discreetly materialised in the delicate china cup. He knew he must make a decision now or he probably never would.

"Monique, look at me." His tone was commanding. "Before we go any further, I have a serious question to ask you."

She stared at him, her emerald eyes startled and enquiring.

He hesitated a moment, saw panic fill her eyes.

"Will you marry me?" he asked, softly.

Her squeal of delight made everyone in the restaurant turn their heads. She rushed round to Jimmy's side of the table, hugged and kissed him fiercely, completely unabashed by their surroundings.

"Is that a good enough answer for you, James?" she asked teasingly, her green eyes sparkling with happiness.

Everyone in the restaurant started to laugh and clap. Jimmy, his face split in a wide grin, returned her enthusiastic embrace. He felt a surge of relief. He could start living once again.

Chapter 18

Long Island, New York. June 1957

Jimmy grabbed a wire-basket full of tennis balls and strode across the tennis court towards the base-line. Whenever he had a spare moment in his busy work schedule, he tried to keep trim with exercise and sport. Tennis was his favourite outdoor activity and he worked hard to improve his game. Today he intended to practise his serve. He bounced a ball several times in front of him, but as he threw it up to serve, he spotted Monique walking determinedly towards him across the lawn of their Long Island estate. Deftly he re-caught the ball.

"James, darling!" she called as she approached, her face alight with excitement. "David has just telephoned. He wants me to go back to Hollywood to audition for another part." She sported a pale-blue cashmere sweater and a beautifully cut white linen skirt. As usual, she managed to look both elegant and voluptuous.

"But your film contract's already run out," protested Jimmy. "You were going to spend this year at home – we were going to start a family."

"An opening has come up with another studio for a fantastic new film. I have already read the script. It is a wonderful opportunity, James – I must do it if I can." In her agitation, her husky French accent was more noticeable.

"I thought you wanted a child, Monique," said Jimmy, his normally soft voice raised in scarcely repressed anger. He strode across the tennis court, impatiently smashed the tennis ball against the wire-netting surrounding the court. Damn Monique! There was always some excuse. He was beginning to believe she didn't really want any children. "You said we'd start a family as soon as your contract ran out," he said, unable to hide his anger. "You've already extended it twice!"

She looked at him archly through the wire, flashed her lovely smile. "Of course I want a child, James, but not for a little while yet."

"What do you mean, not for a little while?" He started to bluster, knowing he was lost once Monique became persuasive. She would use every sexual trick in the book and invariably get her own way in the end. Angrily he threw his racket down. "In case you've forgotten, we've already been married nearly five years. I seem to remember a child was the main reason you put forward for our marriage."

"Please, James, do not get so angry. You must see I cannot interrupt my career just at this moment!"

"Fiddlesticks, Monique! I have no desire to ruin your career, but you must admit you've gone about as far as you're going to – as a screen sex-kitten! It's time you settled down, accepted your family responsibilities. After all, you're not a spring chicken any more." He tried to pull himself together, to appear more reasonable. "In any case, having children won't mean the end of your career."

"But James, this new role – it is a tremendous character part, not another stupid sex symbol."

"Character part! But you can't act, Monique!"

Her face went white. She turned on her heels and strode angrily away across the lawn.

Grabbing his tennis gear, he rushed out of the court after her.

"Come back, Monique. I'm sorry, darling, I didn't mean to sound as harsh as that. But you know what I mean. You've only ever played light parts till now. It's quite different taking on a demanding character role."

"I know that, James. That is why this part is so important to me." She turned to face him, her green eyes wide and appealing.

But he wasn't about to give in.

"Monique, you promised. I'm not a young man any longer – I'll be forty-three next birthday. Old enough to be a grandfather, let alone a father. You're thirty-two. You can't wait forever to have your first baby. Remember what the doctor said."

"I have plenty of time yet to have many children," she said, obstinately.

He took her by the arm. They walked in angry silence across the lush grass towards the mansion's sweeping drive and main entrance.

"What about us, Monique?" he said, determined not to give in this time. "We've hardly seen anything of each other during the last couple of years."

She shrugged his arm away.

"That is not all my fault, James. You have been just as busy as I have."

"Yes, but I've been working for us – for our future."

"And so have I," said Monique with a swish of her black curls. "In any case – that's not the real point. We both work and play hard because we like doing it. We don't need the cash. You have far more money than we shall ever need. Why did you have to branch out into real estate, start building those huge apartment blocks?"

Jimmy sighed.

"You're right. We both seem to have this compulsion to tie ourselves up with work. What's the matter with us, Monique?"

"I like my work, James. When I am in front of a camera, I know I have everyone's attention. That is more than I can say when I am with you." Her cat-eyes flashed at him, challengingly.

"I'm sorry you feel that way, darling. I've always tried to treat you well."

"Oh yes, James. You have been the perfect husband in many respects." Her voice had an edge of bitterness and her mouth, under its gloss of crimson lipstick, curved in a sardonic smile. "But I never feel you are giving your whole self. There is a coldness about you, James – and I don't mean sexual. Always you seem to be holding back from me in some way."

Clasping her roughly by the hand, he turned her to face him. "Monique, don't you think a family would help? If we could spend more time together, have a child ... become more of a family unit ... Surely that should bring us closer together?"

Her eyes softened.

"You can usually get round me, James. But not this time. Still, I will make you one promise. If I don't get this part, we can start making babies."

Jimmy's hugged her to him. "In that case, I certainly shan't wish you good luck on this particular trip!"

* * * * * *

Monique never got the part.

Giles was born in May the following year. A large lusty baby, he grew excessively demanding and headstrong. Monique tried her best with him at the beginning, but soon gave up. A succession of nurses and nannies took over. Even the toughest of these found him a difficult child. Hyperactive and full of boundless energy, his behaviour was invariably directed towards mischief. Unusually big and strong for his age, at each stage of his growth he required ever-increasing attention.

Monique had christened him after her father. The boy certainly took after that side of her family. Though Jimmy had never known Monique's father, Giles often reminded him of her powerfully-built rumbustious uncle, Pierre, who had rescued him when he first landed in France. In no way, he thought, did Giles resemble himself physically or mentally. Jimmy, slimly-built and softly-spoken, could find little in common with his sturdy boisterous son.

Like his mother, Giles had dark curly hair, but his eyes blazed a vivid aquamarine. A handsome boy, broad and large-limbed with never an ounce of fat on his body, even as a baby he seemed tough as a lion. He rarely cried, even when he hurt himself, but his constant demands and unceasing energy exhausted everybody around him.

Jimmy often wondered if his son's demands for attention were rooted in insecurity. Monique had little time for Giles. Perhaps, if he had been an easier more amenable child – more sensitive and loving – she would have felt closer to him, spent more time with him. As it was Giles overwhelmed her with his energy and waywardness. At times she seemed half-frightened of her son. She certainly had no control whatsoever over him. Monique had been used to bending men to her own will, to being the centre of their attention. Giles confused and frustrated her. Eventually she gave up with him, went back to her film work, accepting smaller and less important roles as time went on.

Jimmy tried to compensate for her absences, spending as much time as his work allowed with Giles. But however much he tried, he found it impossible to get close to the boy. Emotionally Giles seemed completely self-contained. He showed little warmth and affection, even for his father. A tyrant in miniature, he was bent on following his own energetic will. Attempts at discipline made him more rebellious.

* * * * * *

Obviously distressed by her disastrous relationship with Giles, Monique showed no inclination to have any more children. Jimmy could hardly blame her. Their own relationship had grown worse, not better, following the birth of their son. Deep down he blamed himself more than Monique. He had always known his second wife to be self-centred, almost childish, in her need for attention but he was equally aware that he had failed to give her the security and love she deserved.

He still found her physically exciting. Their separations were punctuated by passionate reconciliations. But these never seemed to last long. He knew he had never really loved her. There was no warmth or rapport between them other than on a purely sexual plane.

Monique turned more and more to her other friends and activities. Jimmy suspected she was unfaithful to him when away in California. He heard rumours of wild parties at their Hollywood home. Even worse, he found he didn't really care much anymore. Strangely enough, despite his own promiscuity before his first marriage, he remained faithful to Monique – even when it became apparent his loyalty wasn't reciprocated. It eased his conscience, feeling as he did that the failure of their partnership stemmed largely from his own shortcomings.

Paradoxically, or perhaps because his domestic relationships had deteriorated, he became even more successful in business. The fifties and early sixties were a period of boom. Financially he couldn't put a foot wrong, whatever enterprise he took on. Money made more money. His personal fortune grew by leaps and bounds. Unfortunately happiness didn't follow his increase in wealth.

His unsatisfactory existence took another downturn when, at the tender age of eight, Giles was expelled from his expensive private school in New Hampshire. Jimmy reacted with a mixture of fury and remorse. His life now revolved about his son and heir, despite his problems with the boy, the lack of easy communication between them. He had been convinced that time and a good education would sort him out.

He admired so much about his son – his powerful body and energetic mind, his indestructible enthusiasm and complete lack of fear. Jimmy had heaved a huge sigh of relief when he realised Giles would never suffer his own tragic disability. His son showed no trace of fear. Jimmy had watched the boy during times of risk and challenge. He knew his bravado was not a front as it had been with himself. Giles thrived on danger; his eyes would sparkled, his whole body come alive with excitement when confronted by any physical challenge.

It wasn't a matter of courage or bravery – Giles simply knew no fear. If his boundless energies could only be properly channelled, Jimmy felt sure he would develop into a son to be proud of.

As soon as he heard the news of his son's expulsion, Jimmy went alone to collect him from school, driving the Rolls himself. He didn't want even the presence of a chauffeur to interfere with their reunion.

Giles stepped into the limousine silent and defiant, refusing to even look at his father. Jimmy felt an overwhelming desire to strike the boy but managed to restrain himself. He hated violence and wanted to hear his son's side of the events leading to his expulsion. The silence between them continued as the Rolls purred smoothly along the highway home.

"Well, Giles. Have you nothing to say for yourself?" he asked, impatiently. "What actually happened? I've heard your headmaster's version. I think it only fair I hear yours. Mind you – you must have behaved pretty abominably for them to expel you, considering the amount I pay in school fees!"

Still Giles refused to speak. He sat defiantly in the front passenger seat, his blue-green eyes cold as steel, his face immobile. Jimmy felt an uncontrollable shiver pass through him. The self-possession of the young boy was almost uncanny. He might have been ten years older. Jimmy found his son's cool presence more threatening than a confrontation with a board of hardened businessmen.

"I'm waiting, Giles. Being expelled may not seem very important to you. But I can assure you it is a most inauspicious start to your academic career. Have you no remorse? You don't look at all sorry."

"I have nothing to be sorry about," retorted Giles coldly.

"Nothing to be sorry about?" yelled Jimmy in exasperation. "How then do you explain your extreme rudeness to a master – the fact you struck him with a riding crop?"

"He asked for it. He was rude to me first," declared Giles, his voice hard and implacable.

Jimmy felt the cold fury return.

"Don't be impertinent Giles! Whatever the master said or did, there was simply no excuse for striking him. You are eight years old – you must show due respect for your elders. In any case, there's never any excuse for unnecessary violence. You're not stupid, Giles! You must realise you can't go around hitting people, especially those in authority."

"I don't believe in authority," said Giles, as if that were the end of the matter.

"I don't care what you believe, Giles," said Jimmy, white with anger. "I've given up reasoning with you. From now you will do as I say, abide by my authority." He softened his tone, trying to get through to the boy. "I can understand your feelings of rebellion to a degree, Giles. But you must start to exercise restraint and self-control. You can't go through life striking out at people, just because you don't like or don't agree with them. I have no intention of spending the rest of my years baling you out of trouble. You will be on your own." He paused to emphasise his next words. "I mean that, Giles – on your own!"

Giles sat impassively in the passenger seat, refusing to answer. But glancing surreptitiously at his son, Jimmy felt sure he saw a shadow of apprehension pass over the boy's normally inexpressive features. Giles was no fool. He must realise he needed his father's support and financial backing.

"I'll try not to get expelled again," said Giles eventually, his tone still grudging and completely lacking in contrition.

Jimmy sighed inwardly, not knowing how to get through to the boy.

"I warn you – if it does happen again – you will be sent to the local day school," he told him coldly. "There you won't enjoy the same privileges and facilities you've grown used to – especially as far as sport is concerned."

Giles looked at him in consternation. The last remark had really hit home. His son adored and excelled at every form of sport.

"OK Father, I understand. It won't happen again."

Giles stayed true to his word. He was never expelled again, but at times he came close to it.

It upset Jimmy to see the way his son was developing. Giles had an excellent brain, a strong lithe body – he could have accomplished so much. But utterly selfish and self-seeking, he stretched the bounds of authority to their limits, somehow seeming to know intuitively when he had reached the breaking point. Then he would stop – just in time.

To Jimmy it was like reining-in a headstrong colt. Soon the young animal would grow into a powerful stallion. One day the brute might realise its own strength and bolt! Then who could prevent anyone crossing his path from being hurt!

Chapter 19

Long Island, New York. February 1967

Jimmy was sorting through his desk drawers searching for some old papers when he came across the snapshot – a picture of himself together with some of his closest friends from his old squadron taken during the time of the Battle of Britain. They stood in a group in front of his Hurricane fighter. Next to him in the photo, his arm around Jimmy's shoulder, was Simon Carstairs.

Jimmy's heart missed a beat. He hadn't seen the photograph for years. Yet he'd always kept it with him, even in France, where it could have proved fatal, revealing as it did his true identity. It was the only snapshot he had of the old days, except of course the photograph of Cathy, which he always kept somewhere on his person – usually in his wallet. Not a week passed when he didn't study it in detail and think about her.

But he hadn't seen this photo for some time now. He stared at it, suddenly conscious of the rapid passing of time. They all looked so young in the picture – little more than boys – yet they had been fighting a cruel adult war. All the airmen were grinning cheerfully into the camera. From their jaunty demeanour they might have been a group of young cadets who had never undergone the rigours of deadly air battles. But their gaunt tired faces betrayed the stresses and strains of those war-time days. Nostalgia flooded over Jimmy.

Monique swept into his study.

"James, you won't forget the Sassoons are coming to dinner tonight." She stopped short, seeing the expression on his face. "Whatever is the matter? You are not feeling well?" Then she spotted the photograph in his hand. Moving to his side, she stared at the slightly-faded picture.

"Oh, James. You – in that very sexy uniform! Just as I always remember you, that very first time in France." Her voice softened. "May I have a closer look? I never knew you had such a wonderful old photograph."

Wordlessly he handed her the snapshot.

"My hero-airman," she mused. "You look so young, so innocent. But you have not changed so much, my darling." Affectionately, she stroked his dark-blonde hair. "How do you say in English – some 'distinguished' grey hairs at the temples, thinning just a little on top, but nothing you would really notice." She looked down again at the snapshot. "Who is this by your side? He looks very nice."

"That was my best friend, Simon Carstairs."

"Was? Did he die in the war?"

"I'm not really sure what happened to him. As far as I know, he's probably still alive and kicking. He was flying with me that day I was shot down but I don't think the Huns got him. Dear old Simon! He was a tremendous chum."

"Poor James! You must miss your old friends. Do you think often of those terrible flying days?"

He realised her concern was genuine. In recent years, since her film career had finished, she had spent more time with Jimmy in their Long Island home. The two of them had grown closer. Although there would always be something lacking in their relationship as far as he was concerned, they seemed to have reached a workable understanding.

Jimmy shrugged.

"I try not to. It would only make me miserable." He had never told Monique the truth about those days in France – his desertion! He had led her to believe he had spent the rest of the war in a prisoner-of-war camp, moving to America after his discovery that his wife had died in an bombing raid.

"We must frame it, darling! You should be proud of your flying days." Monique's firm tone booked no argument. "It is always good to be reminded of old friends. I will see it is done straight away. Now don't forget the Sassoons." She glided gracefully away to organise dinner.

Jimmy sat quietly behind his desk. Simon! he thought. Why had he never considered contacting his old friend before? He could have trusted Simon, and Simon might have been able to provide him with information about Cathy's death. For some reason, in his devastation at learning about both Cathy and his mother, Jimmy had never thought of tracing him. Yet Simon had been his best friend and a link with Cathy. He might have been able to tell him more about his wife – how she had taken his loss, how she had died.

Even as he grew older, Jimmy never ceased to dwell on her. If anything, during the last few years he had thought about her even more, though he tried not to let it interfere with his improved relationship with Monique. It was a strange phenomenon. He had known Cathy so little time – days in total, not even months, such a short fraction of his life-time. Yet their relationship was the one shining period of his existence – what his life had been all about. He had lived the rest of his years in the shadow of those glorious brief moments with Cathy.

He knew it was the reason he had never been able to give himself fully to Monique. Their marriage had suffered from his everlasting obsession with his first wife. No, it wasn't an obsession, he decided, just the purest love he'd ever known.

He desperately wanted to know how Cathy had fared after he was shot down and the full details of the bombing of their home. Had she suffered terribly over him before her death? Was there the slimmest of chances she might have survived the raid? With a new sense of urgency he reached for the telephone, rapidly dialled the number of his Manhattan lawyer.

"John, it's Jimmy Pritchard. Could you do me a favour ...? Yes, I'm fine. But I want you to put me in touch with a private investigator, as soon as possible. Oh ... and he's got to be red-hot. Not some sleazy character dealing in divorce and muck-raking ... Thanks a lot, John. Tell him I'll look forward to hearing from him."

He slammed the phone down and stared for a long time at the faded photograph.

* * * * * * *

Investigator Brian Daniels was British not American, though he had lived in the United States since 1946. During the war years, he had apparently been involved in some branch of Military Intelligence.

He didn't look at all like Jimmy's idea of a private investigator. A small plump man, neatly dressed with a rather fussy manner, Daniels reminded him of an enthusiastic assistant in a clothing store. John Baxter had assured him Daniels was one of the best in the business and Jimmy soon realised his lawyer's assessment was correct. Brian Daniels, for all his disarming manner, had a razor-sharp mind and a keen persistent eye for detail. He asked all the right questions and had that wonderful gift of being able to extract information without appearing to do so. If anyone could find Simon Carstairs, thought Jimmy, it was Daniels.

"As I said before, Mr Daniels. Expense is no problem. Spend whatever's necessary. I'm looking for results, regardless of cost. A considerable amount of travel may be necessary in your investigation. I'll open an account immediately for your special use. Send me a weekly report and a list of expenses. The rest I leave to your own discretion."

"Thank you, Mr Pritchard. That's the way I like to work. I don't foresee any real problems; unless of course this gentleman, Simon Carstairs, is already dead."

"If that's the case, I'm afraid there's probably little you can do. I will leave it to you. My main interest is to discover anybody who might have had anything to do with Mrs Catherine Proctor before she died. Of course I'm trusting to your complete discretion. At no stage in your investigation are you to reveal the identity of the party you are representing."

"Of course not, Mr Pritchard." Daniels sniffed and rubbed his plump hands together. Jimmy had the overwhelming sensation that – at any minute – the man would extract a tape-measure from his pocket and start measuring him up.

"Should you discover anything concrete," continued Jimmy, "let me know immediately – wherever you may be."

"Certainly, Mr Pritchard." Daniels rose from his seat. They shook hands, and Jimmy walked with him to the door of his study.

"Good luck, Mr Daniels."

"Thank you, Mr Pritchard, we all need our fair share of that." Daniels placed his hat on his head and walked softly away.

Action at last, thought Jimmy.

Three weeks later, he received a long distance call from England. It was Daniels. The connection wasn't a good one, but he could sense an edge of excitement in Daniel's otherwise concise reporting.

"I may be on to something, Mr Pritchard." Daniels's voice was distorted for a moment by static on the line. "I'm afraid Mr Carstairs was killed – not in the war, but in an accident during a flying stunt in 1954. His wife remarried. She and her new husband and family moved to Australia."

"Damn it!" muttered Jimmy. Poor old Simon. So his old friend was gone too – his last link with Cathy.

"Are you still there, Mr. Pritchard?"

"Yes ... yes, I'm sorry. Please carry on."

"Following your instructions, I did make further investigations into the death of Mrs Proctor. The building at the address you gave me was definitely demolished – a direct hit from an explosive bomb. I've been there myself, as well as checking out the air-raid and fire department reports. The remains of three bodies were found, just as you were informed previously."

Jimmy's heart sank. His last glimmer of hope – that perhaps there might have been some mistake, that Cathy might have miraculously survived – was finally shattered. It seemed all links to Cathy had been cut. Was fate repaying him for his abandonment of his wife?

"However," continued Daniels briskly, "although your friend, Simon Carstairs, is no longer alive, I was able to make contact by telephone with his wife, Mrs Vanessa Carstairs, in Australia. Apparently she was a close friend of Catherine Proctor."

God, thought Jimmy! Nessie – it must be Nessie! It was she who had married Simon. What a turn up for the books!

"Can you hear me, Mr Pritchard? I'm afraid the line's very bad."

"Yes. Yes, I can hear you. Please carry on."

"Vanessa Carstairs was extremely helpful and her information proved most interesting. I am pleased to be able tell you that I have every good reason to believe Mrs Proctor is alive!"

Jimmy couldn't believe his ears. He sat down hard on the chair. "Are you sure, Mr. Daniels?" His heart thumped so loudly, he was sure it could be heard at the other end of the telephone. Could he trust Daniels's information? It seemed too good to be true. He couldn't bear another bitter disappointment. "What about the bombing of the flat?"

"As I said before, the flat was definitely bombed; but by a stroke of good fortune, Mrs Proctor wasn't there at the time. Mrs Carstairs was quite adamant about this. Apparently Catherine Proctor remarried during the war. She and her second husband went to live in Oxford. From further enquiries, I discovered that two of the people who died in the bombing had only recently moved into the ground-floor flat – the flat you believed to be empty. With them and the Mrs Dauncey you mentioned, who lived upstairs, that accounts for the three bodies."

Jimmy was scarcely listening. All he could understand was that Cathy was alive! Relief surged through him, swiftly followed by a new sense of apprehension. Cathy – remarried! Of course – it was only natural. Yet he couldn't prevent a feeling of nausea rising in his throat. He felt ecstatically happy she was alive. But married! It wasn't only jealousy, but a sickening fear. Who was the man? Had he been right for Cathy? Did he mistreat her? Was she happy? More than twenty-six years had passed since the bombing; God knows what might have happened to her.

"I can't hear you, Mr Pritchard." Daniels was shouting to him down the phone. "Would you like to know Mrs Proctor's new married name?"

"Yes ... Yes please, Mr Daniels," stammered Jimmy, "and any other information you may have."

"She now goes under the name of Mrs Bourne – Mrs Leslie Bourne. I'm afraid that's all Mrs Carstairs could tell me – except that the last she knew Catherine Bourne was both fit and well. They have three children, by the way."

Relief and happiness flooded through Jimmy. Cathy – married to her old friend, Leslie, who doted on her. He couldn't have hoped for anything better. He knew she would be safe, happy and well cared-for. And with children of her own. He smiled to himself. Cathy would make a superb mother. Of course, the children would be grown-up by now. He wondered if Cathy's off-spring resembled her or Leslie.

"Thank you, Mr Daniels. That's marvellous news!"

"Shall I continue further with my investigation, Mr Pritchard?"

"Yes please, Mr Daniels. "I should be grateful for confirmation of all this information and any further news about Mrs Proctor – I mean Mrs Bourne – and her family. But don't forget my original stipulation. On no account may you disclose my interest in the subject."

"Of course not, Mr Pritchard. Goodbye."

* * * * * * *

For the first time in nearly twenty-seven years, since his desertion of both Cathy and the Air Force, Jimmy felt content. A warm satisfaction glowed inside him. The knowledge she was alive, and in all probability happy, changed his whole attitude to life.

He longed to see her but knew his greatest gift to her would be to stay out of her life, not interfere in what should be a fine marriage to Leslie. He couldn't wait to hear more news from Daniels, just to be sure all was well.

In the meantime his attitude towards Monique became more mellow and understanding. His wife blossomed under his new attention.

Giles, however, was another matter. His son went from bad to worse, as if driven by some internal demon – as if he resented Jimmy's new closeness to Monique. Yet the boy's personal magnetism and handsome good looks had only improved as he developed towards manhood. Jimmy was at a loss to know how to handle his wayward son.

* * * * * * *

Three weeks after his original telephone call, Daniels called again. Recognising his voice on the line Jimmy trembled with anticipation.

"Yes, Mr Daniels. What news do you have?"

"It appears Mr and Mrs Bourne are safe and well – still living in the university city of Oxford. So far I've only seen two of their children. The eldest, of course, would be married or living away from home. In view of the need for discretion, I didn't like to pursue my enquiries without speaking to you first. However, I have come across one rather strange piece of information which you never disclosed to me in my briefing, Mr Pritchard. I wondered if you yourself were aware of this fact."

"What fact – what are you talking about, Daniels?" demanded Jimmy, impatiently.

"Were you aware, sir, that Mrs Proctor gave birth to her eldest child before the apartment was bombed?"

"Before?" Jimmy was stunned and perplexed. "You're mistaken, Daniels. That's impossible. You must have the wrong woman!"

"I can assure you my sources are most emphatic in this respect, Mr Pritchard. Two neighbours of Mrs Bourne when she lived in South Kensington, a Mr and Mrs Jenkins, made contact with me recently, following my enquiries in the area. The information they provided included the fact that Mrs Bourne – or Mrs Proctor as she was then – gave birth to a baby some time before the bombing incident. They remember it well. Mrs Proctor had lost her husband several months before the baby was born. They thought the circumstances very tragic."

Jimmy sank into his chair. His body flashed hot and cold, he found he was trembling all over. His insides churned, as if he had been struck in the stomach with a sledge-hammer.

"I see ..." he said, still in a daze.

"Would you like me to continue with my investigations, Mr. Pritchard, perhaps see if I can trace more details about this older child? I could of course contact Mrs Carstairs again in Australia ..." Daniel's voice was discreetly understanding. Jimmy sensed at once that the investigator was probably all too aware of his relationship with Cathy.

"No, I think you've discovered all I need to know, Mr Daniels."

"You were right about the Somerset House records," continued Daniels quickly. "They were destroyed for that period, but the child's details may have been submitted at a later date."

"Yes, of course. Thank you, Mr. Daniels, for all your efforts. I'm most grateful. Please let me have your final accounts. I'll include a substantial bonus for your excellent work. Tell me ... just one thing – did the Jenkins happen to mention if the baby was a boy or a girl?"

"A boy it was, sir. Although the Jenkins couple never actually saw the baby. Apparently they weren't close friends of Mrs Bourne, and because of the Blitz, they moved to the countryside very soon after the baby was born. But they had heard his name mentioned several times and remembered it especially. It seems Mr Jenkins has exactly the same Christian name! The child was called Sam!"

PART THREE

SAMANTHA

A pair of star-cross'd lovers.

William Shakespeare

I was a child and she was a child,
In this kingdom by the sea;
But we loved with a love that was more than love
I and my Annabel Lee.

Edgar Allan Poe

Chapter 20

Oxford, England. September 1958

"Hi, Mother, I'm home!" called Samantha. She threw down her satchel in the hall and walked through to the kitchen.

Cathy, her sleeves rolled up to her elbows, stood at one of the marble surfaces making pastry. "Hello darling. Had a good day at school?"

"Fine, thanks. I've got some good news for you." She leant to kiss her mother on the cheek. Giggling, she gently wiped a smudge of flour from Cathy's nose.

"Mother, why do you always end up with flour all over your face."

"I'm a self-taught cook, Sam dear. There were no domestic science classes at my boarding school, and the war put paid to any flash cordon bleu courses. Nobody ever taught me how to keep myself flour-proof!"

Samantha laughed.

"Never mind. You're a great cook and that's all that matters." She glanced around. "Where are the twins?"

"They're at a football practice – they should be home soon."

"I thought it seemed remarkably quiet! Those two create havoc when they're around. Boisterous isn't the word for it – they're like an accident looking for somewhere to happen. I don't know how you cope. And they're still only nine. Can you imagine them as teenagers!"

Cathy smiled indulgently.

"I can handle them, darling, as long as they leave me enough time to spend with my lovely daughter."

Samantha smiled shyly. "Well, if you do have a spare moment, mother, I'd love a little chat while the boys are out of the way."

"Of course, darling – just two ticks." Cathy kneaded the pastry into a ball, wrapped it in grease-proof and placed it in the refrigerator. She was pleased Sam wanted to confide in her. It was always difficult knowing what went on in her daughter's lively mind.

"I'm all yours!" She pushed her hair back with a still-floury hand, leaving another white smudge on her forehead.

Samantha smiled.

"Come and sit down, Mother."

"Oh, this sounds serious."

"Don't worry, it's good news, but there's something I wanted to discuss with you."

They wandered into the living-room. It was a room Cathy loved – large and airy, comfortably furnished with French windows which ran along most of one wall. These gave onto a sunlit terrace and a long stretch of immaculate lawn. The view over Oxford and its dreaming spires was magnificent.

Cathy settled into a deep comfy armchair. Samantha, as usual, relaxed on the carpet, tucking her long slim legs beneath her. Cathy stared expectantly at her daughter, feeling pride well up inside her. Now seventeen, Samantha had grown into a beautiful young lady. Physically she took after her father, Jimmy, and Cathy's own mother Denise, Samantha's French grandmother. Extremely slender, almost fragile, with delicate features and Denise's slightly turned-up nose, her hazel eyes were Jimmy's, as was her fine dark-blonde hair which she had grown long and now wore in a pony-tail. Sam also displayed many of Jimmy's mannerisms, yet she had never known her father. It never ceased to amaze Cathy. Each time Sam shrugged her shoulders or smiled knowingly at her mother, she would feel a slight wrench inside. It might have been Jimmy.

Samantha beamed at her, pride shining in her eyes.

"Mother, I'm so happy – I've won our Form Prize again."

"Well done, Sam! That's absolutely marvellous. It's the fourth year running, isn't it? Poor Chris must be feeling upset. You always seem to pip her to the post." Christine and Sam were not only great friends at school, but keen rivals for first position in their form.

"Chris will get a special progress prize, so she's not too disappointed." Sam smiled. "I'm glad – she really deserves it."

"And so do you, darling. You've worked very hard."

Sam looked down, seemingly embarrassed. "Oh, it wasn't too bad, Mother." But Cathy knew how hard her daughter worked at school, as if driven by some strange force inside her. Not academic herself, Cathy admired but couldn't wholly understand Sam's apparent pre-occupation with her studies, her determination and ambition to always be top. Her daughter was naturally intelligent and didn't really need to push herself so hard.

"I've also got your invitations to Speech Day," continued Sam, happily, "so you'd better buy a new hat and get Dad organized. He's not to go in his corduroys!" Then her smile faded. She fidgeted with loose strands of her hair and started to blink rapidly, a sure sign to Cathy that her buoyant mood had changed to nervousness or apprehension. "I also had a chat with Miss Davis today." She looked hard at Cathy.

"Oh yes?" Cathy smiled and tried to keep her tone light. She sensed something bothering her rather complicated daughter despite the good news of her exams. She found it difficult to get Sam to speak about her deeper feelings and often the more concern Cathy showed, the more Sam would retreat into herself.

She wants me to take two of my subjects at Scholarship level, as well as 'A' Level ..." said Sam, hesitantly "... try to get into Girton College, Cambridge, her old Alma Mater."

"But darling, I thought you were going to try for Oxford, so you'd be near home."

"That's just the point, mother. I don't want to try for either. I want to study in London." Sam's expression was serious, her voice determined.

"London? I don't understand, Sam."

"Mother, I've spent all my life cosseted by you and Dad. You've both been absolutely marvellous, but when I finish school, I need to get away – make my own life for a while, without your help."

"But Sam, you're still so young."

"I shall be eighteen when I finish my 'A' Levels. Most girls are out earning a living at that age, often far from home." She stared hard at Cathy. "You joined the WAAF when you were eighteen, Mother."

"*Touché* darling. But you forget – things were different then. There was a war going on."

"It doesn't make any difference. I want to see more of the outside world. You must admit we have an 'ivory towers' existence here in Oxford, with Dad lecturing at the University."

"But it's a good life, Sam," said Cathy, gently. "Darling, it's not as if you're an extrovert sort of person. You're really quite shy. Don't you think you'd be a little overwhelmed, living in a large city where you know nobody?"

Sam thrust out her slim chin.

"That's one of the reasons I want to go. I need to get out of myself more, see how the rest of the world lives."

Cathy knew that for all her mild almost fragile appearance, Sam could be tough and determined. At times she also proved remarkably stubborn. Once her daughter had made up her mind, there was little likelihood of anybody changing it. Cathy felt a sudden chill inside but tried to disguise the extent of her concern.

"Leave it with me, will you Sam, dear? I'll have a chat with your father tonight. In the meantime, please think about it carefully. It's a very big step. You have the opportunity of a brilliant career ahead of you. Don't spoil it. You'll have plenty of time to see the world, once you've finished your studies."

Sam leapt to her feet.

"Mother! Oxbridge isn't the only education in the world you know. I want to read something interesting, something relevant to everyday life – like sociology or business studies."

"You can always read PPE at Oxford," said Cathy softly. She rose and put her arm round Sam's shoulder, was surprised to feel her daughter trembling beneath her touch. She gently pulled her down onto the sofa by her side and stroked her hair.

"It would still be ivory towers ... don't you see, Mother?" Sam's tone had changed to pleading and Cathy saw tears in her eyes. But the moment was broken by the sound of shouting and scuffles from the hallway – the twins, obviously home from school. A plump black cat rushed into the room, leapt onto Cathy's lap, quickly followed by a sleek and graceful Siamese. Roger, the retriever, gambolled in their wake and sat tongue lolling out, staring in rapt attention at Cathy.

Her daughter sighed and pulled away but continued to gaze imploringly at her. Cathy could sense the frustration in her voice.

"Mother, you have Dad who absolutely adores you, the boys, the dog, the cats, the horses, the birds in the garden, plus every waif and stray that ever comes near you – human or animal! You also have half the University eating out of your hand. Can't you let me go?"

Caught unawares by Sam's vehemence, Cathy felt hot tears start to well in her eyes. How awful that her daughter should feel so trapped and over-protected! She took a deep breath, managed to stem the flow of tears, but she could hear the tremor in her voice as she spoke.

"You're right, Sam, quite right. You need to make your own life." She swallowed hard. "We'll have a proper talk about it later, when your father gets home and the boys have gone to bed." She wiped a hand brusquely across her eyes and stood up. "You must be hungry, darling."

"Absolutely starving."

"Good, it's your favourite tonight – steak and kidney pie."

With a muffled sob, Sam fell into her arms. Cathy could feel her daughter's body shaking uncontrollably, the wetness of tears on her own cheeks.

"I love you, Mother." She rushed out of the room – just as the twins piled in.

"What's the matter with Sam?" asked Timothy, the elder by a matter of minutes. He gave her a puzzled look.

"Oh, nothing, darling." Cathy tried desperately to sound matter-of-fact. "She's just a bit overcome – she's won the Form Prize again."

"Girls are so silly!" chimed in Adrian. "Fancy getting upset when something nice happens. If I won a form-prize, I'd go and climb my favourite tree and eat all my chocolate ration at once."

"Not much danger of that!" said Tim, digging his brother in the ribs. "You're too stupid!" They started to wrestle.

"Out in the garden if you want to horse-play," said Cathy firmly.

The boys and Roger bounded out through the French windows onto the lawn. Cathy ran her fingers nervously through her hair. Had she really been over-protective of Sam, smothered her daughter with too much love? She had so wanted her to be happy and secure, never to suffer her own lack of family love. She couldn't wait to see Leslie and discuss it with him. He would sort everything out.

* * * * * * *

Cathy lay in bed staring at the ceiling. Leslie held her hand and gave it a squeeze.

"Don't worry, my love. You have nothing to reproach yourself for. Sam adores you – we all do. It's natural she should want to spread her wings, now she's getting older."

"But I never realised how she was feeling all this time!"

"Cath, we're both to blame in that respect. I've cosseted her as much as you. But I don't think it will do her any harm. She's an extremely sensible, capable young lady, and we have ourselves to thank for that."

"I just wanted her to have all the love and affection I missed, when I was younger."

Of course you did. Darling, you are the most loving sensitive person in the whole world – that's why everybody adores you. But sometimes with those closest to you, you don't seem to see the light."

"What do you mean, Leslie?"

"Sam isn't like you. She'll never be satisfied – even with the most loving husband and family. She's had all the security she needs, thanks to you. Now she wants something more. Our daughter is a determined ambitious young lady. She's capable, intelligent and extremely self-contained – she'll want more from life than a cosy family."

Leslie was right, she thought – as usual! They had both given Sam a solid base for her life. Now their daughter could spread her wings, discover a rich new life. She started to feel warmer inside.

She loved the way Leslie always referred to Sam as their daughter, never just hers. Soon after Jimmy had died, Leslie had happily taken over her first husband's responsibilities, emotionally as well physically. Yet he had never denied Sam her true father. When Leslie adopted her as his own daughter, he had insisted Sam should keep her father's name, as well as his own. Their daughter was known as Samantha Proctor Bourne. Both of them talked naturally and happily to her about Jimmy, telling her all they could about him – the love and respect they had felt for him. Sam had never known her father but she grew to understand him as a real person, not some ephemeral figure in the past. She came to dote on his memory and never tired of hearing about him.

"There's just one thing, Leslie. I know Sam's self-contained, but she's still rather shy with strangers. Don't you think she'll be lonely in London?"

She stared up at the ceiling, trying to sort out this new concern.

"She's always been rather serious-minded. I wanted to encourage her to have fun at college, enjoy herself – as well as working hard at her studies. I'm frightened that on her own, without family and friends, she might become introspective, too wrapped up in her work."

"You're underestimating her, Cath. She'll soon make new friends – she'll have to. It might be the very stimulus she needs."

"I hope she meets some nice young man," mused Cathy, snuggling down beside Leslie's warm body. "She's such a wonderful girl – talented and so beautiful. The boys all chase her, but she doesn't seem to have found anybody special in Oxford. I was hoping that nice young boy, John, might have roused a spark."

"You'll never change, will you Cath?" murmured Leslie, tolerantly. "Nice young men indeed! Samantha will be looking for more than that."

He's right, thought Cathy, as she settled down to sleep. She gave his hand a squeeze. Trust Leslie to reassure her! But she still couldn't help worrying about Sam.

Samantha's bedroom, at the other side of the house, was small but tastefully and delicately furnished in tones of blue. Sam lay in bed, unable to sleep. She hoped she hadn't upset her mother too much with her outburst. She doted on her and would hate to hurt her. She only wished she had her mother's easy charm and captivating way with people. Everybody loved Cathy. They all fell under her spell. She had the art of instantly understanding other people's feelings and needs.

The strange thing was her mother seemed blissfully unaware of the devastating effect she had on others. She often bemoaned her shortcomings, her lack of beauty. It was true Mother wasn't physically stunning. She carried herself well, but her figure was unremarkable. She had a warm pleasant face, which had scarcely aged, and it was highlighted by good cheek bones.

But she couldn't be described as beautiful. Her mother's beauty came from inside. But of course, looking in the mirror, she could hardly be aware of her natural charm, the winning personality behind the ordinary features.

Tossing and turning, still unable to sleep, Sam caught sight of the war-time photograph of her parents on the bedside table. How she wished she could have known her real father. Often she would fantasise that he was still alive. She knew she looked like him and she felt akin to him in many more ways than to her mother.

"I wish I could be brave and fearless like you, Father," she murmured to the man in the photograph. "Please help me to stop feeling nervous and insecure all the time. I know I'm not wonderful in the way mother is – I can never compete with her – but I know you would have loved me too. I'll try hard to make a success of my life, like you would have done if it hadn't been for that awful war ..."

Her eyes misted over. He looked so handsome and debonair in the snapshot – obviously a one for the ladies. Yet she could easily understand how he'd fallen for the young unassuming brunette who stood by his side. With one innocent smile and a few understanding words, her mother could quite innocently become as seductive as any pin-up girl.

Well aware of her own physical advantages, Sam gave a wry smile. Boys seemed to find her attractive yet John, the only boy she had ever really liked, had eventually rejected her for a girl who according to her friends at school wasn't half as pretty as Sam. She had never said anything to her parents about her disappointment over John, preferring to give the impression she didn't really care. But inside she deeply envied her mother's charm and appeal. She would have given anything to exchange her own slim figure and good looks for her mother's easy way with people. She wished she could be more like her – just as easy to love – and more able to show her own feelings in return. Sam felt painfully shy and insecure with strangers and somehow unable to capitalise on her physical assets. Despite her looks and academic successes she still lacked confidence in herself. It was a shortcoming she had to overcome.

She gritted her teeth. It couldn't be that hard. During her short lifetime she had found that tenacity, hard work and determination could overcome most difficulties – and she had a plentiful supply of those virtues. London and a fresh environment would surely make all the difference. Even if she didn't have the talent for inspiring love, if she could never compete with her mother as far as relationships were concerned, she could be highly successful like her father in her chosen career, and that was where she intended to direct her attentions.

She stared again at the happy snapshot of her parents, doubting she would ever marry or have a family of her own. She could never understand why the girls at school spent so much time chatting about weddings and children. Was it because she had somehow always felt the odd one out, despite all the love and attention she had received from her mother and her step-father. Leslie was wonderful and she adored him, but she deeply regretted never knowing her real father, and once the twins came on the scene, she seemed further estranged from the mainstream of family life. She felt that somehow she was different from the rest of them. Yet they continued to overwhelm her with their love. And despite her envy of her mother, she knew deep down that she likewise loved her mother more than anything in the world.

An unexpected thought brought a sudden smile to her face. Her mother might have everyone eating out her hand, but thank goodness there was one person who – though he adored her – controlled Cathy with an invisible hand! That was Leslie. Dear old Mother, she thought. Even she, for all her wonderful intuition, didn't realise that!

She was lucky to have a stepfather like Leslie and sometimes she felt guilty for idolising and dreaming so much about her real father. Leslie was marvellous to her and despite his devoted quiet manner, certainly the real power behind the throne. She, the boys and her mother would be lost without Leslie's steady presence, his enduring wisdom. She knew he would convince her mother tonight on her behalf. Now she could make plans for the future without feeling guilty. She couldn't wait to get away to London!

"Thank you, Leslie," she murmured into the darkness. Feeling suddenly drowsy she turned on her side, curled up in a ball and fell into a deep dreamless sleep.

Chapter 21

London, England. October 1959

Samantha strolled along Gower Street in the direction of Senate House – a tall graceful white building which served as the administrative centre of the University of London. She planned to visit and familiarise herself with the library there, before moving down to the Strand and the famous London School of Economics where she would be studying. The LSE was one of the four largest colleges incorporated in the University of London – an obvious choice for Sam, once she decided to read Economics.

She had arrived in the capital the day before and spent the day unpacking and settling into her digs in Swiss Cottage. Living in digs was part of a compromise with her parents. They had wanted her to move into one of the university halls of residence. But for Sam, determined to maintain her freedom and independence, halls of residence reeked of authority and school-type restrictions. She would have preferred to rent a flat; but apart from the expense for a person living alone, her parents seemed terrified that left to her own devices she would either starve, fall ill alone and unattended, or be raped by some predatory male!

Eventually she agreed, that for the first term at least, until she made friends and was able to share rented accommodation, she would stay in digs. A list of recommended landladies and their addresses had been sent to her by the college. She had made a lucky choice. Her digs were comfortably furnished and conveniently situated near Swiss Cottage tube station. She found her landlady, Mrs Fowles, pleasant enough and a fair cook – if the supper and breakfast Sam had sampled were anything to go by.

Travelling on the tube, then strolling through the busy London streets, she felt happiness and excitement well up inside her. Now a part of this vibrant fascinating city, she could already identify with its pace and bustle. On her own at last! She realised with a sudden thrill as well as a certain apprehension that almost overnight she had become an independent adult.

The day was crisp and sunny. Leaving the bustle of Tottenham Court Road, she wandered past the British Museum into the heart of the Bloomsbury area, immediately sensing a change in the atmosphere. The streets became quiet and residential, interspersed with graceful tree-lined squares. There was an air of past gentility – almost as if she had been transported back forty years, to that period when Bloomsbury had been the social and intellectual, as well as the bohemian, centre of London.

As she approached the impressive white stone entrance of Senate House, a tall exuberant young man rushed up to her. He sported the same purple and yellow college scarf that she wore.

"Sorry to bother you, but I see from the scarf you're also at the LSE. Could you direct me there?"

She blushed, feeling suddenly shy and self-conscious.

"I'm afraid I'm a fresher. I haven't set foot in the college yet." She hesitated, but before she knew it, the words came tumbling out. "I do know where the college is though. I can show you on my map."

"That's absolutely wizard – I'm a fresher myself. I only came up today." He gave a warm smile. "I had a feeling you might be a new student – you looked a little lost."

"Oh, did I?" said Sam, disappointed. She had desperately wanted to look part and parcel of this sophisticated city.

"Don't worry about that," laughed the friendly young man. "Perhaps we can help each other. What wonderful luck to find another LSE fresher – and such a pretty one at that! My name's Douglas, by the way."

She blushed again, but she couldn't help but like the enthusiastic and amiable young man. Tall and well built, he had thick sandy-coloured hair, vivid blue eyes and pleasant even features. Despite the college scarf slung casually around his neck, he was elegantly dressed and his warm cultured voice revealed traces of a Scottish accent.

He held out his hand. She smiled and accepted the handshake, trying to be equally friendly and outgoing.

"My name's Samantha Proctor Bourne. I'm from Oxford. I take it you're from Scotland."

"How did you guess?" laughed Douglas. "Yes, I'm Scottish through and through – from the highlands. But what's a genteel young lady like you doing studying at the LSE – the 'hot bed of socialism'?"

Her interest was immediately aroused. "I could ask you the same question. In any case how do you know I'm 'genteel'?" she asked, her tone slightly waspish.

"Ah, a girl of spirit, too. But I'm afraid everything gives you away – your voice, your dress, your general demeanour. I would bet your father's a don!"

"You're far too clever by half," laughed Sam, "but you're wrong in one respect. He's my stepfather, not my father ... My father died in the war – before I was born."

"Oh, I'm sorry." His laughing blue eyes flashed instantly sympathetic, then started to twinkle again. "I have to confess my family are members of the awful landed gentry, but I'm afraid they're rather poor now. I decided a degree in Economics would be more useful as a career-opener in this day and age than a BA in History. I'm not academically minded in any case."

"Snap!" said Sam. "I was pretty fed up with my family's cloistered existence in Oxford. London and the LSE seemed to be a good way to find out more about the real world." She found it surprisingly easy to chat to this friendly attractive young man. Her customary shyness with strangers had already disappeared. "Do you think we'll be outnumbered by all the radicals at the LSE? Politics don't bother me, but my stepfather was rather worried – he's a staunch conservative. Actually I'm rather looking forward to meeting some revolutionaries!"

"I don't think there's much chance of that – at least no more than at many other universities. Friends have told me that though the students tend to be politically active, the college now has a pretty fair cross-section of all shades of opinion – not like the Sidney and Beatrice Webb socialist era. Apparently the current president of the Students' Union is an active Tory."

"How intriguing! I'm really looking forward to it. I was just going to look at the Senate House library, then go on down to the college."

"Good idea! Mind if I join you?

"Of course not! I could do with some moral support."

"Perhaps we could have bite together afterwards? There are some super Indian and Chinese restaurants here in town, and they're not expensive."

"What a lovely idea! I've never eaten exotic foods in a restaurant before. My mother makes excellent Indian curries, but I'd love to sample the real thing."

"That's settled then. What a day! The prettiest fresher and I find her my first morning!"

Laughing and chatting, her niggling self-doubts for the moment forgotten, Sam walked with him through the gates of Senate House and up the steps to the main entrance.

* * * * * *

Two days later – at the Students' Union Freshers' Party – she and Douglas met Tom. Sam hadn't been too keen on going to the welcome party. Not much of a party person, the idea of being bundled together with a crowd of embarrassed first-year students filled her with horror. But Douglas in his usual flamboyant fashion soon persuaded her to join him. His easy companionship gave her the confidence she needed – with him at her side she felt she could face anything.

They climbed the winding rickety wooden staircase which led to the Students' Union bar. All the Union offices and social rooms were located in an antiquated Dickensian type of building in Clare Market, just down the road from the main LSE building. She had already explored this part of the college when visiting her tutor, whose study was in the same quaint but musty warren of ancient buildings.

They pushed their way through the crowded entrance into a room bursting to the seams with noise and activity. She turned to Douglas in surprise, taken aback by the scene which met their eyes. Every Union society and club had erected a colourful stall. Each was hawking its wares, propounding the advantages of their respective activities. The competitive banter and background noise was deafening.

Gazing around in bewilderment, she decided this was obviously the time of year the societies went out of their way to win new members from the ranks of the freshers. She was amazed by the variety and scope of activities they offered: political societies, sports clubs, special interest groups – drama, music, Gilbert and Sullivan, wine & food, travel exchange and many more. The noise and hustle were overwhelming.

With a helpful shove here and there from Douglas, they managed to progress through the *mêlée*. The room had a carnival atmosphere about it – noisy, lively and colourful. The enthusiasm of the students was infectious. Sam had had no intention of becoming heavily involved with extra-curricular activities, fearing they might be detrimental to her studies. But as one of the few new women students – and a pretty one at that – she soon found she was the focus of attention and overwhelmed by invitations to join every available club and society.

"Come along, darling. We need an attractive girl like you in Dram. Soc.," said one lively young man with a thatch of auburn hair, deep-set eyes and a wide expressive mouth. He gave her a saucy smile.

"I'm no good at acting, I'm afraid."

"Doesn't matter darling, we need plenty of help backstage." He grinned again. "If you're not interested in Dram. Soc., what about the European Society? If not, just tell me what does interest you. The two of us can make our own society."

She laughed nervously and looked appealingly at Douglas, who came instantly to her rescue.

"Sorry, old fellow, we're just off to join the Wine & Food Society. More up our street, I think."

They pushed through the crowds to an inviting-looking stall, where members were offering students glasses of wine and tit-bits of cheese. Douglas took a glass for Sam and one for himself.

"Quite an evening, isn't it?" observed another student drinking at the stall. He was lean and dark, not much taller than Sam, softly-spoken with sensitive features and a neatly-chiselled nose. Despite his slim stature and bone structure, there was a certain presence about him. Beneath the urbane exterior, Sam sensed an aura of power, of taut unleashed energy.

Taking a long deliberate sip from his glass, the young man swished the liquid around in his mouth, then swallowed with obvious satisfaction. He eyed them both, his grey eyes confident, all-seeing.

"How are you two coping – have you joined much yet?" he asked.

"Not so far. It's difficult to decide – too much to choose from," said Douglas. "Still I think this one is very much up my street." He took another piece of cheese. "What about you, Sam?"

"I don't know what to do, Douglas – it's all rather bewildering. I don't want to get too involved with societies. But I think you're right – I wouldn't mind a bit of wine-tasting!"

"Good!" said the other young man. "I've just joined myself. By the way my name's Tom Evans." He shook hands with both of them and they made their introductions.

"I take it you're a fresher too?" said Douglas.

"Yes, but I'm quite a bit older than you two – I haven't come straight from school. I've already been working for a few years – what they call a mature student. I was lucky to get a place here." He gave Sam another penetrating stare. "What are you reading, Samantha?"

"Economics, specialising in Industry and Trade." She felt slightly uncomfortable under his gaze, finding his direct almost demanding manner disturbing. Yet she was strangely fascinated by his forthright approach, his quiet air of confidence. He seemed a very self-possessed young man, more mature than other boys she had known.

"Great!" said Tom. "I'm reading the same as you. That's a relief. I was feeling bereft of female company. Most of the girls here – and there aren't that many – seem to be reading Sociology or some such subject. What about you, Douglas, are you on the same course?"

"Yes, but my special's International History. Still we should see quite a lot of each other during Part One. Well, Sam, shall we sign on the dotted line?"

They both signed up and paid their Society dues.

"Our first meeting's at seven p.m. next Wednesday, in the Beatrice Webb room," a society official told them. "French wines from the Bordeaux region."

"Can't wait," murmured Tom, appreciatively. The three of them moved off, continued their round of the stalls. Douglas joined the Conservative Society, inviting Sam and Tom to do the same.

Sam smiled, but shook her head. The last thing she wanted to do was get tied up with university politics.

Tom also declined.

"Afraid I'm a socialist a heart," he said with a wry grin, his grey eyes serious. "But I'm not that interested in politics, certainly not enough to join a society." He gave Sam another searching glance. "Anybody fancy a beer and bite to eat?"

"Please," she said. "I'm starving!"

The two men gallantly linked arms with her and they headed for the bar. From that day on, the three of them became inseparable.

* * * * * * *

Over the course of the next few weeks, several other young men attached themselves to their group – Teddy, a plump cuddly character who loved to play the fool, although Sam suspected he had hidden depths; Justin, from North London, with an unfortunately pompous manner but a heart of gold; Jishnu a slim, aristocratic Indian of great charm with a fervent love of politics and intrigue; and blond Barry, a huge ape of a man, a street-wise cockney with a mind sharp and brilliant as diamond.

Sam found herself the centre of their little *coterie*. Flattered and encouraged by their warmth and friendliness, she blossomed and quickly overcame much of her previous shyness, finding her self-confidence growing by leaps and bounds. The boys all treated her with deference and respect. She became their lucky mascot; they demanded her presence, protected her from the unwanted advances of other male students.

Instead of being wrapped up in her studies, she fell into a social whirl of parties and society activities – orgies of eating, talking and laughing with other students, discussing every subject under the sun. They made the most of living in London: visited cinemas, theatres, museums, pubs and parks. They studied together in the quiet opulent comfort of the library reading-rooms, comparing and exchanging notes and textbooks; attended lectures in a group, using the same seats each time in the gallery of the lecture-theatre where they could safely laugh together and ape the professors.

Her parents continued to telephone her regularly, still apparently worried about how she was coping on her own.

"I'm just fine, Mother," she would laugh into the phone.

"Now you're sure you're not working too hard, Sam," asked her mother one morning, her voice sounding unusually tinny as she fought the static which had suddenly affected the telephone line.

"Mother, if anything I'm not working hard enough," she replied with a laugh. "There's just too much else to do!"

"That's good news, Sam." She could almost hear the smile in her mother's voice. "And how are those nice young men-friends of yours?"

Sam grinned to herself.

"They're all fine, mother, and they look after me very well."

Her mother chuckled.

"And no unwanted advances? I find it difficult to believe they all want a purely platonic relationship with my beautiful daughter."

"Oh, they've all made advances – at some stage – but I made it clear from the start that I'm not looking for either romantic or sexual adventures." She had in fact been flattered by the attention from all the boys, but was determined not to be hurt by anyone at this stage. She had to admit she felt particularly close to Douglas and Tom – the three of them had been nicknamed 'the three musketeers'. At times it would have been easy to let her relationship with either one of them slip into something closer, but she was determined to retain her hard-won independence and not become involved.

"Douglas, Tom and I have been nicknamed 'the three musketeers'," she told her mother, "because we're always together and such good friends."

Her mother laughed.

"So you've become one of the boys! Well, you're probably right not to get involved, darling. You seem to have a very nice arrangement at the moment. There's plenty of time for deeper relationships when you've finished your degree."

Not even then, thought Sam, but she said good-humouredly, "Yes, mother, there's plenty of time."

Not long after that particular telephone conversation, Sam was almost relieved when Douglas met a 'debbie' kind of girl from one of the women's colleges, and became involved in an affair with her. It didn't seem to affect the closeness of the 'musketeers' nor of the group in general. Tom, on the other hand, remained strangely aloof to other women although there was invariably some girl chasing after him.

"Didn't you see that brunette on the other side of the lecture theatre today?" Sam would tease. "Whoever she was, she could hardly keep her eyes off you."

"You mean Judy," replied Tom airily and unperturbed. "I suppose she has been rather attentive lately, but you know I'm waiting for you, Sam." He raised his eye-brows quizzically.

She dropped her eyes, never knowing how to respond to Tom when he was in one of these moods. She found it difficult to know when to take him seriously. In some conversations he insinuated he was deeply in love with her, then at other times he would act in his usually cool detached way.

"Don't look away, Sam, I mean it. I'd marry you tomorrow, but I don't think you're ready. Nor do I want to stifle your individualism. But you'll come round in the end, you wait and see."

"Don't be silly, Tom." she said, laughing nervously. She knew he was teasing her again, yet his eyes held a serious gleam. "You shouldn't joke about things like that. One day somebody's going to take you seriously. Then look at the mess you'll be in."

At that moment Douglas strode up.

"Come on you two – stop huddling in corners. We'll be late for Forsythe's lecture, and I've almost got his little dance off 'to a T'." With great aplomb and dexterity, he performed a caricatured version of the professor at his lectern, cleverly mimicking Forsythe's complicated routine of ambling steps and exaggerated movements with his eye-glass.

Sam could never resist his clever mimicry. She and Tom dissolved in laughter.

"Come on, you idiot!" grinned Tom, grabbing Douglas in mid-routine. "Forsythe himself will be along any minute. If he sees you ..."

" ... he'll probably join in," finished Douglas. "I've heard he has a great sense of humour."

"I wouldn't bet on it!" giggled Sam. She looked down at her watch. "God, we will be late! Come on, you two."

She grabbed them both by the hand and they all rushed off to the lecture theatre.

Chapter 22

London, England. October 1961

"You've got to stand for vice-president, Sam. You'll win hands down!" Douglas gazed imploringly at her, his vivid blue eyes alive with excitement.

"He's right, my love," said Tom. His tone, as usual, was cool but Sam could sense a certain tenseness and expectation beneath his urbane veneer.

"Me – Vice President of the Students' Union? Impossible!" She could feel a hollow in her stomach at the very thought of it.

"Rubbish Sam," said Douglas, impatiently. "The only candidates at the moment are a couple of waffling second-year students whom nobody's ever heard of. It would be a walkover."

"Well, if it's so easy, why don't you stand, Doug?" she retorted in self-defence.

"Don't be silly, Sam. I'm one of a thousand male students. You're a beautiful female, bright as a button, with tremendous charisma. You can't fail to be elected." He brushed a piece of fluff from his otherwise immaculate blazer. "In any case, I'm too tied-up with LUCA this year – I want to try for a position on the national committee."

Sam nodded, knowing Douglas had become increasingly involved with his work for the London University Conservative Association. He was hoping to make a career in politics.

"You've got a good track record with your work for AISEC, and on the committee of the European Society," Tom told her, sounding as confident and determined as Douglas.

"Come along you two – that was completely different," she said, defensively. "Purely administrative work. And we all did a certain amount for AISEC to ensure good student exchanges during the summer vacs. As for the European Society, I was only treasurer and the work was quite straightforward."

"It doesn't matter," insisted Tom. "The other two candidates have done nothing within the Students' Union except attend a few meetings."

"That's just it!" wailed Sam. "Can you imagine me on the stage of the lecture theatre with the rest of the Student Council, holding forth on some topic. I'm no good at public speaking. I'd be completely terrified." She felt weak at the knees with just the thought of it.

"Nonsense, Sam, you're just a little shy. You'd soon get the hang of it."

"But the union debates! – The attacks on Council from the floor get so fierce. I wouldn't be able to handle it." Even as she said it she could feel the apprehension building up inside her, but also a strange sort of excitement that set her nerves tingling. Could she do it? A year ago she would never have entertained the thought, but now ... ?

"Of course you could handle it," insisted Douglas. "Remember how coy and introverted you were when we first met. And now look at you!"

Sam giggled.

"That's true. I've certainly come out of my shell a lot, thanks to you lot. But it doesn't alter the fact that basically I'm not an aggressive political animal. I'm still very nervous in public and I prefer the quiet life."

Perfect!" said Tom. He lit up a cigarette and inhaled deeply. "We'll capitalise on the fact that you're not aggressive and self-opinionated – present you as an attractive feminine candidate, who's already proved herself quietly capable and highly efficient – ideal for the requirements of the job of vice-president." He smiled, encouragingly. "You'll score even higher on the PR side, Sam – a beautiful, intelligent and classy woman. What a great image for the LSE! A complete change from noisy aggressive males who spend most of their time promoting themselves, rather than the interests of the students and the college itself."

He looked challengingly at Sam.

She shook her head, but inside felt again the stirrings of excitement. Perhaps she could win the election, even cope with the job itself? It would be a great challenge, the experience invaluable! It would certainly help in her curriculum vitae when she went for a job. More important, she felt sure she could bring a lot of new ideas to the post.

She looked long and hard at both Douglas and Tom.

"Do you really think I can do it – get through the hustings and everything?"

"No problem," said Tom, calmly.

"Look! I've got a great idea." said Douglas, his voice full of excitement. "This is how we'll handle the campaign. We take a sexy shot of Sam's superb calves and ankles – you know, to go alongside the photos of the candidates on the notice and hustings boards. We blow up the photo and add the following caption: 'Which would you prefer to see on your Council platform – this? Sam's beautiful legs. Or this?, pointing to the ugly mugs of the other candidates. Then we simply list Sam's credentials below. It can't fail!"

Tom's face split in a wide grin.

"You're right, Doug. Just think of the hours we've wasted gazing at all those ugly Council members on stage at Union meetings. Anybody would prefer to look at Sam!"

"You're being flippant and chauvinistic," she told them primly. "Some students take these elections very seriously."

"Which is precisely why our approach will work," said Tom. "Douglas is right – it's simple, amusing, tongue-in-cheek and COMPLETELY NEW! And anyone studying your credentials will see you're more than a pretty face – not to mention the legs, of course," he added, laughing.

She couldn't prevent her stern expression changing to a smile, then as the idea caught her imagination, she started to laugh out loud.

"You know – I think you're right." She shook her pony tail, gazed at them thoughtfully. "But I'm still not sure I want to be on Council. It's a lot of work – and this is finals year."

"Finals are nothing compared to what we went through for Part One," said Douglas.

She nodded in agreement, relieved like them that the nightmares and horrors of the Part One exams were over. During the first two years of their degree course no important examinations had been held. Then at the end of the summer term of the second year the vital Part One exams had taken their toll. Covering a total of eight widely differing subjects, ranging from psychology and politics to economics and history, the width of subject matter covered was immense. Since no exams were held at the end of the first year many students, including Sam and the boys, took it easy during their first few terms. The quantity and pace of work was consequently that much worse at the end of the second year. Anyone failing any subject in Part One was sent down, with no chance of continuing their degree – two wasted years with nothing to show for it.

The summer term of their second year had been a nightmare for them all. When the crunch came, they all worked together exchanging notes and tips, spending hour after hour in the college library trying to catch up on the piles of work. Their close camaraderie had helped them cope. Some students had fallen by the wayside under the intense pressure – nervous breakdowns, even suicides, had been hinted at.

Sam remembered living through two months of purgatory before the exams, her stomach permanently churning with worry, her brain in a whirl from so much cramming. During the period of the actual exams, she hardly slept more than two hours a night and when it came to writing the exam papers, she would sit paralysed for several minutes, her hand shaking too much to control the pen. With panic welling up inside her she would see all the other students around her, writing feverishly. Only by a tremendous effort of will was she able each time to calm her nerves, recall her examination number, force her trembling hand to write. Then within seconds she would be away, writing as fast she could, racing to put her ideas and thoughts onto the paper in front of her, ruing the precious minutes she had already wasted.

They were days she would never forget, but suddenly it was all over. And every one of their group had passed!

"I never want to go through anything like that again," moaned Sam. "Thank goodness we can specialise in our final year. I'm finding it much easier, though I must admit I eventually realised how closely interlinked the Part One subjects were – how each one helped with the others. But by that time I was one hour through the first paper!"

"You're right," agreed Tom "I scored best on the Government paper, yet none of my prepared subjects came up. I had to draw on everything else I knew, try to salvage something from the whole course, drag in anything I thought relevant bits of sociology, statistics, applied economics. But it worked!"

"Enough of Part One sufferings," said Douglas. "Back to the VP elections. What do you reckon, Sam? Will you have a go?"

"I'll think about," she said, ambition and excitement already starting to conquer her fears.

"Knowing Sam, that means yes," smiled Tom. "And knowing her determination, I think you and I, Douglas, should start treating our future VP with a little deference."

Douglas dropped immediately to his knees, reverently kissed her hand.

"You're both idiots," laughed Sam. "What am I letting myself in for?"

* * * * * * *

They took two photographs of her. One was the required passport shot; but Sam's fine features and flowing dark-blonde hair shone through to make it something special. She looked like the girl every man would like to have living next door. The other photo was elegant yet provocative – Sam seated with her slim legs crossed to one side, a favourite modelling pose. The photo was cropped so that all that was visible, beneath a flowing skirt and a teasing glimpse of lace petticoat, were Sam's neat calves and ankles and an elegant pair of high-heeled shoes.

It took the college by storm!

Her two rivals immediately stepped down and she was left without a fight. However, to show willing, she made a short speech at the hustings which hardly anybody heard amongst all the clapping and wolf-whistles.

"We made one mistake," said Tom at the group's celebration dinner after the election.

God, what did I do wrong, thought Sam to herself in panic. As far as she was concerned everything seemed to have gone better than expected. But had she in her inexperience made some silly error?

"Mistake?" queried Jishnu. "The campaign went perfectly – almost too perfectly. I would have relished a little more intrigue." He grinned, wolfishly.

"You Indians are all the same," laughed Teddy. "But I have to agree – it couldn't have gone better. Mmm ... this Chinese food's fantastic!" He took another large helping of sweet and sour prawns. "Well done, Sam. I can't wait for the first Union meeting with you up on the platform."

"Yes, brilliantly done, Sam," said Justin.

Barry said nothing, but blew an exaggerated kiss across the table.

Sam smiled at them all with gratitude and relief.

"What mistake, Tom?" persisted Douglas, looking baffled. He had been so proud of her success. Even he hadn't foreseen the extent of it when he first conceived the idea.

"Yes, please explain what I did wrong, Tom," she said, as worried and puzzled as Douglas by his comment.

"You should have stood for president – not vice president!" declared Tom, with a triumphant grin. "It would have been a cinch."

"Here, here!" they all shouted. She blushed, thrilled and proud with the success of the campaign. But inside her a little voice still insisted: Don't forget next Friday's Union Meeting!

* * * * * * *

The meeting went without a hitch. Sam had little to put forward in her first speech to the house, but what she did say was accepted with a mixture of curiosity and tolerant amusement. Apart from the inevitable wolf-whistles, on the whole she was treated with restraint. They were waiting for her to show her paces!

* * * * * * *

Sam grew to love her work on the Student Council. She enjoyed the thrust and parry of debate at the Council meetings, taking delight in the thorough preparation of motions and proposals and her ability to see them through. She came to be accepted as a positive force on the Council and as such was able to expand the traditional role of the vice-president. Bryan Smith, the president, took her fully into his confidence leaving many of his own duties in her capable hands.

At Union meetings she was a huge success. The student body came to accept that besides being a pretty girl with a figure to match, she knew her stuff. Any smart guy from the floor was quietly and politely put down by Sam in such a way he almost believed he'd won the point. At times she would hug herself with glee. Didn't they realise, she thought, that the Council had all the facts at their fingertips, knew what arguments to anticipate from the floor. Her public speeches improved and she developed a keen wit which proved invaluable at critical moments.

During a period of student protest and marches, she took it upon herself to ensure Union members were presented with all the facts when political activities were proposed. She was determined LSE students shouldn't be used as pawns by any of the political societies, that the Union shouldn't be led astray in a wave of emotion and misinformation.

Union attendances increased. Some of the more moderate students, previously put off by the heavily political slant of student affairs, began to take a more active part in Union activities.

When the External Affairs Vice-President resigned over a political issue, Jishnu was duly elected to replace him. Sam enjoyed having another member of their group on the Student Council, even though Jish tended to complicate issues with his love of intrigue and dislike of the President, Bryan Smith.

Life became more hectic and busy. She hardly had a spare moment to herself and at times feared her studies were suffering. But she found that by rising earlier and going to bed later she somehow managed to cram everything into her busy schedule.

Unfortunately she had to cut down some of her weekend visits to Oxford to see her mother, Leslie, and the twins, but apart from worrying that she might be taking on too much, her parents now seemed to accept that she had her life well-organised and was happy and fulfilled in what she was doing.

"Just don't make yourself ill by overdoing it, darling," her mother warned. "You look a little pale and you seem slimmer than ever."

As usual, Leslie quickly allayed Cathy's fears.

"I think she can cope, can't you, Sam? I get the feeling you thrive on hard work!"

"I seem to, Dad," she agreed, giving him a grateful smile.

Her mother beamed at her. "We're so proud of you, darling. You've already accomplished so much. Now both the boys want to follow in your footsteps, but I think they'll find it difficult – they're not as clever as you."

As always Sam basked in her mother's praise, but this time she felt an extra warm glow inside and realised that with her new-found confidence and popularity, the aching envy of her mother was slowly diminishing.

She hugged her and kissed Leslie on the cheek.

"Thank you both for being so wonderful and giving me your support. I only hope I manage to live up to everybody's expectations!"

"Oh, Sam darling! You'll never change!" laughed Cathy. "We know you'll always do you best. But our hopes and expectations are that you should be happy, nothing more. Always remember that."

"I'll remember," she replied, but she knew – deep inside – that she had far greater expectations of herself.

* * * * * * *

The annual Commemoration Ball featured as the highlight of the social year. Sam worked actively with the social vice-president to ensure this year's Ball should be a greater success than ever before. London's Festival Hall rang with the music of Ted Heath, The Temperance Seven, Ken Colyer's Jazz Band and a popular steel band. The all-night affair, with its magnificent buffet, ran until five in the morning.

After the first few nervous moments, she watched the lively proceedings with growing satisfaction. In her capacity as vice-president, Sam had attended most of the Commem. Balls – or their equivalent – at rival London Colleges, not to mention those of universities throughout England. She knew the LSE Ball was definitely the success story of the year.

* * * * * * *

The months passed with the speed of days. Spring came and with it the approach of finals. Work was hard and demanding, but with little of the drama of Part One. Like old hands, they took the exams in their stride – until it came to the results!

These were due to be posted in the college at eleven o'clock one sunny summer morning. Nervous and apprehensive, she wandered into the LSE entrance hall at ten, planning to meet the boys first in the canteen for a fortifying cup of coffee. It had suddenly dawned on her that this would be one of the most important moments of her life. Today she would graduate or fail. The last three years had all led to this final moment. Had the hard work been for nothing? Had she spent too much time on union affairs? Dreading the next few hours she walked through the door, her stomach in turmoil, her head pounding.

Hundreds of frenzied students were already milling around the notice boards. Goodness, the results had been posted ahead of time! She rushed up to the nearest board, headed UPPER SECOND HONOURS. Upper Two – the pass she had been aiming for! Her Part One results were good enough. Ignoring the pushing from all sides, she scanned the list, desperately searching for her name. It was in alphabetical order, but no mention of her name under either Proctor or Bourne. Oh well, it had been a hope! Please God – let her have a Lower Second!

She scanned the hallway, searching in panic for the Lower Second Results. Suddenly spotting the list, she eased her way through the crush which had grown worse as the news flew round that the results had been posted. She read and re-read the Lower Second list. No luck. Oh God! Had she even passed? Something must have gone terribly wrong. Feeling sick at heart, she fled in desperation to the list of Thirds. Another blank! She had definitely failed! Oh Mother, Leslie – I should never had wasted my time with that stupid union!

"Sam! Have you seen the results?" It was Tom. "Isn't it great! I got an Upper Second!" He must have spotted the tears in her eyes. "Come on love, this is no time for silly emotion – it's time for celebration. Have you seen Douglas? He's got a Lower Two."

How could he be so insensitive, thought Sam. Just because he and Doug have passed, he assumes I've done the same.

"Tom," she sobbed, breaking down. "I've failed ... I've failed!" She fell into his arms.

"What are you talking about, Sam?" He pulled away from her, studying her expression. "This is no time for jokes."

"No ... it's true, Tom," she managed to stammer. "I've searched all the lists, very carefully. I've definitely failed."

"You idiot, Sam! You can't have looked properly – you got a First!"

"A First?" She sank down on the steps, shaking all over. "A First – I can't believe it! Tom, are you absolutely sure? I never even looked on the list of Firsts."

"You beautiful idiot. Of course I am!" He lifted her high in the air, whirled her around. "Come and see for yourself."

"Tremendous, Sam!" yelled Douglas, suddenly appearing at her side. "You've got a First!"

"Yes, I know," said Sam, tears streaming down her face. "Well done, Douglas. You've passed as well."

"A Lower Second. But I'm more than content."

"Excellent, Doug." Tom pounded him on the shoulder. "I'm quite surprised – considering the time you've spent this year down at Tory headquarters in Smith Square."

"No cheek from you, Tom – just because you got an Upper Two. Just wait till I'm Prime Minister!"

"You're both marvellous," yelled Sam. "But please – can I go and see the list – actually see my name, with my own eyes."

They carried her shoulder-high to the board. Happiness and pride bubbled up inside her, then the old feeling that it couldn't really be happening to her.

"You don't think they've made a mistake, do you," she said hoarsely, gazing in awe at the list.

"The same old Sam," chuckled Tom. "When are you going to believe it, my love. You're a success!"

It was true, she thought. Happiness welled up inside her. She turned to Tom and Douglas.

"I'll meet you shortly in the canteen."

"Where are you going?" said Douglas. "It's time to celebrate and open the 'bubbly'!"

"I know," she said with a twinkle in her eye, "but I have one important telephone call to make. You two go ahead and line up the bottles! I'll catch up with you in a moment."

She squeezed Tom's arm and ran quickly to the public telephone. Trembling with anticipation, she picked up the receiver, dialled and listened eagerly as the number rang out.

She heard the phone picked up, couldn't stop blurting out:

"It's me, Mother ... I've passed! You won't believe it – I've got a First!" She listened, gloriously happy, to the barrage of congratulations. Tears of happiness slipped down her face. The whole family wanted to speak to her, tell her how proud they were of her. They all talked excitedly about the degree ceremony which would be held in London's Albert Hall when the Queen Mother, who was Chancellor of the University, would present Sam with her degree. She could already see her name on the diploma – Samantha Proctor Bourne BSc (Econ) First Class Honours. She hugged herself with glee.

When she eventually wandered up to the canteen to see the boys, only one tiny cloud marred her euphoria. If only her father could have been alive to share her success. He would have been so proud of her.

But she still had a long way to go!

Chapter 23

Oxford, England. September 1962

"Well, Sam, I suppose this is goodbye?" Tom looked at her intently, his dark eyes as penetrating as ever, but Sam could see a veil of hurt shrouding their depths.

"That sounds very final, Tom. Can't we still be good friends?" She could have bitten her tongue off. "Sorry – that sounds hackneyed and trite, but you know what I mean."

"I know what you mean." Tom's fine lips parted slightly in what she knew was a forced smile. He stubbed out his cigarette and stared across at her, his normal air of quiet confidence finally deserting him. "I don't think I could go along with that, Sam. I'm not being melodramatic or silly – God, I would love to see you as much as possible! But I don't think it would be right – at least, not for me. Better a clean break. Otherwise I might start to kid myself again, think I stand a chance."

"Tom ... dear Tom. Why do things have to work out like this?" She walked over to the sweeping French windows, feeling a great sense of loss.

Quite unexpectedly, Tom had taken advantage of a weekend visit to Sam's parents in Oxford to formally propose to her. Although shocked and dismayed at the thought of hurting him, she had been unable to accept. But she couldn't imagine life without Tom around – she would miss him terribly.

The steady beat of the rain on the windows seemed to echo their gloom. "I can't imagine never seeing you again, Tom." She turned back to face him. "Do you remember those people we used to call 'professional' students at college – the ones who never graduated, or if they did, kept taking more and more degrees? I used to think they were feeble – afraid to face up to the real life outside a university environment. Now I understand how they felt. If only everything could stay the same. Now we've all left college – gone our separate ways. Our group has broken up, Douglas is back in Scotland and now I'm losing you."

"You can never stand still, Sam."

"I know. I just hate goodbyes. Especially when it's from you, Tom." She felt utterly forlorn. Much of her misery, she knew, came from a sense of guilt. She was surprised at the depth of feeling Tom had revealed after what she had thought to be three light-hearted years together. How could she have failed to realise his true feelings. Her mother, with her unerring intuition, had hinted at it but Sam had airily dismissed her warning. Now she had hurt Tom terribly – he had been shattered by her refusal. She looked sheepishly at him. "I never led you on, did I Tom?"

"No – never. I led myself on. I believed you wouldn't be able to resist me in the end!" He gave a wry laugh. "There's no deception worse than self-deception."

She walked towards him, placed her hands on his shoulders.

"I'm so very fond of you, Tom. I probably love you, but not in the way you love me. Quite frankly I don't think I'll ever fall in love. I shall certainly never marry! I wouldn't be any good at it. I'm just not that sort of person."

"Everybody's that sort of person, Sam. It just depends on the timing and the chemistry. I got them both wrong." He rose slowly from the armchair. "I'll go and say goodbye to your parents – thank them for the weekend. They've been really kind. You're lucky, Sam. Cathy and Leslie are wonderful people."

"I know," she whispered.

"Don't come to see me off – I'd rather you stay here."

He walked slowly to the door. Seeing his languid movements and downcast head, Sam felt a sharp wrench inside – how different from Tom's usually light confident gait.

Reaching the door he turned suddenly, stared at her long and hard – feasting his eyes on every part of her face and body. She stood mesmerised as the seconds ticked by.

"Goodbye, my love. If you're ever in trouble or if you should change your mind – call me. If not, please don't ..." His voice broke; he turned swiftly and was gone.

Sam felt a sense of loneliness and emptiness she'd never experienced before. Sitting quite still, she could feel the sobs rise from deep inside her.

"Anything I can do, darling." It was her mother. She came swiftly to her side, held her tight, rocking her like a baby.

"Oh, Mother. He's such a super boy. What's the matter with me?"

"Absolutely nothing!" Holding her at arm's length, she smiled her lovely warm smile. "You're a wonderful girl, Sam, and Tom's a fine man. In some ways he reminded me of your father. But he's obviously not the one for you. Don't worry – one day the right man will come along."

"That's just it, mother. I'm not really interested in getting serious with any man. I love their company. I'm attracted to them physically. But I've never been to bed with anybody – not even Douglas or Tom, the people I've been closest to. I was tempted with Tom – I'm so fond of him – but somehow it didn't seem to be right. You and Dad taught me the importance of pride and respect for myself. As far as I'm concerned, that includes my body! I don't feel I should give myself physically if I can't give my heart. Am I strange and old-fashioned?"

Her mother's eyes were moist and shiny.

"In no way, Sam, darling. I'm proud of you. I admire your integrity, your sense of responsibility. Those qualities are never old-fashioned."

"But there's another thing, Mother. I just don't feel I need a man in any permanent way. I don't even want a family!"

She'd admitted it at last! She studied her mother's face. Would she be shocked, even horrified that her daughter lacked any basic maternal feelings.

Mother was such a traditionally feminine and domestic person – her whole life revolved around her home and family.

She needn't have worried – her mother's eyes were warm and tender.   She gave Sam a swift hug.

"I do understand, darling. Mind you – we have Leslie to thank for that. He was the one who told me what to expect from my remarkable daughter! There's nothing wrong with you, Sam. It's as normal to feel that way, as to pine for motherhood. We all have our own priorities and needs. Follow your instincts, not the crowd. It's your life!" She chuckled. "But mark my words: one day some marvellous young man will come along. You'll fall – just like the rest of us."

"Ever the romantic, aren't you, mother?" sighed Sam. "I do love you." And she meant it with all her heart. Once again she found herself wondering why she couldn't be more like her mother. Life would be far simpler!

* * * * * * *

A week later the letter arrived which restored Samantha to her previous good spirits. From the advertising company Pinkerton Telford and Partners, the largest British owned agency in the UK, it informed her she had been accepted as a graduate trainee, with a view to becoming an Account Executive.

Sam hugged the letter to her. Following countless interviews with various government departments and commercial companies, she had received several offers of career openings. But this was the one she had been waiting for. As soon as she walked through the doors of PTP, she had sensed an unusually intense buzz of excitement, electricity and camaraderie in the air. She had known immediately this was the career she wanted.

"Mother, Dad!" she yelled in delight. "I've got it! I've been accepted by PTP." She rushed into the kitchen where her mother was washing the breakfast dishes. Leslie, as usual, stood by her side, helping with the drying-up.

"Hold on, young lady. Calm down. What's all the excitement about?" His eyes twinkled with expectation.

Her mother, sensing the importance of the occasion, quickly dried her hands on a towel and sat down at the breakfast table.

"Is this the one you've been waiting for, Sam?"

"Yes. PTP. I'm to start in two weeks! Isn't it marvellous?"

"Are you sure this is what you really want, Sam, dear?" Leslie couldn't disguise the concern in his eyes. "It's not quite what we'd expected for you. With your qualifications, you could choose anything."

"Yes I know. But this is what I want. So many of those other places where I went for interviews, they were so stodgy, so old fashioned, so dead! – especially that Civil Service post you were both so keen on."

"You could make a fine career in the Cabinet Office," he said. "But of course it's up to you. You know we'll back you – whatever you choose."

"I'm still a little worried, darling," said her mother. "Advertising is a rather flashy, unpredictable sort of career."

"It's challenging, exciting and full of opportunities," said Sam, firmly as if quoting from a brochure. "There's no silly rules on seniority – the sky's the limit. Advancement depends only on you and your ability."

"'Hire 'em, fire 'em' – or so I've heard," said Leslie. "What about security, Sam?"

"Dad, you don't understand. I'm not interested in security and pensions and all that nonsense. I'm only interested in today. The rest will look after itself. I know I can make a success of it. If I do well, I won't need a pension!" She could hardly believe what she was saying, how confident she felt. What a change from just a few years ago when she had set off for university in London with so much determination but with so many self-doubts.

Her parents exchanged worried glances.

"It's an extremely extrovert, almost brash sort of existence, isn't it darling? Do you think it will suit you?" asked her mother, dubiously.

Sam laughed. "You've been seeing too many American films, mother. PTP is a very British kind of firm. In any case, I can cope. I'm no longer the little mouse I was before I went to college. I know I can handle it."

"Of course you can, darling," said her mother. Her face broke into a wide smile. "We have to act the devil's advocate at times, Sam – just to be sure."

"I know, Mother. And I appreciate it."

"Good luck, Sam," said Leslie, giving her a brisk hug.

"Thanks, Dad."

* * * * * * *

Samantha loved every moment of her work at PTP She spent several months in each department of the agency – media, marketing, creative and production – discovering how every aspect of an advertising campaign was planned and executed by the agency. As an account executive it would be her job to liaise between the different departments of her agency, as well as the advertising teams of the companies whose products they handled. It was vital she should understand the intimate workings of each department.

A highlight of her new career was finding a wealth of new friends and colleagues. She loved the emphasis in advertising on youth. Surrounded by young energetic people with fresh dynamic thinking, she found her work exciting and stimulating.

Two other graduate trainees, both men, were taken on at the same time as Sam. They all found life at the agency fast, lively, full of fun and humour. Despite the relaxed informal atmosphere, the work burden was heavy, the pressure constant. Overtime was accepted as part and parcel of the job. Sam might spend ages over a business lunch, but on other occasions she would still be working at the agency late at night, or arriving at seven in the morning at the whim of an exigent client.

Her parents took to telephoning her at work when they couldn't find her at home in her flat.

"It's gone ten o'clock, darling," her mother told her, calling her at the office one night several months after she had started at PTP "Are you still working? I bet you haven't had any dinner. You must be starving!"

"I'm fine mother. I'm currently working in Media on the Rover car account and today we had a fantastic lunch with the ad. manager of *The Sunday Times*. I didn't get back to the office till nearly four!"

"It seems a rather strange way of working, darling, but you obviously relish it."

"I love it, mother! The unusual hours don't bother me – I enjoy the lack of routine, never knowing what's going to happen from one day to the next. It's a wonderful challenge!" she continued breathlessly.

"Even as a trainee, my opinions are welcomed. New ideas are encouraged and accepted for their intrinsic value, whoever they come from. Seniority hardly counts – only the excellence of each new idea!"

"OK Sam, slow down – I'm convinced!" laughed her mother. "But what about your social life?"

"I don't need a social life. I get enough enjoyment out of my work. It's tough, but it's fun." She wished she could explain it all better, but realised her mother wouldn't be able to understand without experiencing the nature of the work. Sam was now attending campaign meetings where the creative, media and marketing teams assigned to each product would plan their respective campaigns. Each product had its own individual team made up of representatives from each department. Different teams worked on different products. She loved this ever-changing mix of personalities and knew it kept the executives on their toes, ensuring fresh interplays of people and ideas.

She enjoyed the thrust and parry of campaign discussions, watching how ideas were thrashed out, how flashes of individual brilliance were welded into a single theme. It was satisfying to see a campaign come to life in a matter of months, witness it in action, then later judge its degree of success.

And she didn't lack for male attention. Light-hearted flirting was a constant factor at the agency, without the need to get involved. To a degree the bright youthful atmosphere was similar to college, but at PTP urgency and excitement filled the air. For Sam this was life at its best, breath-taking – even terrifying at times – but always challenging and fun.

* * * * * * *

After fifteen months of training she was summoned to the personnel office. Head of Personnel was Evelyn Baker, a striking black-haired eagle-eyed female in her mid-thirties. Sam admired her efficiency and style. Evelyn had a perfectly-maintained figure, was always impeccably dressed, immaculately coiffured. She had great charm and a gracious presence, but beneath the urbane smoothness, Sam knew her to be acutely perceptive, aware of every undercurrent in the agency. Evelyn's sharp eyes and ears never missed a trick.

She smiled warmly as Sam walked in.

"Good morning, Sam – please sit down." Her keen eyes took in every aspect of Sam's appearance and she gave a slight nod of approval. "You're a lucky girl, Sam! Beautiful and talented." She leaned back in the deep luxury of her executive chair.

Sam waited expectantly. Was she to get her promotion from trainee or was this Evelyn's diplomatic way of breaking the news that she hadn't quite come up to standard? She felt suddenly very nervous.

"Well, Samantha, I'm glad to tell you we shall be taking both you and Philip Mitchell onto our permanent staff. The other trainee didn't quite meet our requirements. You will be assigned to work as an account executive under Paul Wilson. He's one of our top Account Directors, so you should do well."

Sam heaved an audible sigh of relief. Evelyn smiled.

"Don't worry, Sam – we're more than pleased with your progress. Continue as you have been, and you have a bright future ahead of you in advertising. You're a natural – intelligent and creative. Your work is fast and efficient and you get on with people. I have to admit I wondered originally if you lacked the mental and physical tenacity, the toughness the job requires. Your appearance is deceptive."

Puzzled, Sam wrinkled her brow, wondering where she had gone wrong.

"Oh? In what way, Mrs Baker?"

"I don't know how to explain it, Sam. Physically you are very feminine, even delicate in appearance, and in personality you seem rather shy – at times almost vulnerable. Yet underneath it all I suspect you're as tough and determined as the most macho of my executives. Your appearance should work to your advantage."

"I'm sorry, Mrs. Baker. I thought I'd got over my inborn shyness."

Evelyn laughed her throaty laugh.

"Don't worry, Sam. As I said – it's an advantage. Don't look so perplexed! You see you're a woman, and a pretty one at that. Whatever anyone tells you about equality of the sexes, it's just not true. It's still a man's world we're working in. You will have to prove not only that you do your job as well as a man – but far better. The problem is that men can be put off by pushy women. What they consider strength and dynamism in a man is often resented in a woman."

Sam listened, fascinated, as Evelyn continued.

"Advertising is a young profession. It prides itself on its acceptance of talent, whatever the age, background or sex of the employee. But as a woman myself, I know we are still up against it. My advice is – capitalise on that quiet charm, that unassuming manner. Once they realise you're good at your job, it will be that much easier for them to accept your talent."

She brushed back an imaginary wisp of hair.

"Incidentally, Barry Clarke is account executive in the office next to yours. He fancies himself as something of a lady-killer. You've already caused quite a stir among the young males in the agency – so he'll be after your scalp. Watch it!"

Sam laughed.

"Thanks for the warning. But don't worry. He's already made a few passes. I think he's got the message I'm not interested."

"Good for you, Sam. Office romances cause more trouble than they're worth. Have fun, but try to steer clear of any involvement. I have great hopes for your future." She held out her hand.

Sam shook it, warmly.

"Thank you. I appreciate your help and advice. I'll certainly try to live up to your expectations!"

"I know you will, Sam. Good luck!"

Chapter 24

London, England. March 1964

Paul Wilson strode purposefully into the outer office, his expression grim. He looked across at Samantha who was busy dictating an action report to their secretary.

"Sorry to interrupt, but could I have a chat with you, Sam?"

"Of course." She turned to the girl seated on the other side of her desk. "Carry on with the letters, please Dawn. We'll finish the report later." She followed Paul into the inner cubicle comprising his private office. Sam, her assistant Jonathan White, and secretary Dawn Davenport, all had desks in the outer section of the office.

Sam wondered what was up with Paul – why hadn't he wanted to speak to her in the main office?

She sat down opposite him, noting his fierce expression. She had rarely seen him look so angry. Paul Wilson's self-control and easy cool were as legendary in the agency as his smooth looks and laid-back charm.

"That wretched man! I could cheerfully wring his neck!"

"I take it we're talking about the dreaded Dennis Payne," guessed Sam, with a wry grin.

"Payne it is, and a pain is certainly what he is!" muttered Paul, his brown eyes flashing. "I'm sure he does it on purpose – just to annoy us. He thinks it keeps us on our toes, but it's really just to boost his own ego – playing silly power games. He loves to see us squirm and hop." He passed an impatient hand through his light brown hair. Slightly thinning on top, it did nothing to mar his elegant aristocratic looks. His ascetic features, slim build and upright bearing were matched by a perfectly modulated almost hypnotic voice.

"What's he done this time?" enquired Sam, crossing her slim legs and smoothing down her skirt. She loved hearing the latest stories about Dennis Payne, Advertising Manager for The New Mode Group. The NMG, which represented a string of top fashion houses throughout Britain, were one of the agency's most important clients with advertising billings over a million pounds a year.

Paul gave a snort of contempt.

"He's insisting all client meetings should be held at seven in the morning at the group headquarters off Trafalgar Square. I don't mind urgent meetings at seven or even six in the morning, but there's no earthly reason why it should be a regular occurrence. In any case, holding all client meetings away from the agency is a perfect bind. Our presentation material is here – it's far easier for him to come to Knightsbridge, than for us to move the whole team lock, stock and barrel to the middle of town."

"How does he get away with it?" she enquired. There seemed no end to Payne's petty practices.

"Because he represents one of our most important and prestigious clients. Lots of other agencies are after the account – it has tremendous potential. But don't worry, our chairman George Pinkerton, is assembling a file on him – every unnecessary problem he causes, his ridiculous requests and outright rudeness. Little does Dennis know it, but he's digging his own grave."

Paul smiled at the thought of it, then his expression became grim again. "But we can't move till we have enough on him. You can't tell a big outfit like the NMG they have a lousy ad. manager. But Payne will make mistakes – he already has – and I think he's upsetting people within his own company. In the meantime, we've just got to hang on tight – smile and not let him know he's getting through to us."

"I don't understand how he ever got the job," mused Sam. "He's arrogant self-centred and domineering. He even looks so dreadful – fat, gross and ugly!"

"Yes, but he can turn on the charm and the chat when he wants too, and he does know the business backwards. He used to work on the agency side, before he got too big for his boots and was kicked out. That's how he knows all our wrinkles – knows just how far he can turn the screws."

"I see. Well, what's the plan now?"

"I'm afraid there's an important meeting lined up for next Tuesday – at seven in the morning, of course! And I simply can't attend. You'll have to handle it on your own, Sam."

"Oh, no!" She groaned inwardly, felt panic well up inside her. Her first client meeting without the support and backing of Paul, and it had to be with the dreadful Dennis Payne. What if she messed it up and they lost the account? One million pounds of advertising! She had only met the client a couple of times at meetings. Although Payne had eyed her figure appreciatively, he had directed all his questions and instructions via Paul, effectively snubbing her whenever she took any part in the proceedings.

"Is there no way you can make the meeting?" she pleaded.

"I'm afraid not. I have to go up to Manchester on Monday night. Our final presentation for the Tender Tissue account is on Tuesday. That really is a priority."

Despite her dismay, Sam giggled at the mention of Tender Tissue, the brand name for a new toilet paper about to be launched on the market.

"Promise me, if we win the account, we'll change that terrible name."

Paul chuckled.

"I'll do my best. Now Sam, look on the bright side. This could be your opportunity to win over Dennis. He won't be able to ignore you if I'm not there. Use your charm, but make sure you anticipate every point he may bring up. He's bound to test you out – try to find your weakness."

"Hell!" said Sam. "Do you really think I can do it, Paul?"

"Of course you can. Just make sure you set your alarm clock!" He gave a warm encouraging smile.

Sam bit her lip and walked through to the outside office. She felt like a bullfighter about to confront the bull. The moment of truth was certainly at hand. Had she got the guts and the ability? Her confidence had certainly increased tenfold. New responsibilities had been continually thrust upon her and it had been a case of coping or falling by the wayside. So far she had responded well to each new challenge, but it was rather like walking a trapeze wire – there was always the niggling doubt that the next step might be beyond her capabilities. If she could handle Dennis Payne she could probably handle any client. IF! It was a big word. She made a wish and crossed her fingers.

* * * * * * *

The day of the New Mode meeting Sam dressed with even greater care than normal. She wanted to look feminine, but smart and efficient at the same time. The night before, having explained the problem to her flatmate Paula, she paraded before her in a number of outfits. Paula, a good-humoured girl who worked for the BBC, watched half-serious, half-amused. After much laughter and discussion they both settled on a navy-blue Chanel suit with simple classic lines. As accessories they chose Sam's best silk scarf and a pair of matching court shoes which showed her ankles off to perfection. That morning Sam swept her long, dark-blonde hair into a neat French pleat and completed her outfit with the simplest of gold jewellery.

The morning was dark and chill but she managed to park relatively easily due to the early hour. She met the rest of the PTP team, laden with the presentation material, in the company foyer. They all gave her reassuring smiles before taking the fast lifts to the conference room at the top of the building.

She found she was trembling; her stomach was in turmoil and she felt an overpowering desire to turn on her heels and flee. As they came out of the lift, her assistant Jonathan gave her a jaunty grin of reassurance. Brian Jason, the burly chief from the Production Department, squeezed her hand.

"Sock It to 'em, baby!" he said, with an outrageous attempt at an American accent.

She had to grin. Brian, in his early forties the oldest member of their team, had left school at an early age and worked his way determinedly up the agency ladder. Sam found great reassurance in his calm, experienced and sturdy presence. She took a deep breath and they walked together into the board room.

Dennis Payne strode eagerly to the door to greet them, exuding charm and bonhomie.

"Miss Proctor Bourne! You look charming! What a refreshing change from dear Paul – delightful though he may be."

He eyed her speculatively, rather like a shark eyeing its prey before the final attack, thought Sam. She managed to smile sweetly at him and settled into the chair he gallantly offered her by his side.

The rest of the team waited with bated breath. They were used to Dennis Payne and his moods – his sudden flashes from charm to boorishness, from calm to flaring anger, most of it done for effect.

The meeting started auspiciously. Payne was charm itself to Sam, listening attentively as she put their proposals before him. She began to relax and gain confidence. Perhaps he wasn't quite the ogre she had supposed. Maybe he sympathised with her position, was prepared to let up on this occasion until his old adversary, Paul, returned.

Then abruptly his questions became more demanding, his tone sharper. The tension mounted in the air as the team recognised the tell-tale signs.

Payne turned suddenly to Samantha, his double chin wobbling with anger.

"Is this the best media schedule your agency can offer me, Miss Proctor Bourne?" She was taken off-guard. During the first part of the meeting, Payne had accepted the media schedule without comment.

"Of course," she answered spiritedly. "The agency offers its recommendations only after full consideration – when agreement has been reached by the entire campaign team." She was pleased to receive a reassuring wink from Brian. That's it – don't let him bully you, girl, it seemed to say.

"Including Mr Paul Wilson?" said Payne, his tone acrimonious.

"Of course," said Sam, falling into the trap. "Mr Wilson is the account director. His is the final word."

Payne pounced on the slip.

"Then why isn't he here?" he snapped, belligerently. Gone were the soft flattering words and manners. He had succeeded in catching her off-guard. Now he had her where he wanted her – he was poised for the kill.

She tried to remain cool, not to panic.

"Mr Wilson has already explained why he cannot attend this meeting."

"Explained!" Payne shouted. Perspiration started from his brow. "All I know is that your agency considers a loo-paper account more important than the whole of the British fashion industry!"

"But Mr Payne, this is a routine meeting. Mr Wilson's presence isn't essential. But he is required at a new business presentation."

Payne's face turned black as thunder.

"So you admit it! You consider touting for new business more important than handling my account? Your agency would be better advised to look after existing clients – before attempting to attract new business. If not, you may find those same clients will go in search of a new agency!" He thumped the table, then knowing he was winning, gave an evil grin.

"Hell!" thought Sam. Was he bluffing, just bullying as usual? She realised she would have to change tactics. Smiling sweetly at Payne she spoke softly, forcing him to listen.

"Of course we consider your account to be of prime importance, Mr Payne. That is why we have undertaken our planning with great care and attention, under Mr Wilson's firm control. These are the agency's proposals which I, as account executive, am presenting on his behalf.

She drew a deep breath.

"I should be obliged if you would allow us to continue with our proposals. I'm sure you will agree we have a superb Autumn campaign planned for you. We shall be happy to answer any queries you may have." She gave him a dazzling smile. "If you are still not completely satisfied, I am sure you can discuss any unresolved points with the Account Director at our next meeting, or before, if necessary. After all Mr Wilson will be back in London by tomorrow." She looked him straight in the eye.

Payne's eyes narrowed cunningly, but she thought she spotted a glint of respect lurking in their depths.

"So I'm to work with a young inexperienced woman, am I, Miss Proctor Bourne?" he asked artfully.

"It's true – I am young and relatively inexperienced, but I have behind me the skills and experience of the whole agency I represent. One thing I can assure you, Mr Payne, you will have all my enthusiastic efforts and my complete involvement in your product. I believe in your Group and will do everything possible to advance their interests."

"Right," said Payne, slightly mollified. "We shall see." He looked down at the superb art-work in front of him. "This isn't too bad, I suppose," he admitted, grudgingly. "But I'm still not happy with the media schedule."

Of course not, thought Sam. That's where your strength lies. You worked in media before and know all the angles. She said out loud, "Is there anything you specifically wish to discuss?"

"Certainly," said Payne. "For instance, I see you're proposing to put a hefty sum into this new magazine, *Elegance*, which hasn't even been launched yet. I consider that far too risky."

Sam nodded towards Bill Harvey, the Media Group Head.

"I'm sure Mr Harvey will be able to reassure you on that point."

Bill Harvey went through all the motions, explaining the excellence and experience of the publishing group producing the new magazine, the guaranteed print run and their special launch rates."

"It's still an unknown factor," persisted Payne.

Bill looked at Sam in desperation.

"I've seen a dummy issue of the proposed magazine," said Sam, with her most winning smile. "It just the kind of magazine that we need for the fashion group – beautifully produced, chic, elegant. As Mr Harvey explained, we've received guarantees of circulation for the first six issues and reduced rates. It's a bargain."

"But if it doesn't work out ..."

"We also have a guarantee that we may cancel at any time if the magazine disappoints us in any way," she said. Payne looked stunned. She waited a moment to give full impact to her final ace. "Mr James the ad. manager of *Elegance*, is simply dying to meet you, Mr Payne. He's heard so much about you. He would love to take you to lunch at the earliest opportunity. By the way," she added casually, "he plans to give extensive editorial coverage to the New Mode Group."

She knew she had him. Payne adored free editorial coverage, hob-knobbing with Fleet Street cronies and good lunches – in that order!

His eyes softened.

"Your media department certainly seems to have things well worked out, Miss Proctor Bourne. May I call you Samantha?" He placed his big paw over her slender wrist and grinned wolfishly. "I think you and I are going to get on just fine."

There was an almost audible sigh of relief around the conference table. The rest of the meeting went like clockwork. Sam got all their proposals approved.

Later in the local pub the whole team congratulated her, thumping her on the back. Only Bill, the Media Group head, stood apart from them, smiling knowingly at Sam.

"I guess I've got a big job ahead of me, Sam?"

"You certainly have, Bill."

The rest of them looked at her in surprise.

"You mean you haven't got all those guarantees, the editorial coverage and so on from *Elegance*?" said John, his mouth opening and shutting like a fish.

"No," said Sam, "but we soon shall have, shan't we Bill?"

"No problem," grinned Bill. "I'm sure they'll jump at it to get a nice slice of billing from a prestigious account like the NMG."

"Even the lunch, Bill?" she said, smiling archly.

"No problem there, Sam. Fred James is one of my very best friends."

"That I did remember – from my weeks working in media," said Sam, reminding him of her trainee days in his department.

"You little minx!" Bill's face split in a wide grin and they all joined in the laughter.

* * * * * * *

Early the following day, Paul called her into his office.

"Congratulations, Sam. I heard all about it. And I've just had a call from Dennis Payne himself. He insists you service his account with only token assistance from me. His excuse is you're much prettier! But I know Dennis. You seem to have won him over. Mind you, he'll always be difficult so it certainly won't be all plain sailing. You'll have your ups and downs. But you've got to him, all right."

Sam left Paul's office in a dream. I've done it, she thought. Outwitted Payne! But she doubted it would always be that easy. She had been lucky yesterday with Payne – acting on inspiration, taking a flyer which he hadn't challenged because of his own greed and self-absorption. Next time she might not be so fortunate! In future she would be prepared for anything. She would study not only the product, but the clients themselves – their strengths and weaknesses. That way she could anticipate their every need, their every foible. Like one of her idols, Good Queen Bess, she might have only the body of a weak and feeble woman, but she was determined to be the best at her job!

Chapter 25

Oxford, England. May 1965

"We'd love you to come with us, Sam," her mother said. "In any case, a holiday is just what you need – sun, sea and relaxation!"

"You know you can't wait to show Sam the villa," teased Leslie, with a conspiratory wink.

Sam smiled indulgently at the two of them. They were like a pair of eager children, dying to share a secret. Her mother had grown a little plumper in recent years, but her face was as unlined and youthful as ever. Leslie sat by his wife's side on the large sofa, his hand on her knee. Ever-conscious of his long tall frame, he stooped a little more as he grew older, but was still as sprightly as ever. They're becoming a real Darby and Joan couple, she thought. Twenty-four years married and they still hold hands like a couple of teenagers!

She wanted to please them, share the thrill of the new villa they had bought in Spain.

"I'd love to come, Mother, but I just can't take the time off."

"Of course you can!" Leslie insisted. "Everybody has to have a holiday at some time. You work like a slave in that agency!"

"I know," she admitted with a smile, "but I do love every minute."

"You are looking a little peaky, Sam," said her mother, concern in her voice. "You've hardly had more than a few days off during the last couple of years. You know what they say – 'all work and no play'...."

She laughed.

"I know, Mother, but I get as much fun from my work as I do from any holiday. Mind you, I must say I'd love to see this fantastic island of yours and the villa – it looks gorgeous on the photos."

During the last three years her parents had taken frequent holidays on the Mediterranean island of Ibiza. They had fallen in love with this tiny Spanish paradise, and the previous year had decided to buy a holiday and retirement home there. Sam had to admit that from the photographs both the island and her parent's new house looked breathtakingly beautiful. For the first time she felt tempted to see it at first hand. She could certainly do with the rest, some time to wind down a little.

"When do you plan to visit next?" she asked.

"We've already booked our boat tickets," said Leslie eagerly. "We're driving down at the beginning of July. The twins will join us by air when their term ends. Come on, Sam. You'll love it, I promise you!"

"It all depends how soon we can get this new chocolate bar account sorted out," she said. "I daren't leave till then. It's still rather short notice ... but it might be possible ... I'll have a chat with the MD" She was reasonably certain he would agree – once, of course, the Star Bar campaign had been approved. She was already being head-hunted by half a dozen London agencies and now earning an unusually high salary for her age. PTP, anxious to keep her happy and settled, had already promised her promotion to account director as soon as the agency won another account.

"Oh, Sam, that would be marvellous!" enthused her mother. "The boys will be so thrilled. They always complain they never see enough of you. They'll insist on taking you water-skiing – they spend most of their time in the sea."

She crossed to the study desk and returned with a large map. Spreading it out on the carpet before them, she started to show Sam places of interest on the island.

"Look, there's the walled city of Ibiza. It's thousands of years old, founded by the Carthaginians ... full of atmosphere and history! Our villa's here!" She pointed with a forefinger to a position on the other side of the island. "There's the Bay of San Antonio – it lies just below our villa. We overlook the whole bay and the islands beyond. Some days you can even see to the mainland ..."

"OK. I'm sold!" Sam interrupted, laughing, "as long as I can get the time off. I'll let you know straight away."

"You're welcome to bring one of your young men with you," remarked her mother, a shade too nonchalantly.

Sam giggled.

"Mother! You'll never change. I shall be perfectly all right on my own. It'll be refreshing to get away from all those smooth London types. You never know," she added, mischievously, "I may fall for some dark passionate Spaniard!"

Her mother shook her head.

"Don't tease so, Sam!"

"The only dark passionate thing Sam will ever fall for is the latest chocolate bar that needs advertising!" said Leslie, dryly.

"You said it, Dad!"

"Sam, you're starting to sound quite American," her mother reproved.

* * * * * * *

Six weeks later, they boarded the evening-boat from Barcelona to Ibiza.

The crossing lasted the entire night. The ferry, a converted royal yacht, had seen better days. Their car was hoisted aboard by an ancient crane with a creaking winch and chain. Sam chuckled to herself seeing Leslie's expression of horror as he watched his beloved car dangling precariously twenty feet above them. Eventually it landed on deck with an unceremonious thump!

They all shared one of the two available staterooms aboard. Once settled in, they wandered up to the tiny bar situated outside on the main deck. It was a delightful evening – balmy and still – the stars twinkling brightly above as the boat creamed its way through the gentle swell. She smiled as she watched Leslie and her mother gazing entranced at the night sky, like a pair of young lovers. It was lovely to see them so happy.

Relaxing in deckchairs close to the bar, they slowly sipped icy-cold gin-and-tonics. Sam began to unwind and enjoy herself. She had spent a hectic few weeks before her departure from the office and wondered if she would be bored just lazing around on holiday. At the moment the contrast was soothing and relaxing. Three weeks ahead of her with no worries or responsibilities, she thought – it couldn't be bad!

At seven-thirty the following morning she was rudely awakened by the steward thumping loudly on the cabin door. Sunshine streamed through the porthole. She saw her parents were already up. Feeling free as air – like a bird, newly released from its cage – she quickly changed into a light cotton dress and went to join them in the tiny salon-dining room.

"Good morning, Sam!" said her mother. "We didn't wake you – you seemed so fast asleep. Sit down and have some breakfast before we polish off all the *ensaimadas*! I'll order more coffee."

"I feel absolutely ravenous," said Sam. "It must be the sea-air. God! – I sound like the typical tourist!" She took a huge bite from a delicious whirl of pastry dusted with icing sugar. "Mmm ... these are gorgeous – even nicer than croissants. Could we order some more?"

Having demolished two more of the fluffy pastries the moment they appeared and two cups of steaming coffee, she sat back with a sigh.

"Lovely! Most mornings I don't even have time for a coffee before leaving the flat – not that I'm ever that hungry. How wonderful not to have to rush off somewhere! What time are we due to arrive?"

"Fairly soon," said Leslie, glancing at his watch. "We'd better get on deck. We mustn't miss the view of the Old Town as we sail into harbour – it's magnificent."

As they wandered out on deck she drew in a deep breath of the fresh tangy morning air and gazed about her. The boat was now cruising close to the hazy Ibiza coastline. The silhouetted coastline and purple hills rising mistily from the sea had an almost magical aura. Gosh, she thought, it's enchanting – like a fairy-tale island in the South Seas. I'm beginning to see what Mother and Dad like about this place.

The boat rounded another headland. It was then she saw it! Rising sheer from the calm translucent waters stood the ancient walled city of Ibiza, its steep stone and terracotta ramparts shimmering in soft shades of pink and gold as the early rays of the sun reflected from its ancient battlements. On the summit the Cathedral stood aloft, like an enchanted castle.

Her mother and Leslie turned towards her, their eyes proud and shining.

"Well, Sam what do you think?"

"It's lovely!" said Sam. "One of the most beautiful sights I've ever seen. The whole setting seems unreal, almost theatrical – I can just imagine the Moors and Spaniards fighting on those ramparts. Yet the city looks impregnable from the sea."

"It's nearly as unassailable from the land-side – steep walls and fortified entrances." Leslie told her. "Don't worry, we'll take you all round the Old Town and the ramparts – even show you the secret passage!"

"I can't wait," she said, thoroughly captivated. "Thank you both for persuading me to come. I know I shall love it. Now! – where are all those dark handsome Spaniards?"

"*Ibicencos*," corrected Leslie, with a laugh. The local people are known as *Ibicencos* and they speak their own *Ibicenco* language – a dialect of Catalan. It's quite different from Spanish."

"Hell, I'll be lost", said Sam. "I know a few phrases in Spanish, but not a word of Catalan."

"Don't worry," said her mother. "Most of the locals understand and speak Spanish, except some of the older generation. Most youngsters also speak a fair amount of English." She looked proudly at Leslie. "Your father's already picked up some Spanish, but I'm just not bright enough."

"You get by as well as anyone, my dear," Leslie defended her. "One smile from you and they're all eating out of your hand."

"I can believe that," said Sam with a grin. "Typical Mother! Now don't look embarrassed – you know it's true!"

The ferry started to pull into the bustling harbour. Scores of people on the jetty shouted and waved to friends and relations on board. The weekly arrival of the Barcelona boat was obviously an important occasion in the island's weekly calendar, thought Sam.

"Have you brought any heart pills with you, Dad?" she teased. "They'll soon be unloading the car!"

Leslie groaned and they headed back to the cabin to collect their luggage.

* * * * * * *

The next week flew by in a whirl as her parents showed her all over the tiny island. Each fresh discovery was an unexpected pleasure. She fell in love with her parent's new home – a converted island finca, or farmhouse, with low Moorish lines, thick stone walls and arches, wooden beams and wrought-iron balconies. Parts of the house had been rendered and whitewashed; the brilliant white of the lime contrasted brilliantly with the soft red-brown of the dry-stone walls. Colourful geraniums and vivid purple and red bougainvillea adorned the walls and terraces.

Despite its typical design and architecture – parts of the house were three-hundred-years old – the interior had been modernised with an eye to comfort. But the alterations had been made with meticulous care to retain the traditional farmhouse atmosphere. Sam adored its cool rooms, shady balconies and sunny terraces, the sweet aroma of the climbing honeysuckle, the tangy scent of the pine-trees and herbs which drifted on the breeze from the surrounding countryside.

The views to the sea were superb. To the north sparkled the cove and beach of Cala Salada, the looming headland of Cap Nono; to the south stretched the whole of the magnificent Bay of San Antonio and the island of Conejera, where – they told her – Hannibal was reputed to have been born.

"The Romans christened San Antonio Bay 'Portus Magnus' or The Big Bay," Leslie told her. "It's one of the largest natural harbours in the world." He put his arm round her shoulder as they gazed out to sea from the covered balcony. "That natural advantage, plus its strategic position in the Mediterranean, made Ibiza a crossroads for all the great commercial sea-faring nations in the ancient world – Carthaginians, Greeks and Romans. Of course, its sea-salt industry was also important to them – as were the pine forests. They offered a plentiful source of wood for the ancient fleets." He gave a wide grin. "I love it – the whole island simply reeks of history!"

"What better place for a history professor to retire!" laughed Sam. "I'm glad you both love it so. I have to admit the island has a rare fascination. I can't explain exactly what it is ... it's not only its beauty and antiquity.... I just feel it in my bones."

Her mother stared at her, her face full of emotion.

"I'm so glad you said that, Sam. You see – Leslie and I and many of our friends feel exactly the same. It's a fatal fascination impossible to explain. The Ibiza magnet! You either feel it or you don't. I think it accounts for the wonderful cross-section of people you find here – all types of people and nationalities – attracted by the same island magic! I'm so happy you've felt it, too."

"So am I," she said, kissing her mother gently on the cheek.

She meant it. She was fascinated by the island, adored the way it attracted such an unusual mix of people from all different cultures and backgrounds. They all seemed to meld here in Ibiza. In such a small place, everyone seemed to know everybody else, yet the friendly village atmosphere was spiced with an arty cosmopolitan flavour Sam found unique and exciting.

She loved the lack of class and status-symbols. Millionaires and paupers alike drove around in rickety old cars – the most sensible thing to do in a place where most roads were rocky dust-tracks or dried-up water courses! Dress was casual and simple – nobody stood on ceremony. Film stars and business tycoons hobnobbed with artists, writers, islanders and hippies. Each person seemed to start afresh in Ibiza, accepted – or rejected – for their personal qualities, regardless of their previous background. The one thing they all had in common was their love of the island.

Soon she was caught up in the swinging social scene. Before leaving England she had visions of lazy hours basking in the sun, of boredom even, but she was soon immersed in a lively round of barbecues, beach parties and pool lunches. They spent balmy evenings dining out in delightful restaurants, others quietly at home enjoying a light supper in the cool of the terrace, gazing at the moon and stars.

It was ages since Sam had felt so relaxed, so happy in herself mainly, she thought, because she had a successful and satisfying career waiting for her back in England. But she had to admit that this idyllic break in Ibiza had revealed another aspect of her character which she had never allowed to surface before - the ability to relax and be content, to take time off from the continual striving, the desire to excel.

She also felt more at ease than ever before with her parents, discovering a new empathy with her mother. Secure and confident of herself, Sam found her long-standing envy of Cathy had vanished. Instead of being in awe of her mother, she now felt only love and the need to humour and protect – as if their roles had been reversed. Here in the island paradise of Ibiza where her mother and Leslie had found a new wide-eyed enthusiasm for life, they had become like children with her playing the role of the world-wise, indulgent parent!

Before she knew it, more than half her holiday had flown by. She hadn't had time to read a single book or worry about any of her clients at the agency. The twins were arriving the next day, and she knew they would pester her to join in their maritime adventures. It would be fun. The Ibiza spirit was getting to her and she didn't care – at least not for the next ten days!

Chapter 26

Sam met Barry Johns at a pool party in a villa near Ibiza Town. The only son of their hosts, he was powerfully-built and extrovert with dark hair, flashing eyes and a neat black beard. Swarthy complexioned and deeply tanned, he could have passed as a Latin except he was taller than most of the local men.

He quickly took Sam under his wing and proved to be excellent company – except when he had been drinking too much! Even then, he had an indefinable charm and could invariably worm his way out of trouble.

He turned up at the villa one hot sunny morning, whistling loudly. Sam, engrossed in weeding the garden despite the intense heat of the day, wore only a tiny bikini and a large protective straw hat.

"A sight for sore eyes!" boomed Barry. "Wish we had a gardener like you! Can you stop for a cold beer or am I being presumptuous?"

"Of course not," laughed Sam. "It's almost too hot to work today, but I felt I ought to do something useful for a change. I've been living the proverbial lotus-life ever since I arrived in Ibiza!"

"That's what it's all about," Barry said.

"Is it?" she asked, more seriously.

"Of course it is!"

"But I mean, every day – not just on holiday. Do you enjoy living like this all the time – never feel the need to do anything more ... well ... more responsible, I suppose?"

"My! We are getting into deep waters today."

"Sorry. I'm just not used to this sort of existence."

"Well, it's time you did get used to it," he said amiably, refusing to take her seriously.

Sam wondered if it was a front or if he really was the complete hedonist.

"You're bright and intelligent, Barry," she persisted, "with an excellent education. Don't you ever get tired of never using your talents, of doing nothing in particular except enjoy yourself?"

"Isn't that what everyone wants to do – enjoy themselves? I've travelled the world, met plenty of people. I like this life." She noticed his tone had become slightly defensive.

"You're probably right," she said, not wishing to upset him. Not everyone was as workaholic as herself, she realised – she should be more diplomatic. She smiled her disarming smile. "To what do I owe the pleasure of your visit?"

His good-natured face broke into a teasing grin. He gave an extravagant bow.

"In my usual self-indulgent way, I wondered if you'd join me for dinner tonight?"

"I'd love to," Sam said, suppressing a giggle. She ought to know better than to try to talk seriously to Barry. She walked over to the garden fridge, pulled out two icy-cold beers. Pouring them carefully into long slender glasses, she passed one to him and raised her own glass.

He gave an enormous wink.

"Here's to the lotus-life!" he toasted.

* * * * * * *

Barry picked her up that night at eight on the dot.

"We're eating at El Refugio," he told her as they drove into town. "I hope you don't mind, but I've asked another couple to join us. My oldest friend, Peter Radcliffe, has just arrived here on holiday. He and I were at school together and our parents are very chummy. I thought it would be fun if he and Jane made up a four."

"Of course I don't mind – it sounds fun. I haven't been to El Refugio before but I've heard good reports."

As soon as they walked into the typical-style restaurant, charmingly decorated with trailing grape-vines and huge wooden wine-casks, she knew she was going to enjoy the evening. The manager ushered them enthusiastically to their table, helped them into their chairs. He obviously knew Barry well and gave Sam a beaming smile of welcome.

Within seconds a waiter approached the table. "Suckling pig, as usual, Señor Barry?" he enquired.

"We shan't be ordering for a few minutes, Juan – some friends are joining us. In the meantime, two gin-and-tonics, please, with plenty of ice and lemon?"

The waiter bustled away.

"Like it?" enquired Barry.

"It's lovely. I adore the garden setting, and the aroma from the kitchen is gorgeous! My taste buds are already screaming for attention."

"Don't worry, we shall be ordering soon. Peter's never late even when he's in Ibiza!" He looked over his shoulder to the door. "There they are now." He rose from his chair to greet the attractive young couple approaching their table.

Sam's attention was immediately drawn to the man. She stared dumb-founded at his striking blond hair and deep brown eyes, the latter now crinkled in a broad friendly smile which seemed to take in everyone in the restaurant. Tall and broad shouldered, his white open-neck shirt revealed a magnificent tan. What a marvellous combination, she thought – dark eyes and blond hair!

Almost reluctantly she turned her gaze to the girl by his side. Of medium height with long chestnut-coloured hair and a neat figure, she too sported a deep tan set off to perfection by a low-cut vivid green dress. Her jade eyes and slightly freckled, upturned nose gave her an almost impish appeal. Attractive and lots of fun, thought Sam.

"Peter ... Jane ... this is Samantha Proctor Bourne, better known as Sam!" said Barry. "Sam, let me introduce Jane Thorpe and Peter Radcliffe. They all shook hands and Jane and Peter sat down at the table. The waiter quickly reappeared and more drinks were ordered.

"I'm ravenous, Peter," said Jane, brightly. "Could we order soon?"

"A girl after my own heart," laughed Sam.

Peter looked at her approvingly. "Good! I like girls who enjoy their food instead of picking at it. Mind you, you two have nothing to worry about figure-wise." His voice was teasing and friendly, but for some reason Sam found herself blushing.

"Gazpacho soup and suckling pig?" suggested Barry. "They're both specialities here."

"And we can finish with the Soufflé Alaska," added Peter. "It's out of this world."

"Perfect," said Sam, scarcely able to stop staring at Peter.

"That's settled then! Now where's that waiter?" Barry beckoned to Juan, who rushed to his side, pencil in hand.

Sam found the meal delicious, the company lively and entertaining, felt herself drawn more and more to Peter and Jane, both of them friendly and full of fun. A super couple, she reflected, with a twinge of jealousy she had never experienced before. They seemed very close, even acted a little proprietarily towards each other. Jane wore an emerald ring on her wedding finger, so she assumed they were already engaged. Lucky girl, she thought. Peter was a dear and very attractive – the perfect combination of masculinity and sensibility.

For some reason she found herself recalling an observation her flatmate Paula had once made. The nicest, most attractive men are always attached, she had bemoaned to Sam. Strange! Sam had never considered it before, never been so drawn to somebody else's husband or boy-friend. Trying to keep her gaze cool and withdrawn from Peter, she returned her attention to the light banter around the table.

Later in the evening the conversation took on a more serious tone. Peter, it seemed, worked hard in the family business, gradually taking over more responsibility from his father who would soon retire. Sam guessed he was about twenty-six-years-old. He spoke affectionately about his married younger sister and her two small children, whom he obviously adored. Jane on the other hand worked in a boutique in Chelsea and clearly loved the fashion business.

"I hear you and Barry are old school friends," she said to Peter, intrigued by their relationship. They obviously got on well, but were entirely different characters – Barry the complete hedonist, Peter for all his fun and good-humour, more serious and responsible in his approach to life.

"Even before that. Our families were neighbours," explained Peter. "So we knew each other as boys. My parents eventually moved, but Barry and I were at the same boarding school. We've been close friends for years – spent our profligate youth together!"

"But Pete's so tied-up with the business in England, I hardly ever see him now," complained Barry.

"There's always the holidays," grinned Peter, "but they do shoot by so quickly. How soon do you have to go back, Sam?"

"I've only got about ten days left. You're right – time here simply flies by."

"Well, let's make the most of it!" said Barry, eager to move on. "Where would everyone like to go tonight?"

"Could we drop into the Music Bar for a spell?" suggested Jane. "I love the guitars there, and the atmosphere's very friendly."

"OK We can go on to a night-club afterwards, or finish up at the Playboy – that's an open-air disco, Sam. Which would you girls prefer?"

"Let's do both," laughed Jane. "The night's still young. Is that OK by you, Sam?"

"In for a penny, in for a pound," agreed Sam, delighted to spend more time in their company.

* * * * * * *

She had a terrible hangover the following morning. Normally up bright and early, on this occasion she felt justified in luxuriating longer in bed. The fuzziness in her head had just started to recede when she heard a car draw up outside the villa.

The sound of muffled voices came from below, then her mother called to her.

"Sam, it's for you. We'll be out on the patio."

She staggered out of bed. Damn it! It must be Barry, but it was unusually early for him, especially after their lateness the night before. She threw water over her face, quickly cleaned her teeth and slipped into casual white slacks and a navy top. A few minutes later she was running down the tiled staircase, and out onto the patio.

"Good morning, Sam!" said a deep friendly voice. She stopped dead in her tracks. Peter Radcliffe! What was he doing here? She was suddenly aware of her dishevelled appearance – she must look terrible! It would have to be Peter!

"Hello, Peter. What a lovely surprise!" Her heart stirred as she stared again into his dark eyes. "Thank you for a super evening last night. We did enjoy your company."

"I was just going to fetch some fresh orange juice for Peter," said her mother diplomatically. "Would you like some, Sam?"

"Please, Mother, I've got a terrible thirst!"

Her mother smiled. "You were rather late last night." She headed off to the kitchen.

Sam looked around the patio.

"Where's Jane?" she asked him. "Still the worse for wear? I must admit I've a terrible head this morning!"

Peter looked mildly surprised at the question. "Oh, I expect she'll be off to the beach today. She loves sunbathing at every possible moment. She only wants to know about me when she needs an escort."

Sam shook her head in puzzlement.

"I ... I thought you and she ... well I thought you were engaged or something?"

Peter gave a laugh of delight.

"Jane and I? Well I guess we are pretty close, but my dear cousin's engaged to an extremely handsome young man who works in the City."

"Cousin?" queried Sam, her heart starting to pound.

"Didn't Barry tell you?"

"No ... well, I suppose the subject really never came up."

"I thought you treated me a little coolly," said Peter, grinning happily. "Very polite and charming, I hasten to add, but a little aloof. I thought it was because you were so taken with Barry. Then I had a little chat with him last night – after we'd dropped you off. You see – I desperately wanted to see you again, but I didn't want to tread on Barry's toes." He hesitated, passed a hand through his thick blond hair. "He ... he didn't seem to think you were that interested – in him that is – just good friends as they say. So I thought I'd take a chance and try my luck. At least ask you out one night. As you can see I didn't waste any time!"

His dark-brown eyes twinkled as he watched her reaction.

Sam sat down with a jolt in the cane chair. "And I was so sure you and Jane ..." She gave an embarrassed laugh.

"Here you are you two," said her mother suddenly appearing with the fresh orange juice. "Best thing for a hang-over – it helps cure the dehydration! What's the matter, Sam? You look as if you've seen a ghost."

"Nothing, I'm fine," she said, pulling herself together and feeling suddenly outrageously happy. "Mother, we had a super time last night. We went to El Refugio, then to the Music ..." Wild shouts interrupted her from the garden. "Oh no! Here come Tim and Adrian. Peter, you haven't met my younger brothers yet. I call them the terrible twins." She found she couldn't stop smiling. "You have a treat in store."

"I certainly do," he grinned, "and another if you'll agree to come to lunch with me."

"I'd love to," she said, trying not to appear too eager.

Her mother, in the process of pouring Peter's orange juice, gave him a knowing wink.

"Just wait till you meet Sam's brothers," she teased him. "You might change your mind about this family."

Sam saw her mother's eyes were full of laughter. She's obviously taken with him too, she thought happily.

Peter flashed his irresistible smile.

"I haven't invited them to lunch! But I'll certainly take them out on the boat one day. Do they like skiing?"

"They love it!" said Sam. She smiled shyly at him for once strangely tongue-tied – then raised her glass of orange.

"Here's to Ibiza!"

"Here's to us," Peter said, softly.

"Yes, to Peter and Sam!" agreed her mother. "Let's drink to that." Her face was one wide happy smile.

Chapter 27

During the last few days of her holiday, she and Peter were inseparable. They spent mornings at the beach, sometimes just lazing in the sand, sometimes exploring the paths through the cool tangy pine-woods, where the silence was intensified by the ceaseless hum of the cicadas. They bounced down forgotten cart-tracks in Peter's battered Seat to discover hidden coves where nobody would care Sam was getting an even tan all over.

In the evenings they frequented the tiny 'tapas' bars and romantic restaurants, spending hours simply chatting together over aperitifs and simple island dishes. With a sinking feeling inside, Sam realised her time in Ibiza was running out. She would miss the island but at least she would still be able to see Peter when he returned to England a week or so after her.

The day before she was due to leave they took the car to the top of Atalaya, the highest mountain on the island. The old Seat laboured its way up the steep fissured track to the undulating summit. The views over the island in all directions were magnificent. To the west they could even see the hazy outline of the Spanish mainland.

"That's Cabo San Antonio, a headland near Denia," explained Peter. "It's called that, because from the top they can see over here to San Antonio."

He fell silent and they lay in the grass, for once at a loss for anything to say to each other. Dusk fell, slowly painting out the surrounding countryside. The whitewashed houses turned pink in the soft light of evening, the honey-coloured stone of the terrace walls jealously holding on to the last moments of the day's heat.

Peter took her in his arms, stroked her hair. She found she was crying. He rocked her in a gentle embrace before wiping her eyes with his handkerchief.

"Sam, I love you very much," he said simply. She put her finger to his lips, willing him to say no more.

He shook his head.

"You know I want to marry you, don't you?"

She nodded, dismay showing in her hazel eyes. She realised she had been living an unreal existence, assuming her glorious relationship with Peter could continue indefinitely, with no commitment from her. She knew she loved Peter, but couldn't reconcile herself to the idea of marriage, of losing her independence and trusting her future to somebody else. And she could never handle a family. The very thought of it frightened her, left a stifling sensation in her nose and throat.

Peter gazed at her, the hurt showing in his tender brown eyes.

"Why Sam ... why don't you want me?"

"I do want you, Peter. I just don't want to get married," she said in a small voice.

"What's that supposed to mean?" he said, impatience slipping into his voice. "Do you love me, Sam?"

"You know I do – at least as much as I'm capable of loving anybody." She put her arms around his neck, ran her hand through his blond hair, her body aching for him.

"Love me, Peter, just love me," she whispered.

With a groan, he drew her closer to him, held her so tightly it hurt. She didn't mind – she wanted him with an intensity she had never felt before.

She had made love to one other man before Peter. Although fond of her first lover, Mark, she hadn't been in love with him. She had found him sexually exciting, and after so many years of fending off male attention, her body screamed for fulfilment. Eventually her mind, too, surrendered.

Mark had sensed the ambiguity of her feelings, her fear of involvement. But aware his love-making inflamed her, he had tried to satisfy her every whim, hoping by captivating her body, to win her mind. Once aroused, her body demanded more and their relationship continued for several months. But mentally she knew they weren't right together. Eventually they had split up, both of them hurt and disillusioned.

But with Peter everything was different. From the minute she met him, she was captivated, knew she wanted him in every way. She adored every inch of his body, wanted to explore every crevice of his mind.

Now she clung to him in desperation, her body crying out, her senses reeling. Her excitement mounted as his hands and tongue began to explore her body. She began to quiver uncontrollably, felt her body juices flow freely. She wanted to crawl all over him, never let him go.

His love-making became harder, more demanding, yet it never lost its sensitivity. She had known, intuitively, it would be like that. It was the embodiment of Peter's character: his unique combination of strength and gentleness.

She felt a surge of euphoria when he finally thrust into her. He spoke to her – words of love, words of passion – his voice, low and compelling, arousing her further. She twisted beneath him, trying to take over the rhythm herself; felt herself floating, floating up, into the midnight blue of the dusky night-sky above. Paradise, she thought, as a tremor of ecstasy convulsed her whole body. She heard a voice shouting out loud.

"Don't ever stop loving me!" It was her own.

Their passion spent, they clung to each other for what seemed an eternity, willing time to stand still ...

* * * * * * *

As they drove quietly home, Peter took one hand from the wheel and grasped her slender fingers.

"When can we get married, Sam?" he asked, tenderly.

Her heart sank.

"Peter, I did mean what I said before. I'm not ready for marriage yet. I love you – more than anything else in the world – but I'm just not the sort to get married."

173

"Don't be ridiculous, Sam. How can you say that after the days we've spent together; after this evening? I can't believe you can just walk away from me?"

"I don't want to walk away from you," she said, distressed. "Why can't we carry on the way we are?"

"That's not enough for me," he said firmly. "I want you, I want you one hundred-per-cent, not as your boyfriend, not even to live with you. I want you to be my wife. It may sound outrageous, but I made that decision within minutes of meeting you. What are you frightened of, Sam?"

"I don't know exactly. Marriage is so confining, so final."

"You mean you want to be free to have other men-friends?" he asked grimly.

"Of course not. I'm not promiscuous, Peter, you know that. You satisfy me completely, physically and mentally. I've never wanted any man as I want you."

"I don't understand you, Sam. Most girls of your age want to get married."

"I don't," said Sam, equally firmly. "You forget, Peter. I have a wonderful career which I love. It takes up most of my time. I'd make a terrible wife."

"You wouldn't have to stop working Sam, you know that. I'd be more than happy for you to continue your career."

"And if a baby came along?" she said quietly. "You do want a family, don't you Peter?"

"Of course I do. I love kids – you know that – but we have time."

"How long? You're twenty-seven – I'm already twenty-four." She took a deep breath. "You see, I don't think I want a family."

He shrugged.

"A lot of girls are frightened of motherhood – until it happens to them. Don't worry, you'll make a perfect mother."

"Peter, you can't change me! I don't want to get married, and that's final."

His brown eyes flashed.

"Your mother warned me you could be stubborn," he said angrily, "but I didn't think you were stupid! You may love your career now, Sam, but what happens in years to come – when you've forfeited your happiness for a sterile career. Can you imagine yourself old, alone, with no family – an empty, bitter woman."

"Don't be so melodramatic, Peter. You're exaggerating. Don't you see – everything has happened too fast for me. Think about your own experiences. You've had other serious girl-friends before – you told me about them. Why did those relationships never come to anything? Obviously because you changed your mind. What's to say you won't change your mind about me in a year or two?"

"You're different, Sam," he said, his usually wide friendly mouth set in a bitter line. "You've been different from the start. What you mean is you might tire of me."

"I'm not saying that." She sighed, knowing he would never understand. "Only that everything has happened too fast. In any case I don't think I shall ever marry."

"So what's in this relationship for me?" he asked his voice rising in frustration. "What am I supposed to do? Hang around, waiting for you to spare me a few minutes from your precious career – with no prospects of you ever becoming my wife? You can't expect that, Sam. It's cruel and selfish, and you're not that sort of person."

"I'm not so sure," said Sam, sadly.

He looked at her in amazement.

"In that case, Sam, I think this is where we part ways."

They didn't speak again until they reached the villa. Peter's face was set white and hard beneath his golden tan. She'd never seen him so angry. Before today they had never had the slightest quarrel.

He came round to open the car-door for her.

"Goodbye, Sam. I wish you luck." He turned on his heels, got in the car and drove away.

She cried herself to sleep.

* * * * * *

The following morning she went down to breakfast trying to put on a brave front. But her mirror had told her she was red-eyed, her face pale and drained. Her mother approached her without a word, put her arms round her shoulders.

"Don't worry, darling," she comforted. "It will all turn out right in the end."

"Oh, Mother. I hope I haven't done the wrong thing."

"Only time will tell," said her mother simply.

"Come and have some breakfast," said Leslie, gruffly. "The boys asked you to join them for a ski on Cala Gracio beach before you leave. Why don't you pop down after breakfast?"

"Thanks, Dad. I'll do that."

* * * * * *

She never heard any more from Peter before she left. She understood why, and in a way admired him for his firm stand. As he said, he was a hundred-per-cent man. Peter never did anything by half measures. It was one of the qualities she admired in him.

On the flight home, he filled her thoughts. Already missing his good company, his ability to make her laugh, she recalled his delicious deep laugh and irresistible smile, his hard tanned body. Then she remembered deeper qualities – his kindness, consideration and sense of humour, his inner strength and dependability. Oh, Peter, Peter! What shall I do without you? Work, she decided, she would immerse herself in her work. She would soon forget him.

* * * * * *

Somehow it wasn't that easy. She drove herself harder and harder at her job. She got her promotion, but still she kept up the pressure. Eventually even David Telford, the managing director, told her it to take it easier.

"You're working too hard, Sam. It's not that necessary. You'll only make yourself ill."

But she didn't know what else to do. Every moment on her own – when she wasn't working – the emptiness and ache for Peter returned.

She became snappy and short-tempered. At the flat, Paula handled her with kid gloves. Sam hadn't explained any details to her but Paula obviously assumed she had been let down by some man in Ibiza, and went out her way to be kind to her. It only made Sam feel worse. She stayed later at work in the evenings, went into the office earlier in the mornings.

Her parents were now back in England, but she avoided visiting them, unable to answer their enquiring glances, to let them see the state she was in. Her mother telephoned her regularly and she found that a great comfort. She never revealed the depth of her suffering, but she knew her mother, as usual, sensed her distress.

* * * * * * * *

She sat in her office one day staring into space, when the phone buzzed on her desk.

"It's a Mr Barry Johns," said Dawn, on the intercom. "I tried to put him off, but he said it was most urgent. Shall I put him through?"

Panic seized her. Barry! Why was he ringing? Something must have happened to Peter. Her voice seemed to dry up in her throat.

"Put ... put him through please, Dawn," she managed to stammer at last.

Barry's voice boomed down the line.

"Is that you, Sam?"

"Yes ..." Her voice faltered. "What is it, Barry? Has something happened to Peter?"

"Yes," he said, his voice grave.

She winced, felt her stomach tie in a knot. A terrible cold fear crept through her.

"Tell me, Barry ..." She paused, unable to put her terror into words. "Has he ... has he had an accident?"

"No, Sam. It's you! You've happened to him. What have you done to the poor chap? He's a shadow of his former self! I've just got over to England and I've never seen him looking so terrible. He's lost weight – looks as if his about to give up the ghost. It's all your fault, Sam!"

Relief flooded through her.

"Oh, Barry I thought something terrible had happened."

"It has – unless you're prepared to see sense," Barry insisted, grimly. "You love him, don't you, Sam?"

"Yes," she whispered.

"Well, what are you playing at? Or have you found yourself a new man?"

"Oh no," she said in horror.

"Well, you'd better buck up and see him, before the poor chap finally goes to pieces."

"Did he ask you to speak to me?"

"Of course not. You know Peter better than that. I found your name in that advertising manual – BRAD, I think it's called." His voice went hard again. "What are you going to do, Sam?"

Suddenly she knew – what she had wanted to do all the time.

"I'll ring him," she said simply.

"Good!" said Barry. "Make it fast." The line went dead.

She felt the hot blood surge through her veins again. What a fool she had been – so determined to be independent, so frightened of being hurt that she couldn't even trust a man like Peter, so prepared to accept half a life, when she could have it all. She understood now what her mother had meant all the time, how she had wanted Sam, too, to enjoy the fulfilment of a true love relationship. Feeling almost light-headed, she buzzed her secretary, gave her Peter's business number. "Put me through as soon as you can, Dawn."

Please let him be in she prayed to herself, suddenly nervous and afraid. What if he refused to speak to her? He had been so hurt, angry and disillusioned the last time they were together. He might never want to see her again!

"Mr Radcliffe on the line for you," came Dawn's cool voice.

She tried to stay calm.

"Hello ... Sam, is that you?" It was Peter, his voice hollow and strained.

"Yes, it's me," she said softly, then realising there was no use beating about the bush. "Peter, darling, just two questions: Will you forgive me ... and will you marry me?"

"I thought you'd never ask," he said, hoarsely. She heard his sigh of relief which echoed hers. "Gosh, Sam, don't let's ever to do this again."

"Never again," she promised. "Never again!"

✳ ✳ ✳ ✳ ✳ ✳ ✳

They were married a month later at Sam's local church in Oxford. Barry stayed on in England to be best man, and an overjoyed Paula was chief bridesmaid. Peter's cousin, Jane, and his two nieces made up the bridesmaids. Tim and Adrian, the terrible twins, proudly acted as ushers.

Her parents were over the moon with happiness. During the ceremony her mother couldn't stop weeping. Sam could hear her sobs from the pew behind as she and Peter made their vows. Dear mother, she thought, she must be really happy to be crying so!

Most of her friends from the agency attended the wedding, and many of Peter's friends, including some from Ibiza. It made a large gathering. Even Douglas and Tom, and the rest of the group from college, managed to turn up for the wedding to wish her luck. She was touched.

"You're a lucky man," Tom told Peter, clapping him on the shoulder.

"I know," beamed her new husband.

"You realise you're walking off with our lucky mascot?" teased Douglas. "We shall demand compensation."

"There's plenty of champagne in the marquee," laughed Peter.

"Sold!" said Douglas, blowing Sam a kiss.

Tom gave her a swift hug.

"All the luck in the world, Sam!"

"Thanks, Tom," she said. "I shall never forget you."

* * * * * * *

In July the following year, her baby girl was born.

They decided to christen her Kate, after her grandmother. Cathy and Leslie were thrilled to bits.

"My own little name-sake," cooed her mother to the baby. "Sam – I'm so very happy for you both!"

"So am I, Mother," she said and meant it. She adored her tiny daughter, her wonderful husband. Life couldn't be better. She lay in hospital, her baby clasped to her breast, her slender face one big smile.

Peter grinned.

"Who said you weren't maternal?" he teased.

"OK," you win," she beamed. "But I shall be back at work in a few months!"

"Of course, darling! I never doubted it!"

Her mother smiled across at Leslie. "I think we´d better leave these two lovebirds together with their off-spring. We'll see you tomorrow, Sam." They all exchanged embraces and her mother and Leslie left with a final wave from the doorway.

Sam gazed up at Peter, a great wave of happiness flowing through her. She grasped him by the hand.

"Oh, Peter, I can't believe it. I've got it all – you, the baby, my family and my wonderful career. I didn't believe it possible before. I never seemed to inspire the kind of love my mother did, so I tried to make up for it with my career. Now I've got everything and all because of you." She put her hand to his face, gently stroked his cheek, knowing she needed his love more than ever. "You'll never leave with me, will you?"

He hugged her tight.

"I'm afraid you're stuck with me for ever, Mrs Radcliffe. We'll always be together – a real Darby and Joan – and when we reach a hundred we'll die together in each other's arms." He smiled his lovely warm smile.

"Rather like Romeo and Juliet," she mused, "except they died far too young. But I know what you mean – I couldn't bear to live a moment of my life without you beside me and I don't intend to."

"So it's a pact," he said with a twinkle in his eyes.

"Yes, my darling, from here to eternity!"

"From here to eternity," he echoed.

Chapter 28

Ibiza, Spain July 1967

As soon as they stepped down from the Caravelle at Ibiza airport, Samantha gave a sigh of contentment. They were back on their magical island, the place they both loved best; where they had first met and later spent their honeymoon – and every holiday since.

She raised her head, took a deep breath and sniffed eagerly at the hot air, feeling like one of the kids on the old 'Bisto' billboards. Yes – it was still there, all around her. The Ibiza smell! – a pungent aroma, which never failed to fill her with excitement and nostalgia.

She had often tried to explain the island scent – and the emotions it aroused – to friends who had never visited what had become her Mediterranean paradise. As pervasive as that mixture of garlic, perfume and perspiration, which assaults every passenger on the French metro, the Ibiza scent was something different again. It encompassed delicious culinary odours; the heady perfumes of honeysuckle, jasmine and mimosa; the tangy scent of the sea; the fragrance of a million pines and the rosemary and thyme which covered the island's hills.

She linked arms with Peter as they started across the hot tarmac towards the airport building, searching his face to see if he remembered as well. Their faces widened in smiles, as they spoke the words simultaneously.

"The Ibiza smell!"

He stopped there and then, lifted her high into the air, whirling her round until she felt quite dizzy.

"Stop it, Peter!" she said, loving every minute. "Everyone can see us – they'll think we're quite mad!"

He dropped her gently to her feet.

"Sorry, Mrs Radcliffe – it was the old smell that did it – sends me potty, you know."

She burst out laughing. Peter could always make her laugh. She'd been married nearly two years to her tall blond husband, but still felt the magic of their first days together – the physical magnetism, their unusual closeness of thought and spontaneity of affection. Peter was good for her, anticipating her moods and needs, lifting her spirits with his good humour, never letting her get too bogged down with her responsibilities at work. He adored their daughter Kate and beneath the fun and lightness, there was a solidity and strength in her husband which she knew she could always rely upon.

How lucky she was! She grabbed his arm and they half-ran across to the airport building.

"Look, Sam, nothing's changed." He squeezed her hand. "And there's Pepe! I knew he wouldn't let us down." Pepe, their general factotum, kept a watchful eye on the family villa when they were away from the island.

She glanced across to the airport gate and spotted the small dark, rather stocky Ibicenco, beaming and waving to them from the side of an old cart-wheel built into the white stucco wall. Waving happily back, she gazed round her, drinking in the scene, appreciating once again why this airport was reputed to be one of the most beautiful in the world. Most international airports, austere and clinical, gave no real indication of their geographical location. Ibiza airport shouted its island history and heritage.

She gazed fondly at the low white walls and dark sevina wood beams, the adorning water wheels, wine presses and cartwheels – all redolent of a peasant culture which had farmed its rich red soil and terraced hillsides for generations.

The vibrant colours of blazing geraniums and purple bougainvillea contrasted brilliantly against gleaming-white patio walls. Ancient anforas, paintings and ceramics reflected the ancient culture of a host of invaders over the centuries – Greeks, Romans, Carthaginians, Moors, and of course, the Spanish themselves.

Most of all, the airport gave evidence of an even more recent invasion – that of the international tourist. It teemed with foreign visitors!

They greeted Pepe and strolled into the airport lounge. Peter gazed around him at the now familiar bustle, his dark-brown eyes sparkling with amusement. "Gosh, Pep, how things change! Remember the airport as it used to be? – just a dusty landing strip and a wooden hut!"

Pepe's weatherworn face lit up. He loved to reminisce, especially about his native Ibiza.

"*Sí, sí*, I remember. And not so many years before, we had only the ferry boats to join us with the outside world."

"I came on the ferry, the first time I visited the island with my parents," recalled Sam. "Archaic, but very romantic!" She nudged Pepe. "Did Peter ever tell you about his first arrival at the old airport?"

The Ibicenco shook his head, looked enquiringly at Peter, who raised his brown eyes in mock bafflement.

"You can't have forgotten, darling," she teased, turning to Pepe to explain. "He walked twenty yards from the plane, straight into the wooden hut and ordered a drink. Before his luggage was dumped outside the hut, the barman had treated him to at least another four 'on the house'. He left the airport completely sloshed!"

"Never tell your wife your drinking stories!" laughed Peter. "Unfortunately the barmen aren't so generous now."

Pepe grinned, revealing two dazzling gold teeth. "I remember that barman. He liked very much to give visitors samples of the local *hierbas.*"

"Well, I certainly got hooked on it," admitted Peter, "and Sam doesn't do so badly, when I can wean her off the vino and gin-and-tonics. The first time I met her, she suffered such a hangover she could only drink orange-juice for the next twenty-four hours." He winked. "Remember, Sam?"

"You make me sound a complete alcoholic. In any case, you were just as bad!" She gave a wide grin. "Mind you, at this moment, I'd love an ice-cold gin-and-tonic – with a healthy slice of lemon, of course!"

Pepe pounced on the suggestion.

"And a *coñac* for me, please. Chop-chop!"

She smiled and winked at Peter as he ordered the drinks, enjoying Pepe's quaint use of English. He absorbed foreign phrases like a sponge, then squeezed them out in subsequent conversations, invariably quite out of context. But she admired his quick retentive mind, knowing he had undergone few years of formal schooling. Like most locals, he had a remarkable ability to assimilate languages – his German and French were nearly as good as his English. He made a point of showing off his mastery of foreign colloquialisms whenever he could, his English peppered with phrases he had painstakingly picked up, but wasn't quite sure where to put down. She loved him for it!

"Bottoms up and down the hatch," chanted Pepe. He downed the rest of his brandy in one rapid gulp, but was careful to leave a little in the bottom of his glass. An example of his Spanish pride, she realised – a sign he could afford more. Glancing across to the baggage area, she spotted signs of activity. "I don't believe it. Here comes the luggage!"

They strolled across to collect their bags, Sam laughing in amazement when their cases were the first to appear, giving the lie to her eternal complaint that at whatever stage she checked in, her luggage was sure to be the last to materialise. Still, this was her lucky island, and for once her haven was renouncing its mañana complex, its habitual delays.

Since she and Peter had been making regular visits, they had suffered agonies of frustration over the locals' complaisant, but good-natured philosophy of mañana, whether it related to the repair of a burst water-pipe or payment of an overdue bill.

"I don't know which is worse," she once complained, "waiting weeks for the plumber to call, or having to use all my powers of persuasion to extract a bill from him – months after he's done the job."

Gathering their bags together, they headed out of the airport into the fierce sunlight. After the relative cool inside, the heat hit her with an almost tangible intensity. She could feel it penetrating her very bones, but for all its fierceness, it was a dry heat – just as she liked it!

The men piled the bags into the boot of Peter's old Seat and, with Pepe driving, they trundled off in the direction of San Antonio.

They planned to spend their whole fortnight's holiday at her parents' villa. A swimming pool had now been installed, but Sam was most looking forward to bathing in the translucent waters of the tiny twin coves of Cala Gracio, then stretching out on the clean white sand in the shade of the cool pines. She could scarcely wait!

She turned to smile at Peter in the back seat. He blew her a kiss.

* * * * * * *

Half-an-hour later the Seat reached the end of the heat-shimmering highway, started to climb the hill which gave access to the dirt-track leading to the villa.

Peter took advantage of his position in the back of the car to study his wife. Sam's dark-blonde hair was caught up in a pony-tail. She seemed younger, more vulnerable – not her usual capable self – more like a teenager than a twenty-six-year-old wife and mother. She gazed in rapt attention at the passing scenery, her slim sensitive face alight with happiness, her tawny eyes glowing with anticipation – like a young child embarking on a new adventure.

He knew she loved the island as much as he did. Here she would relax completely, become another person – her usual serious temperament changing to gaiety and lightheartedness.

He adored his wife, whatever her mood – enjoyed both facets of her personality. On one side he loved and respected her intelligence, her independence and competence, but he also relished what he nick-named her 'Ibiza moods', when she became frivolous and girlish again.

She must have felt his gaze on her. Turning and leaning across the seat, she kissed him tenderly on the cheek, then traced the outline of his blond beard with her finger.

"I've definitely decided I love your new beard. Very sexy!" She sighed. "Peter, I'm so happy. Do you feel the same?"

"You bet!" he said. "There's just one thing missing."

"I wish Kate were here!" They said it in unison, and laughed.

"Don't worry," he said, "next year we'll bring her. You needed a complete break as much as I did. She'll be perfectly happy with your parents."

"That's true – they'll spoil her rotten as usual. But I didn't think I'd start to miss her quite so quickly!"

"We'll have a barbecue tonight and you'll soon get back in the swing."

"Oh, Peter, isn't it wonderful to be back?" Her eyes shone with excitement beneath their thick velvet lashes. "I just know this is going to be the most fantastic holiday!"

As she said the words, he felt a strange sense of foreboding he couldn't explain. He shook his head to clear his mind. What was the matter with him? Life couldn't be more perfect. They had their whole holiday ahead of them!

* * * * * * *

The barbecue was a relaxed and intimate affair. At such short notice, they could only make contact with a few neighbouring friends. Telephones in Ibiza were not only a luxury, but in outlying areas, non-existent.

Sam hastily prepared a delicious crunchy salad with a tangy dressing and some garlic bread, then selected the potatoes for baking.

As she was drying her hands, Peter grabbed her from behind.

"That's enough, Sam. You've done your bit. Now, go and relax. I'm the expert with the barbecue, and I'm sure nobody will mind helping themselves to drinks. This is your night off."

"OK boss. It's all yours." She gave him a quick kiss on the cheek, then joined their friends on the terrace by the pool. Sinking back on a sun-bed, luxuriating in the balmy air of evening, she caught a delicious waft of honeysuckle in the passing breeze. This was the life!

* * * * * * *

When all the guests had left they sat quietly on the terrace enjoying the peace and tranquillity of the night. They were so close, she felt she could confide the silly premonitions which for some reason, had been building up inside her that evening.

"Peter," she whispered. "I'm so happy, I'm frightened."

He laughed.

"Now stop getting all serious, Sam. You're on holiday you know."

"Yes. It's wonderful – almost too good to be true. Most of my life has been the same, except that period when I nearly lost you. Everything has turned out so well, I don't feel I deserve it."

"You're really serious, aren't you Sam?"

"Oh yes. You see, other than losing my father, I've been fortunate all my life. Mother and Leslie doted on me and smothered me with love. I had one stupid complex – that I couldn't compete with my mother. Everybody adored her, while I was always shy and awkward with people. But at college and work I got over that. Then I was lucky enough to meet you. Now I have not only you, but Kate, the most perfect one-year-old in the world. I really don't deserve it all."

"Don't be a silly ass, Sam. Of course, you do. You've worked hard all your life – sometimes too hard. Everybody knows that. You deserve all you've got. What could possibly spoil it? As long as we have each other and Kate, it doesn't matter what happens."

"Yes, I suppose I'm being very silly. Love me, Peter. Make these ridiculous notions go away."

"With pleasure, my darling!" he said. "Remember, Sam, whatever happens to you, happens to me. We'll be together – always." He lifted her slim body into his arms and carried her towards the bedroom.

* * * * * * *

The days continued hot and sunny. She and Peter spent their first week quietly, lazing by the pool, swimming in any deserted little cove they could find. Then one morning Barry arrived!

She heard the powerful car from some distance away as it growled its way up the hill to the villa. She stared at Peter in puzzlement, wondering who it could be.

"It can't be for us," he said. "Far too powerful an engine. Perhaps it's going on to the Reynolds' house."

But the car stopped outside their villa and within seconds she recognised Barry's tuneful whistle. He appeared quite suddenly beside the pool like an overgrown genie, black eyes gleaming, a smile all over his face. He gave Sam a bear-like hug and thumped Peter on the back.

"Where have you been, you old devil?" asked Peter. "The place hasn't been the same without you."

Barry tweaked at Peter's beard.

"I like it," he said. "Nearly as good as mine! Now before I go into any explanations, come and see my latest acquisition."

He led them round to the front of the house. There in their drive stood a magnificent white Lotus.

"Isn't she beautiful?" he gloated, his dark eyes shining.

"Fantastic!" said Peter. "But can she cope with the rough roads of Ibiza? You could ruin the suspension, even rip out the sump."

Barry nodded.

"I'll only take her on the tarmac roads, use the Renault for the rough tracks. I get so fed up not having an open car on the island – the climate's perfect for it.

"She's beautiful, Barry," said Sam, her eyes sparkling. "Take great care of her."

He nodded.

"Hop in. I came to take you both for a spin."

"You said you wouldn't drive her on rough roads," teased Peter. "It isn't exactly the M1 up here to the villa!"

Sam chuckled seeing Barry's sheepish look.

"I did drive very carefully over the ruts," he said, defensively.

"I know. We could hear you coming for ages," said Peter, with a grin. "I thought it was a tank – that the invasion had started."

"She goes like a bird on a good surface," said Barry, his face lighting up with enthusiasm. "I've already done the San Antonio-Ibiza run in no time at all. I'm sure we could break the six-minute record – if the time and conditions were right.

"The six-minute record?" queried Sam.

"Yes," Peter explained. "John and Jenny Longford did the trip from San Antonio to Ibiza Town in only six minutes in their Jaguar. It was night-time of course, with nothing on the road."

"We'll have a go if we get a chance," said Barry. "But I'm only here for a few days before I have to go over to Mallorca. I'm helping a friend sail his boat over from Palma. You're welcome to use the Lotus while I'm away."

"Thanks, Barry. We'd love to," said Peter, his eyes gleaming.

"Are you ready for a short spin now?" asked Barry, obviously dying to show off the car's paces. "Then tomorrow we can go to Portinaitx for the day."

"Super!" said Sam. "We'll take a picnic."

"Don't bother. There's a great restaurant there – specialising in suckling pig. How does that sound?"

"Perfect!" she said. "But if we're going for a spin now, I'll need a T-shirt. I shan't be two ticks. I'll bring your shorts for you, darling."

"Thanks," said Peter. "Now let's go and inspect this fantastic machine!"

Sam ran excitedly inside to fetch their clothes. Before Barry's impromptu arrival, she had been planning to tell Peter some unexpected news. Still, the spin in the Lotus would be great fun. Her news could wait till later, when she had Peter all to herself.

Chapter 29

Sam hugged her secret to her all day. After their spin in the car, Barry spent the rest of the afternoon with them, then left early in the evening for what he explained would be a 'heavy date'.

Sam and Peter grinned at each other. Perhaps Barry had at last come under the spell of some femme fatale. They decided to have a quiet evening at the Miramar, an attractive restaurant in the heart of San Antonio specialising in French and Belgian cuisine. It would be a tempting change from the grills and barbecues they had recently been enjoying. Her mouth began to water at the thought of escargot, pepper steak and crepes suzettes. A candlelight dinner at the Miramar would be the ideal opportunity to disclose her secret to Peter.

During the early part of the meal, dying to tell Peter her news she could scarcely contain herself, but decided to wait until they'd settled into their coffee and brandy.

She couldn't fool Peter so easily. He quickly spotted her pent up excitement. They had only just started on the steaks when he sat back in his chair and eyed her speculatively.

"Come on then, Sam. Out with it."

She looked at him in mock surprise.

"Out with what?" she questioned, smiling sweetly.

"Whatever you've got up your sleeve. You can't fool me. Ever since we sat down you've been like a Cheshire cat confronted with a saucer of cream. In fact you've been a bit twitchy all day. What are you up to?"

"Nothing much," she said, munching on the steak, determined to keep him in suspense a little longer. "In fact I didn't plan to tell you till we got to the coffee stage."

"That's sounds ominous," he groaned. "You must be trying to butter me up. What are you planning, Sam? A new house?"

"Well, it might come to that," she said, enigmatically.

"A new job?"

"Wrong!"

He pulled at his golden beard. "Come on, Sam, the suspense is ruining my steak!"

"I'm not one-hundred-per-cent sure ... but nearly ... She looked at him coyly, watched his expression change as understanding suddenly dawned.

"Do you mean ...?"

She nodded her head emphatically.

"Sam, I don't believe it!" he said in amazement. "Another baby, so soon."

"Isn't it wonderful? Aren't you thrilled?"

"Of course I am, but I still can't believe it. After Kate, I thought you said we should wait a while."

"Yes, I know. But the more I got to thinking, the more I thought it better to get this child-bearing over once and for all. You did say you wanted at least two.

While we're going through the fun and trauma of one, we might as well go the whole hog."

"But what about your career?"

"I'd already decided I wanted to spend more time with Kate, especially while she's little. Don't worry. I'll go back to work when the two of them are in school."

"In your line of business, Sam, that won't be so easy. A few months' leave is one thing. Four or five years is something else. Yours is a fast-changing, competitive business – you'll be way out of date. You won't be able to pick up where you left off."

"That's why I married a rich man," she teased. "Don't worry Peter, I'm sure I'll always be able to get a good job. Perhaps not quite the whirlwind career I've had to date – but that won't worry me too much."

He gazed at her, fondly. "Are you sure you mean that, darling? I know how important your work is to you."

"I shall have more than my hands full the next few years with my family. Golly. I'm beginning to sound just like mother!"

"That can't be a bad thing," laughed Peter. "I adore my mother-in-law."

"Everybody does," said Sam simply. "Before I met you I used to envy her charm, her easy relationships with people especially my father and step-father. I never dreamt I could inspire the kind of love and support you've given me."

Peter let out a guffaw of laughter.

"There speaks a girl who took London by storm, littered the world with broken hearts and won mine in a matter of minutes! Sam – you're a case. Will you never acknowledge your own capabilities?"

She blushed.

"I suppose I've always been a little lacking in confidence ... that's why I can never really believe my luck, why I have to keep trying."

Peter's good-natured face broke into a wide grin.

"In actual fact, my darling, you have the edge on your mother as far as our relationship is concerned."

She stared at him, wondering what on earth he meant. "Mother and Dad have been married twenty-six years. Theirs is a fairy-tale marriage."

"I'm not so sure. Damn it! We've been talking so much my steak's gone cold."

"What do you mean, Peter?" she asked, anxiously. Did he know something about her parents she didn't?

"Oh, don't get me wrong. They both love each very much and they have a tremendous understanding."

"So what's the problem?" she said, relieved.

"Well since we've been married, I've talked a lot with Cathy. I'm sure she believes she's still in love with your real father – even though he's been dead for yonks. She's never said anything, of course. It's just a feeling I have."

Sam was stunned.

"But she adores Leslie."

"Of course she does. She just doesn't realise how much. She still has this romantic memory of your father, and of course, over time, that has probably become more glamorised."

Sam shook her head.

"I never considered it before. I know she doted on my father – he was very attractive and heroic. But she seems so obviously devoted to Leslie, I never thought anymore about it."

"Perhaps I'm wrong. It's just a feeling."

"Poor Leslie," she said, her heart going out to her adored step-father, remembering her own obsession as a girl with her father's memory. Did her mother still hanker after her glamorous first husband?

"Oh, Leslie's OK" said Peter, confidently. "Now let's get on with this fabulous steak. In view of your wonderful news, I think champagne's in order with the dessert!"

"Champers it is!" she agreed, "but just one glass for me. I have to take good care of our future son. I'm sure the baby will be a boy! Don't let me forget to call mother with the good news as soon as we get home. She'll be thrilled to bits!"

* * * * * * *

Barry picked them up early the next morning. They all squeezed into the car and the Lotus set off with a throaty roar. They headed to the north of the island, making the most of the good roads. Soon they were high above the coast on the narrow winding road to Portinaitx. Stopping for a delightful swim in the turquoise waters of the tiny bays, they later enjoyed a delicious lunch in a restaurant with panoramic views across the hills and coastline.

In the soft golden light of late afternoon they drove along the rugged coast to Cala San Vicente, then south again, this time via the picturesque village of Santa Eulalia.

"I'm off to Palma tomorrow – on the early morning plane," Barry told them as they headed home. "If you'd like to drop me at my villa, you can take the car – look after her for a few days. I've got a taxi coming for me in the morning."

"Don't be silly," said Peter. "We'll give you a lift to the airport."

"Thanks," said Barry. "I'd like that. But do hang on to the car. And don't forget. Have a try at the San Antonio-Ibiza record if you get the chance!"

"We will!" said Peter and Sam, simultaneously. They grinned at each other.

"Talk about like minds ..." said Barry.

* * * * * * *

"Hurry up, Sam, love," called Peter. "We'll be late."

"I'll be right down." She quickly finished her simple make-up with a glowing pink lipstick. One thing about a tan, she thought, it saves an awful lot of time making-up – a dash of lipstick and a brush of mascara, and you're there! She gazed at her reflection in the mirror. Not bad, she thought. Her dark blonde hair, streaked platinum by the sun, set off her golden tan to perfection. Her cheeks were flushed from the sun; her whole face radiant and glowing. A combination of motherhood and plenty of sunshine, she thought contentedly. Plus lots of plain happiness.

She hurried down to Peter.

"I'm all set!"

"You look super!" he said proudly.

"What time are we meeting Jane and Bill?" she asked, looking forward to seeing Peter's cousin and her new husband, Bill Reynolds. It was over a year since they'd spent any time together.

"The table's booked for eighty-thirty to nine, but we're meeting for a quick drink first in the Montesol. We want to try this new restaurant up in the Old Town."

"Oh yes – I've been recommended the blinis," said Sam, dreamily. "and there's lobster thermidor and ...."

"Stop dreaming about the food again," laughed Peter. "We'll be late!"

"No we won't. Don't forget, we're using the Lotus, not the Seat."

"Good job, too, with a slow coach of a wife like you!"

She dug him in the ribs with her elbow.

"Race you to the car," she said.

The Montesol Hotel, where they met Jane and Bill Reynolds, was situated in the centre of Ibiza Town. Sitting on the outside terrace they sipped long cooling drinks, watched the bustling night scene with its colourful fashions. Later making their way towards the new restaurant, they strolled lazily through the narrow streets, up through the ramparts and main gates into Dalt Vila, the old fortified part of the town.

Sam adored the new restaurant on sight. Situated in a small cobbled square within the old ramparts, its ancient stone walls oozed atmosphere. The setting was elegantly simple. They dined outside by candlelight, the candlesticks overflowing with melted wax producing grotto-like formations of waxen stalactites. The wine, served in huge balloon-shaped glasses, encouraged frequent topping-up by Jane and Bill, who would be walking back to their yacht. Strains of Mozart wafted softly in the background. Sam felt so happy, she couldn't stop smiling and squeezing Peter's hand.

Jane and Bill were also in vivacious form. They chatted together for hours over dinner, then strolled down the cobbled streets to the fisherman's quarter in the harbour – an area Sam loved. Wandering slowly along the front she was captivated by the life and colour, the eccentric fashions of the cosmopolitan port area. The water-front cafés were doing a bustling trade. On the quay towered the huge white form of the overnight ferry boat.

"The Barcelona boat! She's just about to leave," enthused Sam. "Let's watch her going out."

In the noisy animated scene, passengers lined the railings of the boat throwing colourful streamers to their friends on the quay. As the boat glided majestically from its mooring, the streamers stretched, trailing precariously across the widening gap of inky water.

She turned to Jane.

"You realise what the streamers are, don't you?"

Jane's impish green eyes twinkled with merriment. "My goodness, you're right! They're coloured loo rolls!"

"Yes – it's a tradition. If you can stream the whole roll before it breaks, between you and the person on the quay – you'll definitely come back again to Ibiza. But now the island's become more sophisticated the loo rolls come with perforations and they break apart much more easily." She gave Peter a conspiratory smile. "So we always go to a little shop at the back, where you can still buy the unperforated rolls."

There were cheers and shouts as the last streamers broke their tenuous links with the shore. Sam found she had tears in her eyes.

"How about coffee and liqueurs at Clive's Bar?" suggested Peter. "Then we can go on to Lola's for a dance." He led them into the tiny cave-like bar, and they all peered curiously at the colourful clientele.

"My goodness, there's 'unwanted Tom'", said Sam, nudging Peter. "I wonder how long he'll last this time." 'Unwanted Tom', renowned in his more drunken and violent moods for his ability to empty a bar in a matter of seconds, was hardly a sought-after client, hence the nickname! Tonight, however, he seemed relatively calm and mellow. Sam knew the barmen in the port would tolerate him in these moods, but woe-betide him, the moment his demeanour changed for the worse.

"And there's the artist Ernesto," said Peter to the Reynolds. "He's an incredible character and very talented!"

"Why does Ibiza attract so many writers and artists?" asked Bill Reynolds.

"I think it's the easy-going cosmopolitan atmosphere of the place," explained Peter, "the free spirit, tolerance – even love – of eccentricity and individualism. Of course, the artists all rave about the marvellous light and colours and the wealth of subject matter."

Absorbed by the scene around them, Peter and the Reynolds sipped at liqueurs while Sam kept to fruit juice. Seeing that Jane and Bill were enjoying the lively atmosphere as much as they were, she winked across at Peter.

"I suppose we might as well make a night of it!"

Peter grinned his agreement.

"Are you two game to go on to Lola's?"

Jane and Bill nodded enthusiastically and they all strolled off in the direction of the Club.

It was nearly three o'clock when, flushed and perspiring, they left the hot dusky interior of Lola's. Jane glanced down at her watch.

"We'd better be getting home, Bill. We've a busy morning tomorrow ... I mean today."

"I can't believe it's so late," said Sam. "The evening's flown by. But I don't feel at all tired."

"You will tomorrow," said Peter.

They said goodnight to the Reynolds and headed back to the car. Sam had rarely felt so exhilarated. Climbing into the open vehicle, she gazed up at the magnificent night sky. The balmy Mediterranean air was quite still, the sky clear and bright, sparkling with stars.

Leaving the narrow streets of Ibiza Town, they were soon speeding along the highway to San Antonio. Sam's sun-streaked hair streamed in the wind, her eyes gleamed with excitement. She could feel her cheeks glowing with excitement, sensed the magic of the night had infected them both. She gazed up at the glittering night sky. Fantastic! So many stars – so bright and clear. She felt she could reach out and touch them.

A sudden awesome feeling of splendid isolation enveloped her, as if the two of them were completely alone in the world, speeding towards some unknown destiny. She turned eagerly to Peter, shouted to him above the roar of the engine.

"Darling, there's not a soul about. Let's try to beat the six-minute record!"

He grinned, his teeth reflecting luminous white in the darkness.

"What about the timing?"

"I already set my stop-watch at the starting point – it's become a habit." She gave him a mischievous, sidelong glance.

She saw his foot was already to the floor, but the Lotus seemed to find some extra source of energy from their excitement and the sparkling night air. It sped even faster down the gleaming stretch of road.

"Don't forget the bend at San Rafael!" she yelled, suddenly remembering the only bend on the otherwise straight stretch of road.

"Don't worry, I know exactly the speed I can take that one."

The car flashed on, slowed marginally as it approached the sharp San Rafael bend. Nearly round, Peter put his foot to the floor again, accelerating smoothly out of the turn.

A sharp explosive crack resounded like rifle-shot through the still night air, swiftly followed by a fierce hiss. The car slewed wildly across the road. White-faced but deadly calm, he fought to regain control.

"A front-wheel blowout!" he yelled to Sam. "Hold tight!"

Terror seized her – she suddenly felt icy cold. A thousand thoughts rushed through her brain. This couldn't be happening to her, to Peter, to the baby inside her!

He struggled frantically to rectify the steering, but the car continued to lunge to the left. She sat still as a statue, completely mesmerised by the speed of events, too terrified to utter a sound. Her sun-tanned face blanched with fear.

The Lotus careered on down the road, bounced along a dry-stone wall. The slim dark shadow of a telegraph pole loomed suddenly in front of the bonnet. Sam managed a fierce squeeze of Peter's hand before everything went very black.

Her scream pierced even the harsh strident sound of shattering metal and breaking glass. Its ghastly echo continued to reverberate through the still starlit Ibiza night.

Then ... silence once again.

* * * * * * *

It was six o'clock in the morning when the shrill ring of the telephone awakened Cathy and Leslie in the bedroom of their Oxford home.

Cathy stirred sleepily, saw Leslie pick up the receiver. Who on earth could be calling at this early hour? Then Leslie's face seemed to crumple up and turn ashen. She heard his stricken groan:

"Sam, Peter – both of them? They can't be dead! It's not possible!"

A scream rose uncontrollably from inside her, but no sound came out. She sat upright in bed, stared at him in horror, wanting to grab hold the phone, smash it on the ground. Instead she hid her head in her ice-cold, trembling hands and started to rock to and fro. Leslie continued talking, his voice now more controlled, but she tried not to hear his words. Sam and Peter – they couldn't be dead! This wasn't really happening, it was all a dreadful nightmare. In a moment she would wake up.

She felt Leslie's arms around her, his voice soft and soothing.

"Cathy – I'm so sorry – darling I'm so sorry ..." His voice broke with emotion.

She wanted to clasp her hands to her ears, refuse to listen anymore. Gradually, as he gently rocked her in his arms, she fought back the panic and nausea welling up inside her.

"They're not really dead, are they Leslie?" she managed to whisper, still in shock, still refusing to believe. "Tell me it's all some dreadful mistake."

He shook his head, his eyes full of pain.

"That was Bill Reynolds on the phone. It was a car accident ..they died instantly. There was no suffering, my love."

"Oh God. I just can't believe it!" she wailed, trying to control the screams and hysteria which threatened to engulf her.

"Sam, my darling Sam, and dear Peter. They were both so young, so beautiful – their whole lives before them. It's not fair! And Kate – she's only a year old and both her parents dead!" Suddenly the tears came and she started to sob uncontrollably.

"Yes, cry my love, cry We both need to cry. If not, we'll go crazy."

He held her in his arms and together they wept.

* * * * * * *

First my father, then Jimmy, now my daughter, thought Cathy in despair during the black days following the accident. They've all been torn from me, all much too young.

But a little voice chided within her. Don't be ungrateful. You still have Leslie and the twins who love you dearly, not to mention darling little Kate.

Cathy never knew how she got through the next few weeks. With the death of Sam it seemed as if one part of her life had been cut off completely. Sam had been her last link with Jimmy. Her stomach churned as the memories flooded over her: Sam as a beautiful baby, her presence relieving some of the pain of the loss of her beloved husband. In looks and mannerisms her daughter had reminded her so much of her first and only real love.

Then recollections of Sam growing up, successful at school and college, triumphant in her career. How proud both she and Leslie had been of her and all she had achieved. Then memories of those glorious days after Sam's marriage to

Peter, both of them so happy and fulfilled, culminating with the arrival of Kate. Finally, and bitterly aware of the irony of the situation, she recalled their last conversation together on the telephone shortly before the accident, when Sam had confided that another baby was on the way. They had both been so thrilled. Cathy had not mentioned it to Leslie at the time. Sam had wanted to tell him the good news herself when they got back to England. Now, Cathy decided, she would probably never reveal Sam's pregnancy to Leslie. It would only upset him more.

Dear Leslie! As usual he had been a tower of strength supporting and comforting her through the tragic days, just as he had done after her father had died, when her flat had been bombed, when Jimmy was shot down. This time it must have been even more difficult for him. He had adored Sam as much as she, had known her from the minute she was born, raised her as his own child.

In her darkest hour after the funeral, he had held her in his arms, comforted her in the only way he could.

"Remember what Sam and Peter always said, my dearest, that they never ever wanted to be parted. They died together, gloriously happy in their love. It's how they would have wanted it."

In her heart she knew he was right. But that same heart screamed out: Jimmy, Sam – why did I have to lose you both?

PART FOUR

GILES

My only love sprung from my only hate!

William Shakespeare

Oh, when I was in love with you.
Then I was clean and brave.

A.E. Housman

Chapter 30

Long Island, New York. September 1975

Giles Pritchard swung his tennis racquet in a high arc above his head, made scorching contact with the ball. Slamming a powerful service into the right-hand court he raced to the net. His opponent managed a short weak return. Giles hammered the volley, but in his eagerness the ball clipped the net, losing its impact and dropping short the other side. With a brave lunge his rival reached the ball, sent up a high overhead lob. Determined this time to make certain of the point, Giles smashed with all his muscular might, aiming directly at the other player. The ball struck the boy's face with such force he was thrown to the ground.

Giles rushed to the net, faking concern. His opponent lay still on the ground, groaning and clutching at his right eye.

"I'm sure sorry, sir," said Giles, looking up the umpire. "I was aiming for his feet." He ran to the other side of the net, helped the boy to his feet.

His opponent removed his hand from the battered eye.

"I can't see," he moaned. The eye was already closed and swollen, the flesh around it red and puffy. The boy's coach appeared on the court and started to examine the injury. He turned ruefully to the umpire.

"I'm sorry – my boy will have to retire."

Giles hung his head in shame, but inside he felt smug. His opponent deserved it. Giles would have beaten him in any case. He was sure of that. The boy lacked his own power and athleticism, but he was a good touch player. He had made Giles look a fool with a couple of superb drop shops.

"I don't know how it happened, sir," he repeated apologetically. "I was going for the feet."

"Don't worry, son," said the coach. "Accidents will happen. You obviously didn't mean it. I have to admit you've sure got a vicious forehand."

"Thank you, sir," said Giles, brightening. He knew the coach was well-connected, always looking for fresh talent. He wished for the hundredth time he'd taken up tennis at an earlier age. He had a natural talent, as he had for all sports. He'd probably ignored tennis because of his father. His father loved the game so Giles had deliberately avoided it; until he happened to pick up a racquet with some friends one day. Then he'd become hooked. But it was probably too late – you had to make it young these days.

The coach eyed him keenly.

"See me at the end of the afternoon. We can have a talk."

Giles nodded enthusiastically, giving the coach the benefit of his infectious smile. The grin changed to a smirk as he watched the two of them walk off the court, the coach supporting the still-dazed and injured boy under one shoulder. Only two more rounds to go!

* * * * * * *

He reached the final, but then lost in straight sets. When he met the coach in the dressing rooms after the tournament he was feeling angry and depressed.

"How old are you, boy?" asked the coach, eyeing him up and down.

"Seventeen, sir," he said, despondently.

"Don't worry about losing today, son. You're big and strong for your age. You've a lithe body with a good natural eye for a ball. More important – you're enthusiastic and determined, you really wanna win! I can see that with every stroke."

"Yes, sir!" said Giles, his spirits rising. "I see no point in playing, if it isn't to win."

The coach nodded.

"You need to think more about your shots, plan your tactics, find your opponent's weakness. It's no good going out there and just hammering the ball. Your strokes need sharpening up. How long have you been playing?"

"Eighteen months, sir."

The coach looked suitably impressed.

"You could make it, but it would require complete dedication and all your time; no other interests, no distractions. What are your school plans?"

"I'm afraid I just missed making the Ivy League, sir," said Giles, modestly brushing back his dark curly hair, not adding that though his high-school grades had been good enough, the necessary references for the prestige universities hadn't been forthcoming from any of the educational establishments he'd attended. "Right now, I'm at a bit of a loose end," he said, hoping the coach wouldn't go into details.

"Any other sporting interests?"

"Snow-skiing, water-skiing, sailing, squash."

"You'll have no time for those, especially the squash. Too much wrist. It'll ruin your tennis game. What about team sports?"

"I've played them all. Now I prefer to get out there on my own." He flashed his blue-green eyes determinedly.

The coach smiled.

"Well – think about it, boy. It will take time and money, of course." He looked at Giles quizzically. "How are you fixed on the dollar stakes?"

"I'm OK, sir. I can get by."

"Good! Contact me when you've decided. But think about it carefully. I'm not prepared to waste my time on anyone who isn't completely committed. Another thing ... To be good, you've gotta be brave."

"I'm not afraid of anything, sir."

The coach looked at him thoughtfully.

"No, I don't believe you are. Think about it. Let me know within twenty-four hours."

"Yes, sir!" A bossy pants, he thought to himself. Still it was worth kow-towing for a while – if it got him what he wanted. Then the coach would have to go. He had learned the hard way over the years that it was best to go along with authority when necessary, make use of his beguiling manner, his personal magnetism to get what he wanted. Then, like the worm, he would turn.

* * * * * * *

Driving home he gave careful consideration to the coach's words. A career in tennis was a tempting prospect. He loved the game, enjoyed the outdoor life in general; but he wondered if the requirements would be too demanding. Sport to him had always been easy and entertaining, never requiring vast amounts of practice or personal sacrifice. But he knew the coach was right. If he wanted to make it to the top, it couldn't be done in his usual casual way – it would need considerable time, effort and hard work. Was that what he wanted?

What if he didn't make it? There was no guarantee he would. He shuddered. He couldn't face failure. Better not to try, than to fail. That would be one more nail in his coffin as far as his father was concerned.

He felt sure his father would be thrilled if he became involved in his favourite sport. To date he didn't even know Giles played the game. He had entered the tournament on impulse, not even telling any of his friends – just in case he lost. He'd staked a lot on winning, if only to present his father with the trophy – see the surprise on his face. It would be the first time he'd ever bettered his father at anything.

But what if the training got boring, restricting – too much like hard work? His father believed in effort and dedication – whatever the cost. Stiff upper lip and all that. His damned British upbringing, of course! If Giles didn't stick at it, there would be more trouble.

And what about the financial returns? There was hardly any big money in tennis, unless you made it right to the top. He desperately wanted to make money, big money – to become financially independent of his parents. He loved money and what it bought. Curse his father for deliberately keeping him short! Thank God his mother helped out from time to time, though Dad would be furious if he knew.

By the time he reached the long drive to the house, he'd already made up his mind. Tennis was out – at least except for fun. There must be an easier way to make a fortune!

* * * * * * *

He lay on his bed staring at the ceiling. The telephone buzzed irritatingly at his bedside.

Lazily he lifted the receiver.

A shrill female voice roused him from his reveries.

"Giles, it's me, Tracy!"

"Tracy! Goddamn it! What d'you want now? I said I'd call you. Can't you give a fella a break?

Her voice broke into sobs.

"Giles! I've got to see you!"

"I'm busy, Tracy. I'll call you."

"Don't ring off, Giles! Please ..."

He sensed the panic in her voice, felt suddenly apprehensive.

"What's the matter, Tracy?"

"I can't speak to you over the phone." She started to weep hysterically. "I must see you, Giles ... Could you come over? Mom and Dad are going out at seven-thirty."

"I'll be there at eight," he said shortly and rang off.

He cursed loudly, his eyes flashing angrily. Damn Tracy! Why was she in such a state? She wasn't the sort to weep and wail like most of the others, just because he didn't call. A good-time girl, she'd had no qualms about jumping into bed with him. Women! They were all the same. They loved every minute of it, then screamed like stuck pigs if you didn't spend every minute at their beck and call.

He showered and changed, loped down the stairs two at a time, calling to his mother as he left.

"I'll be out for dinner."

"Giles! You promised you would stay in tonight," she said, reproachfully.

That was true. He'd hoped to win the tournament that day, present his father with the trophy.

"Sorry, something came up."

His mother sighed, resignedly.

"Don't be too late, darling ..." Her husky French voice showed signs of despair.

Why did she always make him feel so guilty? He felt sure she wasn't such an innocent herself. He knew there had been other men, even if Dad didn't ...

He slammed the door and strode out to the garage.

At eight on the dot he reached Tracy's house – a beautiful colonial-style mansion. Tracy opened the door before he'd even rung the bell. She must have been waiting, seen him coming up the drive. Her eyes were red, her face gaunt and tear-streaked, her normally shiny dark hair hanging dishevelled round her shoulders. Seeing his expression change to dismay, she stared down at the ground.

"God, Tracy. You look terrible!"

She started to cry again.

"Did your parents see you in this state?"

"No," she stammered through the tears. "I called to them when they left, said I had a headache." She made a pathetic attempt at drying her eyes, ran nervous fingers through her hair. "Come through, Giles. There's chicken in the ice-box."

"Forget the chicken," he said impatiently. "What's all this about?"

She broke down again.

"Giles, I'm pregnant!"

"I should have known – it had to be that!" he said, furious. "God, are you sure, Tracy? I thought you were on the pill. What went wrong?"

"Sometimes I forgot to take it," she said, biting her nails. "But I always tried to make it up. I've never been caught before."

"You're an idiot," he said unrelentingly. "You can't just make it up. How could you be so fucking stupid!"

Her tears turned to anger.

"It's your fault as much as mine, Giles! It takes two to tango, but I'm the one left with the problem." Her voice had become challenging and defiant. "What are you going to do about it?"

"How do I know it's mine?" he sneered.

"You don't. But I never lie, Giles – you know that. So does everyone else."

That was true. Tracy might be stupid but she never lied. He had to believe her, damn it!

"Then you'll have to get rid of it," he growled, overcome with fury at being trapped. How could she have been so naive and stupid!

"Is that all you've got to say?"

"What else did you expect?"

"We could get married," she said, slyly. "I've always fancied you, Giles."

"Marriage! You must be mad! I'm still only seventeen, Tracy. You're eighteen."

Her blue eyes flashed. "You don't have to be so adamant!" she yelled. "Lots of kids marry young. There's plenty of boys who'd jump at the chance to get me. I'm pretty good-looking, wealthy parents ..."

"Then pick one of them," he said angrily. "I've no intention of getting married and you'd be a fool to even consider it. Do you wanna waste your youth on some silly little brat?"

She sank into a chair, her voice suddenly quiet.

"Giles, it's our baby you're talking about ... I can't believe it. You're not human!"

He stared at her, his eyes narrowed. Who the hell did she think she was, talking to him like that?

"I meant what I said, Tracy. You'll have to get rid of it!"

She glared back at him, her eyes blazing. Her tone changed and she spat out the next words.

"All that apparent charm and charisma! Underneath it all you're a perfect rotter, Giles Pritchard! What a fool I've been. You don't have a decent feeling in you!" She stood up – white with fury – as if to strike him.

"Just get rid of that baby," he told her coldly, "as soon as possible."

She flopped back into the chair, defeated.

"OK" she said, her voice suddenly flat and unemotional. "You fix it. Just let me know when." She turned on her heels. "Let yourself out, Giles. I never want to see you again."

She walked out of the room, slamming the door behind her.

He drove home in a fury. Another fucking abortion! Where was he to get the money this time? The first time it had been that little tramp, Maureen. Mind you, he couldn't expect her to know any better. Ever since then he'd stuck with girls of his own class. But it seemed they were all the same. What God-awful luck! He'd have to go to that cheating moneylender again!

Furious, he put his foot down hard on the gas, gave vent to his anger in his driving. His whole evening was messed up! Now what could he do? He was fed up with the local girls. He'd blown dinner at home.

Wait a minute. That girl he'd met at the tennis. What was her name? Ah, yes – Karen. Great-looking, sexy and she'd really given him the eye. He might just give her a call. His lips twisted in a sardonic smile. It could just turn out to be a good evening after all.

Chapter 31

Two weeks after Tracy's abortion, his father called him into his study. It had to be bad news. Dad never summoned him this way, unless there was trouble brewing. He walked jauntily into the room, determined not to show his nervousness.

Jimmy's lean, still-handsome face flashed dark with rage.

"Sit down, Giles," he said coldly, motioning with his hand to the chair in front of his desk.

Who the hell does he think I am? thought Giles – some ten-year-old, snotty-nosed kid?

Jimmy smoothed back his silver-grey hair, stared hard at him for several minutes without saying a word.

He stared back, defiantly.

"I've just had Tracy Canning's father on the line." His hazel eyes glittered dangerously.

He couldn't prevent a start of surprise. Damn it! Tracy had ratted on him.

"You obviously know what I'm talking about," his father continued grimly. "I'm profoundly shocked. I just can't fathom you out, Giles. Getting a girl into trouble is one thing. I'm not condoning it, but things like that do happen. But why did neither of you tell your mother or me – or at least confide in Tracy's parents." He drummed his fingers on the mahogany desk-top. "It's the height of callous irresponsibility – cold-bloodedly arranging an abortion for a girl, without a word to anyone. Tracy's parents are distraught. Do you realise what you've done this time, Giles?"

"We didn't want to worry you," he said sullenly. Why was Dad taking it so hard? – he'd already paid through the nose for his mistake. "I took care of everything – there was no need for anyone to get upset. I suppose Tracy babbled."

Jimmy's face changed to thunder. He half-rose from his chair, as if to strike him. Giles flinched uncomfortably in his seat, not that he felt physically scared of his father. He was heavier, stronger than him any day. But he feared his own hot fury if Jimmy did dare touch him. He still needed him at the moment – he daren't push him too far.

His father drew in a deep breath.

"Tracy said nothing. But she wasn't so well afterwards. Were you aware of that? News of the abortion got back to her doctor through the medical grapevine." He shook his head despairingly. "But that's all irrelevant now. It's the principle I'm trying to get through to you!"

Giles remained silent. Receiving no response, Jimmy stared at him in exasperation.

"There's no reasoning with you, is there, Giles? You obviously have no concept of the depravity of your actions. What you did was completely amoral. How could you be so selfish, so insensitive?"

He looked down. He had to assume a degree of penitence this time, or goodness knows what might happen.

Jimmy was having none of it.

"I don't believe you're the slightest bit sorry, Giles. Worse still, you don't seem to consider you've done anything wrong." His face seemed to crumple and he suddenly looked years older. "What is it with you, son? You're lucky enough to have every natural advantage – a strong and handsome body, an excellent brain. You've had everything you've ever needed or wanted and the best education I could buy. Only your own bad behaviour and stupidity prevented you getting into a top college."

Still he said nothing. There was no arguing with his father in this sort of situation. He just hoped his allowance wouldn't be docked; he was heavily in debt with the moneylender.

Jimmy seemed to read his thoughts.

"I've been making further enquiries. It seems you're also heavily into debt – not for the first time." His voice hardened. "Listen to me carefully. I'm going to settle those debts – set you straight. I won't have my name dragged through the mud. But I promise you – this is the last time. If you don't change your ways, I'm afraid I shall have to take other measures."

Giles continued to look down, but inside heaved a sigh of relief.

"I mean it, Giles. Don't think you've got away with it scot-free. I want you to spend the next few days thinking hard about your future. Make up your mind what you want to do with your life. I'm not prepared to let you loaf around any longer."

He took a chance.

"Dad, I've already been thinking. I might try my luck abroad, work my way round the world and all that jazz."

"That's fine by me, Giles. It might be the best thing for you. But in the circumstances don't expect any financial help from me, and I mean it. You'll be on your own."

His heart sank. He'd certainly no intention of working his way around the world, that had been a figure of speech.

"I'll think about it, Dad," he said quietly.

"OK, son. We'll have another chat in a few days."

He walked dejectedly from the study. Damn it! What was he going to do now?

* * * * * * *

Later that night Jimmy was wondering the same thing. What could he do with Giles? His son had an excellent brain, a strong athletic body. Yet he never seemed to achieve his full potential. He was impatient and intolerant and given to vindictiveness when thwarted. Hence his dreadful treatment of this girl, his generally amoral attitude to life.

Even on the sports field his efforts were marred by an excessively aggressive approach, verging on the violent. There was a wildness, even savagery about the boy which Jimmy could never understand, let alone contend with.

Yet Giles had a powerful magnetism and charm which he could switch on at will – an indefinable charisma which led people to admire him, even when they half-feared him. His zest for life, his strength and determination and his apparent invincibility attracted others to him particularly among his contemporaries. His son was a complete enigma!

He wandered morosely into the bedroom, still brooding over their conversation. Monique lay on top of the bed, her arms behind her head. Obviously naked under an exquisite ivory silk robe, her figure, though a little fuller, retained its voluptuous appeal. She stared up at Jimmy, concern in her still-beautiful green eyes.

"It did not go well, darling – your talk with Giles?"

"It couldn't have been worse," he said flopping down beside her on the huge four-poster bed. "Monique, he worries me so. He wasn't at all sorry – didn't seem to realise he'd done anything wrong. How do you get through to somebody like that?"

"Don't worry so, James," she said, stroking his hair. "It is probably his age. All teenagers go through defiant, rebellious periods."

"It's not just that, Monique. There's something basically wrong with him – something bad inside him. It frightens me!"

He turned to her, stared earnestly into her eyes.

"Where did we go wrong? He has so much potential, so much going for him, but I know he's going to blow it. Somehow I feel it's all my own fault."

"Hush, my darling. Don't blame yourself. Giles has always been a wild one – ever since a baby. He is my son, yet even I recognise he is a demanding selfish boy. But he is beautiful, he is talented. Most important – he is a survivor!"

"I'm not so sure, Monique. I don't want to be melodramatic, but I sense within him the seeds of his own destruction."

He felt her involuntary shudder. She lay quiet for several moments before she eventually replied.

"No, James. I think I understand him better than you – he has a lot of me in him. Giles is not completely bad. One day he will see the light."

Jimmy hugged her to him, but his concern didn't leave him. We can't both be right, he thought, or can we?

* * * * * * *

Two days later Giles walked into his study, neatly dressed and smiling his winning smile. It's going to be all right, thought Jimmy. He's realised his mistakes.

"Do you have a spare moment, Dad?"

"Of course, son." He put down his pen.

"I've been thinking – you know, about what you said the other day."

"Yes?"

Giles grinned again.

202

"You're absolutely right, Dad. It's time I knuckled down to some hard work."

Jimmy smiled with relief.

"I'm glad you think so, really glad."

"I've got some great ideas," Giles carried on enthusiastically. "But I'd like your advice."

In this ebullient mood, he was hard to resist. Jimmy felt again the power and sheer animal magnetism his son could radiate. If only his talents could be properly channelled!

"I want to go into the business, Dad, your business – work my way up. I don't expect to go in as the boss's son, but the opportunity's obviously there. It'd be stupid not to take advantage of it!"

"What about the rest of your education, Giles? You're not eighteen yet."

He frowned.

"I don't fancy some tin-pot college, Dad, and I've blown it with the rest. In any case, it isn't necessary." He used his trump card. "After all ... you never went to College and it hasn't harmed you." His blue-green eyes gleamed as he saw the barb go home.

Jimmy couldn't help laughing.

"OK Giles. You win. We'll give you a try. You can always go on to college, do a business course at a later date if you change your mind."

"Thanks, Dad. Perhaps we could have a chat about it now – where I should start and when."

"Sure, Giles. But let's get one thing straight before we go any further. Don't expect any favours, any special treatment from me ..."

"I've already said I'm prepared to start at the bottom."

"Good, but there won't be any sudden rises to fame. You've got to earn your promotions. Don't worry – I'll place you with some good people. Then it'll be up to you. Stick at it Giles! Don't let me down. What I said the other day still holds good. This is your last chance."

"Don't worry, Dad." The boy's tone was sincere. "I've learned my lesson. I won't let you down."

Giles felt a moment of triumph. Why hadn't he thought about it before? His father's business, his father's empire! All the money in the world at his fingertips. Dad couldn't go on for ever – he was sixty already. Then it would be his – all his.

But he needed to get into the heart of it now, get established. He didn't want any fuddy-duddies telling him what to do when his father retired. He knew he was smart enough; he'd work hard for a while, get the necessary experience. Then when he'd gained control he could leave the work to the underlings, enjoy the good life. His father's work was boring and uninteresting – all that stupid PR and advertising, not to mention the building and real estate. Unfortunately that was where the money was. It would be worth a few years of effort. After that, he'd have them all just where he wanted them – his father included.

* * * * * * *

During the first three years Giles kept his promise. He knuckled down, working hard and efficiently. With his sharp brain he picked things up fast, exploiting his charm and charisma to the full. The rest of the staff were quickly drawn to him, particularly his own generation. Some of the older company members remained sceptical but Jimmy put this down to jealousy, fear even of Giles's influence over his father, for the safety of their jobs. He realised that despite his winning ways, the more perspicacious of his employees sensed a ruthlessness in Giles which his father had never displayed despite his astute, even hard-nosed commercialism.

Yet even these older members of staff showed a grudging admiration for Giles. They reminded Jimmy of his son's classmates at school. Even those who instinctively feared him, never ceased to admire his strength and energy.

Pleased with his son's enthusiasm and rapid progress and sensing in him a certain impatience, a need for some recognition of his achievements, Jimmy decided to take him into his confidence. That afternoon as they were discussing a project for the expansion of the Public Relations Groups, he raised the subject.

"Giles, I've never spoken to you before about long-term plans for the future. I didn't consider you mature or involved enough to be taken into my confidence. However ..." he smiled proudly at his son, "you've now apparently turned over a new leaf. I'm extremely happy with your progress. You seem well prepared and able to take on new responsibilities."

A broad smile spread across Giles's face.

"Thanks Dad. I wondered when you'd really start to trust me."

Jimmy looked at him sharply.

"Confidence has to be earned, Giles. Your previous record was scarcely conducive to winning my trust. However – as I said – that's all changed. I've decided to appoint you to the board of the PR companies ..."

"That's great, Dad!"

Jimmy held up his hand.

"But not until next year, when you turn twenty-one."

Giles's face fell.

"Not until I'm twenty-one? I thought that now I'd started to take over certain responsibilities ..."

"Be patient, Giles – let me finish." He smiled at him indulgently. "I shall be semi-retiring in less than two years. You will then have to take over many of my duties. I shall, of course, retain overall control but when you become twenty-eight – as long as you show yourself fit, you can assume control yourself." He paused. "In the event of my premature death the company stock will be held in trust for you, again until you are twenty-eight. Management of the companies will also remain in the hands of the Board until you reach that age.

"Twenty-eight!" choked Giles. "Dad, that's not fair. You're effectively tying my hands for years to come."

"That's right and with every good reason. Think about it, Giles. Even at twenty-eight, you'll be extremely young to be in control of such a large financial concern. I hope by then your highly-commendable energy and dynamism will be tempered by the necessary experience and a certain degree of prudency. In any case," he added wryly, "I'm not planning on dying quite so soon, so should you show your worth before you may be able to take over a certain amount of control at an earlier date."

"You think I'm too rash," said Giles truculently.

"Not at all. That's what youth's all about. I admire your fire and zest. But I also recognise the occasional need for caution and restraint. That comes with experience – knowing when to take the chance and when not to. With all the best intentions in the world, Giles, it's ten times easier to lose money than to make it." His eyes twinkled kindly. "In any case, you seem to forget what I said. The Board arrangement only applies should I die prematurely. All being well, I shall live to see you assume control well before you're twenty-eight. I certainly shan't hold you back. You can gradually assume a place on all the boards, including the Holding Company."

He stared expectantly at his son. Giles still didn't seem convinced. He fidgeted in his chair, his usual buoyancy and confidence no longer so apparent.

"Dad, you're handing over the responsibility without the rewards," he said agitatedly, but Jimmy also detected a hint of menace in the hard glitter of his aquamarine eyes.

"You've had rewards enough, son. And there'll be plenty more to come. You're already earning an incredibly high salary for your age; you have a life-style any young man would envy. Don't be too greedy."

"You still don't trust me." Giles eyed him challengingly. "That's what it comes down to, doesn't it?"

"No, Giles. Anyone in my position of responsibility would do exactly the same." He kept his tone firm and confident, but inside knew that in a way his son was right. Despite his incredible reformation, Jimmy still didn't trust him. An intuitive but indefinable apprehension constantly gnawed at his stomach.

Giles glared at him and stalked out of the office.

Jimmy shook his head, hoped he wasn't being unfair on the boy. He couldn't help it, but he still wasn't sure about him. Hopefully time would prove him wrong.

Chapter 32

Giles left his office in a fury, stumped to the car. The brandies he had downed after his conversation with his father hadn't helped lift his mood. How could he treat him this way after all the hard work and effort he'd put in during the last three years? He had worked at his apprenticeship more seriously than anything he'd ever done in his life before, conscientiously taking on more and more responsibilities. Still his father wouldn't yield.

As he got into the car another terrible thought crossed his mind. Would Jimmy really semi-retire in a couple of years and gradually hand everything over to him? His father loved his work – it was in his blood. He enjoyed every minute of it. He'd certainly be reluctant to relinquish, not only the pleasure it gave him, but the power he wielded. Giles felt sure of that. Who was to say how long he, Giles, was to remain in the wings waiting for his father to die or eventually decide to hand over power.

He had to admit he'd started to succumb himself to that same fascination his father had for the business world. He hated the ties of work, its more humdrum aspects; but the excitement and power involved in running a large commercial empire handling millions of dollars had started to get to him. He'd become so enthralled with the thrills of the business world, even his love-life had suffered. Not completely, of course. He certainly hadn't become a monk, and had no intention of doing so. But now he preferred to dally with one woman at a time, rather than play the field. The hunt, the juggling – they were all too time-consuming!

He smiled as he thought about his current lady-friend – Janey – a raven-haired beauty, small and petite, except for extravagant breasts. They had a date tonight! He licked his lips at the thought, increased his speed not wanting to arrive late.

Then his conversation with his father forced its way back into his mind. Hell! He couldn't face all those years ahead slaving away at someone else's beck and call. The thrills of the boardroom, policy making and power building were one thing. But the prospect of a dull office-bound future, spent as self-sacrificingly as the past few years, filled him with horror. If he couldn't be in charge there had to be another answer. He jammed his foot angrily to the floor.

Damn it! His fury and frustration had aroused him sexually. He had to see Janey, work out his passion on her lush and pliant body.

The night outside matched his present mood – pitch black and freezing cold. An icy drizzle started to play on the windscreen of the car. Irritated, he turned on the wipers, increased his speed. The streets of the city outskirts seemed deserted on such an inhospitable evening. He swung round the corner into the next block, felt the wheel shudder at the violence of the manoeuvre. The turn seemed sharper than he remembered, or perhaps it was just his extra speed tonight.

Without warning the car slid away on the greasy surface. Automatically he slammed on the brakes. The skid worsened. Damn it! He should never have

206

braked. He tried to correct the skid but the car swerved erratically, mounted the sidewalk.

A frail dark figure loomed like a ghost in front of him. It smashed into the car, the sickening crunch of impact astounding him – the figure had looked so slight, so wraith-like. The body bounced along the hood of the car like a discarded puppet. For one horrifying moment he saw, just inches from the windscreen, a gaunt face and staring eyes, thin wisps of grey hair, a grotesque toothless grin. Christ! Some old crone. But he couldn't even tell if it was male or female – or some foul figment of his imagination. The hideous image slid from sight as the car crashed down from the sidewalk.

Shaken and trembling, as if waking from a terrible nightmare, he straightened the steering, managed to continue down the road. Screeches and screams echoed in his ears, but he knew they all came from inside his head. He had to get away, escape the ghoulish imaginary form that had attacked him.

He'd gone another mile before the real horror of the accident hit him. It hadn't been his imagination. He'd run somebody down. He pulled into the side of the road, sat silently in the car, his body quivering all over.

After what seemed hours – when he could at last control the tremulous shaking in his legs – he slipped from the car, staggered round to the front of the vehicle. The fender was smashed, the bodywork of the hood severely dented. He ran nervous fingers along the line of the dent. Something wet and sticky! God, no! He looked at his fingers. Jesus Christ! they were covered with thick slime and traces of hair. He turned his head, vomited violently. But his whole stomach continued to churn. Five minutes later, his insides bruised and heaving, he got back into the car.

Panic hit him again – he had to get away! He'd probably killed someone! Not only that, he'd been drinking. Not drunk, of course – he hadn't had that many brandies. In any case he'd been quite fit to drive. What bad luck – the greasy state of the roads, that crazy skid.

But would anyone believe him? He knew he was quite capable of driving with any amount of booze inside him, but would they? He'd done it any number of times before – no problem. But those crazy police tests – they'd be sure to prove he was drunk. He'd lose his licence, be indicted for manslaughter.

He tried to pull himself together, to think clearly. At last his mind started to clear. Christ! Who was to know? Who the hell would even guess he'd been involved? The nervous flutters of panic started to calm.

There had been nobody about except him and that crazy old hobo. God knows why he'd been out walking on such a foul evening. Nobody could have seen the accident. He could clean the car up himself, then smash it into one of the trees on his own drive. He'd use his sports car for a while; leave the repair for a few weeks, just in case there were any checks.

In any case there was nothing to connect him with the accident – he lived miles away. He could say he'd left the office earlier than he actually did. Nobody knew he'd stayed on to prepare that report, to drink away his frustration with his father. His parents were out early to dinner that night, the servants wouldn't be around. No one would know what time he got in.

His mind made up, his escape route planned, he felt relief surge through him. It would all be OK. What a fool he'd been to panic – he was plenty smart enough to get himself out of this mess.

Then he remembered his date with Janey. Now he wouldn't be able to see her, but there was always another time. The important thing at this moment was to get back as soon as possible, clean up the car, work out the finer points of his alibi. Calm and reassured, he drove rapidly home.

He had just finished cleaning the battered fender, was about to start on the hood, when he heard a car pull into the drive. Who the hell could that be? His parents wouldn't be home so soon – it was far too early. The car pulled right up to the huge garage; he heard the automatic doors swing open. A car-door slammed. He stood, transfixed, seconds later saw the figure of his father silhouetted against the darkness outside.

"A funny time to be cleaning the car, Giles," he teased. "You normally leave it to the gardener. I thought we were being robbed!"

"Hi, Dad – you're back early."

"I've an important call to make to Paris – before the office closes over there. You know – about the take-over bid. I left your mother chatting with the Simmonds. They'll drive her over later."

"Sure, Dad. Hope you had a good evening." He tried to sound casual, but he could hear the nervous ring in his voice.

His father must have sensed it, too. His face turned serious.

"What's the matter, son? Trouble with the car?" He walked into the garage.

Giles laughed, nervously.

"Oh, just a bit of a bump, Dad – an argument with a tree!"

"That's not so funny, Giles – you're always having bumps and bashes. It's not just the cost. One day you might do yourself ... " Drawing closer, he noticed again the cloth in his son's hand, the bucket of water. "Why on earth are you washing it – if it's got to be repaired? God, Giles, that fender's in a hell of a state. And look at those dents on the hood."

"Must have been the lower branches," said Giles, quickly. "I'll leave it now – I'm tired. Let's get inside."

But his father was already running his hand along the hood.

"What's this?" He stared at his fingers. "Looks like blood, congealed blood." He looked up, suddenly concerned. "What's the matter, son? Have you hurt yourself?"

"No, I'm fine, Dad. Must be something off the trees."

"Rubbish, Giles. I know blood when I see it – saw far too much of it on our fighter planes after the dogfights." Suddenly his face turned grim. "It's not yours, Giles – the windscreen's intact. What's been happening? It looks like a nasty accident!"

"Oh, nothing much, Dad ... It's all been sorted out." He knew he was waffling, but his brain seemed to have seized up.

"Has anyone been badly hurt, Giles?" demanded his father, his voice cold and hard.

"Nothing serious, Dad."

"Tell me the truth, God help me!" he yelled, his face white, his hazel eyes boring into him. "You can't fool me – somebody must have been seriously injured. Why else is there blood all over your hood, not to mention the fender – before you washed it? Or are you going to tell me it was a dog?"

I should have thought of that one, mused Giles. But his heart sank – he was done for. Once his father got his teeth into something, he'd never give up. He'd better come clean.

"It wasn't my fault, Dad – the road was slippery from the rain, I got into a skid ... It couldn't be helped."

"Who was hurt in the other car?"

Giles shuddered.

"There wasn't another car," he whispered.

"Tell me the truth!"

"It was just some crazy old pedestrian. He ... she – I couldn't see which – stepped out in front of me ... I tried to miss, but skidded in the wet, lost control ..."

"How bad is he?"

Giles looked at him in dismay.

"I think he's dead ..." His voice faltered.

"What do you mean ... think?" thundered his father. Giles had never seen him so angry, even during the worst of their rows.

"Dad ... I panicked, I was scared – didn't know what I was doing."

"You mean you drove on without stopping...?" Even in anger his voice sounded incredulous.

Giles looked down, caught sight of the cloth in his hand, let it slip to the ground.

His father stared at him, his face drained of blood, his lips twitching in fury. "But you know what you're doing now, don't you, Giles?

He remained silent.

"Destroying the evidence, I think the police would call it." He leant heavily against the car. "Did you ever consider the poor unfortunate person who was injured? He or she might still be alive, needing urgent medical attention. If you didn't kill him outright, Giles, you've probably succeeded by your subsequent cowardice and negligence."

"Sorry, Dad. I didn't want to get you in trouble – create bad publicity for the Group."

"I'm not stupid, Giles. You had no tender thoughts for anyone but yourself. All you thought about was saving your own skin." He grabbed him by the shoulder. Giles was surprised at the strength in his father's lean hands. For the first time in his life he felt weak and helpless. For the only time he could remember, he wanted to weep.

"Come inside, Giles," said his father, his voice merciless. "We have a phone call to make, right away – to our friends, the police." He dragged him into the house.

Giles sat silently in the library while Jimmy made the brief call to the local cops, explaining his son had been involved in an accident, was in a state of shock but would be coming in shortly to make a statement. He gave details of where the accident had taken place, asked for an ambulance to be sent immediately to attend another person who had been injured.

Giles felt a moment of intense hatred for his father. He obviously couldn't care less what happened to his son. All that concerned him was some stupid old hobo and his own holier-than-thou sense of duty. As long as his conscience was clear, it obviously didn't matter what happened to Giles.

His father put down the telephone. Giles stared sullenly at him.

"Well, you've really set me up, Dad," he said hoarsely.

"What did you expect me to do, Giles? Help in your nasty little cover-up? Your behaviour was despicable – quite brazen. You even tried to lie to me, after I'd caught you in the act."

Giles shrugged his shoulders. "Sure. I knew I'd get no help from that quarter."

"Of course I'd help you. But, it wouldn't be the sort of help you wanted. You've committed a terrible crime, Giles. Forget for the moment the ethics of the matter, the demands of common decency. Hit-and-run is a serious crime. If you'd stopped right away, there'd have been no problem at all. In the circumstances, as you've explained it to me, it seems a complete accident. Had you looked after the victim, there would have been no repercussions."

Giles said nothing – there was nothing he could say. His father's words were quite logical.

"Why didn't you do just that, Giles? I have no illusions about your finer instincts as far as the injured party was concerned; but for your own sake, why did you panic? You're smarter than that."

"I don't know, Dad. It was the shock, I guess."

"Have you told me the whole truth?"

"Of course," he lied, glibly.

His father looked doubtful.

"Had you been drinking, Giles?"

"Only a couple."

"Now I see," he said angrily, leaning back in his chair. He gave a deep sigh. "Why didn't you tell me this right away, Giles. I have to know the whole truth, or I can't help you. Don't you see it will all come out in any case? This isn't the time to lie to me. I can't help you if I don't know all that happened."

Giles bit his lip. He daren't tell his father everything. He started to sob.

"Are you sure you've told me the whole truth now, Giles?" This time his voice was more gentle.

He nodded, miserably.

"On your honour?"

He nodded again.

His father relaxed a little.

"I can understand you panicked at the time. But why – once you came to your senses – did you continue to do nothing, except try to save your own skin. There was certainly no panic when I found you, calmly cleaning the car. You made your decision in cold blood. I can't explain how disappointed I am in you, Giles!"

"What are we going to say to the police, Dad?" he pleaded. "Please help me."

"I'm not going to say anything! You, Giles, will tell the truth about the accident. You don't have to mention the alcohol, just say you were deeply shocked by the accident and panicked as a result. When you reached home and calmed down, you immediately realised your mistake, told me, and we informed the police straight away. It will be serious, but I think the police will be understanding in the circumstances." He eyed him, coldly.

"I will certainly not lie to the police, Giles, but neither will I volunteer the fact you had no intention of reporting the accident – that you intended to cover up your involvement. That's all I can promise you. In a way I despise myself as much as you, but you are my son. There's nothing else I can do. I shan't mention your intentions to your mother, either. It will be our secret."

"Thanks, Dad!" He felt weak with relief. He hated his father at times, but he ought to have known he'd never let him down. When it came to it, his father could never deny his one and only offspring. After all, Giles was all he had!

Chapter 33

The police officer at the precinct who took Giles's statement was large and bear-like with a tough craggy face. He looked a hard nut, thought Jimmy, yet beneath the harsh exterior, his grey eyes peered out surprisingly gentle, almost benign. They suggested he had seen a lot of evil in the world, but hoped to find excuses for it. He seemed duly impressed by Giles's clean-cut appearance, his polite deferential manner. Before taking the statement he spoke respectfully with Jimmy, obviously familiar with his name and status in the community.

Returning to Giles, he quickly noted his personal details and those of the car, then asked the location of the accident, nodding thoughtfully as the boy gave the details.

"It's just as well your father called and you came in, young fella," he said. "The accident had already been reported. We were about to list it as 'hit-and-run'." He stared hard at Giles, watching his reaction.

Jimmy had to admit it – Giles played the part perfectly. Even he would have been convinced, if he hadn't known better.

"I'm real sorry, officer – I know I should've stopped ..." Giles stammered, looking contritely miserable. "I don't know what came over me. I guess ... I just panicked." His voice broke. "How... how is he?" He gazed searchingly at the officer, his eyes earnest and sincere.

The cop shook his head.

"It was a she, son," he said gruffly. "Not that you could tell beneath the grime and old clothes – the poor old thing was wearing an old pair of men's pants and an anorak. I'm afraid she died outright – multiple fracture of the skull, internal haemorrhaging." He looked down at the papers in front of him. "Mary O'Connor, age 72," he recited, "no fixed abode, no next of kin, no friends as far as we can make out ..."

Giles broke down, held his head in his hands. Jimmy wondered if the gesture was genuine – you never knew with Giles.

The cop's eyes flashed suddenly steely. He barked out the next question.

"How did your car come to mount the sidewalk, son? We found the skid-marks."

Jimmy's heart froze. Oh God, Giles had been lying! He'd said nothing about going off the road. What else was there to come? The cop seemed polite enough, but he was no fool.

Giles raised his head, spoke without guile.

"I couldn't help it, sir. A dog – it ran out, right in front of me as I came round the block... I swerved to avoid it – missed the dog, but the car went into a skid. It was drizzling, you know, the road was greasy."

The officer nodded encouragingly, seeming to find the explanation satisfactory.

"Next thing I knew I was on the sidewalk," Giles continued, "the old woman right in front of me ... There was nothing I could do. I can still see it, now." He bowed his head. "I'll never forget it. I thought at first I'd imagined everything ...

it was all some terrible dream. I drove on. Then realised it had been for real. I knew I had to report it. I drove straight home. I had to see Dad." He looked proudly across at his father, "I knew he'd handle it right."

"Sure, son." The officer's grey eyes stared at him, kind but penetrating. "But remember if anything like this ever happens again your duty is to stop, help the injured, then report the accident immediately. As luck would have it, nothing on this occasion could have saved the old girl."

"I've learned my lesson, sir. Don't worry – it'll never happen again." Giles shook his head, morosely. "That poor old lady, she never stood a chance. God, if only there was something I could do..." He looked eagerly across at the police officer. "You're sure she has no family, sir? Nobody I could help, perhaps financially ...? I know that's not everything in the circumstances, but...

The cop shook his head sadly.

"Hell! There must be something I can do." Giles said, thoughtfully. He turned to his father. "I think the least I can do is see she gets a good funeral, with all the trimmings."

"That's a nice thought, son." The officer looked relieved. "I'm sure that can be arranged. If you'll just sign this statement, then you can go home. In view of your explanation about the dog and considering the weather conditions, we'll give you the benefit of the doubt. Nothing can help the old girl now. We'll drop the hit-and-run and manslaughter counts – charge you only with dangerous driving."

Jimmy heaved a silent sigh of relief.

The cop abruptly looked up from his report.

"I think I should tell you something else, young man. There was a witness, you know?"

"Someone saw the accident?" queried Giles, his tone surprisingly casual, but Jimmy could detect a note of apprehension. So there was something else Giles hadn't told him. His heart sank. The cop was obviously playing cat-and-mouse with him, catching his son off-guard just when he thought he was in the clear, waiting for a mistake.

"Not to the accident itself, but a resident heard the screech of brakes, saw a car drive away. They took the licence number – yours, of course, son. So you see, we'd have found you in the end." He grinned with satisfaction at this proof of the long arm of the law, then stared hard at Giles. "Not, of course, that that was necessary in your case." He looked back at the papers in front of him, then looked up again at Giles. "But you'd be surprised at the number of people who think they can get away with these things."

Giles stared back at him, wide-eyed.

"The witness didn't happen to see the dog, did he officer?" he asked coolly. "That animal needs care and attention. It shouldn't be allowed to wander."

"Nope," said the cop sharply. "There was no mention of a dog." He rose to his feet. "Thank you for coming in, Mr Pritchard," he said, shaking his hand. He gave Giles a nod of dismissal.

The two of them strode across the room to the exit.

"Just one thing, young man." The police officer's voice rang out, stopping them in their tracks. He smiled shrewdly at the startled Giles. "Drive carefully in future, won't you, young fella – not quite so fast!" He looked back down at the papers in front of him.

When they got outside Giles was exultant.

"We did it, Dad!" He turned to look at his father, but Jimmy's answer was a stony silence.

"You don't seem too happy about it," said Giles, annoyance in his tone.

"I'm not," Jimmy said, coldly.

"But it's all over! I'll have a helluva fine to pay and lose my licence for a while – but otherwise everything's going to be OK"

"That doesn't change what happened though, does it Giles?"

"Oh, come on Dad. Give me a break."

"You got away with it because there was nothing to prove your story wrong. You were lucky."

"You sound disappointed I wasn't put in jug," he said, bitterly.

"You've still not told me the whole truth, have you, Giles?"

His son's eyes glittered as they bore through him.

"I know I didn't tell you about the dog, Dad. But don't get mad. I swear I forgot all about it – until that cop mentioned the skids on the sidewalk."

"The dog was my idea, or rather my sarcastic remark at the time when I realised you were lying to me." Jimmy felt the anger rise inside him. Did Giles think he was a complete fool? "I have to admit it," he said dryly, "you were quick-witted – remembering a throw-away line like that. But there was no dog, was there, Giles? You were drunk. That's why you skidded, why you went up on the sidewalk."

Giles stared at him, his blue-green eyes hard and clear.

"There was a dog, Dad. You heard what I told the police."

"Yes, I heard," sighed Jimmy. "But I'm not the police."

"There was a dog, Dad."

"Yes, Giles."

* * * * * * *

The more Jimmy thought about it, the more he knew he had to face up to the truth. Giles had cold-bloodedly lied to him, was still deceiving him as he always had. An inveterate liar, worse still, he lacked all common decency and social conscience. Could he ever trust him again? Time and again he had forgiven him, offered him another chance – a fresh start. On each occasion Giles had failed not only Jimmy, but himself.

Could he entrust his commercial empire to such an unscrupulous person? The power he would wield would be a temptation for the most upright of individuals. Power corrupts and Giles was already far down the road to corruption. What damage might he cause, not only to himself but others? He shivered at the thought of it.

He knew most of his son's failings, but he had been surprised and shattered by Giles's lack of moral and mental courage, by his obvious panic at the time of the accident. He'd always admired his son's courage, his utter fearlessness in the face of physical danger – the very quality he lacked himself. But he knew he would never have acted as his son had done after the accident. He might fear the searing bullets of a Messerschmitt, but he would never flee a scene of horror of his own making, cold-bloodedly leaving the victim behind to die in the gutter. And he would never make a deliberate attempt to cover up such an affair. It shocked him that Giles could be capable of such callous behaviour.

* * * * * * *

What could he do now? After all the hopes he had for Giles! No way was his son ready to take on the responsibilities he had planned for him. Would he ever be? He had long suspected, but now he had to face the fact that Giles was a bad lot, completely lacking in moral fibre and personal integrity.

True to his promise to his son, he didn't tell Monique the entire truth about the accident, but somehow she seemed to guess there was more to it than Giles's glib version of the occurrence. She probably understood their son better than he did.

"I do not want to know the sordid details, James," she told him. "I am sure there are some. The atmosphere reeks of intrigue! But what do you intend to do about it?"

Jimmy shook his head.

"I'm at a loss to know what to do."

"James, you have to accept your son for what he is. He will never have your nobleness of spirit. Perhaps time and your example and encouragement will help."

"I can't risk it, Monique. I daren't put him in a position of power. But don't worry, I shall see he's provided for."

"James, he is our son. I know he is difficult to love." Her emerald eyes glistened with unshed tears. "But he is all we have!"

Her words rang in his brain, sent his mind reeling. Of course she had no other child, he thought, but he did – another son – somewhere! Guiltily he brushed the thought aside, caught her hand.

"I'm not disowning him, Monique. But I can't entrust him with the future of the Group."

"There is time, we still have plenty of time. Please, my darling, wait before you make a final decision."

He smiled at her reassuringly, hating to see her upset. Perhaps she was right. They had time – no need to make an irrevocable decision right now.

"You win, Monique. I'll give him a shock, but I won't make any final decisions, at least for the moment. In the meantime Giles is going to have to work hard to win his inheritance. I'll either make him – or break him!

* * * * * * *

Giles slammed the tennis balls around the court, viciously punching volleys, hammering his ground strokes, serving like a demon.

"Easy, Giles!" called his opponent, Max, an old school friend who had come up to visit. "You're annihilating me! There soon won't be any fluff left on the balls".

Giles breathed deeply, tried to calm the anger still seething inside him. It felt great battering the hell out of the balls, easing the white hot fury and hatred burning inside his chest. He'd almost forgotten it was Max at the other side of the net. He grinned across at his opponent.

"Come on, Max, you usually get a few games off me."

"Not when you're in one of these moods. Who do ya think you are – that McEnroe guy?"

I could have been, mused Giles.

"OK," he said out loud. "Let's call it a day." It was stupid wasting his time and energy on a tennis ball. Better to save it, harbour his talents and use them against his father. He was the enemy now!

He felt the bile rising inside him. Dad had betrayed him – gone back on his promises. For some reason the accident had really shaken his father's faith in him. From now on, he told Giles, he was on his own. He had to prove his reliability, his sense of responsibility, before his father would allow him any further progress or power within the corporation.

What's more, Dad had refused any guarantee, let alone a time schedule. It could be years before he'd allow him an appointment to any of the boards – perhaps never. The thought infuriated him. There had been no mention of disinheriting him, but Giles could read the threat in his father's eyes. He was on probation!

Fuck that stupid accident, that silly cow who'd caused it all! Dad's original conditions had been bad enough – now the situation had grown impossible. He wasn't prepared to waste any more of his life trying to live up to some crazy standard set by his father. Yet what was the alternative? There had to be some way he could outwit him – Giles knew he was stronger, smarter, more ruthless than his father.

The idea came to him a few nights later. Divide and rule! He couldn't beat his father on his own, but with the support of other powerful members of the group, it might be possible. If he could set the other directors against him ... It would need meticulous planning, time and energy. But the prize was certainly worth it. He smiled to himself. It could also prove quite enjoyable – getting his own back on his father. Giles loved a challenge. He would show him who was the smartest!

Chapter 34

Long Island, New York January 1980

"Giles! Giles! Quickly, come quickly!" His mother rushed into the music room, screaming above the stereo which boomed out a heavy metal number from his favourite Led Zeppelin album. Dressed only in a night-gown, she looked distraught – her face ashen, her normally immaculate black hair hanging dishevelled around her shoulders. She hadn't even bothered to put on a robe. He'd never seen her so agitated, so lacking in composure. She put her hands to her ears in wide-eyed desperation, trying to ward off the cacophony of sound resounding through the room.

"What the hell's the matter, Mom? Calm down." He moved across to the music centre, turned down the sound.

"Your father! He's collapsed – on the bedroom floor," she cried, her low husky voice now shrill, fringing on hysteria. "Giles ... he's unconscious. I can't lift him!"

His heart sank. Please don't die on me now, Dad, he whispered to himself. I'll lose everything. Just when I'd gotten it all set up! He spoke sharply to his mother.

"Pull yourself together, mom. You phone the doctor. I'll look after Dad."

He raced, two steps at a time, up the long ornate staircase, rushed into his parent's suite. His father lay stretched out, face down, on the white carpet where he had fallen.

Icy fingers tore at Giles's stomach. It had to be a heart attack, perhaps a stroke. He knelt by his father's side, pressed his ear to the side of his face. The skin was grey and ashen, but he could hear a slight rasping sound of breathing. Thank God! He was still alive!

Drawing on his rudimentary knowledge of first aid, he gently turned him onto his side to allow any fluid from the mouth and throat to drain out to prevent him choking, then grabbed the duvet from the bed, carefully covered the inert form. He knelt again by his side, full of apprehension, saw with relief his father's hazel eyes flicker open, his mouth move as he tried to speak – but no sound came out.

"Don't worry, Dad. You're gonna be all right."

He's gotta be all right, he thought to himself. Otherwise all this last year's efforts had been in vain. He had been cut out of his father's will – except for a pittance, and that had been put in trust for another eight years until he turned thirty.

He had skilfully worked on most of the board members and several of his father's lawyers and accountants, steadily trying to gain their confidence. Ostensibly fiercely loyal to his father, he slowly let fall the odd poisonous words and intimations, managing to infer all was not well with the older man: his father was ageing, losing his touch and judgement, and for some strange reason held an irrational prejudice against his son.

Cunning and subtle in his intimations, he worked slowly and artfully, never overdoing the malice in his words, always apparently excusing and covering for his father, appearing loyally concerned for his well-being. He had managed to find one lawyer in the legal team he judged to be corruptible – a man, who with promises of lucrative future rewards, now actively supported him in the subtle insidious insinuations.

Now this had to happen!

He stared down at his father, willing him to live, took hold of one of his hands and rubbed it between his own strong fingers to restore the circulation. He'd never felt so completely helpless!

His mother appeared suddenly at his side.

"The doctor and an ambulance are on their way." She spoke breathlessly, but seemed a little calmer. Kneeling by her husband's side, she stroked his hair, made a low moaning sound. Tears started to course down her cheeks and her whole body shook.

Suddenly aware of the depth of her love for his father he felt a rare sense of compassion and put his arm round her lovely shoulders.

"Don't worry, Mom. He's gonna be fine!"

His father seemed to hear his words. His eyelids flickered open again and he managed a wan smile.

"Thank God! Oh, thank God!" breathed Monique.

* * * * * * *

Unbelievably, a couple of months later, his father had returned to the office! The stroke had been minor and he made a rapid recovery. A slight loss of muscle control in his left hand and leg seemed the only apparent damage, and this improved daily. His speech was perfect and full control had returned to the left side of his face, where the cheek and eye muscles had shown temporary signs of paralysis during the first few days after the stroke.

Giles couldn't believe his luck – his father back to health, but the stroke providing him with every excuse for the alleged lapses and idiosyncrasies in his father's behaviour.

Several weeks later, with everything going to plan, he decided to take the bull by the horns and approach Ken Griffith, one of his father's top advisers – a powerful figure within the group.

"Sorry to bother you, Ken," he said striding into the chief executive's immaculate office.

Griffith looked up from the single sheet in front of him, the remainder of the surface of his vast mahogany desk shiny and clear with not another paper in sight. It irritated Giles that this man could work in such an orderly fashion. His own desk was always strewn with papers.

Ken gave a warm smile, his cherubic face kind and avuncular.

"What's the problem, Giles?" He indicated an easy chair. "Sit down – make yourself comfortable."

Ken was one of the least prepossessing characters Giles had ever met. His chubby face gave him an innocuous appearance and his stocky unimposing body never looked good in clothes, his garments seeming to cling to him, protesting his stout form.

Yet Giles knew him to be the shrewdest of all the top executives, his simple demeanour utterly misleading. He had accompanied Ken to vital meetings, had seen the condescending smiles on people's faces when the older man was introduced. Then he had watched those same faces straighten, become alert, then alarmed as Ken took over in his cool calm voice, smiling sympathetically at them – even as he tied them in knots.

Ken Griffith was no fool. It was vital for Giles to win him over to his side. He gave a friendly smile.

"Ken – I need your advice."

Griffith nodded, smiled back at him encouragingly.

"Sure, Giles. Fire away."

"It's about Dad."

Ken looked puzzled.

"He seems to be making fine progress, Giles. Almost back to his old self. What's the problem? Is there something I should know?"

"I'm not sure I should tell you this, Ken ..." He paused, dramatically. "Of course, it's not Dad's fault, and I'm sure with time he'll improve ..."

"What are you saying, Giles?"

"I guess I'm being disloyal to him, speaking to you like this, but then again, I have to consider the Group. I know you'll be discreet, Ken. Hopefully with time ..."

"Damn it, Giles! Don't beat about the bush. This isn't like you. You know you can trust me – I've worked with Jimmy now for twenty years. If he needs help, if anything's wrong, let me know. We'll soon get it sorted out."

"I know he seems better, Ken, but at times in our chats and discussions, his judgement ... well, it's way out – he can't seem to grasp the essentials. He's desperately trying to cover up, of course. That concerns me too – the last thing he needs at the moment is undue stress. I'm worried the pressure's starting to get to him."

"I sure appreciate your concern, Giles. But I must say again, I haven't noticed anything wrong with your father. Quite the reverse – the other day at a board meeting, he was top-notch, really on form." He looked worriedly across at Giles. "Mind you, I have to admit, you're not the first person to mention something like this over the last few months."

"Oh?" He tried to look surprised.

"Yes, I've been hearing various rumours, but I've always put it down to envy, or the usual reaction of younger people to an older superior. You know me, Giles – I prefer to act on my own judgement. Personally, I haven't spotted any change – even since the stroke."

He looked down at the paper in front of him, thought for a few moments.

"Of course I could be letting my respect and admiration for your father cloud my judgement. I certainly wouldn't like him to be under any unnecessary stress."

Inwardly Giles blessed Griffith for his fair-mindedness. However devoted he might be to his father, he wouldn't let personal considerations cloud his judgement.

Ken eyed him, keenly.

"Can you give any concrete examples of this unusual behaviour?"

"Sure, Ken, but I don't know as it'd be fair to Dad."

"I understand that, Giles. I respect your loyalty but there's your father's health, as well as the future of the Group, to consider."

"That's what I've been thinking, Ken – what finally convinced me to come to you." He coughed nervously and moistened his lips. "Well, for example, just last Thursday I was discussing the Eezy-Cleen account with him – the one that's just come up for bids. As you know, they're looking for new agents. Dad said it wasn't worth making a presentation. He had some crazy idea we didn't have the capacity for a new account. I reminded him that some of our other campaigns have been cut recently – so we could easily handle Eezy-Cleen. It took over an hour of argument before he finally come round to my way of thinking."

Seeing Ken hanging on his every word, he drew a deep a breath and continued.

"Then a week ago he was talking of selling off the new Garden City apartments – for some ridiculous price! You know as well as I do, they'll be worth a fortune once that new highway comes into operation. It seems like he doesn't want the extra work, the responsibility ..."

"This is serious," said Ken. "He seemed so enthusiastic with me about both those ventures."

"Only after I'd made him see the light," insisted Giles, shaking his head. "I'd never have told you, but I'm frightened one day he'll make a fool of himself – in front of all the directors. I'd hate that."

Ken nodded and frowned, plainly perturbed.

"Leave it with me, Giles. I'll make some discreet enquiries ... check things out a while."

Great, thought Giles, satisfied. If he'd done his groundwork properly, there should be plenty of substantiating comments from other members of the staff. He looked sheepishly at Ken.

"Don't say anything to Dad, will you – about the two cases I've mentioned. I'd hate him to think I'd gone behind his back. In any case, he's now convinced they were his ideas all along. Don't disillusion him."

"OK, son. I appreciate your concern and I'm more than happy you confided in me. You're a fine young fella – a real chip off the block!"

"I wish my father thought as much," said Giles, ruefully.

"Of course he does. I've never heard your father say a bad word about you, other than the obvious – that you need a little more maturity and experience."

Giles stared at him in surprise. He'd always assumed his father would have confided his misgivings about him to Ken Griffith, his confidant. Yet it seemed the old man had kept most of his son's problems to himself. A piece of unexpected luck! Now there would be no apparent reason for Ken to suspect him of wanting to discredit his father.

He flashed his most winning smile.

"Dad's quite right in that respect, but I'm learning fast! I just hope one day I'll be half as good as he used to be."

"So do I, Giles. Your father's a brilliant businessman, and with time I'm sure you'll be equally good."

"Thanks, Ken. I'm sure glad I came to see you. It's a relief to be able to leave it with you."

* * * * * * *

The cold damp November morning did nothing to improve Jimmy's mood. He flinched visibly as he sat in the library, listening intently to Ken Griffith's startling words.

"I just couldn't believe what Giles was saying, Jim, but I had to investigate – you can understand that?"

Jimmy nodded and lowered his head in abject misery. It seemed Giles had been up to his old tricks again. Even worse – this time he was the victim!

"At first quite a few people seemed to back up his allegations," explained Ken. "It was only when I probed further, went into exact details, that it seemed that all the stories could be traced back to Giles himself. At first I couldn't think why your son would act in that way. It just didn't make sense." He shifted uncomfortably in his chair. "It was young Peter Price who gave the game away."

"The bright new boy in the legal department?"

"Yes. He let something slip when I was questioning him. I knew he didn't have access to that information, unless through Giles. I questioned him further. He eventually broke – Giles picked the wrong man there! I'm afraid you're not gonna like this, Jim."

Jimmy reached for the brandy bottle, poured another drink for them both, finding himself strangely unshaken by Ken's revelations. He smiled grimly at his colleague.

"I'm sure I'm won't, Ken."

"It seems Giles had got to Price, promised him all kinds of rewards for his support and inside information. The idea was to completely discredit you over a period of time, enabling Giles to slowly slip into your shoes. Of course, the fact you had that stroke played right into their hands, gave people a reason to believe you might be partially incapacitated. But Giles moved too far too fast, especially with me. How he thought he could ever get away with it, I don't know. Mind you, he'd already gotten quite a few people convinced."

"I can believe it," said Jimmy, dryly. "He can be most convincing!" Was nothing beyond Giles's machinations?

"What I still couldn't understand, Jim, is why he did it. Your share of the business would've come to him in time – he'll be an extremely wealthy and powerful young man."

"Yes, but he didn't know that, Ken. He thought I'd cut him out of my will. He must have figured he'd have to wait a long time to get anywhere in the Group. I'd better tell you the whole story ..."

Griffith listened in obvious astonishment and dismay. When Jimmy had finished, he shook his head.

"I can't believe it, Jim. Giles is such a talented youngster – so enthusiastic, so plausible in all he says and does." He shook his head, sadly. "I just wouldn't have believed he could be so callous. I still can't believe it – after all he's your son! You've done everything for him."

"It's taken me nearly fifteen years to accept it, Ken. Each time, I've tried to believe he'll grow out of it. That's why, after the car accident, I told him I'd disinherited him – that he had to make his own way within the business, prove himself before he could take on any position of trust. I thought that might force him to change. Now I have to accept he never will."

Ken nodded.

"As far as I'm concerned, Jim – if a boy betrays his father the way Giles did, there's no hope."

"I agree, Ken. This is definitely the last straw – I've made my decision. I'll see the lawyers tomorrow, get it sorted out. Have another brandy and I'll tell you what I have in mind." He sipped at his own drink, settled further back in the leather chair. This time he had to put Ken completely in the picture. There would be no turning back.

Chapter 35

Long Island, New York January 1981

When Jimmy learned all those years ago that Cathy was still alive, he made a conscious decision not to become involved with her or the son he had never seen. Reluctantly he tried to forget he had another off-spring living in Europe.

He originally made this decision for Cathy's own protection, not to mention their child, Sam. As far as he knew, she was happily married with a family of her own; any interference from him or reminder of their past together would scarcely help her peace of mind. Even worse, his return from the dead would render her whole relationship with Leslie bigamous, not to mention his own with Monique! His loyalty to Monique and Giles, as well as his sense of guilt over his lingering affection for Cathy, reinforced this decision.

He had been forced to admit a further reason for ignoring the existence of his first-born – a purely selfish one. He feared becoming emotionally and personally involved with the child, felt the permanent ache for Cathy would return to haunt him more sharply. The old wound would be re-opened, this time aggravated by a yearning to know his other son.

But in the wake of Giles's latest betrayal, he decided to take drastic action as far as his estate was concerned. He had given up with Giles. He would ensure the boy's future was financially protected, but in his will the bulk of his estate would go to Cathy's child, Sam. With a sudden shock he realised his first-born would now be thirty-nine years old, almost certainly with a family of his own!

It wouldn't be such a risk. He had a gut feeling Sam would be intelligent and competent, and more important, a man of warmth and integrity. In the event of his own death, Monique's future welfare would be assured. He had already settled a large amount on his wife and she would be free to enjoy a luxurious old-age. Cathy wouldn't be harmed in any way. When the will came into effect, he would no longer be a threat to her and her family.

As further protection for all concerned, he stipulated his true relationship to his new heir should not be revealed. Cathy, of course, might guess the identity of her son's unexpected benefactor, but the choice would be left to her. She could decide when and what to reveal about her first husband. By that time he would be past hurting not only Sam, but any grandchildren there might be. She would have the sense and the sensibility to know what to do the in the circumstances – he could rely on that. At least he could die knowing he had done something for the family of the only woman he had truly loved.

Ken Griffith, who featured as one of the trustees, was in full agreement with the terms of the new will.

"Don't worry, Jim, the trustees will make sure your wishes are carried out. I'm certain you've made the right decision."

Jimmy smiled gratefully. He had felt a certain shame recounting the full story of his past to Ken – knowing his colleague had always held him in high esteem and regard. But for Ken to be able to understand the intricacies of the situation, he had to know the whole truth . Ken scarcely blinked an eye when Jimmy recounted the story of his desertion from the RAF.

"I could never figure how any of you guys managed to handle the strains of the Battle of Britain – I reckon it was enough to send anybody off their rocker. I take my hat off to any pilot who fought in that scene, regardless of what might have happened afterwards. You were a bunch of heroes, as far as I'm concerned!"

That's a real friend talking, thought Jimmy, thanking his lucky stars. Throughout his life he'd been blessed with loyal friends and colleagues. That at least he had to be thankful for, besides those glorious months with Cathy.

"I've had another thought, Jim," Ken said, "something I reckon you should consider. It may seem a pretty unlikely occurrence, but it should be taken into account."

"What's that, Ken?" said Jimmy. He'd thought he and his lawyers had covered every detail within the intricate terms of the will.

"You haven't heard anything about your first wife and her family since 1967?"

"That's right. I thought it best at that stage to let sleeping dogs lie. It would have done more harm to both my families to get involved." Besides breaking my own heart, he thought to himself.

"I understand that, Jim. But have you considered that something could've happened to your first wife or her child, by now? Was Cathy the same age as you?"

"You think she might have died?" The words were like a knife in his heart. Cathy – dead? It wasn't so long ago he'd discovered she was alive and well. Of course, it was always a possibility.

"She was six years younger than I, Ken – only nineteen when we married. That would make her fifty-nine now – her birthday was in April. Our son, Sam, will be nearly forty."

He felt sure Cathy was still alive. Funny, he couldn't even imagine her as an older woman. For him she would be always be sweet nineteen, with soft brown hair, innocent blue-grey eyes. And he certainly couldn't imagine a nearly middle-aged son!

"Don't worry, Ken, the will's quite clear. If Sam should die, the estate automatically passes to his family – our grandchildren."

"And in the event of anything happening to the grandchildren, assuming there are grandchildren?" persisted Ken.

Jimmy shook his head. He couldn't accept that possibility – that there might be no living reminder of his union with Cathy.

"You've gotta consider it, Jim," said Ken, firmly. "I know it's pretty unlikely, but awful catastrophes like airplane accidents do happen. Whole families can be wiped out. We must cover all eventualities."

"Of course," he said, reluctantly. "In that case, I suppose the estate must revert to Giles, but in that eventuality I want it held in trust until he's thirty-five. Just one other thing, Ken. I've written a letter to Cathy, to be sent in the event of my death. Will you see it's done for me?"

"Sure, Jim," he agreed, his eyes understanding. "I think we've covered everything. When will you break the news to Giles?"

"Right away. I'll need your help," said Jimmy grimly. "It's only fair he should know the situation. From now on he has to run his own life, fend for himself. He'll have enough money to be comfortable. Beyond that I don't want to know about him."

"How's Monique taken it, Jim? I guess you've told her the details?"

"Of course. Monique's a strange woman – she took it all very calmly, accepted it as inevitable. She always has, as far as Giles is concerned. She adores him, as you know. But she's always faced up to his shortcomings, been more aware of them probably than I ever have. She seems fairly confident he'll survive – even prosper – in the long run."

"Sure, Jim – I can believe that. Knowing Giles, she's probably right. Monique's quite a dame, you know. I gather you've still got a soft spot for your first wife, but don't ever underrate Monique. Not only is she still a stunner, she's gotta lot of guts – and she adores you." Ken's voice was kindly reassuring. He'd obviously guessed Jimmy's true feelings, but wanted to help him all he could in his uneasy relationship with Monique.

"I know that, Ken. She was pretty upset when I told her about Cathy, but as long as I stay well clear of my first wife, I think she can handle it. I'll look after her, don't worry. Monique and I have developed a good understanding."

"What about love, Jim?"

"That's something I threw away many years ago, Ken," Jimmy said, sadly.

Ken smiled wanly, gave a helpless shrug. He stood up and walked to the door.

"Good luck! Jim."

"Thanks, Ken ... for everything."

* * * * * *

After his colleague had left Jimmy sat pondering his words. He couldn't bear to think something might have happened to Cathy or to their son, Sam. In his heart he felt sure Cathy was alive and well – he could feel it in his bones. As for Sam, his son would be approaching the prime of life – he had to be fit and well. Jimmy didn't dare investigate any further. Until he died he could be nothing but a threat to them.

In any case, deep down he knew he didn't want to hear any bad news about Cathy or Sam. After his heart-wrenching disappointment with Giles, he couldn't face any more disillusionment. He no longer trusted the vagaries of fate. At least this way he could enjoy his hopes ... his dreams.

* * * * * *

Giles realised he was in trouble when Ken Griffith called him into the president's suite. Within minutes he knew the game was up. In tones of disgust, Griffith referred to his 'appalling schemes against his father', told how his plan of deceit and betrayal had been exposed. Giles knew that had his father been prepared to forgive him, he would have handled the interview himself. That he wouldn't even speak to him, demonstrated the strength of his rejection, his determination not to give Giles the opportunity to persuade him otherwise. Giles didn't blame him. Dad wouldn't be frightened of telling him, but the process would be all too painful for him. What the hell would happen now?

Then Griffith dropped the bombshell!

"With regard to the future disposal of the estate, I have to tell you your father has willed the Group, or its proceeds, to a third party. He wishes to discuss this matter with you, personally.

"A third party?" gasped Giles. He'd been prepared to expect restrictions, harsh controls, years of trusts and delays, but not substitution by another person. "But there isn't any possible third party," he croaked in disbelief.

"I'm afraid there is, Giles," said Jimmy, entering the room from his private access door, his voice forceful and cutting. Gone were the normally soft smooth tones. His hazel eyes stared at him hard and unblinking, his handsome face seeming to have aged ten years.

"What the hell are you talking about, Dad? Surely you're not gonna leave everything to this bunch of bureaucrats?" He waved his hand in the direction of Ken Griffith. Christ! Why had he tried to involve that sonovabitch in his schemes?

Griffith rose hastily to his feet.

"I'll leave you to it, Jim," he said in obvious relief, walking swiftly to the door.

Jimmy took over the vast leather chair. He met Giles's defiant stare with an expression of contempt.

Giles could feel the pounding of his heart, had a strong sense of foreboding. What the hell did his father have up his sleeve this time?

"Giles, I don't quite know how to break this to you." Leaning thoughtfully back in the chair, he steepled his fingers in front of him. "Throughout your life, I've always tried to protect you from the knowledge I'm about to disclose to you. I'm afraid it's your own fault I have to do this now – your own deplorable behaviour has led me to change my plans."

Giles started to shake, both from nerves and a silent fury he couldn't explain. He realised it was anger, directed not only at his father, but at himself.

Silence hung in the air. His father took a deep breath and stared across at him, his eyes gleaming clearer and more penetrating than he'd ever seen them before.

"Giles, be prepared for a shock. I have to tell you that... you're not my only son! I have another – older than you."

He couldn't believe his ears. "But Dad ... that's not possible ..."

"I'm afraid it is. I'm not prepared to go into details just now. Suffice it to say, that in view of your consistently deplorable behaviour, I've changed my will in favour of my elder son."

Giles threw his head back, utterly flabbergasted. He'd been prepared for virtually any twist of fate, but not this. For once his defences tumbled around him – he was at a complete loss for words. Another son? It couldn't be true.

Why hadn't his father mentioned it before? But if it was true ..? If only he'd known before – now it was all too late!

Hot tears began to slide down his handsome cheeks. Impatiently he brushed them away – tears of anger and frustration, but his father would see them as signs of weakness, shame even. And he had nothing to be ashamed of. It was his father who had deceived and betrayed him.

Another son! He realised it had to be true. Dad would never lie to him. Shocked and furious, he leapt up from his seat, fled, choking, from the office suite. He drove home in rage and desperation. Reaching the house, he burst through the front door. His mother stood waiting for him in the hall . He fell into her arms, his head resting in defeat on her firm breasts. She stroked his hair, murmured to him French – she hadn't spoken to him in her mother-tongue since he'd been a boy.

"Mom ... you know?" He raised his head, stared searchingly into her green feline eyes.

She nodded.

"Yes, my darling. I am so sorry."

He could see the hurt and sadness in her eyes.

"It's true then?" His heart sank as she nodded again.

"Would you like me to explain?"

"No!" He wrenched free from her embrace. "I don't wanna know anything about his bastard son!" He saw her start and tears welled in her eyes. "He is a bastard, isn't he, mother?" he pleaded.

She didn't answer, just stared ahead, her body trembling.

"Oh, God! Why didn't he tell us!" He stared at her accusingly. Had she known the truth all the time?

She read the question in his eyes.

"Darling, I promise you – I never knew. I suppose I should have guessed – it explains everything."

"Everything?" He shook his head in puzzlement. "What do you mean?"

"Nothing, darling." She clasped him by the arm. "Giles, I think you should go away ... travel, the way you have always wanted to. You have an income. If you need more, I have some money."

He narrowed his eyes, immediately suspicious. Why did she suddenly want to be rid of him?

She seemed to sense his doubts.

"Don't you see, Giles? Your father needs time. With time he may mellow, change his mind. There is nothing for you here now – you will only be an irritation to him. But I know your father. He will not be able to refuse you forever." Her voice broke. "Giles, you cannot blame him – you are at fault, *mon chéri*, you know that."

"He deceived me, mother, betrayed us both!"

"He did what he believed best. You may not understand that now, but it is true. He tried to do everything for you." She grasped his arm. "You must go, Giles! Go now, before you are hurt any more."

"You're as rotten as him," he shouted, hating her for siding with his father. "But you're sure right about one thing. I should go! I'm obviously not wanted here any more." He pushed roughly past her, strode angrily up the staircase.

She started to weep. He heard her husky, tear-ridden voice call after him.

"Giles, my darling, I love you. I will always love you. Please remember that!"

He cursed her under his breath. Women! They thought love was the answer to everything. What fools they were! Yes, he'd leave. But whatever they might think, he wasn't done for.

Not yet!

Chapter 36

London, England. June 1981

Giles strode through Immigration at London's Heathrow Airport, well aware he was causing a number of heads to turn. He felt in tremendous shape, knew his striking good looks were set off to their best advantage – his normally unruly dark curls neatly trimmed, his tall sturdy body tanned deep-bronze by the Mexican sun. His athletic frame bounded with vitality as he walked, his cheeks glowing with health and fitness. Hip-hugging designer jeans, a crisp damask shirt, Gucci shoes and travel bag gave an overall impression of casual elegance with distinct overtones of wealth.

The overweight, pudgy-fingered immigration officer eyed him speculatively, then smiled in icy politeness. Barely disguised envy gave his words a patronising edge.

"Purpose of your visit, sir?"

"Pure pleasure," replied Giles, with his most disarming smile. His teeth flashed gleaming white against the golden tan.

"I'm sure you'll find plenty here, sir," responded the immigration officer, dryly. "Enjoy your holiday!"

Giles grinned and took his passport. Holiday! Little did that fat fool know that for him, life was all one big vacation.

He reflected over the events of the last few months. How he'd lived it up! Mexico had been fantastic. He'd made the right choice – going there to lick over his wounds. He had fled the States, mentally and physically defeated. But Mexico had been marvellous for his damaged ego, for overcoming the anger and self-recrimination eating away inside him following his final rupture with his family. Mexico had been sun and sea; delicious spicy food, strong cheap liquor; scores of exotic voluptuous females – all practically falling into his arms. It had been like picking ripe cherries from a tree!

His Mexican life-style had been as therapeutic for his body as for his spirit. Physically he felt totally regenerated. Nearly all his time and activities had revolved around the beach, the sea and the tennis court. Hours in the water – surfing, skiing and sailing – had left his muscles rippling, his body hard as nails. Floodlit hours on the tennis courts had honed his reflexes, perfected his co-ordination. His superb fitness had enabled him to drink and womanise with impunity. He couldn't remember the last time he'd had a hangover – he felt he could take on the world!

That was when he had decided to come to London. Despite the gratifying months of hedonism and self-indulgence, Mexico had started to pall. Revived and invigorated, he had felt the need for new stimulation, new challenges. He was also running short of cash, despite frequent loans from his mother. His father, damn him, had provided him with an income but it didn't match the life-style Giles would like to become accustomed to! Fast cars, yachts, expensive women and luxury sports all cost big money, and that was something he didn't have – as yet!

His agile mind had already started to calculate his next move. Where to go, what to do next? He had considered South America, but his various talents didn't include fluent Spanish or Portuguese. He sensed his strength would lie in the field of communication – where he could make best use of his personal charisma and previous experience. To succeed in this field without fluency in the language would be impossible. He also lacked faith in the political situation in the majority of South American states.

That left Canada, Australia, parts of the Far East or the UK itself. The thought of visiting Britain left him trembling with excitement. After all he was half-British by birth and the rest of Europe – with its myriad of fascinations – lay just a stone's throw from the shores of his father's native land. France itself hovered just across the water – a chance, too, for him to investigate his Gallic roots.

The more he thought about it, the more he felt an itching desire to visit the country where his father had been raised, which had imbued him with that elegant veneer, that almost indiscernible air of understated superiority. If he, Giles, could acquire the patina and gloss of British style and distinction, it must help him when he eventually returned to the States to claim his inheritance – as he fully intended to do one day.

Brimming with confidence and anticipation, he sauntered into the baggage hall, whistled a porter to collect his luggage, cleared customs and stepped out into the fresh air.

So this was England. A bright sunny day! – who said it always rained? He grabbed a taxi and enjoyed some entertaining banter with the cockney cab-driver who drove him to his hotel – the Ritz on Piccadilly.

Passing through the smart residential areas of West London, he began to fall in love with the city. It had a charm and atmosphere he couldn't explain, redolent he supposed, of its rich historic past. Strangely drawn to its unusual mix of quaintness combined with the energy of a modern metropolis, he could scarcely repress the feeling that this ancient city with its roots in the past, was the civilised heart of the modern world. New York, even Washington, suddenly seemed garish, almost provincial by comparison – like upstart children.

Checking into an exquisite suite, he showered and changed, then refreshed from his journey, strolled down to the elegant tea room. Tea at the Ritz! His first taste of British style.

In leisurely mood, he soaked up the coolly refined atmosphere of the tea-lounge, enjoying the impeccable yet unobtrusive service. He relished every course of the superb tea menu, even requested more of the wafer-thin sandwiches, mouth-watering scones with jam and cream, the delicious gateaux and delicately-served aromatic tea. If this was the British lifestyle, he couldn't get enough of it!

Hovering over his second helping of gateaux, he felt a familiar hair-prickling sensation at the back of his neck – sensed he was being watched. He half-turned, slowly looked behind him. A strikingly beautiful woman, seated alone on the table to his rear, gave him the benefit of a magnificent flashing smile. He half-grinned, half-gaped in astonishment, turned quickly back to his raspberry gateau, desperately trying to regain his composure.

God, what a stunner! Fancy him missing a female like that. He usually covered most of the occupants of a room with one sweeping glance when he walked in. But he hadn't spotted her then   she must have come in since, had probably been watching him ever since from her vantage point behind.

He flushed, recalling his obsessive preoccupation with his English tea. Pouncing on every mouthful in a beano of unashamed gluttony, he hadn't once looked round, or even paused since the first tempting morsels were served on the delicate bone-china plate. She must be laughing at him – thinking what an uncouth pig he was.

He couldn't resist turning once again to check. She might not be quite as exquisite as he'd first imagined in his embarrassment.

But she was! Choice, really choice. Shiny black hair and dark smouldering eyes, high cheek bones and a wide voluptuous mouth. What he could see of her figure matched the face. She smiled at him again, revealing perfect white teeth, the smile friendly and teasing. He obviously hadn't put her off!

His confidence restored, he gave her the benefit of his own flashing grin and challenging eyes, then toasted her with his teacup. Her eyes crinkled, her mouth quivered as she tried to stop laughing; then she looked demurely down.

Ah! So now she was now playing the coy ladylike role, but he'd bet any money she was an approachable broad. He might as well try his chances. But he'd certainly play it her way.

He caught the waiter's eye, asked for a piece of note-paper which materialised instantly. Scribbling down a few quick words, he asked him to relay the note to the woman behind. Within seconds the waiter had returned to his side.

"The lady would like you to join her, sir," he said politely.

"Certainly," said Giles, enjoying the byplay. Smoothing his hair, he rose slowly from his chair and approached her table.

"Marvellous to see you, Melissa," he said in a loud voice, aping his father's Oxford accent. "Hardly recognised you after all these years. I must say you look absolutely spiffing! How's your pater?"

The raven-haired beauty nearly choked on her tea. The waiter moved diplomatically away.

The girl continued to gurgle over her teacup.

"What's the matter?" he asked, raising his eye-brows in mock surprise. "You didn't want it to look like a cheap pick-up, did you?" He started to laugh himself.

"To begin with," she chortled, "my name's not Melissa, and the waiter's known me for years. In any case, nobody says 'spiffing' and 'pater' anymore – you sound like something from a Noel Coward play!" She began to laugh again, a high-pitched tinkling laugh which reminded him of storybook elves.

He looked at her approvingly.

"How long have you been watching me?"

"Practically from the start," she said, then added mischievously. "You really enjoyed your tea, didn't you?"

He flushed slightly. "It was great!" he said, using a heavy Texan accent to cover his embarrassment. "I just love your little old English tea."

"So you are American."

"Is it so obvious?" he asked in his normal voice.

"Yes," she said, her dark eyes sparkling.

"Don't you like American men?"

"I don't know any American men," she said ingenuously.

"We can soon remedy that." He placed his hand over hers.

She moved it away – though not immediately, then looked down.

He felt sure he was scoring.

"Actually – as you British would say – I'm strictly European by birth ... half-British, half-French, but I have lived most of my life in the States." He offered his hand across the table, this time to shake hers.

"Giles Pritchard's the name. Now tell me yours. Or shall I ask Jeeves, the butler, to introduce you?"

She smiled and shook his hand, her fingers cool and soft.

"Penelope Smythe," she said, looking directly into his eyes.

"I see there's no Mr Smythe," he remarked, looking pointedly at the fingers of her left hand.

"Not yet, although I am unofficially engaged." Her eyes flashed at him, almost challengingly.

Strangely the information didn't put him off, if anything adding a touch of spice to the chase.

"Perhaps I could invite you and your fiancé-to-be to dinner this evening?"

She didn't turn a hair.

"Are you sure you can manage dinner – after all that tea!" she teased.

"Sure. I'm a big man. I need plenty of fuel!" He stared at her hard, deliberately trying to project his own magnetism.

She fell silent.

"Your boyfriend surely can't object to improving Anglo-American relations. After all I am a lonely tourist in a strange city."

"I can't imagine you being lonely for long!"

"No, but I'm very selective with my friends." He spoke earnestly, his bantering approach changing to tones of sincerity. The contrast usually worked with women, throwing them off-guard – they never knew when to take him seriously.

"Thank you, Giles," she said in mock formality. "I'm sure Perry and I will be happy to accept your invitation." She rose abruptly to her feet. "Will eight o'clock be all right?"

"Great!" he said. "But where shall I pick you up?"

She had already started to walk away, but turned slightly to answer him. "Oh, here in the foyer will be perfect."

"You're staying at the hotel, too?" he called after her. But she had already glided away. Giles feasted his eyes on her slightly swinging hips, her elegant figure. As she left the lounge, she turned and gave a little wave.

A real classy dame, he thought, but why the sudden disappearing act? Typical woman – wanting to seem mysterious and unattainable! He still reckoned he'd have her in his bed within the next twenty-four hours, boyfriend or no!

* * * * * * *

They were already waiting in the foyer when he came down, Penelope looking even more stunning than before, her ebony hair swept up to one side, giving a swan-like elegance to her lovely neck. She was dressed entirely in black and gold – harem trousers and a wide-shouldered, almost diaphanous blouson top which showed off to perfection her firm swelling bosom.

The man standing beside her – as ugly as she was beautiful! – took him completely by surprise. He was a good ten years older than Penelope, of average height, with dark slightly-receding hair. His beautifully-cut clothes failed to disguise narrow shoulders, thick hips and a beer-swollen belly. He had a jowly face, unhealthy and dissipated, the skin almost grey in tone, the eyes small, the lips loose and flabby under a fleshy but strangely upturned nose that would have looked better on a girl. Despite his unfortunate physiognomy, he still retained an air of superiority verging on the arrogant. What on earth did Penelope see in this weird creature?

She gave him a warm smile as he approached them.

"Giles, I'd like you to meet Peregrine Dalton, better known to his friends as Perry. Darling, this is Giles Pritchard from America!"

"Extremely happy to make your acquaintance, Mr Pritchard. Penny's already told me so much about you – you quite made her afternoon! May I call you by your Christian name?"

Giles couldn't help but admire the man's sudden flash of charm, his rich beautifully-modulated tones. The voice – deep, resonant and cultured – completely belied his physical appearance. Giles had never heard such superb articulation. His father's voice had been one in a million, but this man's was something different. He could understand Penelope falling in love with the voice alone.

He answered him with a wide grin.

"Sure – if I can call you Perry." He shook his hand, was surprised by the strength in the man's grasp.

"And please call me Penny," laughed the girl. "Only my parents call me Penelope."

"Sure, Penny, though I did prefer Melissa," said Giles, giving her a side-long wink. "But Penny and Perry it is. You sound like a couple of Walt Disney characters!"

They all laughed, Perry's laugh as rich and distinctive as his voice. He immediately involved Giles in captivating small talk and before he knew it, they were outside the hotel and in a cab heading in the direction of Piccadilly Circus.

Scarcely knowing what had hit him, Giles enjoyed one of the finest evenings of his life. Perry was charm and intelligence personified. He had a ready wit, but never directed it against Giles. Penny sparkled and shone like a jewel, her soft tinkling laugh and alluring appearance drawing everybody's eyes to their table. To cap it all, the food was superb – the cuisine French, the service impeccable.

233

Captivated by their excellent company, he began to feel he had known them both for years. The evening seemed to fly by. He was more than sorry when they eventually had to leave the restaurant.

On the way back to the hotel, he decided not to make a play for Penny. At least, not that night. Perry had been far too nice to do the dirty on him that same evening. He wanted to enjoy more of their company before doing anything which might spoil the easy stimulating relationship they had established this evening. But quite astonishingly, after Giles and Penny alighted at the Ritz, Perry stayed on in the taxi.

"Have to go, Giles," he explained. "I've an early start in the morning. Thoroughly enjoyed the evening. See you tomorrow." He gave a friendly wave as the taxi drew away.

Penny took him firmly by the arm.

"I'd love a good-night drink, Giles," she said. "Won't you invite me up to your suite?"

"Sure," he said. He never looked a gift horse in the mouth.

He surpassed even his own prediction of a twenty-four-hour conquest. Penny was in his bed – within twelve hours of their first meeting!

Chapter 37

He spent the next three days in a whirlwind of activity with his newly-found friends. Perry seemed completely blind to Giles's affair with his girlfriend; or if he was aware of their sexual antics every night – which Giles thought he would have been a fool not to have been – seemed happy to ignore it.

Together, the three of them visited every highspot and attraction in London from the Tate Gallery, the Tower of London and St. Paul's to the meanest dive in Soho. They cruised the canals of Little Venice, visited Kew gardens and drank at the traditional Thames-side pubs.

For Giles it was the happiest period of his life. The weather held good, Penny satisfied his every sexual need, whilst Perry never ceased to amaze him with his razor-sharp wit, genial conversation and boundless fund of knowledge. Giles found he paid most of the checks when they were out, but it was well worth it. He couldn't have hired a more knowledgeable, attentive and entertaining pair of guides.

In an incredibly short period of time he discovered the heart and soul of London, in the process making valued friendships with two of the most attractive and stimulating people he'd ever known. He found Penny delightful in body and mind. As for Perry, he no longer even considered the man's physical ugliness. His natural charm made him forget everything about him, except his scintillating personality.

One night, he lay in bed with Penny, exhausted but blissfully content after a particularly acrobatic session of love-making. Consumed with curiosity about Perry's seeming indifference to their affair and confident of her affection for him, he decided to broach the subject.

"Are you really unofficially engaged to Perry, or was that just a way of fending me off?" he asked casually.

"Oh no! We have a definite understanding." She stretched out languorously on her back, raised her arms and crooked them behind her head. Even in that position her large breasts seemed scarcely any less lavish. Munificent, he decided, was the word for them!

"So why are you sleeping with me?" he challenged. "And why doesn't Perry seem to care?"

She turned her huge dark eyes on him.

"Have you always been faithful to your girlfriends?"

"That's different," said Giles, annoyed.

She laughed her tinkly laugh. "The typical male chauvinist! It's normal for a man to be promiscuous but not acceptable for a woman, I suppose." She turned on her side, faced him directly.

"Don't you realise, Giles – you and I are very much alike. We have the same physical needs. Perry satisfies me mentally, but as you've seen, he doesn't exactly excel in masculine libido, and he's far from being the perfect male specimen – not like you!" She eyed him, provocatively, started to fondle him again.

"But he must get jealous," he murmured, trying not to be distracted. "He obviously adores you."

"Quite honestly, I really don't think he realises what's going on. It may sound strange. But Perry doesn't think much about sex, so it never occurs to him that other people do. I doubt he's even considered we might be lovers. And if he did, it wouldn't bother him so much. He'd probably accept it as a need I have to fulfil."

"So I'm just satisfying your physical requirements?" he growled, offended by the remark. Most of the girls he made love to ended up head over heels in love with him.

"Don't be silly, Giles. It's just that Perry is different. You must admit it. He's extremely intelligent – and one day he'll be very rich!"

"So will I!" he retorted, even more riled.

She laughed softly. It reminded him of the delicate tones of the wind-chimes some friends had brought his mother from the Far East.

"Perry's extremely wealthy, already," she said, pursing her full lips. "And he's about to become filthy rich."

His irritation reverted to curiosity.

"An inheritance?"

She shook her head.

"Oh no, through his own efforts, or at least through those of his contacts." She looked sideways at him, suddenly coy. "I shouldn't really be saying all this ..."

He started to caress her ample breasts, felt the nipples harden beneath his adept fingers.

"He wouldn't mind you telling me – we're good friends. Perhaps I could help, or if it's a really good scheme, invest some money myself."

She shot up from the bed, her eyes shining.

"Why didn't I think of that before? If you do have money, I'm sure Perry would be glad to advise you – put you in the way of a fantastic opportunity. He's an extremely generous person. Mind you, you would need a sizeable amount. He doesn't fool around with small sums."

"That could be arranged," he said, grandly. Christ! He had to get hold of some money quickly. He couldn't miss a golden opportunity like this. He'd hock his investments, borrow from his mother. "Tell me more about this get-rich scheme of Perry's. Are you sure it's legal?"

Penny chuckled. "Of course... though you could say it involves stretching the law a little. 'Insider information', they call it. Perry has lots of contacts in the financial world. He's had a hot tip about one big company – there's a take-over bid in the offing. The company shares should increase dramatically."

Giles's blue-green eyes glittered. This sounded more like it. No risk, no crime, no hard work – just knowing the right people. Even if the proposed take-over didn't come off, the shares were bound to gain from the interest raised. They certainly wouldn't lose. He couldn't go wrong!

"Don't let's talk about it now," whispered Penny, her voice growing hoarse, a sure sign she was physically aroused. "Discuss it with Perry tomorrow. I'm sure he'll help you. But don't let him know I spilled the beans. He'd be furious."

She threw a shapely leg across his body, knelt above him and started to fondle him the way she knew he loved best.

* * * * * * *

He managed to raise the subject with Perry the following day during a drink between matches at Wimbledon's Centre Court. Penny had opted out for the afternoon. Tennis didn't interest her, she said, and the strawberries and cream weren't as good as they used to be. She had winked at Giles, obviously cueing him to make the most of his time alone with Perry.

He took a long sip from his glass of Pimm's, grinned across at Perry.

"How did you manage to get Centre Court tickets at such short notice? I thought we were going down to Henley today."

"The match on Centre Court looked a corker, so I decided to transfer our plans."

"And the tickets?"

"I have my contacts," said Perry mildly.

He sighed.

"I envy you your contacts. At times over here I feel a fish out of water. I'd hoped to make use of the visit, to make some new investments. The dollar's at a high and I don't know how much longer it will last."

"Oh, I think you have time yet," Perry said slowly. "Are you really looking for investment possibilities here? I thought your visit was purely for pleasure."

"I always have my eyes and ears open," he said, his tone nonchalant. He didn't want to frighten Perry off by being too eager.

"You have a large amount of cash readily available?" asked Perry, equally casually.

"Sure," lied Giles. He'd damn well see it was available – if the right chance came his way.

"I've got my fingers into a rather interesting pie at the moment," said Perry, softly. "If you're really interested, I could try to put some of it your way."

"Sounds interesting," he said, his tone noncommittal, but he could feel the adrenaline rising.

"Let's go and see the rest of the tennis. We'll talk about it later."

Giles nodded. He smiled to himself as he followed Perry back to the court. His friend had taken the bait – he was on his way to some fast dollars!

* * * * * * *

They discussed the matter in greater depth later that evening. Giles was staggered at the sum Perry proposed to invest in the company. It must be a sure thing for this intelligent urbane man to be risking so much of his own money though from what Penny had said, it was probably only a relatively small part of his overall wealth.

Giles spoke later that night with his accountant in the States, instructing him to realise all that was left of his assets and transfer the proceeds to the UK immediately. The accountant sounded dubious, but Giles had the last word.

Then he rang his mother.

"Mom! You've gotta do it! It's the chance of a lifetime. I'll never be able to make so much money so quickly – with so little effort."

"But Giles, I do not have that sort of money. It is all invested to give me an income should anything happen to your father. I have already given you all the spare cash I had."

"Come along, Mother. I've never had a chance like this before."

The line went silent.

"Mom ... are you there?"

"Yes, I am still here."

Her voice had gone tinny and hollow. Damn these long-distance lines!

"Mom, please ..." he pleaded.

"I will see what I can do, Giles," she said, still sounding hesitant.

"I need the money fast – otherwise the chance will go. The news could break any time now!"

"I will do what I can Giles," she repeated, impatiently. "I can do no more."

"I'll call tomorrow, as late as possible to give you time. Please try, Mother!"

"Yes, Giles."

He sensed the resignation in her voice. She would do it, he was sure. She could never refuse him anything.

* * * * * * *

Within five days he had raised both his own money and a considerable sum from his mother. He made out a banker's cheque in favour of Peregrine Dalton, which he passed on to Perry for the purchase of the shares. Perry winked conspiratorially as he gave him a receipt for the money. Before he left, they celebrated the deal with a bottle of champagne.

He sat back waiting for the money to come rolling in!

* * * * * * *

Matters started to go wrong a couple of days later. Penny rang to say she and Perry would be unable to make the concert that night at the Royal Festival Hall.

"I'm terribly sorry, darling, but it's this big financial deal you know. Perry has to go dinner with his stockbroker – see everything's been sorted out properly. Apparently the takeover's imminent."

"But there's nothing to stop you coming over – or have you got to see the stockbroker as well?" He couldn't keep the sarcasm from his voice.

"Of course," she said sweetly. "After all it is a social occasion as well."

"You've never bothered to accompany Perry before, when it's a business matter," insisted Giles.

"Don't be so possessive, Giles. I promise I'll come to dinner tomorrow night."

"But what about the Henley Regatta? I thought we were all going down tomorrow."

"Darling," she chided. "You can't expect to make a fortune and not miss out on some of the social scene. Don't worry. I'll see you tomorrow evening at eight." The line went dead in his hand.

She didn't show the following evening. Instead, a messenger delivered a hastily-written note.

Giles darling,
Great news! Everything is going to plan. We shall all be rich – isn't it exciting? Watch the papers tomorrow or the next day.
Sorry about tonight. Will call tomorrow. Save your energy for me!
Love, love, love ... Penny.

He stared at the note in disbelief. What was she playing at? And what was Perry doing all this time? He hadn't heard a word from him for nearly three days. Still it seemed everything was going to plan. Tomorrow – the note said – watch the papers tomorrow. It wasn't so long. He knew much of his bad temper stemmed from the fact that he was missing their company. Life without Perry and Penny was slow and boring. He grinned to himself as he studied her last words again. Save your energy! If he didn't see her soon, he'd explode!

* * * * * * *

The following day he scanned every financial newspaper. But there was no mention of the big takeover. The company price was still listed the same, in fact a few points down on the previous day. He started to feel scared. Could anything have gone wrong?

Nervously he paced his suite, frightened to go out in case Penny called. Why hadn't she given him a fixed time for her call?

Later in the afternoon he realised he hadn't eaten anything all day, only coffee in the morning. Despite the nervous churning of his stomach, he felt pangs of hunger. He ordered a light meal of smoked salmon and scrambled eggs. It arrived in minutes, together with the evening papers.

Again he scanned the pages. Nothing! And no call from Penny. Worse still, he had no telephone number for either her or Perry, no address, no means of making contact with them.

He went cold inside. Perry's receipt would be worthless if he couldn't trace him! Why had he never gotten a telephone number or an address from them? The question answered itself. Because it had never been necessary. He'd always been in the company of at least one of them, if not both, during the last few weeks. They always made contact with him, picked him up at the hotel.

At one time, that first day, he'd assumed Penny was staying at the hotel, too. The memory made him lunge for the 'phone.

No, said Reception, there was no record of a Miss Penelope Smythe staying at the hotel, nor of a Mr Peregrine Dalton. Then, in desperation, Giles remembered the waiter in the tea-lounge.

Asking the receptionist to take careful note of all telephone messages, he rushed down to the tea lounge. They'd almost finished serving. He soon spotted the same waiter who'd served him that first day, the one Penny said had known her all her life.

He walked over to him.

"Excuse me, but could I have quick word with you? I need some information urgently."

"We're rather busy at the moment, sir – clearing up, you know," replied the waiter apologetically.

"It won't take a minute." He slipped the man a five-pound note.

"Of course, sir."

"You do remember me?"

The waiter smiled.

"Yes, sir. I hope you enjoyed your tea."

"Yes, yes ... it was great. But I wanted to ask about the lady."

"The lady, sir?"

"Yes. The one I joined... you know, the one you've known for years?"

The waiter frowned in puzzlement.

"I remember the young lady, sir. She does visit the hotel occasionally to meet friends – but only over the last six months or so. I never saw her before that."

"You mean you don't know her name."

"Of course not, sir. It's not my business. But I could check her name from the table reservations. However, I don't think I could disclose it to you, sir, without permission."

"It doesn't matter – I know her name," said Giles, impatiently. "But she insisted you knew hers!" The light suddenly started to dawn. "Those friends of hers you mentioned – were they always male?"

"Oh yes, sir, it was always gentlemen she met here." He coughed discreetly. "Mind you, sir, she always seemed a most respectable lady. I don't want you to get the wrong idea."

Giles looked grim.

"Don't worry – I'm just starting to get the right idea."

He strode furiously out of the tea-room.

Chapter 38

Pattaya, Thailand. February 1985

Giles woke with a start, blinked his eyes against the bright Thai sunlight which had managed to penetrate the room despite the grime on the window. God it was only eight o'clock in the morning! Even more surprising, his head was clear – he didn't have a trace of a hangover! He rose and walked over towards the door, caught sight of his own reflection in the cracked mirror on the nearby wall and recoiled with horror. His face, drawn and haggard with lines he'd never seen before, might have been the face of a man fifteen years older. His golden tan had turned a dirty black, his hair lay matted and filthy, his strong chin hidden by an unkempt beard which looked like the nesting place for a whole range of wildlife.

He looked down at his grubby body, realised he could actually smell his own uncleanliness. The fit athletic body he'd once been so proud of had deteriorated into flab and sag. He no longer even held himself erect, but stooped as if apologising for his poor shape. He felt utter disgust at himself. No wonder he no longer made it with the girls. He thought about taking a shower. There was rusty apology for a shower-unit in the bathroom down the hall, but again a strange malignant lethargy took control of his limbs. It all involved too much effort, and what was the point?

He felt in his pockets for some Baht coins. Nothing! God – he'd better tidy himself up a bit, get back on the beach and try to get a hire for the boat. That was all he had to live on now – the money from the hire of an antiquated speedboat which a richer hippy friend had left him when moving on from Thailand. It just managed to cover the cost of his food and drink plus the rent for a room in this hovel of a building which called itself a boarding house at the back of the Pattaya tourist strip. Not so many yards away, along the front, the visitors indulged themselves in the luxury and opulence of the magnificent beach hotels. Still, at least the room was dirt-cheap – that was the main thing. He also knew the cheapest places to eat and drink. What a bit of luck he'd discovered this cosmopolitan resort on the Bay of Thailand, just a hundred miles south of Bangkok.

* * * * * * *

It was a poor working day – only one rental – but at least he'd have enough for a good meal tonight. He spent the rest of the day lazing on the sand, watching the happy carefree holiday world go by. Then just when he was thinking of leaving, he saw her coming up the beach – a striking brunette with a pert nose and large innocent dark eyes which gave her prettiness a waif-like quality.

But it wasn't this which drew Giles's attention. She had the most fabulous legs he'd seen for a long time – long, lithe and shapely. Most long-legged girls had a tendency to knobbly knees, or their limbs would err on the skinny side, lacking form. The legs on this water-maiden were gorgeous, both in shape and texture. They glistened smooth and golden-tanned with a shiny sheen which didn't come from greasy sun-oil. He shifted his position in the sand to get a better look at her. She was a complete change from the soft gentle Thai girls with their beautiful oriental faces but much shorter limbs.

The girl had just emerged from the sea. She'd obviously been swimming – really swimming, not just taking a cooling dip. Water streamed from her hair and body. She shook her short curls and droplets of silver spray sparkled around her in the pink and golden light of the late afternoon. Her body, slim and taut, glowed with radiant health; her young, unblemished face shone with the satisfaction of recent energetic exercise.

She started to move up the beach towards him, her movements graceful and exquisitely feminine – her hips undulating, her small well-formed breasts rising and falling in a ripple effect.

He sat upright on the golden sand knowing she would pass right by him. He gave a seductive smile as she brushed lightly between him and the small speedboat pulled up on the beach by his side. She stared at him momentarily but continued on her way scarcely seeing him, her only reaction a compassionate widening of her eyes – as if he were some unfortunate stray dog she pitied but didn't want to become involved with.

He turned to watch her go, felt sobs rise within his chest. He could have accepted it – if she'd ignored him completely. Most of the foreign girls did now. Even the young, ever-available Thai girls who worked the beach road and its bars – normally so gently persistent and smiling when they offered themselves to their prey however old and ugly – had given up where Giles was concerned.

He had no money. They tolerated him and though they still bestowed their shy inscrutable smiles, they allowed him to pass, unmolested.

But this European girl's obvious pity for him struck at his innermost pride. Damn it – he was a wreck! Why hadn't he realised it before? It had taken the shock of his own reflection this morning in the mirror, the pity of the beautiful girl to bring him to his senses. But he knew it wasn't only that. He'd seen himself as he really was, mainly because for just once he hadn't woken up suffering from the after-effects of drink or drugs – or both. Not that he'd ever gotten into the hard stuff. Just enough to help the alcohol provide an escape from reality. When sober, he had been forced to acknowledge his failures, his total disillusionment with life. The continuous haze of intoxication seemed less painful than a state of sobriety.

He couldn't recall why he hadn't got stoned last night, why he'd awoken cold-sober this morning. But it was just as well. Now at least he realised how low he'd sunk. He! – Giles Pritchard – who once could have had the world, and any girl in it!

Abruptly he rose to his feet. He had to get himself clean – he couldn't live with his filthy body any longer.

* * * * * * *

He sat in the noisy bar enjoying hot spicy Thai soup, followed by delicious crab and his favourite charcoal-grilled chicken with sticky rice. Eating in the steamy resort was still incredibly cheap. At least he'd manage to provide himself with the occasional good food, despite his lack of money. When he wasn't completely stoned that was. He couldn't remember how he'd eaten at other times. But tonight, freshly showered, shaved, squeaky-clean and cold-sober, he relished every mouthful. Determined to stay that way, he asked for a fruit juice instead of his usual Thai beer or local whisky.

The Thais, according to their Buddhist religion weren't supposed to drink alcohol – it was one of their Five Commandments. But a ready supply of liquor was always available for visitors and the less stoic of the natives. The only thing he'd really missed had been a decent glass of wine. The wine, all imported from abroad, had been too exorbitantly priced for his meagre pocket.

He started to reflect when and where it had all gone wrong. When he'd been conned, of course, and lost all his money. He shuddered now, even at the thought of it, ashamed of his lack of guile and perspicacity. He'd fallen for the oldest trick in the world – he should have known better.

What had happened to his normal smartness, his worldly, sceptical approach to life? He'd been deceived by that same British urbanity which his father had always used against him. But his father had never robbed him – except of his inheritance, of course. He supposed it was the same thing in the end.

He'd lost not only his own money, but his mother's as well. She'd been furious. He knew his father would see she was all right financially, but she'd complained about being let down, betrayed by her son's stupidity. Now she – who had always admired his cleverness, his instinct for survival – was as disillusioned as his father

How could he have let Penny and Perry get away with it? He'd been a complete fool! He squirmed as he remembered it all. He must have stood out like a sore thumb – obvious prey for Penny lying in wait at the Ritz for some fresh-faced young idiot to fall into their trap. They'd led him by the hand all the way, and he'd followed, like some naive trusting child; stunning Penny with her alluring body, ugly Perry with his wit and bewitching sophistication.

Even when he'd discovered how they'd deceived him, there'd been little anyone could do. The British police, though polite, treated him like the idiot he was, obviously sympathetic but tut-tutting at his foolish, credulous behaviour throughout the affair. There had been little they could do. Penny and Perry, obviously operating under pseudonyms, were by that time well out of the country, Perry leaving first with the cash, while Penny covered for him.

Penny and Perry – God! His Walt Disney characters! He should have been suspicious of the names alone! How they must have laughed at him behind his back! He'd realised Penny wasn't in love with him, but he'd been confident of her fondness for him, her admiration of his physical and sexual prowess. He'd been immensely flattered by the attention of the brilliant Perry. In a state of utter euphoria, all his normal caution and common sense had flown out of the window. They'd certainly been masters of their trade.

The worst fall-out from the affair wasn't the loss of the money, but of his own self-confidence and self-esteem. He could blame nobody but himself. Gathering together the meagre remains of his resources, he'd fled with his tail between his legs to the Far East – Hong Kong, Singapore, India and finally Thailand.

But it had been downhill all the way. In each place he'd met similar young gypsies – European and American youngsters, all seeking something different, a new answer to their problems in the mystic atmosphere of the exotic East. His own tenacious instinct for survival, and a certain degree of luck, had saved him from the worst of the drug scene. He'd moved in the society of hopeless young addicts, but somehow never succumbed to the temptation, despite the pressures and his own feelings of desolation.

The young Thai waiter roused him from his reveries. Did he want anything else to eat? he asked, with a cheeky grin. Giles shook his head, despondently. He'd had enough – of everything! He knew now what he really wanted to do. Go home! Back to the States and make a new start. This time he'd learnt his lesson. He knew it would be hard – he'd have to start from the bottom again. But there was no alternative.

He strolled back along the colourful thronging streets, drinking in the sounds, sights and spicy aromas of the night scene. It might be his last evening in the noisy jostling streets of the Thailand he'd come to love. He smiled tolerantly at the breathtakingly beautiful transvestites, gently declined the attentions of the nubile young bar-girls, some of them, he suddenly realised, little more than children. Now that he'd cleaned himself up, looked more affluent, he was immediately accepted as ready prey.

Delicious aromas wafted up from the noodle stalls along the busy street. He sniffed the tropical air – hints of jasmine and honeysuckle mingled with the culinary fragrances. Then a waft of something less sanitary assaulted his nostrils. He grinned to himself, felt suddenly nostalgic. He'd miss the Far East; but he couldn't wait to get home!

He strode briskly to his friend, Spang's traditional Thai house on the outskirts of town where he intended to telephone his father. He knew Spang would lend him the money for his ticket home. He'd met the young doctor soon after moving to Pattaya, when he'd gone down with a severe stomach bug. Whatever Spang had given him had settled his alarming diarrhoea in a couple of hours. After that, they became close friends. Spang had been educated in the States and loved to talk about America. He'd tried to make Giles change his aimless lifestyle and go back home.

"This is not the life for an intelligent young man like you, Giles. It is a criminal waste. You disappoint me."

He hadn't wanted to listen. Eventually his visits to Spang's house grew less and less frequent. His friend had probably given him up for lost by now. But he'd always promised to lend him money – as long as it was for him to return home.

Spang gave a start of surprise when he saw him, but noting the change in Giles's appearance, his mild gentle face broke into a warm smile.

"So you want to go home, my friend?" he said, immediately understanding the reason for Giles's visit.

He nodded.

"Good," said Spang, simply. "How much will you need?"

Impulsively, Giles grasped his hand in gratitude. It was so like Spang not to say any more, to refrain from 'I told you so' – anything which might harm his pride. He hadn't even mentioned the words 'borrow' or 'lend'.

"Thanks, Spang. I'll check with the agency. But first could I phone my father?"

"Of course!" said Spang, grinning in obvious delight at his friend's transformation. "And I insist you take some refreshment with us before you leave."

Giles smiled in admiration at Spang's immaculate English, his innate hospitality, then saw the young Thai's expression had changed to one of sadness.

"Does this mean I shall not see you again?" asked Spang.

"Of course not! I'll always come back to visit, and you must come as my guest to the States."

Spang's face relaxed.

"Good, good. This is a time then for celebration. But please – first make your telephone call."

Hearing the number ring out, Giles felt suddenly nervous. Please, Dad... please be in, he thought. I have to know it's ok. Now I've decided and made my plans, I wanna get back right away.

A woman's voice answered, one he didn't recognise, obviously a new maid.

"Who shall I say is calling?" she enquired.

"Mr Giles Pritchard," he replied. He heard her catch her breath. She obviously knew who he was, had heard something about his lurid past.

"Just one moment, sir."

"I'm ringing long-distance – from Thailand. Put my father on the line as soon as you can."

"Just one moment, sir," she repeated, obviously not sure the father would want to talk to his prodigal son.

Dad must be there, thought Giles, otherwise she'd have said so immediately. He waited impatiently. After what seemed an eternity, there was a flurry on the line. Then with relief he heard his father's smoothly-measured tones.

"Well, Giles. This is something of a surprise – after all it's only two years or so since we heard from you."

Damn him! Why did his first words have to drip with sarcasm. He tried to keep his voice under control, polite enough, without being too obsequious.

"Hi, Dad. Sorry I haven't been in touch before, but I think you understand why."

"Yes, I understand, Giles, but I certainly don't approve. Still at least you have called now. I take it you need money?"

Giles winced.

"No... well at least, not right now. But I wanted to tell you. I'm coming home."

"Oh!" He spoke the word quietly. Giles couldn't tell if his tone was one of relief or resignation.

"How's Mom?"

"She's all right. Always worried about you, of course. She hasn't been the same since you both lost all your money in that ridiculous affair in London. Your flight to the Far East didn't help matters! You've been most cruel and inconsiderate as far as she's concerned. I may not care what happens to you anymore, Giles, but your mother's different."

"Sorry, Dad. I should have got in touch before, but I've been having a tough time myself. Still, I'm over the worst. Tell her I'm just fine."

"So I imagine," said his father, dryly. "When shall we expect you? You're in Bangkok, I gather?"

"Pattaya – a resort to the south. I'll be back on the first flight I can get tomorrow. I'll call you when I land. Must go now – I'm using a friend's phone. See you, Dad."

"Giles? Just one thing. Your mother will be happy to see you, but don't think you can return ... just start back ... as if nothing had happened."

"No, Dad. See you soon." He rang off. His father couldn't mean those last words. Even if he did, he would show him that this time he really intended to reform and change his ways. Surely his father would take him back.

Relieved at his decision and full of plans for the future, he went to tell Spang the good news.

PART FIVE

KATE

Those have most power to hurt us, that we love.

John Fletcher

'Tis better to have loved and lost
Than never to have loved at all.

Tennyson

Chapter 39

Ibiza, Spain. July 1985

Eighteen-year-old Kate Radcliffe drove along the winding mountain road to Cala Vadella in an open Citroen Mehari. The car had seen better days. Noisy and uncomfortable, it roared and rattled its progress despite the smooth tarmac surface. But she loved this battered old apology for a jeep. With the side and back panels down and only the fringed, surrey-style roof above her, she could enjoy the cooling rush of air as she drove, smell the heady scents of the countryside which she adored. She felt giddy with happiness. Home at last in Ibiza!

Her long pale-blonde hair streamed behind her, occasionally whipping across her cheeks with the back draught. Her bronzed face radiated her happiness, her topaz eyes sparkling with anticipation and a simple joie-de-vivre. This road through the hills from San José to the sandy beach and deep bay of Cala Vadella, on the island's south-west coast, was one of her favourite drives. Cathy, her grandmother, had told her that in its days as a dirt-track, it had been the most beautiful of the island's scenic routes. The new asphalt road made it more accessible, less dramatic, but she had to admit the views from her mountain vantage point were still magnificent. Stunned by one particularly breathtaking sight, she pulled in to the side.

The new road had created a water-shed between craggy peaks on one side and an undulating fertile valley which fell gently towards the sea. Young fresh pines grew in abundance by the steep road-side. More pine trees, in that incredibly fresh emerald colour, dotted the stretches of neatly-worked terraces which descended the valley slopes in mathematical progression. Olive, almond and carob trees grew in profusion. Patches of russet-brown earth and verdant hillocks glowed in the softness of the early evening light.

Kate had found the day intensely hot, the sun penetrating even her deeply tanned skin. After the fierce heat and the vibrant colours of the afternoon, she felt refreshed by the cooler breezes of early evening, the softer hues, the earthy aroma of the rich, red terraces.

In the distance, the intense azure blue of the tranquil Mediterranean seemed stolen from an artist's palette. The effect was heightened by the western light which lent the water an effervescent sparkle. She had to crinkle her eyes against the dazzling silver reflection of the sun's rays. Beyond the shimmering streams of light, the colour of the water melted into a softer blue which stretched as far as the eye could see to a hazy horizon of indigo.

No clear distant vistas here as in winter time, no views to the mainland. To the far south-west the towering rock, Es Vedrá, rose stark and precipitous from the translucent waters. It looked unreal – a mystical, dreaming spire suspended in the tranquil sea. This was what the promised land must have looked like, she thought – undulating pine-covered hills, fertile valleys, a sparkling sea ...

The whole panorama had a feeling of space and extension, the magical light of evening bringing out the soft pink tones. It was her favourite part of the day – an opportunity to see the world through rose-tinted glasses!

She heaved a sigh of pure pleasure at the beauty and silence. She only experienced this kind of rapture when in the countryside or out at sea. Kate loved people, but her happiest moments had always been when alone with nature. She felt a kinship, a oneness with natural things, her spirit most in tune with a silver beam of moonlight, a warm breeze in the air, the waves rippling the sea, the soughing of the pinetrees, or the vibrant colour of a geranium. She had missed it all so much while away at school.

The tranquillity of the scene below her was suddenly broken by two speed-boats as they cut through the water leaving foaming wakes in their trail. She wondered if they were friends racing, or had they just happened to meet like two camels in a lonely desert?

The sight of the boats reminded her of her date with the Reynolds family. She glanced quickly down at her watch. She would need to hurry to reach Cala Vadella in time to meet them all when they arrived on the yacht. Almost reluctantly she continued on her way, loathe to leave the magical scene. She had only arrived back on the island the day before, but already she was feeling as if she had never been away.

She had spent all her childhood from the age of six in Ibiza. Attending the local school, she had quickly absorbed the Spanish language in the classroom and the native Catalan tongue from the local children. She remembered those childhood days as a blissful, sun-lit period; her free-time spent with friends, playing like so many young puppies in the pinewoods or on the beaches where they swam, sailed and skied. Life had been a paradise of sea, sunshine, freedom and boundless fresh air. She had wept for hours when, at the tender age of eleven, she learned she was to go to boarding school in England. Her memories of her homeland had been dim – days of Northern greyness compared to the sunlit brightness of the Mediterranean.

Yet Ibiza had been the scene of her parent's tragic car accident. Her mother and father, two young beautiful people in the flush of love, had perished here in one tragic moment of mangled metal and glass. Yet Kate never resented Ibiza for stealing her parents from her. If it hadn't been for the island, they would never have met; she, Kate, would never have been born. She knew her parents had adored the island, spent their happiest hours here. She had inherited that same affection.

Her grandparents, Cathy and Leslie, had moved permanently from England in 1972, to make their home on the island. As far as Kate was concerned, that was when her life had really begun.

She didn't miss her parents too much. Adored and cosseted by Cathy and Leslie, she never went short of love and affection. With no memory whatsoever of either her mother or father, she couldn't miss them as individuals. What she did hate was the feeling of being different – the knowledge that she was, in fact, an orphan. She missed never being able to chat about her parents – even complain about them – as her friends at school did. They all took their parents for granted. Only one of them lacked one parent. As Oscar Wilde's Lady

Bracknell had declared – nobody should be careless enough to lose both of them! It set her apart.

She sometimes felt that having no parents had made it easier for her to become almost a child of nature, as if the countryside around her was there to succour her spirit, comfort and revive her soul. She adored poetry and was particularly drawn to Wordsworth, a kindred being who seemed to echo her own affinity with Nature, sense – like her – the same mystical harmony.

Of course she adored her grandparents. As a little girl, she insisted on calling them by their christian names. They were her substitute parents. If she couldn't actually call them Mother and Dad, she didn't want them to stand out too obviously as her grandmother and grandfather. Referring to Cathy and Leslie by name brought them closer to her generation – people might even think they were her real parents! So Cathy and Leslie they had remained!

She also enjoyed the avid attention of her uncles, or rather half-uncles, Tim and Adrian – they were both like father figures to her. Cathy's twin-sons by her marriage to Leslie had been only eighteen when Kate's parents died. Kate had been just one year old, but in her childhood memories Uncle Tim and Uncle Adrian were two bear-like figures who scooped her up in their arms and spoiled her with presents and treats. Both married now, with children of their own, they still idolised her.

The raucous sound of the car engine became more bearable as she slowed to descend the last steep section of the hill winding down to the golden sands of the beach. From her vantage point above, she could see the Reynolds' yacht coming to moor in the deep lagoon of Cala Vadella. Scores of boats were already anchored in the well-protected bay.

She hooted the horn, waved happily to Roger, Claire and their mother, Jane, who stood at the helm. Jane neatly brought the graceful yacht into its mooring, Roger handling the anchor while Claire put out fenders. They all loved sailing and worked slickly in easy co-ordination.

Although she hadn't seen them for a couple of years, Kate was very close to the Reynolds family. Jane, her father's cousin and an old friend of both her parents, had dined out with her mother and father on the night of their fatal accident.

She had been unexpectedly widowed some three years ago when her husband, Bill, suffered a coronary. Instead of retiring into a sad and bereaved widowhood, she had quickly pulled herself together, determined to make the most of the rest of her life. It was what Bill would have wanted, she explained, and her children agreed.

Kate felt great admiration for this remarkably vital woman. Her chestnut hair and jade eyes set her apart, as did her sense of fun and incredible energy. Her trim figure and impish face – with its girlish freckles and upturned nose – could have belonged to a woman ten years younger. Kate held her in great affection and only hoped she would age as gracefully as Jane! Her aunt had many admirers, but as yet hadn't succumbed to any of them. Kate didn't believe she ever would. Mentally Jane was still bound to Bill, but it didn't prevent her packing more into one day than most people could accomplish in a week!

"Hi! Kate!" yelled Roger from the boat. "I hardly recognised you! Grab a drink at the bar – we'll be ashore in a few moments." The three of them lowered a small tender into the water and Roger rowed the tiny craft steadily towards the beach. As they drew near, Kate left her drink on the beach-bar table and walked to the water's edge to help pull the tender ashore.

They all gave her enthusiastic hugs.

Claire held her affectionately at arm's length.

"It's great to see you again, Kate. You look absolutely marvellous – as usual," she added good-naturedly, without a trace of envy. "How was the weather in England?"

Claire might lack her mother's striking looks, thought Kate, but her sweet temper and good humour made up for any physical shortcomings. She grinned back at her.

"Dreadful! It rained all last week. It might as well have been winter."

Jane studied her with a proud, almost motherly eye.

"Kate, darling – you've grown more ravishing than ever! Your parents were both handsome people, but you've inherited the best of both – your father's Nordic colouring and Sam's lovely features."

Kate blushed modestly, not understanding why everybody raved about her looks. Her hair was too blonde by far, almost a paler shade of white! Her topaz eyes lacked the rich depths of her father's brown eyes. She would have loved to have dark eyes like his! And her figure was fuller than the slim elegant form of the lovely woman she knew from photos to be her mother.

Roger said nothing, just stared at her in surprised admiration. In a rather gangling way, he had his mother's good looks. He hadn't seen Kate for four years and seemed taken aback by the transformation.

"My God!" he managed to stammer at last. "What happened to Kitty-Kat, my tomboy friend of the past?"

"She's still here!" she replied, strangely moved to hear her old nick-name again. "Don't worry, I haven't got too old to push you in the pool – or stuff a crab down your t-shirt! Mind you, you're so big and tall now, it could be more difficult!"

"Just try!" said Roger, obviously pleased she remembered their previous teasing friendship.

"Now you two, act your age," said Jane, a twinkle in her eye. "Thanks for meeting us, Kate. It saved one of us coming by car to pick up the others. We don't get so many opportunities to sail together. By the way, you must come out with us on the boat one day."

"I'd love to," beamed Kate.

They walked in the fading light across to the beach bar.

"Shall we have a drink here," asked Claire, "or should we get on to the barbecue?"

Jane looked at her watch. "I think we ought to be making our way to Cala Carbó. The barbecue will be underway pretty soon. Do you mind if we leave straightaway Kate?"

"Of course not. I can't wait to see everyone again."

They all climbed into the battered Mehari and set off up the steep hill in the direction of Cala Carbó, a tiny beach to the south of Cala Vadella which boasted two attractive beach restaurants. Unfortunately, the cove offered no safe mooring for larger yachts, so Kate had volunteered to collect her friends from neighbouring Vadella.

"I expect you're glad to be home," said Jane as they drove along. "Cathy told me you've been studying at her old boarding school in England, but it's ages since I've had the chance to chat with her and Leslie. I gather they can't come to the barbecue tonight?"

"No, they had a previous invitation to a friend's for dinner and they hate to let anyone down."

"Yes, of course. How are your studies going, Kate?"

"I've just finished my 'A' Levels – that's how I was able to get away before the end of term."

"How did they go?"

"OK, I think, but I'm keeping my fingers crossed! I'm not as bright as my mother was, you know."

"I don't believe that. Any plans for the future?"

"Nothing specific. If my results are good enough, I'll go on to Oxford – my interviews went pretty well, but I'm not counting my chickens until they've hatched!" She changed down as they drew close to the beach and parked among the trees.

Even before they'd climbed out of the car, the delicious aroma of meat sizzling on a charcoal grill reached her nostrils. Dusk had started to fall and the fairy lights in the trees were already lit.

"Mmm," sniffed Roger. "I hope it's not long before we eat. Come on, Kate. Everyone's looking forward to seeing you again. It will be quite a reunion – most of the old gang are out for the holidays."

He was right. Many of her old friends were there – sons and daughters of ex-patriate residents and regular visitors to the island. They had known each other as children, spent their holidays on the island together. Thrilled to see everyone again and busy renewing old acquaintanceships, she quite forgot her hunger.

"Hi, Chris!"

"Hi, Kate You look stunning. Love that t-shirt!"

"Hello, Kate! Haven't seen you for two years! We went to the Far East last summer!"

Soon she was surrounded by friends, all exchanging news and gossip. Eventually with the barbecue ready to be served, the younger generation gathered on one large table, their parents and friends settling around another.

"Where's Big Bob?" asked Kate, suddenly missing the fat, laughing form of Bob Bagley, normally the life and soul of their parties. "Hasn't he arrived on the island yet?"

"He had to put in an appearance at a drinks party at his parent's villa," said Claire. "He's coming on as soon as he can. Knowing Bob, he shouldn't be long."

Even as she spoke, they heard bellows of laughter through the trees.

"That's Bob!" said Roger.

Kate chuckled. She loved Big Bob – he could always make her laugh, even at her own expense.

The fat man himself appeared through the darkness at the end of their table – accompanied by a tall, well-built, darkly-handsome figure. Kate caught her breath. Who on earth could that be?

Bob suddenly caught sight of her and gave a yell. "Kate! You made it! You look more beautiful than ever. How about a kiss for your crazy, fat friend!" He waddled exaggeratedly towards her.

She laughed, stood up from the table and threw her arms around him. As she drew back, he grabbed the arm of the newcomer by his side, pulled him towards Kate.

"Kate, I like you to meet the latest addition to the Ibiza scene!"

The tall man with dark crinkly hair took her hand in a warm firm handshake. His eyes twinkled, knowingly.

"Hi Kate!" He had a mild, rather attractive American accent.

"Hello," she said, immediately captivated.

He gazed admiringly at her, entranced by her pale-blonde hair, her topaz eyes which gleamed cat-like in the darkness.

"Happy to make your acquaintance, Kate. My name's Giles Pritchard!"

Chapter 40

So that was Kate Radcliffe, mused Giles. He sat alone and silent on the moonlit aft-deck of the yacht he was skippering. It was two in the morning and the temperature had at last become pleasantly cool. The yacht lay motionless at its mooring in the black velvet waters of the marina. He looked up at the stars – they seemed to burn with a brilliant incandescence in the clear night sky, their light reflected in the shimmering sea.

He hadn't been able to sleep, his mind still alert and active, eagerly reflecting on the evening he had just spent on the other side of the island – at the barbecue in Cala Carbó.

Kate Radcliffe! At last he'd found her. Even made a date with her! He laughed wryly to himself. Although quite ignorant of the fact, Kate was now the heir to his father's fortune!

He wondered what her reaction would be should she discover his real identity. There was no likelihood of that, he thought grimly, until his father died! It was that very possibility which had brought him to Ibiza. During the years he had spent in the Far East, his father's health had deteriorated. On his return to the States in March, Giles had been appalled at the extent of his father's physical decline. A month later Jimmy suffered another stroke, leaving one side of his body partially paralysed. A further stroke would surely kill him!

Unfortunately for Giles, despite his repentant return to America, his efforts to ingratiate himself with his parents had completely failed. His father remained unmoved, refusing to believe he had turned over a new leaf. He had spelt it out for Giles – the bulk of his fortune would still go to his other son.

Giles gazed across the harbour to the floodlit Old Town of Ibiza. It rose from the inky darkness like a magic castle in a children's fairy-tale. Fairy-tale! There had been nothing fairy-tale about his last fateful conversation with his father which had inspired his search for his rival Sam. He could still remember every word.

They had been sitting on the garden veranda in the early spring sunshine. He had taken advantage of his father's mellow mood to question him about the past. Unwilling to beat about the bush, he came abruptly to the point.

"Don't you think it's about time you told me about this other son of yours, Dad?"

Pain filled his father's hazel eyes. "I'd rather not talk about it, Giles."

"I'm sorry. I guess it's kinda hard on you, but I think it only fair I should know." He knew an appeal to his father's sense of fair-play was the strongest card in his hand.

His father looked down, rubbed his good hand over the partially-paralysed fingers of the other, slowly closed his eyes – as if the very memory was too much for him.

"Does mother know all about it?" persisted Giles.

He nodded, wordlessly.

"So why can't you spill the beans, Dad?" he demanded angrily. "Why should I be kept in the dark? After all, it's my half-brother we're talking about, or should I say brothers. Is there only one, or have you lots of them lying around?"

His father winced and looked up.

Giles looked away. He had expected an expression of anger at his impertinence, but instead there was understanding in Jimmy's eyes.

"I know how you must feel, Giles. But it's not that easy ... Are you sure you want to hear the whole story?" He paused a moment, searching for words. "It will hurt you as much as it will hurt me."

He felt a shiver go through his body, but his jealousy and curiosity about the dark side of his father's life had been aroused. He desperately wanted to get to the truth.

"What's his name, this half-brother of mine?

Jimmy shrugged his shoulders.

"I suppose I'd better tell you. You'll find out in the end, of course, but by that time no harm can come to anyone. Promise me, Giles, that what I'm about to tell you will never be divulged by you to anyone, until I die."

He gave a reluctant nod. Christ! he thought, what was all the drama about? The truth surely couldn't be as devastating as Dad was making out.

His father looked at him, doubtfully.

"Giles – you've deceived me before, but in this case it's in your own interest to keep the secret. I trust you will do so."

"Thanks for your confidence, Dad," he said, his voice dripping with sarcasm.

"Have you ever given me any reason to trust you?" Steely eyes stared across at him.

He glared back, just as hard.

"You don't seem to accept I've changed now."

"I hope so." The voice sounded weary, wanting to believe, but unable. "If you really want to know all the details ... my other son's name – as far as I've been told – is Sam."

"What about his mother? – your fancy woman!" he asked, bitterly.

"She wasn't a fancy woman, Giles, she was my wife."

"Wife?" he gasped in horror. He had never allowed himself to consider his father might have been married before. In his mind the rival son had to be illegitimate. His mother's reaction to the same question, before he went abroad, had led him to believe the same.

"She was an English girl, in the WAAF," continued his father, wistfully. "We married during the war, just before the Battle of Britain."

Giles shook his head, puzzled. "WAAF? I don't understand."

"Women's Auxiliary Air Force," explained his father, his face suddenly soft and pensive.

Giles felt sick. God! Dad had actually loved this other woman.

"Did she die in the war?" he asked, already hating her for having the nerve to join up in the forces, even though she was a female.

"No." His father's voice rang out sharply.

"So why did you get divorced? A war-time romance and all that – it didn't work out?"

There was a moment of silence.

"We didn't get divorced, Giles." His voice sounded hollow.

"What do you mean, didn't get divorced? Was she Catholic? Was the marriage annulled?"

"No, the marriage was never annulled. And I have every reason to believe Cathy – that was her name – I believe she's still alive."

He sat in stunned silence. Christ! – his father's mind must have been affected by the last stroke. But staring at him, seeing his clarity of expression, the unmistakable apology in his eyes, he suddenly realised it was all true.

"You mean you're still married to her – even now?"

"Yes, Giles. I'm afraid so."

"Christ, Dad! What are you playing at? You mean your marriage to mother was bigamous?" He couldn't believe what his eyes and ears were telling him.

His father had the grace to look down – away from the disgust and hurt in his son's face.

"In that case, I'm the one that's illegitimate!" concluded Giles in dismay. It was all like some dreadful nightmare. But he knew he'd never wake from this one. White hot anger overtook him.

"Dad, you're a fucking hypocrite! You – you've always preached to me about my behaviour, told me I was the rotter. How dare you! What a bastard you've turned out to be! No sorry!" He laughed grimly at his own sick humour. "I'm the one – I'm the bastard – quite literally!" He slumped forward, his head in his hands.

"Giles – I'd like to explain ..."

"There's nothing to explain! Christ, Dad! I just can't believe it! You always made out you were so fucking perfect!"

"Whatever I did, I did to avoid hurting other people, not to deceive them.... except one thing. Unfortunately, that deception started it all."

Giles looked up, his curiosity piqued. "Why the hell didn't you divorce her, Dad – before you married Mom?"

"I couldn't – she thought I was dead! I thought the same about her."

He was still mystified. "This is absolutely crazy! Go on – I might as well hear the worst."

His father nodded miserably.

"You see, Giles, I deserted the RAF."

He looked up, shocked, then gave a wry laugh.

"I don't believe it! Our great Battle of Britain hero! Deserting! First his country, then his wife. What other skeletons have you got locked away in that cupboard, Dad?" His voice trembled with disgust.

The bitter words had an unexpected effect. His father seemed to recover his composure, along with the remnants of his pride. He spoke quietly, with a certain dignity.

"You've no right to speak to me in that fashion, Giles. You've never experienced a war, never had to fight for your life in endless, mind-blowing combat. Until you have – don't dare to judge me."

He looked Giles coolly in the eye.

"I shan't make any silly excuses for my actions. I fought as long as I could. I had to bale out in France, after a hell of a dog-fight. But my nerve had gone. I knew I couldn't go back ... to face it all over again. I escaped. The Resistance – they thought I'd been killed. Eventually, at the end of the war, I came over here."

"Leaving your darling little wife to believe you'd died a hero's death ..."

"More or less. I couldn't go back. It would have hurt her more to know what I'd done – deserted her, as well the Air Force."

"So you just left her and her son to cope alone?" At that moment he despised his father more than ever before. A craven coward, a liar, a deserter – that's all he was! God! He'd make him suffer.

"No, Giles," said Jimmy firmly. "I never knew at that stage we had a son. I did check later, but was led to believe Cathy had died in an air-raid."

"How convenient! Pity she didn't," he added remorselessly. "Along with that other damned child of yours."

His father's face went white with rage. "How dare you say such a disgusting thing!"

"How would you feel, Dad, if you suddenly discovered you were a real live bastard, your father a yellow-livered coward – a criminal deserter, who, along with everything else, abandoned his wife and child?"

The taut, upright figure in front of him seemed to collapse.

"I've told you, it wasn't like that ..."

Giles was horrified to hear wracking sobs coming from the slumped form in front of him.

"Dad! You make me sick!"

He sat watching him, his mind in turmoil, for what seemed an eternity.

Finally Jimmy managed to pull himself together. He raised his head, started to speak slowly and deliberately, gradually recovering his composure.

"Whatever's happened, Giles, it's made no difference to you or to my fair treatment of you. As you know, I always intended to leave my entire estate to you. Your own attitude and behaviour forced the change. You even squandered the means I'd left you for a comfortable life-style. In spite of that, you're still my son. I promise you'll always receive a living."

"Gee, thanks," he said in disgust.

"Nobody need ever know the truth about my relationship with you and Sam," continued his father, "unless you tell them. It will be assumed I divorced Cathy. So it's in your interest to maintain the secret."

"This Cathy dame – are you sure she's still alive?"

This time his father ignored his derogatory tone.

"No, not for certain. My last contact with them, or rather with the private investigator I hired, was in 1967."

"But that's eighteen years ago. Anything could have happened since then," he said, his hopes suddenly rising.

"I don't think so. Cathy married again. The last I heard she and Sam were fine. In any case, Giles, I've covered all eventualities. In the event of anything happening to Sam, the estate will pass to his children."

"And if anything happens to his kids ...?"

There was a pause, then a reluctant answer.

"In that case, it will revert to you, once you've reached the age of thirty-five. But don't start dwelling on that, Giles. It's a chance in a million. You've must reconcile yourself to making a good life with what you have."

Giles nodded, in apparent acquiescence, but his mind was already working overtime. He had tried everything with his father – without success. Perhaps he would have more luck with this half-brother of his – Sam. He might be a reasonable guy – more understanding, less astute than his father. Perhaps he'd have no interest in his father's commercial empire; or he might even appreciate his own help and experience in running it.

There was still a possibility Sam didn't even exist. His father had never actually seen his first wife again, or her son. He had spoken of a private investigator – there could have been a mistake. Perhaps the guy had reported what he thought his client wanted to hear. Private investigators were all a bunch of rogues!

In any case, he was running out of time. He had to act fast, before Dad could put any further obstacles in his path – or before he died!

He studied his father's face. Tired, drawn, disillusioned, it was the face of a man who lacked the will to fight any longer. But behind the defeated facade, he sensed an obstinate determination to protect this other family of his.

He spoke again, this time without venom, not daring to let his father suspect his new intentions.

"Sorry I went for you, Dad. But it sure was a shock!"

"I know, Giles. I should have told you everything before. I kidded myself that what you didn't know couldn't hurt you, or your mother .... or them."

"Did you love her very much?" he asked, his tone unusually sympathetic.

"Yes." A simple answer, but Giles's stomach turned over. He instinctively knew this woman had been the love of his father's life. No wonder he wanted to leave everything to her damn son!

"Cathy ... you said her name was Cathy?" Again he kept his tone casual. "Catherine Pritchard?" he repeated quietly.

His father looked up in surprise.

"No...no – Catherine Proctor," he reacted automatically. "Proctor was my real name. I changed it later to Pritchard. But she'll be known as Cathy Bourne now – she remarried. I knew her husband, Leslie, in England – he was an old friend of hers. That's as far as my information about them goes."

"Ah-ha," murmured Giles, the names already firmly imprinted in his memory. He changed the subject quickly, not wanting his father to think it had any real significance.

"I can see you've had a tough time, Dad. The war and all that, losing your first family ... me not turning out as you wanted."

His father looked up, surprised. For the first time in years, he gave Giles the benefit of his warm smile. But now after his stroke, the smile was slightly crooked, the effect almost clownish.

"Thank you for understanding." He struggled to his feet. "I'm sorry, Giles, but I'm very tired now. I think I'll go up to bed. Tell your mother I've gone for a nap." He turned and limped slowly into the house, for the first time stooping slightly, as if in defeat.

Giles felt a rare moment of compassion for the man who had rejected and disinherited him. But it didn't lasted long. He refused to accept defeat at his father's hands. He would find out for himself the truth about Catherine Proctor and her son Sam – his rival. He made a swift decision to return to Europe. It was easy to find a pretext for going – a new UK branch which needed attention.

After exhaustive investigations in London, he discovered Cathy Proctor was very much alive, remarried – just as his father had said – to a Leslie Bourne.

But Sam was dead! The elusive Sam Proctor Bourne had not been a man at all, but his half-sister, Samantha. Beautiful – from the photograph he had seen – and apparently successful, Sam had died tragically young. But she had left a child, an heir. After months of tracking down, the trail had led finally to Kate! Now he was in an even bigger dilemma. When he first went in search of a half-brother called Sam, he hadn't expected to find a woman like Kate at the end of the trail!

Chapter 41

A slight breeze had come up in Ibiza harbour and tiny wave-lets began to lap gently at the side of the yacht. It was a reassuring lulling sound, but Giles, ever watchful of any change in the weather, checked all the mooring lines. If the wind did come up during the night, he didn't want to be caught too close to the jetty wall.

He had been lucky to get this skippering job aboard the ketch, *Sirocco Sunset*. He had qualifications and experience enough from his years of sailing in the States and Mexico; but arriving in Ibiza some time after the start of the summer season, he had been fortunate to find work on such a handsome craft as this. Her original British captain had suddenly been taken ill and returned for treatment to the UK. Giles had turned up at just the right moment to fill the gap. His charm and obvious expertise during a trial run, had quickly impressed her owners and provided him with a base from which to operate during his stay in Ibiza.

The seventy-two foot yacht was owned by John and Barbara Hiscock, a semi-retired British couple who spent most of their summers in Ibiza, where the yacht was based. Both enthusiastic and competent sailors, in their younger days they had handled the boat themselves, with a girl on board acting as cook and assistant-crew.

Now into their sixties, they had found the more strenuous aspects of sailing getting beyond them. Comfortably off, they were happy to hand over the more arduous physical demands and overall responsibility for the craft to a competent young skipper, leaving them to enjoy the fun of sailing, without the hard work and need for a constant watchful eye.

It suited Giles. The Hiscocks were easy charming people. He had a reasonable amount of free time. Although the owners lived aboard the boat, they didn't want to sail every day. Some weekends they went off to the mainland, and occasionally spent a few days in England when John needed to attend company board meetings.

At this critical time in his search for Kate, he was relieved the couple were away to attend a family funeral in the UK. The girl-cook, Janet, had gone ashore for a break, so he had the yacht to himself.

He fixed himself a drink, relaxed again in a comfortable canvas chair on the aft-deck, his thoughts returning once more to his investigations in England. Using his charm to the full, Giles had explained to the solicitor handling his enquiries that he was trying to trace distant members of his family living in Europe. He had been utterly amazed when the lawyer's inquiries suddenly revealed that the Sam he was searching for was not a man but a young woman – Samantha Radcliffe, née Proctor Bourne.

"Mrs Radcliffe was a beautiful, talented lady," the solicitor told him. "Sadly I must inform you that she died in a car crash, along with her husband, nearly eighteen years ago, on the Spanish island of Ibiza.

Giles couldn't believe his ears. He had hit the jackpot!

"I'm very sorry to have to pass on such tragic news about the British branch of your family, Mr Pritchard," continued the solicitor, "but there is a brighter side. Mrs Catherine Bourne, Samantha Radcliffe's mother, is fit and well. She and her husband have retired to live on the same island of Ibiza where the crash occurred. I have their address so you can perhaps visit them and have a family reunion!" The solicitor beamed, obviously happy to pass on good news, as well as bad, to this courteous and amenable young American.

Giles tried to look attentive, although inside he was still busy congratulating himself. Sam, or rather Samantha was dead! His rival was out of the running! All he had to do now was keep quiet; leave his father to his pipe-dreams, then quietly inherit the whole estate when the time came!

It was then the lawyer dropped the final bombshell!

"I realise this must have come as quite a shock to you, Mr Pritchard," he said, obviously mistaking his silence and preoccupation for shocked dismay. "It was an extremely tragic accident, even worse when you consider the poor baby.

"Baby?" queried Giles. "What baby?"

"Mr and Mrs Radcliffe's, of course. You'll be happy to know you have another much younger relation. The Radcliffe's baby daughter was just one year old when her parents died. She was christened Kate, apparently after her grandmother, Catherine. Quite ironic in a way," he mused, "since it was Catherine and Leslie Bourne who brought her up, following the tragic death of Samantha and Peter Radcliffe.

Giles sat in stony silence, his hopes evaporating around him once more.

"Let's get this straight, Mr Ferryweather," he said finally. "You mean Samantha Proctor – Mrs. Radcliffe that is – had a daughter who survived the car crash?"

"Oh, yes! The child wasn't involved in the accident – she wasn't even on the island at the time. Her parents were on holiday. They had left the child with her grandparents in England."

Giles felt a pounding in his head. It couldn't be true! Fate was against him yet again. Just when he thought he'd had one stroke of luck, the fickle goddess laughed in his face and provided another stumbling block.

"I see." He tried to look as pleased as would be expected about this newly-discovered family member. "Do you have any further information, Mr. Ferryweather?"

The solicitor beamed again.

"I actually have a photograph of Mr and Mrs Bourne and their baby, Kate, soon after she was born." He pushed a file across the table to Giles.

On the top of the papers lay a typical family picture – two proud parents gazing adoringly at the chortling child in the mother's arms. The baby, to Giles's inexperienced eye, looked like any other except she actually seemed to be laughing into the camera, unlike the more passive babies he'd seen in similar photographs. But his attention was immediately drawn to the delicate sculpted features of the mother, and the handsome blond looks of the father.

"An attractive couple," murmured the solicitor. "Such a tragedy, their premature death! They were apparently very happy together, and both highly successful in their careers."

Giles nodded, numbly.

"Do you have any more recent information about the baby and her grandparents?"

"Certainly. The Bournes, as I explained before, are now retired to the island of Ibiza. Their grand-daughter, Kate, still lives with them, although in term-time she attends boarding school in England. Our source of information is most reliable; it's Leslie Bourne's brother, Paul, an ex-naval officer who lives here in the UK He kindly gave us the photograph."

"You didn't reveal my identity, I hope," asked Giles, anxiously. "I want it to be a real surprise when we meet."

"Of course not, Mr Pritchard!" He looked shocked that Giles might even consider such an abuse of confidence. "Vague mention was made of an old college friend of Samantha Radcliffe, who wanted to make contact with her. Paul Bourne was extremely helpful. He's obviously very fond of his brother's family. By the way, Catherine also has twin sons – about thirty-five-years-old – from her marriage to Leslie Bourne. Of course there is no blood relationship between them and your family."

Giles rose to his feet.

"Thanks, Mr Ferryweather. You've been real helpful. May I take the file?"

"Of course, Mr. Pritchard. May I say how refreshing it's been, handling these enquiries on your behalf. Most of our work deals with the less attractive side of life – divorce, separation, disputes within families. It's rewarding to be instrumental in re-uniting family members for a change – however distant their ties may be. I wish you well with your reunion."

Giles shook his hand warmly.

"Thanks, Mr Ferryweather. I sure appreciate your efforts and your good wishes."

"It will be interesting to see how young Kate Radcliffe has turned out," mused Ferryweather, as he showed Giles to the door. "She must be about eighteen now."

"It sure will!" agreed Giles, with a cold smile.

* * * * * * *

It had been more than interesting, thought Giles. A revelation, in fact! Looking up again at the Ibiza night sky, a dazzling vision of Kate Radcliffe came to his mind. What a gorgeous unspoilt girl! Absolutely stunning! Kate had an unconscious, unstudied voluptuousness which he had never come across before – her figure lithe and lush, her hair the colour of white gold, her leopard eyes in certain lights almost matching the gold flecks in her hair. She had her mother's high cheek-bones and perfect features; but Kate's cheeks were softer, rounder than Samantha's, her mouth wider, more sensual and expressive. Yet she seemed strangely unaware of her radiant looks and tremendous sex-appeal.

But it was her personality which most amazed him. She was the least complicated girl he had ever met, with no apparent hang-ups. For a girl who had lost her parents at the tender age of twelve months, she appeared as serene and unaffected as any eighteen-year-old could be. Totally natural and unspoiled, as innocent and trusting as a child, she seemed confident the world would treat her well – as it probably would! There was a protective aura around Kate, a luminosity he had never encountered before.

He had been expecting some shy withdrawn orphan girl or at worst a spoiled wretch. Kate was neither, far from it – she was a complex mix of ripe voluptuous body and bright innocent spirit. The more he thought about her, the more confused he became.

What was her relationship to him? He started to work it out. They had one kin in common. His father, Jimmy, was Kate's grandfather! He gave up trying to work out their exact kinship. He was only eight years or so older than Kate, so they were more like cousins, yet their blood relationship was even closer...

He started to feel drowsy, but realised he still hadn't worked out what to do about Kate. Should he reveal his identity, try to befriend her and win her good will, as he had intended to do with Sam? The fact that Kate was a young girl, not the middle-aged man he was expecting Sam to be, put a different complexion on the whole affair. She certainly might be more pliable, more susceptible than an older man.

The problem was he liked her – in every way. If only she'd turned out as expected, he would have no compunction in duping her. Kate was the new threat to his future. But for some strange reason, he felt reluctant to deceive the trusting, beautiful young girl he had met tonight.

Christ, Giles! he thought to himself. Don't be a fool! She's only a girl, after all. Look what the last woman in your life did for you! Penny was enough to put you off women for life! But Kate's different, insisted a small voice inside him. She's young, harmless, no threat whatsoever – except, he thought, she's heir to what should have been my rightful fortune!

Damn it! He didn't know what to do! Give it time, he supposed. He'd handled enough girls in his time to know how to keep them dangling. He would play the situation along for the moment – give himself time to think. He'd already told his father about his move to Spain, ostensibly to investigate new business opportunities. The Spanish economy was surging forward, he explained, offering attractive incentives to foreign investors.

He yawned sleepily. Tomorrow was another day. He had arranged to see Kate in the afternoon. Disturbed, yet excited at the prospect, he wandered down to his cabin and fell immediately into a deep and dreamless sleep.

* * * * * * *

The following morning he awoke to a perfect day, feeling rested, light-hearted and optimistic. Gone were the perplexing anxieties of the previous night. The sun shone brightly from a cloudless blue sky, yet the morning felt pleasantly cool. But he knew from the stillness in the air the day would later be hot. Thank God he wouldn't be stuck on the yacht in the harbour.

He could scarcely wait for the afternoon – to see Kate once again. Where should he take her? She would know the island far better than he. Perhaps he'd better leave the choice to her – she would know the best place to spend a scorching July afternoon.

He heard a familiar whistle from the bows. Janet Manners, the cook, laden with groceries, was staggering along the narrow gangplank linking the yacht to the jetty. Young and plump, with mousy hair and chubby features, he humoured her because she was a superb cook and had a redeeming sense of fun. She was also steady and reliable, able to handle a rope or fender when necessary. Janet might not be worth her over-weight in gold, but she was a useful and pleasant crew member.

He watched her struggle along the deck, the bulging plastic bags matching her own lumpy body.

"Damn it!" she groaned. "These wretched bags have cut right through my fingers."

He grinned.

"Why didn't you ask for a cardboard box?"

"And balance it on my fat stomach?" she said with a giggle. Her over-endowed figure never seemed to bother her. She gazed dreamily at Giles.

"How are you today, handsome? How did the party go?"

"I'm fine and the barbecue was great."

"Do I see tiny bags of fatigue beneath those gorgeous eyes?" She glanced sideways along the deck towards his cabin. "You haven't been entertaining a lady-friend from last night?"

"No such luck!" grinned Giles. "Mind you, there was one there I'd like to have taken to the sack."

"You mean your American charm failed you for once?" teased Janet. She readily admitted to being completely under the spell of her good-looking skipper.

"I reckoned the time was inappropriate."

"My, my! Sounds serious. Not your usual one-night-standers. Are you seeing her again?"

"I sure hope so – we've a date this afternoon!"

"Well, if she doesn't show, remember I'm always available." She fluttered her eyelashes outrageously, at the same time wiggling her ample hips.

"I'll remember," he laughed. "Now you'd better get all that stuff in the freezer." He slapped her on the backside.

"Get away, you mad passionate fool!" she said, loving every minute. Reluctantly she picked up the bags and clumped down the deck. "Are you on board for lunch?" she called, before disappearing down the hatch leading to the galley.

"No, gorgeous. I want to do some things in town. Then I'll have some light tapas – to set me up for my sex-filled afternoon." He growled like a lion on the prowl.

"Don't get your fingers burned!" shouted Janet, as he stepped agilely onto the quay.

"Don't worry. I won't," he called back.

At least I hope I won't, he thought to himself. Today I'll get this Kate girl sorted out. She took me by surprise last night, but she can't really be such a paragon of virtue. Probably just the effect of too much champagne!

Full of confidence, he sauntered jauntily down the quay towards the town.

Chapter 42

Kate arrived early at the Montesol café. From her position on the outside terrace, she saw him approaching from some distance away. He strolled across the square with easy confidence, his long legs clothed in fashionably baggy but neatly-tailored white trousers, lending an athletic bounce to his stride. She saw he wore a loose-fitting navy t-shirt printed with the KU logo and smiled to herself. So Giles was also a fan of the huge open-air discotheque, KU, now renowned throughout Europe for its floodlit pool, dragon-slide and tropical gardens. Kate had fallen in love with KU on her very first visit.

As soon as he caught sight of her he waved, his white teeth gleaming against his darkly-tanned features. Her heart began to pound and her mouth went dry. She suddenly felt nervous. Whatever was the matter with her? She hadn't reacted this way before to any man, not even to Giles when she first met him at the barbecue last night – although she had been immediately attracted to him! What a bit of luck Big Bob had brought him along! He had been easy and entertaining to chat to and within minutes she felt she had known him for ages. She was soon telling him all about herself. Their conversation had been relaxed, yet lively and stimulating. He was exciting to be with – his natural enthusiasm reflecting her own optimistic approach to life.

Not until he said he had to leave, had she realised just how much she liked him, how she wanted to see him again. She had heaved a sigh of relief when he asked her to go to the beach with him the following afternoon. After he left, she joined her friends swimming and moonlight skiing, but her thoughts had been centred all the time on Giles Pritchard and she had scarcely thought about anything since.

The moment she had reached home last night she had rushed into the kitchen knowing there was a good chance her grandmother would be there sipping hot tea or making toast! Cathy would never admit that she couldn't sleep until her grand-daughter was safely home. But whenever Kate returned late at night, she would still be up waiting, with some silly excuse about suddenly feeling hungry or thirsty or wanting to stare at the moon! The two of them would sit together over tea and toast, laughing and giggling, while Kate recounted all the events of her evening.

Last night had been no exception. As she bounded in, Cathy was seated at the breakfast table, one of the cats on her lap and the two dogs at her feet. The kettle on the stove had just started to boil. Kate hugged her with delight.

"I'm so glad you're still up, Cathy," she said breathlessly. "I've got so much to tell you!"

"Well, we felt rather guilty, darling, not being able to come with you to the barbecue on your first night back. But we couldn't let poor Evelyn down – it was her first dinner-party since Gerry died and she's been so lost without him. But come along, I'll make some tea and you can tell me all about it."

"You would have loved it! Everyone was there! I saw lots of my old friends and ..." She took a deep breath. "Cathy, I met the most fabulous man!"

"Did you, darling?" Cathy turned in surprise from her tinkering with the tea-cups. "Now that sounds really exciting! What's he like?"

"I've decided he's simply a larger-than-life person – in every way," she explained. "He's tall and well-built – which in itself is rather strange because I'm not normally attracted by muscle-bound he-men – I prefer the slimmer type. Then again, his hair's dark and curly when I normally prefer the blond Nordic look ..."

Cathy smiled knowingly. "Like your father?"

"Yes," she grinned. "I suppose so. Anyway Giles – that's his name – well, he does have a lovely wide infectious smile and laughing eyes ... they're a startling aquamarine-blue, invariably twinkling ... as if he's recalling something really funny." Her last words came out in a rush.

"From what you say, he sounds quite gorgeous," laughed Cathy, "whatever your previous preferences!"

"Yes, he is rather," she admitted, and couldn't help grinning. "He's also eight years older than me and much more sophisticated than the other boys. But Cathy – I don't know how to explain it – though he's older, more mature, he has none of the trendy cynicism I've come across in some of the older boys I've known. He's full of enthusiasm and energy. He has such a zest for life it's infectious – I got carried along with him ..."

She gave a sigh. "I've never met anyone quite like him before. It's like trying to keep up with a runaway horse. I felt mentally drained at the end of the evening!"

"My goodness!" said Cathy, for once at a loss for words.

"I do hope you and Leslie will like him."

"I'm sure we shall, darling. He sounds quite wonderful!"

And he is, thought Kate, studying him as he approached her table.

She started to fiddle nervously with her cup of *café con leche* – her favourite frothy white coffee. But as he came closer, his face alive with vitality, she suddenly knew it was going to be all right. Her nervousness vanished and she greeted him with a warm smile.

He grasped her hand, sat down in the chair beside her.

"Kate. Thank God! You look just the same."

"The same?"

"Magnificent!" he burst out. "I thought, when I got back to the boat last night, it was all some figment of my imagination – or the effects of too much champagne! But here you are, looking as fabulous as ever. You really do exist!"

"Of course I do!" she laughed. "And so do you! I had much the same feeling about you."

His blue eyes twinkled wickedly, and his grin widened. "Great! I reckon we're off to good start. Shall we move? It's far too hot here, and if I keep staring at you like this, I'll want to eat you up! I guess that wouldn't be on – not here at the Montesol! You're not on their menu."

She laughed, already caught up in the whirlwind of his company.

"Ready when you are," she said happily, knowing they were already attracting more than casual glances from people in the café. "I'm dying for a swim."

"Where shall we go? I guess I'd better leave that decision to you – you're the island expert! Do you have transport?"

"I have my old Mehari – if you can call that transport!"

"Sounds great! Where shall we take by storm?"

She thought for a moment.

"The restaurant at Cala D'en Real?" she suggested. "The pool there is gorgeous and the view superb. Most important – it's quiet and away-from-it-all. The beaches get so crowded at this time of year."

Strolling back through the square to where she had parked the car, she handed him the keys to the Mehari.

"You can drive Genevieve."

"Genevieve?"

"Oh, that's what Cathy, my grandmother, christened the car. Apparently Genevieve was the name given to a cantankerous but loveable veteran car in a favourite old film of hers. She says the Mehari reminds her of the old banger in the film."

He laughed.

"Sounds ominous. Do you reckon we'll make it that far? I don't fancy walking in this heat, especially carrying a red flag!"

"Don't worry. Genevieve always gets there – somehow!"

* * * * * * *

After a light but delicious lunch, they enjoyed a quick cooling dip in the circular pool, then lazed on the sunbeds round the pool-edge.

"Mmm, that was gorgeous!" she sighed feeling replete and content. The hot sun seemed to penetrate right into her bones, soothing her with its rays. She rolled over to look at Giles. He lay stretched out beside her, his dark hair wet and crinkly from their recent dip. Beads of water from the pool still glistened on his bronzed skin, but as she watched, they evaporated rapidly in the hot rays of the sun.

She felt tense and expectant, deeply aware of the electricity emanating from his still form. Her skin began to prickle from the simple excitement of being close to him. It was unusual to see his restless powerful body so quiet, yet magnetic waves still radiated from him, invisibly linking her to him. It was a strange sensation – as if her were weaving a spell over her. She had never felt such an intense attraction for a man before.

He stirred and turned towards her. She might have guessed he wouldn't lie motionless for long!

He grinned, seeing the intentness of her gaze.

"I wish we were alone," he said. "Don't you?"

She felt her cheeks redden, certain he could read her thoughts, sense her growing desire. She sat up on the lounger, brought her knees to her chest, tried to change the subject.

"Tell me about yourself, Giles! I've already bored you with my entire life history."

"Mine's rather longer than yours!"

"Don't be silly. You're not that old!"

"Twenty-seven, but when I'm with you I feel positively ancient. You're so young – fresh as mint." His voice grew tender. "And very innocent, I think."

She looked down, confused. Innocent, yes, but there was no hiding the fire inside her now.

"Enough of me. Tell me more about you."

He laughed.

"Where shall I begin?"

"At the very beginning," she said, simply.

"Sure! Well, here goes. I was born on Long Island, New York, in May 1958 and went to school in New Hampshire," he recited.

"You don't have a very marked American accent for someone born and bred in the States," she interrupted, surprised. She had imagined he had spent most of his life out of America.

"That's easily explained – my mother was French and my father British."

"So you're not American at all," laughed Kate. "You're one of us!"

"Sure I'm American!" grinned Giles. "My father took up US citizenship, and I was born an American. My family's rather rich, so I had what you'd call a 'privileged' upbringing."

"What did your father do?" she asked, intrigued.

"He ran an advertising agency, then branched out into PR and later into real estate."

"Strange," mused Kate. "My mother used to work in advertising."

At the mention of her mother, he stared at her intently, his eyes widening with interest.

"You're talking about Sam – I mean Samantha?" he said, his tone casual, but she knew his curiosity was aroused.

"Yes, that's right. I forgot I'd told you her name. By the way, you were right first time. Everybody called her Sam, never Samantha, except my grandmother, Cathy – when she was angry with her!"

"Tell me more about your mother," he said his voice unusually serious.

"We're supposed to be talking about you!" she said, laughing. "In any case, there isn't so much I can tell you – at least not at first hand. As you know, I was only twelve months old when my parents were killed."

"Poor little orphan!" He seized her hand and squeezed it, affectionately.

"Cathy and Leslie told me all they could about them, but it's not the same as actually knowing a person, is it?"

"Of course not. Still it's interesting – your mother being tied up in advertising."

"Yes?" she asked, puzzled by the comment.

He gave a tiny start.

"Sure ... her being a woman and so forth. It couldn't have been so easy in those days."

"Oh, I see what you mean. But from what I've heard about my mother, she took it very much in her stride. She was very competent and dedicated in her work, very successful. Goodness knows how far she might have gone, if she hadn't died so young."

She thought she saw him wince – perhaps he didn't like career-women? She quickly changed the subject.

"My father ran a pretty high-powered family business. He was about to go public."

He didn't seem so interested in her father.

"How did the accident happen?"

"Nobody knows for sure – except they had a puncture, a blow-out, on the bend at San Rafael. A new highway was built there a few years ago, bypassing that bend – it used to be one of the most dangerous on the island. From the skid-marks, it seems they were travelling very fast which is quite strange. It seems my father was usually a careful driver."

"The quirks of fate!" said Giles, quietly, obviously moved by the story.

"I want to hear more about you!" she said, sensing the talk about her parents had somehow changed his normally buoyant mood.

His face brightened and he was soon regaling her with amusing stories about his travels in Mexico and the Far East. He made it all sound so exciting, she couldn't wait to see the places with her own eyes.

Before they knew it, the sun was sinking fast. It hung like a huge red ball in the western sky. She looked round, saw everybody else had left the poolside.

He grabbed her hand.

"I think it's time for another dip!"

They swam leisurely together, caressing each other lightly in the deep blue of the darkening water, their bodies moulding together in the soft evening light.

He raised her aloft and she felt feather-light in the water.

"What shall we do tonight, and tomorrow, and the next day, and the one after that?" he whispered in her ear.

She laughed softly.

"Let's start with tonight. I'd like to take you home to meet my grandparents."

"Cathy and Leslie – if my memory serves me right!" he said, with a knowing grin. "Sure! As long as I can show you my home – after we've had dinner in Ibiza."

"You mean go on board the yacht? I'd love to!" she said, her eyes sparkling with anticipation.

* * * * * * *

The whole evening seemed to pass like a dream. Giles was charm itself when he visited the villa to meet her grandparents. She hoped Cathy and Leslie were suitably impressed – she wanted everyone to feel the same about Giles as she did.

After a polite couple of drinks, they left the villa and drove into the Old Town of Ibiza for a meal. Giles laughed and joked with her, and the waiters at the restaurant went out of their way to encourage the young lovers and treat them well, obviously sensing their closeness and happiness in each other's company. Now I understand the meaning of that phrase, she thought. The whole world loves a lover!

With Giles she found even the most mundane moments came to life. Everybody they came into contact with reacted with happy knowing grins to their obvious infatuation with each other.

At ten o'clock they wandered down to the port, to the yacht he was skippering, the *Sirocco Sunset*. Proudly he escorted her aboard. She gazed around, entranced. She had sailed on various yachts during her holidays in Ibiza, but this lovely craft was so spacious and luxuriously comfortable, she felt she could have lived on her for ever. She had visions of herself and Giles sailing off on a similar craft to discover the world.

"I'd love to sail on her," she told him, unable to keep the excitement from her voice.

"We'll see what we can do about that," he said, obviously enjoying her enthusiasm. "The Hiscocks are a swell couple – I'm sure they'll invite you for a sail one day."

He led her by the hand to the large double bunk in his cabin, pulled her down by his side. She started to tremble with nervousness and desire, sure he was going to make to love to her, knowing she wouldn't resist him. She had never made love to anyone before, never met anybody who had set her so afire. She was glad she had remained a virgin. She'd always wanted her first lover to be someone special, somebody she really admired and loved.

And she did love Giles – she was certain of that now – and she dared to hope he felt the same about her. Every moment in his company had been magical. With him, the whole world took on a new meaning and significance. She couldn't bear the thought of spending a minute apart from him. She felt herself drifting in a blissful pink cloud of happiness – in a glorious dream – and she never wanted to wake up!

He stroked her hair, her cheeks. His hand moved down and he gently caressed her breasts. She held her breath, but his fingers returned once again to her face. He gently raised her chin and his eyes met hers in the dim light.

"You're sweet, Kate," he said huskily, "so sweet – so innocent. What am I to do with you?"

She couldn't answer. He didn't love her, she thought, desperately. She was a child, as far he was concerned. She felt like crying in frustration but his hands continued to caress her, softly and gently. There was something exquisitely beautiful about his embrace – she felt an affinity between them which seemed above mere passion.

Eventually she relaxed in his arms. Perhaps one day he would realise she wasn't a child. In the meantime, she loved him all the more for respecting her innocence, for not taking advantage of the situation. He must know she was ready to give herself, yet he'd made no attempt to make love to her.

But a little voice inside her raised the doubt. Perhaps he didn't feel the same way as she did, perhaps she wasn't mature and attractive enough. In which case, why was he bothering with her? Could it be that his feelings were so deep, he didn't want to rush her?

Snuggling up against his hard muscular body, she decided it didn't really matter. As far as she was concerned, she loved him more than anything in the world!

Chapter 43

Cathy Bourne sat poised on the edge of her sun-lounger, staring intently at the setting sun.

"How long has it been now, Leslie?" she asked her husband.

He looked carefully at his watch.

"Nearly three minutes."

"Gosh, it's disappearing so quickly, it almost seems to be falling into the sea." The two of them were timing the final stage of the sunset – how long it would take for the fiery orb to disappear completely below the horizon, from the moment its red rim first touched the sea below.

They sat very still, gazing entranced at the scene before them. It had been a magnificent sunset – the whole of the western sky in the direction of the island of Conejera stained blood-red, patches of orange, pink and purple streaking the soft wispy clouds of the stratosphere.

The sunsets as seen from the terrace of their villa were always glorious, but this evening had been something special, the colours particularly vivid and dramatic. There had been none of the hazy cloud which often developed at that time on the horizon itself. They had been able to watch the disappearance of the crimson ball right to the moment of its fiery plummet into the indigo sea.

"Exactly four minutes," pronounced Leslie triumphantly, as the final red-gold arc was swallowed up by the water.

She felt tears prickle the backs of her eyes.

"Leslie, that was so beautiful." She felt a sudden sense of sadness, of loss. The sun's abrupt disappearance left a frightening void in the sky. The colour-streaked sky was still startling – splashes of vivid crimsons and delicate corals lingered there, gradually darkening   but she felt as if something had died.

"You can understand why primitive people thought the sun might never return, once it had set," she said with a shiver. "It seems so final – that moment when it slips away – almost as though there will be no tomorrow".

He rose from his chair and came to put a comforting arm round her shoulders.

"You're sounding very morbid, my love."

"Not morbid, Leslie. I don't know how to explain it. I've been so happy for so long, I'm afraid it's too good to be true – that it can't go on any longer."

He squeezed her hand.

"We have lots more years to enjoy together. You're still an extremely girlish sixty-four and I'm just a skittish sixty-nine!"

She smiled ruefully.

"Yes I know I'm being awfully silly. But since Sam's death – at a time when everything seemed so perfect – I always have the fear that some other awful quirk of fate may suddenly ruin our happiness." She smoothed back her still-thick dark hair. She knew it was streaked with grey now, but refused to colour it. Leslie had told her that her grey streaks looked nicer than the artificial ones some woman paid a fortune for.

He pulled his chair closer to hers.

"Are you worried about Kate – about this new young man of hers?"

"No more than usual, I suppose," she said thoughtfully. "I'm not quite sure about Giles, but then I always worry unnecessarily about Kate – the way most mothers do about their children. I may be her grandmother, but I feel as strongly about her as I do about the boys, as I did about Sam. I suppose that's silly too. Kate's no problem at all. She's as easy and uncomplicated a youngster as any I've known. She's never been any trouble, ever since she was a baby."

"An absolute poppet!" agreed Leslie. "I only hope she finds a young man worthy of her."

She chuckled.

"You sound frightfully Victorian, Leslie."

"I think I am rather Victorian in some respects," he said with a smile. "Born out of my era, I suppose."

"Maybe. But only in the nicest possible way. Do you remember how Sam used to tease us about our 'ivory towers' existence. I think she thought we lived in the past."

He nodded.

"Yes, she was certainly a modern miss, although she still held on to many of the traditional values. It's funny how Kate's so different from her mother. She has little of Sam's driving ambition, seems much more composed and contented. More like you, really.

"But much more beautiful," laughed Cathy. "And I was always so insecure, needing to be loved – yet so frightened when it happened. Terrible things always seem to overtake the people closest to me."

"I know," said Leslie quietly. "Fortunately I'm still persistently alive and kicking, and I have every intention of staying that way!" He chuckled, completely changing the mood. "So stop thinking you're some kind of jinx!"

She joined in his laughter – he always knew how to revive her spirits.

"And stop worrying about Kate," he continued. "In some respects she's been lucky. She lost her parents, but I think we've filled that void. She's an extremely happy and confident young lady. If she wanted, she could take the world apart, but she seems quite content with things just as they are. It's remarkable!"

She nodded, trying to dismiss the premonitions which had been troubling her that evening, feeling tears welling in her eyes.

"Yes, I'm silly to worry so. I don't know why I feel so weepy tonight. Hold me, Leslie." She moved towards him and sat on his lap, taking comfort from his lean strong arms about her.

He lent her a huge cotton handkerchief and she started to dab at her eyes.

"Gosh, I mustn't cry – I always look so frightful! My eyes swell and go red in seconds."

"Do you know something, Cath?"

She raised her eyes questioningly.

"You're more beautiful to me than you've ever been."

"Leslie! I've never been beautiful!"

He put his finger to her lips.

"More important, you're lovely inside."

"Stop it, Leslie – or I shall start to cry."

He squeezed her hard round the middle.

"Just checking the waist-line! Well, at least you haven't put on too much weight!"

She laughed. "I try to stay as slim as I can. But it's not as easy for me as it is for you. You're naturally skinny." She pinched his stomach. "See, not an inch of fat! You don't seem to have changed at all during the last twenty years. You're a timeless person!"

"My love for you is timeless," he said, simply.

"And a poet, too!" she teased, snuggling down in his arms. Dear, loving, dependable Leslie. He was like a rock. Whatever would she do without him?

* * * * * * *

Half an hour later she stirred sleepily in his arms, opened her eyes to find the last of the evening light had slipped away. Night had descended on the warm terrace.

"Gosh I must have dozed off," she said drowsily.

"You did," said Leslie, gently shifting position and stretching his legs.

"Poor darling," she commiserated. "You should have moved me before. It's a wonder you haven't developed a severe case of cramp."

"I have," he said grinning wryly. "But it was worth it!"

She kissed him, then extracted herself from his warm embrace. "I don't know about you, but I'm starving. Are you ready for supper?"

"I thought you'd never ask!" His brown eyes twinkled.

She dug him hard in the ribs.

"If you'll set the table, I'll heat up the curry and prepare the rice."

He licked his lips.

"Had I known it was curry tonight, you wouldn't have lasted a minute on my lap."

"Cupboard lover!" she chastised, as she went off to the kitchen. She placed two pots of curry on the hob to warm, plus some lentil dhal, then pulled a container of boiled rice from the refrigerator. Using her favourite wok, she quickly fried some whole cardamoms, cloves and cassia bark, then added most of the rice, some desiccated coconut, saffron and a few ground almonds.

Scattering the remainder of the white rice as a garnish, she turned the contents into a serving dish. Perfect, she thought, a delicately-spiced and colourful pullao rice, Leslie's favourite! Thank goodness she had prepared the curry in the cool of the early morning. It would have been impossible cooking during the heat of the day. In any case, curry always tasted better for the keeping!

"Mmm!" said Leslie, coming into the kitchen to collect the chutneys and side dishes. "Smells great! What's on the menu tonight?"

"Madras beef and red prawn."

"Can't wait!"

They dined outside on the covered terrace, silent at first, relishing the initial delicious mouthfuls.

"My favourite food!" sighed Leslie, eventually.

"So I recall," murmured Cathy.

He looked puzzled.

"You even chose to propose to me over a romantic curry, if curries can be romantic," she explained, grinning.

"You remembered!"

"I remember the food, better than the proposal," she teased.

"No wonder you didn't accept!" he said, his tone light and bantering, but she couldn't prevent the tell-tale change of expression on her own face. Her thoughts had flown back to the first marriage proposal she had accepted – Jimmy's!

He immediately sensed his mistake, quickly changed the subject.

"I wonder if the old Taj Mahal is still going strong in South Ken?"

"I doubt it. But there's bound to be plenty of others. Curry houses are prolific everywhere nowadays."

He leaned across the table to take a second helping.

"I wonder how Kate's getting on tonight? What did you really think of that young American friend of hers? You said earlier you weren't sure about him."

"I have to admit he's very charming – quite magnetic in fact! And he's certainly a handsome boy. But there was something about him I wasn't sure about. I can't put my finger on it."

"You'd feel the same way about any young man who took Kate's fancy," he teased.

"Perhaps," she said, trying to keep the worry from her voice. "Kate does seem very taken by him. I've never seen her so all-a-flutter. Last night when she was telling me about him she was positively glowing!"

"She'll be falling for somebody else in a month's time. It's quite normal for youngsters to go through several infatuations."

"But she's so young," insisted Cathy. "She looks beautiful and very mature, but inside she's really just a little girl. And she trusts everyone. What if she doesn't get over this great passion for Giles?"

"It won't be the worst thing in the world. He seems a likeable enough young fellow – from a respectable, not to mention wealthy, family."

"You don't seriously think Kate would consider marrying him, do you?" she cried in alarm. "She's only eighteen."

"She'll be nineteen in a few days. Lots of youngsters marry at that age."

Including me, she thought wryly. I'd been married twice by the age of twenty!

"At least he's a fair bit older than she is and quite mature," said Leslie thoughtfully. "Not some young kid straight from college."

"Kate – married!" she mused. "It just doesn't seem possible. You know at one time, Leslie, I even thought she might become a nun."

He let out a huge guffaw of laughter.

"Kate! A nun! Impossible!"

"Yes, I realise that now, but when she was younger she had this sort of ethereal, other-worldly quality about her, a kind of luminous aura. When she wasn't charging around like some young puppy with the other children, she would sit and stare serenely at the sky or the sea – as if she was meditating, rather like a miniature guru, yet she was only a child! I once asked her if she felt any religious calling. She just laughed out loud, the way you did just now. 'No, Cathy,' she said. "My only religion is the wonderful world around me – the birds in the trees, the clouds in sky ... I think Nature is my God!' Then she laughed again and ran off to join the other children. I was completely taken aback. As you know, I've always loved animals and birds and the wonders of nature, but not in such a metaphysical almost mystical way."

Leslie nodded thoughtfully.

"Yes, she's always been different and rather special. But I don't think you have to worry too much, Cath. Kate may be innocent, even naive, but inside I sense a hidden strength and maturity – a kind of serene equilibrium. I'm sure that will always guide and protect her." He gave her hand a reassuring squeeze. "Did they say where they were going tonight?"

"Apparently Giles invited her to look over the yacht he's skippering – before the owners come back tomorrow. They were going to have dinner in the port afterwards." She laughed. "They've already had lunch and spent the afternoon together – it seems they can't bear to be apart. It's all very romantic!"

"Let's hope she doesn't come back at some unearthly hour. It was pretty late last night – half-past-two before she got home."

"So you were awake as well! You know we're both as bad as one another – not relaxing until she gets in. I could have sworn you were fast asleep when I crept down to the kitchen!"

"Had you known I was awake, you'd have thought something really was wrong."

"That's true." She smiled. "I'm glad I was up. Kate was dying to tell me all about the evening. After Giles left the barbecue the rest of them went midnight skiing on the Webster boys' boat. Kate assured me there was enough light from the moon, but it seems highly dangerous to me. Anyway, I had a quick word with her before they left tonight. She's promised to be back reasonably early. Shall we wait up and hear the news?"

"Good idea. What's for dessert?"

"Melon "

"I'll fetch it." He ambled off to the kitchen and soon reappeared with the chilled melon slices. "I've even remembered the ginger," he said serving her, "and I've put the coffee on."

"The perfect husband!" she said affectionately, and meant it. Leslie had to be the kindest, nicest man in the world!

They dawdled over their coffees, he pouring some *hierbas* liqueur for her and a small Magno brandy for himself. As they drained their glasses, they heard the sound of a car, then Kate's light footsteps through the house.

She burst onto the terrace, her face radiant, her eyes aglow.

"I shan't ask if you've had a good time," laughed Cathy. "Your face is more revealing than a thousand words!"

She blushed prettily.

"Is it so obvious?" She rushed over to her grandmother and gave her a hug. "I've had such a wonderful night!"

She moved on to Leslie, kissed him lightly on the cheek.

"Do you think I look pretty enough?" she asked him, anxiously. "Would you find me attractive, if you were twenty-seven years-old?" She whirled round on the spot.

"So that's how old he is," laughed Leslie. "Yes, Kate, you look gorgeous. If I were he, I'd whisk you away before anybody else could get their hands on you."

Cathy felt a catch in her throat. Her grand-daughter looked so lovely. She wore a flimsy turquoise frock in the finest Indian cotton, the beautifully-embroidered fitted bodice cut low at the back and front, held by narrow shoe-string straps at the shoulder. The vivid Mediterranean colour and style set off her pale blonde hair and golden tan to perfection. She shook her head in disbelief.

"You're so blonde, Kate, I don't know how you manage to tan so quickly. You've only been here three days! Mind you, your mother was the same."

Kate's eyes went misty. "I wish she and Dad could have met Giles."

Cathy looked anxiously at Leslie. He nodded at her and took Kate by the hand.

"You really like this young man then?"

She stared at them both, biting her lip.

"Cathy ... Leslie ... I must tell you – if you haven't already guessed." She looked from one to the other, took a deep breath. "I'm in love with Giles!"

"Oh!" they reacted in chorus.

Cathy turned helplessly to Leslie, willing him to say something sensible.

"The trouble is," continued Kate, anxiously. "I'm not so sure he loves me!"

"Oh dear!" thought Cathy, feeling her premonitions were coming true. Please God, don't let her be hurt, please don't let her be hurt!

Chapter 44

On July 10th Kate celebrated her nineteenth birthday.

She awoke that morning soon after eight o'clock with the sun streaming through the open bedroom window which faced east towards the pinewoods. It was already hot. Another scorcher, she thought, happily.

She draped a light robe round her naked form and padded lightly across the room, through the French-windows and onto the balcony. The swimming pool lay below, gleaming translucent blue in the early morning light. The sea beyond stretched calm and mirror-like as far as the horizon. Nothing stirred in the morning air – only the soft twittering of the birds disturbed the warm, almost sensual silence. She took several deep breaths of the fresh morning air before relaxing into a wicker armchair, glad to have these first few minutes of the early morning to herself, with just the sounds of nature about her. Today she was nineteen! That was exciting enough in itself.

More important, she had fallen ridiculously head-over-heels in love. She gave a deep reflective sigh. So much had happened since her last birthday, so much to change her whole outlook on life. And most of it had occurred in the last few days. From the moment she met Giles Pritchard, her whole attitude to life had altered. She had changed from a young girl to a mature woman.

Since that first meeting, they had not spent a day apart. Each day her feelings for Giles had intensified in a scary way; scary because she was still not sure where she stood with him, was still puzzled about his feelings for her. He constantly sought her company, showered her with flattery and attention, yet never spoke of any deeper commitment – not a word about love or any special affection. Had she been sleeping with him, she might have assumed his interest in her was simply a sexual diversion. But strangely enough, although he exuded a powerful virility, his treatment of her remained uncharacteristically chaste.

He made no secret of the fact that he was attracted and aroused by her, yet never pushed their affectionate kisses and caresses to their natural conclusion. Occasionally, he even thrust her roughly away from him, as if frightened where their passion might lead.

Yet from intimate conversations together, she knew he had enjoyed scores of girlfriends and her woman's intuition told her that those relationships had been far from chaste! She clung to the hope that it was some gentlemanly sense of honour which held him back, perhaps some bitter experience in the past which made him reticent in bestowing his affections.

She was apprehensive of taking the lead herself, of even discussing it with him; if his feelings were only superficial, she might frighten him off, perhaps lead him to believe she was a woman of 'easy virtue'. She smiled to herself as the old-fashioned phrase came to mind. Surely Giles, of all people, would never think that. He was too obviously a man of the world. She had had ample opportunity to witness his considerable allure as far as other woman were concerned. She wasn't the only one to find him overwhelmingly attractive – women seemed to fall at his feet.

Even if he were in love with her, she doubted how long she could continue to hold his interest. It was difficult enough keeping up with his voracious appetite for life in general. Full of enthusiasm and vitality herself, she admired these qualities in others. But Giles had the dash and energy of a wild thing. Could she keep pace with a man who wanted to live more in five days than many people did in a lifetime? Could she compete with every other desirable woman in the world, especially when till now, she seemed completely incapable of satisfying his sexual needs?

She sighed again to herself. Only time would tell. But she hoped fervently she wouldn't end up like some rag doll discarded by a hyperactive child, once its appeal had passed.

Looking out at the calm serenity of the morning scene, she found it difficult to remain anxious for long. Her natural optimism and sunny disposition soon re-asserted themselves. Life was wonderful! It was silly to worry. She was nineteen, had her whole life before her. Her grandparents had organised a wonderful party for her tonight. Most important – Giles would be there! She convinced herself that deep inside him, he did love her. He had to!

A familiar sound – the clatter of breakfast plates – drifted up to her from the kitchen below, closely followed by the evocative unmistakable aroma of bacon frying. Mmm! Breakfast was almost ready. She jumped up from the chair, bounced lightly back into the bedroom, slipping off her robe as she went. She stepped into the bathroom and under the shower. Turning the tap fully to cold, she stood beneath the invigorating jet, her chin raised, relishing the icy tingle of cold water as it streamed all over her flawless body.

* * * * * * *

The party was due to start at eight o'clock. Some sixty people had been invited, most of them young people; but there would be a fair sprinkling of older island residents who had known Kate since she was a child. Cathy and her maid had prepared a superb cold buffet. A couple of piping-hot dishes – chicken supreme and barbecue ribs of pork – would also be on offer. Tables and chairs were already laid out on the large poolside terrace where the food would be served.

Sunset was still an hour away when Kate surveyed the scene from her balcony. Fairy lights already flickered in the trees and shrubs, brightly-coloured balloons floated on the surface of the pool and a banner streamed from the covered terrace, proclaiming in huge letters, 'Happy Birthday Kate', followed by a gigantic '19'. The whole effect was bright and festive. The evening felt balmy, the lightest of softly-scented breezes wafting into her room from the surrounding garden.

At ten minutes before eight, full of optimism, she ran swiftly downstairs, floated out to join her grandparents on the terrace. Cathy and Leslie were already standing by the pool, champagne glasses in their hands.

"Perfect timing!" said Leslie, handing her a glass. "We thought it would be a good idea for the three of us to enjoy some champagne – before the mob arrives.

But let's have a look at you first." He held her at arm's length. "Perfect!" he said, his eyes rheumy with emotion.

Cathy came to her side and hugged her tightly.

"You look beautiful, darling."

"Thank you," she said, relieved. "It took me ages deciding what to wear."

She had finally settled for a simple white creation which set off her tan and unusual colouring to perfection. Before leaving her room, she studied herself intently in the mirror, thrilled to see how her leopard eyes flashed golden topaz in the evening light. Not to be outdone, her tanned skin gleamed with a golden sheen, and twirling around, her pale blonde hair glinted first silver, then light bronze in the soft reflected glow of the sun's late rays.

She thought she had never looked better – if he didn't like her now, he never would. But it was reassuring to have her grandparents' instant approval. She smiled at her next thought. Cathy and Leslie would probably have complimented her, even if she looked frightful.

Leslie took the champagne from the ice bucket and opening it with aplomb, swiftly poured the sparkling liquid into their glasses, not spilling a drop.

"Happy Birthday, Kate!" they toasted in unison.

"Thank you. I love you both. Thank you for preparing this lovely party."

She sipped eagerly at the golden bubbles. How typically thoughtful of her grandparents to organise the champagne and a moment of privacy before the rush. For some reason, she felt unusually nervous tonight – the champagne should help.

Within minutes, the first guests started to arrive. She noticed with amusement that it was mainly the older generation which arrived promptly. But soon the youngsters started to appear and the whole scene became one of frenzied activity, laughter and well-wishing. She was surrounded by her guests, everybody complimenting her on her birthday and her gorgeous appearance that night.

Suddenly the crowd around her broke away. In front of her stood Giles. There was a breathless hush from the rest of the guests as they waited, instinctively, for him to speak.

For a few eternal moments, he said nothing, just gazed at her, unsmiling.

Her heart sank.

Then his face broke into a wide appreciative grin.

"Happy Birthday, Golden Girl!" he said, his voice ringing out across the whole pool and garden area.

Everybody started to shout and clap, obviously loving the title he had given her. Golden Girl! She was thrilled. For the first time in her life, she felt she could have reached out and touched the crock of gold at the end of the rainbow.

* * * * * * *

The tempo of the party had never faltered. At two in the morning the majority of the guests were still there enjoying themselves. Some danced romantically to the soft music which, in the early hours, had taken over from the strident echoes of the current rock scene. Some swam lazily in the pool, the ripple of their movements producing phosphorescent sparkles in the floodlit water. She was surprised to see others still eating. Plates of hot sausage-rolls had miraculously appeared on the scene. Her grandmother seemed to think of everything!

Gazing happily around her, she decided it had been the happiest night of her life. Giles had been constantly, yet unobtrusively, by her side. He had disappeared now, to fetch her a glass of fresh orange juice, this time without champagne! She was starting to feel quite lightheaded.

Within seconds he was back, handing her a tall glass brimming with ice.

"Kate, could we take a quiet stroll? I'd like to talk to you."

"Of course. I think I've fulfilled all my duties as the birthday girl." She took his hand. "Thanks for all your help, Giles."

He shrugged his shoulders. "I did nothing, baby. It was a great evening. But you were the star. You look radiant, Kate!"

She paused in her steps, but kept staring straight ahead. "A reflection of you – your effect on me!"

He coughed awkwardly, then catching hold of her other hand, swirled her round to face him.

"Kate – there's something I've got to tell you."

Oh no! she thought. The moment of truth! I can guess – he's married! He's going to tell me he's already married!

"What's her name?" she managed to whisper, her head held high.

"Name?" He looked puzzled. "What the hell are you talking about?"

She stood there silently, her world crumbling about her.

He burst out laughing, his white teeth gleaming in the moonlight.

"I'm not married or engaged, if that's what you're thinking – never have been!" His expression changed to one of concern. "Would you have been very hurt, if I had been?"

She stood quite still, a single tear trickling down her cheek. She brushed it impatiently away, not sure if it was a visible sign of her relief or her frustration with Giles.

"Of course, I'd be hurt. Really Giles, you gave me such a scare. You must know how much I care for you." She looked down, embarrassed. There – she'd said it. Not in so many words. But now he knew. Please God – let him say he felt the same. She raised her eyes and looked directly into his.

He met her gaze, but this time it was he who looked down, seeming at a loss for words. She continued staring at him, as if her gaze could extract the words she wanted to hear.

"Kate – I don't know what to say. You're a wonderful person ... I'm very fond of you – you know that, but it's impossible."

"What's impossible? Tell me, Giles. What's the matter with me? Am I too young, too dull ... not sexy enough? That's what it is, isn't it? You like me, but I just don't turn you on."

"Christ, Kate!" he groaned. "If you only knew ..."

"So what's the problem? It's only fair you tell me."

"I was going to, but now ... I can't."

"So this is the end," she said miserably.

He looked at her, shocked.

"Of course it isn't the end!"

She shook her head.

"Giles, I just don't understand you. What are you playing at? What's the point of all this charade? You either like me or you don't. You either want to go to bed with me or you don't. I want to know what's going on. I can't continue like this – not knowing."

Her voice had become a sob, but the words still continued to tumble out.

"You don't act as if you want me simply as a friend ... I'm not asking you to marry me, or make any promises. I just want to know exactly how you feel ...".

He shook his head.

"I'm sorry, Kate. I don't know what to say. All I know is I must see you again."

Tears now streamed down her face.

"Giles, I never thought you could be so ... cruel!" She broke away from him, ran swiftly back the way they had come.

Her lovely birthday, the happiest night of her life – it had all ended in disaster. She hated him, yet felt powerless to resist him. If he persisted, she knew she would see him again.

Chapter 45

Giles drove home from Kate's birthday party, his mind in turmoil.

He knew he had hurt her deeply, but why should it bother him so much? He had, of course, ruined any chance of building up a platonic relationship with her and taking advantage of her youthful naivety. But he should have realised that from the moment of their first meeting. Now the whole situation was complicated by his own growing affection for her.

He was certainly not in love with Kate, but no longer could he convince himself he was not deeply affected by her. He had no belief in romantic love as such. Intense sexual attraction – certainly; infatuation, obsession – yes. But the blissful selfless dream-world people liked to call love was an emotion he had no time for – it was an illusion. His father certainly didn't love his mother, and although she believed she loved him, Giles considered that a delusion on her part. She desperately needed his father now, he was her life. She called it love – but he would call it self-interest.

So no, he was definitely not in love with Kate, but he could no longer explain the fascination she held for him. Beautiful, intelligent and warm-hearted, she was still a woman like any other. And she stood between him and the life he wanted. He would have to find a way to deal with her.

Ironically enough, she was the sort of woman he could have married. He hadn't considered marriage before; never imagined himself capable of making the sacrifice of freedom it would involve. In any case, he'd never found anyone he liked enough to make a permanent companion. Until he met Kate! He suddenly realised he could quite happily make a life with someone like her. Besides her obvious sexual attractions, she would make an easy yet stimulating companion. Had it not been for the blood-tie between them, marrying Kate would have solved all his problems. It was a provocative thought – marry the heir to his father's fortune and win, along with his inheritance, the delightful Kate!

He swore out loud. It looked like being the greatest irony of his life: to find a girl he could have married – and so doing secure his future – but not be able to go through with it! She was the daughter of his half-sister, she was his niece, damn it! It wasn't possible. He had to accept that.

And so would Kate if she discovered the truth of their relationship. It was the reason he'd never made love to her, though he was sure she would welcome his advances. He had few scruples when it came to satisfying his sexual libido. But in this case, the big ugly letters kept staring him in the face. Incest! He choked on the word, cursing fate for another cruel blow.

Apart from their shared bloodline, there was one further stumbling block to any satisfactory relationship with Kate, equally as daunting, – his father. Should he discover the existence of Kate, he would never let Giles near her for two reasons. Apart from the obvious repulsion at their genetic closeness, he would never allow his despised prodigal son to have any influence over his innocent new heir, Kate.

Then a dreadful thought hit him – with the impact of a thunderbolt. If he couldn't marry Kate, someone else would! He felt disgust and fury well up inside him. Some unknown worthless character stood the chance of walking off, not only with Kate, but with the fortune that was rightly his.

The solution to the dilemma suddenly came to him – the only logical answer to that unthinkable possibility. If he couldn't have her, nobody would. He could never bear the thought of another man making love to Kate, let alone taking over his father's empire.

With a sinking feeling in the pit of his stomach, he realised the only answer was to sacrifice Kate. The thought made him feel sick. But there was no alternative! Something would have to happen to Kate, something that couldn't be linked in any way to him or his true relationship with her.

The more he thought about it, the easier it seemed. Nobody in Ibiza had any idea of the family connection between the two of them. If an accident were to happen to Kate, there would be no possible motive, no reason for him to be suspected. Fortunately, it was accepted by most people that he and Kate were in love. He must try to foster that impression.

He would have to study carefully every detail of his plan – devise a scheme which would leave him absolutely in the clear. Once Kate was out of the way, he could ensure his father was made aware, subtly, that there were no Proctor heirs. The will would be changed in his favour. Even if his father later discovered he had met Kate, as long as he played his cards right, there would be nothing to link him with her death.

The words hit him with sudden force. Her death. Kate dead! It was a sickening thought. But now it was the only answer – the only possible solution.

He shivered. He would have to be so careful from now on – not let any hint of their blood relationship leak out. He was playing for big stakes – and against his finer feelings for the girl.

He had no reservations about behaving unscrupulously, having discovered that in this life, it was everyone for himself. Nobody had cared a damn about him, in fact quite the reverse. Had it been anyone else but Kate, he would have enjoyed the challenge. The risk would have set his adrenaline flowing. But Kate. The only girl he had ever cared for! He shook his head, cursed with the foulest language he knew.

Unfortunately he could see no alternative!

* * * * * * *

Two evenings later, after a light supper, he sat enjoying coffee and brandy in a café in the port area of Ibiza Town. Eventually he decided to ring Kate. Nearly forty-eight hours had elapsed since their quarrel at her birthday party. Previous to that, they had been seeing each other every day, even when the Hiscocks returned from England. On the days he went sailing with the owners, he had still managed to see Kate in the evening.

After so many hours apart, he was confident she would be anxious to see him again. He had deliberately left her with time enough to get over her anger, to feel the vacuum of his absence. He had already worked out in his mind the first part of his plan – to reassure Kate, and as many people as possible, of the depth of his love and affection for her.

He strolled to a telephone cabin and dialled her number.

"Diga! Hello! 341627," answered a female voice, repeating the number in both Spanish and English. He recognised it as Cathy, Kate's grandmother.

"Hello, Mrs Bourne. This is Giles."

"Oh ... Giles." The voice dropped and became hesitant.

"Could I speak to Kate?"

"I'll see if she's in." The tone was doubtful, but he was sure Kate was there.

He switched to his most persuasive manner. "Mrs Bourne – please try to get her to come to the phone. She's probably still a bit upset from the other evening. We had something of a lovers' tiff. It was my fault entirely. I'm ringing to apologise. Please tell her I've something urgent and important to discuss with her."

Her voice softened.

"I'll see if I can find her, Giles."

The line went dead for several minutes. He began to feel alarmed. Perhaps he'd blown it. Kate might refuse to see him again. She must be there or Cathy would have told him by now.

The seconds ticked by. His heart sank further. Suddenly there was a flurry on the line, then a small, quiet voice.

"Hello, Giles."

His heart ached at the sadness of her tone.

"Kate, baby! Will you ever forgive me? Listen carefully. I had to call you. I must see you."

"I'm sorry, Giles ... I'm afraid that's not possible ..."

"Kate... you don't understand. I love you! Do you hear me? I love you. I L-O-V-E Y-O-U!" He shouted the letters out.

There was a slight gasp, then another moment of silence.

"Kate! Did you hear what I said?"

"Yes, I heard." She gave a tiny sob. "Oh, Giles. Do you really mean that."

"Sure! Of course I do. I've come to my senses at last. Forgive me for being such a bastard. When can I see you?"

"Whenever you like, but please make it soon!" He could hear the smile in her voice.

"I have a day free tomorrow. Big Bob says I can borrow his speed-boat. How about a day on the sea, just the two of us?"

"Wonderful! I'll bring a picnic. Where shall we meet?"

"The harbour bar in the Marina in San Antonio. Is nine-thirty OK with you?"

"Perfect. I'll see you tomorrow."

"I love you, Kate." He blew a kiss down the telephone.

"I love you too, Giles," she said, shyly.

The line went dead. He had done it. Everything was going to plan.

When he caught sight of her the following day, he was surprised at the powerful effect she had on him. Every time he saw her, she looked even better than he was expecting, her figure and colouring so striking they took his breath away. But this time the impact of seeing her startled him.

He spotted her standing outside the harbour bar wearing a simple, vivid-pink T-shirt dress and matching sandals. Her pale-blonde hair was tied casually back in a pony-tail with a ribbon of the same colour. Her long tanned legs seem to extend for ever beneath the thigh-length dress. She wore no make-up, except a gloss of matching pink lipstick. As he approached her, her golden skin seemed to glow with happiness, her leopard eyes flashing topaz, flecked with gold. In the glittering sunlight, the colour of her eyes matched the sunshine of her hair.

The effect was stunning. He had never seen her wear a colour which didn't suit her. She looked elegant and chic in pure white or jet black, but he loved her, too, in the vibrant Mediterranean hues – sunshine yellow, burnt orange, turquoise blue and flamingo pink – which provided a perfect foil for her tawny eyes, shimmering tan and pale hair. She reminded him of some rare and exotic bird.

She fell into his arms and he could feel her trembling as he grasped her tightly to him. The soft sweet scent of her perfume filled his nostrils.

"Let's go!" he said, gruffly, unsettled at the strength of his reactions. He took the picnic-basket from her, led her swiftly by the hand down the floating jetty. Drawing level with Bob's power-boat, he pulled in the mooring ropes and stepped onto the bows, holding out a hand to assist Kate. The surface of the boat was still slippery from the dew, but quickly removing her sandals, she stepped lightly and nimbly on board. Without a word, he switched on the extractor fan to pump out any petrol fumes and after a few seconds started the motor. The big Mercruiser engine sprang to life.

Slowly he edged the boat out of its mooring into the waters of the harbour. As they chugged along the harbour exit channel at the mandatory five knots, he watched as she automatically busied herself removing the fenders. Studying her every movement, he hardly knew how to keep his hands off her.

She came and stood silently at his side, her lovely eyes bright with eager anticipation. He winked at her, and as they left the confines of the harbour pushed the throttle hard forward. The power-boat surged forward, the bows rising high in front of them until the craft reached planing speed and levelled off. They skimmed easily across the smooth surface of the water, leaving a creaming wake to mark their passage.

Having reached the middle of the bay, well away from the shore, he pulled the throttle back. The power-boat lost power and sank rapidly into the water. He switched off the ignition. Laughing at the surprise in her eyes, he pulled her towards him kissing her hungrily, feeling his desire mounting.

"Kate, darling Kate!" He held her away from him. "How could you be such a dope. Fancy thinking I didn't find you sexually attractive. You're the most desirable woman I've ever met." As he said the words, he knew them to be true. Her skin felt soft as velvet, her lips sweet and moist, her mouth as demanding as his own. He could feel her body trembling with same desire already running wild inside him.

"Why did you never tell me how you felt?" she asked, her eyes wide and appealing, like a small child. "You can't believe how upset I've been the last two days."

"Yes I can. It's been just as rotten for me. I tried desperately not to get involved with you. My parents don't get on and I've always been dead set against any close relationship. I tried so hard not to fall in love with you. I know it sounds corny, but I suddenly realised I couldn't fight it anymore. I love you. There's nothing I can do about it."

Gently, she held his face between her slim hands, her eyes large and moist with tears.

"I'm so happy, I can't believe it. It doesn't seem possible after the last few days. I was so sure you didn't want me."

"I've always wanted you, but until the night of your birthday, I didn't think I needed you. But you were such a lovely innocent person, I couldn't hurt you or take advantage of your feelings for me. You're incredible, Kate. You expect the best from everybody and somehow – instead of it making you more vulnerable – your very innocence seems to act as a kind of protective shield. Everyone tries to live up to your expectations. I thought I could never hurt you." He kissed her again, long and hard. "But I did, and that affected me more than anything. Then these last two days – I couldn't stand being without you. I love you, Kate, and I need you."

Her face was alight with happiness. He kissed her again, this time with tenderness.

"Now, before we get too excited, where shall we go?"

"The little lagoon on Conejera," she said, without hesitation. She laughed with pure joy. "This is going to be the most fabulous day!"

Chapter 46

Conejera, the island of rabbits, lay beyond the huge Bay of San Antonio some five miles west of the resort itself. Within minutes they had arrived at the uninhabited rocky outcrop of land and with Kate directing the way, he steered the power-boat smoothly through a narrow channel into a tiny lagoon. It was still early with no other craft in sight.

"Thank goodness! We're arrived first!" said Kate. "It's invariably calm and sheltered in here, so it's a favourite with small boats which can get through the channel. But because it's so tiny, there's only a few places to moor. It's a case of first come, first served!"

Looking round at the mirror-calm water, the tiny deserted beach, he could understand why the lagoon was so popular with the boating fraternity.

He raised the out-drive of the motor so they could drift right into the shallows, leapt over the side as they neared the shore, pulling the craft by hand the last few yards. They waded ashore with the bow anchor and picnic-basket, and settled on the tiny sand and shingle beach. Kate sat by the water, trailed her fingers in the translucent waters, then stretched out on the sand like a cat in the warmth of the sun.

He leaned across to touch her. Her skin felt soft and warm in the morning sunlight, her hair rippled with the texture of silk. With reluctance, he eased himself away.

She looked at him, quizzically.

"Not yet, not here," he told her. "I want everything to be perfect and right for you - for us."

"Isn't this perfect?" she asked with her shining smile.

"It's paradise," he admitted. "But it's not right – not yet."

She laughed. "Then let me show you something else." She dragged him to his feet, then ran off ahead of him across rocks which lead up the side of a shallow cliff. From time to time, like an excited child, she looked back teasingly to make sure he was following.

He followed mystified, but enjoying the sight of her slim lithe body ahead of him as she climbed sure-footedly over the large smoothly-wrought boulders towards the highest point of the headland.

Suddenly she stopped and pointed ahead.

"My favourite cave!" she said proudly. She led him by the hand into a small but perfectly-formed cave set into a steep section of rock. It was dark and damp inside and a musty stench hung in the air.

"Smells of old socks!" he said with a grin.

"Yes, I know, but when we were children we loved to come here and we hardly noticed the smell! We would picnic and explore all the crannies, digging in the sand for old bones and fossils. Once we found a very old Phoenician coin here – we were so excited! Leslie took it to the museum in Ibiza town – it's still there now on exhibition."

She smiled up at him, her face so radiant he couldn't stop himself taking her in his arms. "Kate, you're adorable – intelligent and exciting, yet fresh and innocent as a child." He cupped her face in his hands, felt his heart beat harder as he stared into her gold-flecked eyes. "And you're beautiful – my golden girl." He felt himself drifting, losing control. This was ridiculous, he thought. He daren't let his emotions run away with him. He drew slowly apart from her. "Let's go outside. I think I need some fresh air. You kids might have put up with the smell, but my American nose isn't up to it!"

He led her into the brilliant sunlight and together they gazed eastward – back the way they'd come in the boat. The whole Bay of San Antonio stretched before them, a vast panorama extending from Cap Nono in the north to the island of Bosque in the south. Kate smiled up at him and squeezed his hand, obviously pleased to see he was as impressed as she by the scene before them.

"There's another panoramic view from the other side of the island. Would you like to see it?"

He nodded, realising for the first time how much she loved these beautiful vistas, how proud she was of her island home. She took the lead again as they scrambled over more rocks to the south side where they could see as far as the headland of Cala Conta and the tiny islands beyond.

"Fantastic! I've seen a hellava lot of the world, Kate, but this is paradise. I can understand why you're so in love with the island!"

She looked up at him, her eyes growing more serious.

"I'm glad you understand, Giles – it's important to me. This is my home, but it's more than that. Out here, away from the rest of the world, I feel completely different – free as air, completely happy and fulfilled. Sharing it with you makes it even more wonderful. I love you, Giles."

"Not as much as I love you." He kissed her tenderly on the lips. "But after all that charging over the rocks I'm thirsty as hell!"

She laughed.

"So am I! Let's get back to the boat!" She took his hand and they clambered back down to their own tiny beach. Opening the picnic basket with a flourish, she passed him the champagne bottle to open. "Where shall we go next?" she asked eagerly.

"You're the island expert!"

Her eyes gleamed.

"Do you know what I've always wanted to do?"

"Make love to me!" he said between the bubbles of champagne.

"Of course!" She took the glass from his hand and kissed him.

He held her very close, his breath tight in his chest.

"What else?" he whispered.

She drew back from him, tossing her hair in a characteristic gesture, her teeth gleaming brilliant white in the sunlight, her eyes glowing like liquid gold.

"You'll never guess!"

"No I won't. So don't keep me in suspense."

"Climb to the top of Es Vedrá!"

"Climb where?"

"I've always wanted to climb to the very top of Es Vedrá!"

"You mean that fantastic rock that rises sheer from the water – near Cala D'Hort – where they filmed the long shots for *South Pacific*?"

"Yes. The original 'Bali Hai'! But you're wrong. It isn't sheer all the way round. There is a way to the top."

"But it rises nearly 1,500 feet," said Giles.

"I know. Isn't it exciting? I've always wanted to climb it."

"Ok," he said, catching some of her enthusiasm. "But don't blame me if we don't make it. I've never gone in for mountaineering before."

"We'll make it!" she said, confidently.

Christ! he thought to himself. She was a gem – as energetic and in love with life as he used to be, as he was becoming once more under her influence! What would he do without her vital presence?

* * * * * * *

He caught sight of the giant rock the moment they passed through the gap in the reef off Cala Conta. It rose sheer from the water like a misty citadel, its purple hazy outline lending a mysterious magical quality.

He drew in his breath.

"Wow!"

"Staggering isn't it?" said Kate. "Haven't you seen it before?"

"Sure! But not from this angle. I've seen it in the distance from the other side – from Formentera – when I've been skippering the yacht."

"It's supposed to have magical qualities, give off strange vibrations – some for good, some for bad. Lots of UFOs have been sighted here."

"I can believe that. But I can't see how it can be climbed without mountaineering equipment."

"It's supposed to be a bit of a scramble at first, but then there's supposed to be a good path, as far as the cave of Padre Palau."

"Who the hell was Padre Palau?"

"He was made a saint quite recently, but during the last century he was a kind of hermit priest. He lived for months in seclusion on Es Vedrá, just meditating. He had incredible visions of angels, in chariots of fire, descending to the rock, raising him up to the sky with them."

"Sounds like a modern day UFO sighting, or too many nights on the *hierbas* bottle," he commented, irreverently.

She giggled.

"Whatever it was, his visions have been published. There's a bust of him in Es Cubells and the cave he used is still there, near the summit of the rock."

"How did he survive so long without food and drink?"

"Miraculously enough, there's a fresh-water spring at the back of the cave. I suppose he fed on the fish he caught."

"I'd be happier if there were a champagne fountain up there. Still, the water will be damned useful. We won't have to carry so much. You're not really considering climbing in this heat?"

"No, let's moor in the shadow of the rock and have our picnic. We can start climbing when the sun gets lower."

"And drive back in the dark?" he teased.

"Do you think it will take that long?"

"It depends on the state of the path, but I guess it'll take some time to get to the top and back. Don't worry. It doesn't get dark until late. In any case, why not go back in the dark? There's still enough moon to see by, and we've got navigation lights."

"Return in the moonlight?" she said, her eyes shining.

"Sure," he replied, with a grin. "Now, how about a ski? I've a good mono on board – a tunnel!"

She laughed and released her hair from the pink ribbon.

"I told you this would be my perfect day!" She slipped out of her bikini and into a white one-piece. Within seconds she had disappeared like a sylph into the purple velvet of the water, returning glistening to the surface.

He flung her the tow-rope, and set off in the direction of the craggy rock. She rose quickly to the surface of the water, gliding effortlessly along on her single ski. Once she had mastered the intricacies of the new ski, she started to slalom across the wake, her pale blonde hair streaming behind her, her face a wide grin. She was obviously enjoying every moment!

Later, she drove while he skied, working out his physical and mental frustrations with the power and daring of his turns. He leaned further than he had ever done before on an unfamiliar ski, using his superb balance, his strong arm and leg muscles to defy gravity and the whiplash of the rope. Each time he executed a perfect turn – almost grazing the surface of the water with his body, the spray streaming behind him in a peacock plume – Kate would smile and wave enthusiastically from the boat.

Climbing back on board, he felt more relaxed – some of the tension released from his body, his mind clearer. He gave her a swift hug and towelled himself down before moving off to moor in the welcome shade of the towering rock of Es Vedrá. She pointed to the shore, to a section of rocky scree which rose less precipitously from the sea than the rest of the of the craggy mountain side.

"That's where the path starts. You see – there's a red arrow."

She's right, he thought. The climb should be a cinch.

They picnicked on smoked salmon, quiche and salad, washed down with a light white wine and slices of iced melon; then manoeuvred the bows of the boat into the sun, to enjoy a lazy siesta on the sun-deck before setting off on the rocky assault.

They found the going rough at the beginning. The path was fairly steep, and loose scree made it hazardous and slowed their progress. But soon the surface improved and they wound their way steadily higher.

Suddenly the track grew very steep. Kate gave a gasp of surprise, grabbed hold of him. The path had changed into a series of shallow steps, the footing itself safe enough – the steps were cut into rock – but to the sea-side there was a dramatic sheer drop. Hundreds of feet below them, the waves lapped gently at the very base of the craggy island.

"Hold my hand!" commanded Giles, "and don't look down." She smiled at him – completely trusting, utterly vulnerable. Was this the opportunity he had been waiting for? One gentle push and she would be over the edge, her young body shattered on the rocks below.

He dismissed the thought instantly. It was too soon after the birthday scene, the new closeness of their love affair not fully established. More important, he was alone with her. The accident would be easy to explain, but in the circumstances there would be exhaustive enquiries.

He couldn't afford that. When Kate's fatal 'accident' occurred, he wanted plenty of witnesses. Every detail had to be minutely planned. Her accident, or justifiable homicide as far as he was concerned – he refused to think in terms of murder – must be an open-and-shut case.

He held on to her tightly. Seconds later they were past the hazardous section and on the way to the summit.

Her face suddenly lit up.

"Look – there on that rock. 'To the cave of Padre Palau'," she recited.

Seeing the words, plainly written in red paint, he let out a guffaw of laughter.

"It's a bit like Disneyland – directions everywhere. And here we were, thinking we're pioneers!"

"We are!" she said, determinedly. "I'm sure nobody's been up this path for years."

There was certainly no other sign of life, past or present, except the carcass of one dead rabbit.

"Are there no other animals on the island?" he asked Kate.

"I heard there used to be goats, but not any longer."

Before they knew it, they were close to the summit. Sure enough, there was the famous cave, larger than he had expected. He was as thrilled as Kate to see the natural spring at the back. Cold icy water trickled from it and they both drank their full. They had carried food and mineral water with them, just in case, but the spring water tasted like nectar.

Leaving the cave, they edged along a rocky ledge towards the summit, but at the end of the narrow contour were confronted by a sheer rock wall, with no way round. He stared up at the summit -tantalisingly close, some fifty feet away. But there was no way they could scale this last section, without the aid of ropes.

"I'm afraid this is where we have to stop," he said. "Sorry, Kate. You must be disappointed, having got so far."

She shook her head and smiled.

"There is an easier way to the top, I'm sure, but it doesn't matter. We've seen the cave. This gives us something to do next time we come up."

He grinned, admiring the way her outlook on life was always so positive and buoyant. He glanced down at his watch.

"I guess we'd better be getting down now. We'll need good light on the way back."

With only few hundred metres left to descend, he decided to stop on a grassy knoll, a particularly beautiful spot with spectacular views across the sea and the west coast. In the distance, dusk was slowly painting out the dazzling white of the houses, the verdant green of the pinewoods. To the west the sky was already tinted pink.

It was then he decided to give her the present.

She looked at him with surprise when he handed her the tiny box.

"It's your birthday present – rather late, I'm afraid. I was about to give it to you at your birthday party, when we had our .. er .. little tiff." He smiled reassuringly at her. "I wanted to be alone with you when you opened it."

Her eyes went misty and she stared at the box.

"The next thing I give you will be an engagement ring – but that will be official. This is just between you and me."

She opened the tiny box with visibly excited fingers. There on a bed of black velvet lay the exquisite gold locket he had bought in Ibiza Town.

Enchanted, she turned it round and round in her hands. It glittered in the last golden rays of the sun.

"Giles, it's beautiful," she whispered. "I shall put your photograph inside. I'll always, always wear it." She gazed at the simple engraving on the front. "KATE. 10.7.85."

"Look at the back," he instructed.

She turned the locket over to see a further engraving on the reverse side. 'KEEP THAT BREATHLESS CHARM!'

She stared up at Giles, her eyes swimming.

"It's the most beautiful gift I've ever received," she whispered.

"I'm afraid the words aren't original."

"I know," said Kate, and she repeated the verse from memory.

"Lovely, never, ever change,
Keep that breathless charm,
Won't you please arrange it,
Cause I love you,
Just the way you look tonight."

"You see, that was my grandmother's favourite song," she explained, "I remember it from my childhood."

A shiver of excitement went through him.

"So do I," he whispered. "It was my father's favourite, too." Their favourite – he realised – the young lovers, Cathy and Jimmy – his father and her grandmother. He knew he was playing with fire. He took her hand. "The phrase comes to me – whenever I think of you. I don't know who wrote the words but they sum up just how I felt the night of your birthday. How I feel now. Keep that breathless charm, Kate."

He leant towards her, kissed her tenderly.

* * * * * * *

The journey home was swift and silent, apart from the hum of the engine. The powerboat seemed to fly across the water. The sun dropped suddenly close to the horizon and the distant contours of the Ibiza hills and the sea took on the wonderful colours she loved so well. The misty contours of the coastline and the hazy mountains gleamed silver and pearly grey and as she looked back towards to Atalaya it no longer stood stark, but soft and ethereal as it rose from the deep blue velvet water. The sea was so calm it was like driving through cream. Further to the south-west the sun eventually disappeared like a ball of fire leaving behind a sky of pink and gold. The moon rose on the other side of the sky, large and orange, then changed slowly to pale yellow, then white. Its rays reflected silver on the surface of the sea.

Kate snuggled up to Giles´ side and gazed at him with luminous eyes.

"Is it perfect now, Giles?"

"Idyllic, yes. But not perfect." He saw a tiny frown of puzzlement crease her lovely brow.

"When will it be perfect?" she asked in a small voice.

"The moment I slip a diamond solitaire on your finger."

A single tear slid down her cheek and she clutched at the locket around her neck.

"I love you," she said, simply.

He placed her hands on the driving wheel, and standing behind her, covered her fingers with his own large palms, enfolding her body in his. They drove together over the velvet water with only the roar of the engine in their ears.

He felt a strange excitement. It wasn't just the closeness of Kate. Already a plan was starting to form in his mind, and so far he couldn't fault it.

Chapter 47

Over the next few days Giles considered his bold plan from every angle. The more he thought about it, the more perfect it seemed. He was sure he had found the ideal solution – a yachting accident, with other people on board when it happened. It would not be so difficult to execute: an apparently accidental gybe, a heavy boom flying out of control knocking Kate on the head. She would be overboard in seconds. Even if she survived the impact of the blow, he could rely on his own rescue efforts in the sea to do the rest!

He knew all sailors were aware of the dangers of a boom flying out of control and just how easily it can happen – invariably the result of an uncontrolled gybe. Gybing – the method used to change course when the wind blew from behind – involved the rapid swing across the deck of the boom and the sail it supported. It was a tricky operation – even when controlled – and consequently treated with caution, and plenty of warning for crew members to keep clear. If, as a result of a freak gust of wind or careless steering, the gybe went out of control, the boom swinging unexpectedly across the deck became a lethal weapon. The suddenness and power of the movement could catch even the most experienced sailor unaware.

The wooden boom supporting the mainsail on *Sirocco Sunset* must weigh some two hundred pounds; the blow to anyone caught in its path would be tremendous.

Kate had done very little sailing. A few private words in her ear to move to a vulnerable position, clever use of a strong gusting wind from behind, and the mighty boom would do the rest.

His employers, the Hiscocks, had already promised to take her sailing and she was looking forward to it with her usual enthusiasm. He was satisfied the Hiscocks would make perfect witnesses. They knew how much he adored Kate and would certainly attest to that fact. Experienced sailors, who could vouch for the innocence of the accident, they would not be physically able to interfere in any rescue attempt. Janet, the cook, would also be an ideal witness – young, but her plump form far from athletic! He would have liked another friend on board as well – the more the better to witness his heroic life-saving attempt, as long as it wasn't a youthful fit male, who might be tempted to help him!

The result – an unfortunate accident – for which nobody could be blamed!

* * * * * * *

The opportunity to take Kate sailing came quite naturally the following afternoon. Even better, it was John Hiscock himself who raised the subject as he sat relaxing with a drink on the aft deck, after a light lunch aboard the yacht. Barbara and Janet were below, washing up the dishes.

"How's that lovely young lady of yours?" he asked, puffing noisily on his pipe.

"Kate – she's just fine!" grinned Giles. "I've just bought the ring, you know. We're having a quiet engagement party next weekend – just the two of us and Kate's grandparents. It's their wedding anniversary on the Saturday. I thought it would make the ideal occasion to present Kate with the ring and make the engagement official."

"Very romantic!" John nodded, approvingly. "You know, Giles, you're a very lucky man."

"Don't I know it!"

"I can't explain it, but Kate ... she's wonderful – a shining kind of girl."

"I know exactly what you mean, sir," said Giles, and he did. Kate was a shining person, but his clever plan was too important to forfeit at this stage.

"When shall we take her sailing?" asked John, obligingly. "We did promise. And Barbara and I would love to see her again soon."

"Whenever you like, sir," he said, jumping at the chance but trying not to appear over-eager. "I know Kate can't wait. She's pretty handy on powerboats, but she's never sailed on a yacht as big as this before. She's sure looking forward to it."

"We'll need a good wind," said John.

"You bet!" he said, pleased. A strong wind was vital to his plan. "I'd like to really demonstrate the boat's paces. Kate loves thrills. She'll adore some good sailing."

"We'll make sure she gets it! Call Barbara up we'll get something organised."

Within minutes, his wife appeared from below deck. They decided to take Kate out the first day there was a good wind.

"Would it be OK if another person joined the party?" asked Giles, his fingers crossed. "Kate has an aunt she's very fond of, who's on her own at the moment. She's a keen sailor, with a sloop of her own, a thirty-eight footer. She'd love the chance of a sail on a larger yacht." He smiled his winning smile. "She's a real boating person. I'm sure you'd enjoy her company."

"With pleasure," said John, and Barbara nodded. "What's her name?"

"Jane. Jane Reynolds. She's a widow. She has a son and daughter of Sam's age, but they've gone over to the mainland for a few days."

"Fine," said John. "That will make six of us." He turned to his wife. "Make sure Janet prepares a good picnic lunch. Sailing's hungry work for these youngsters!" He raised his glass of gin-and-tonic. "Here's to good winds and happy sailing."

Giles grinned with satisfaction and returned the toast with his half-empty beer-glass. Now it was only a question of time and weather.

* * * * * * *

Three days later, the weather obliged. When he awoke the day was sunny and very clear with no trace of haze, but a brisk breeze already blew from the south. Gazing out to sea with the binoculars, he noted white horses already forming on the horizon.

He telephoned Kate and Jane Reynolds from the Yacht Club, as they'd already arranged.

"It's on!" he told Kate. "A perfect day for sailing!"

"Great!" she said, excitedly. "We'll be at the Club in half an hour."

Little more than an hour later, *Sirocco Sunset* had cleared the harbour of Ibiza, headed on a course for the nearby island of Formentera. The wind had already come up, as he'd expected. Even beating with the sails close-hauled, the yacht made a smacking pace.

Jane Reynolds sat on the forward deck with the Hiscocks. They had immediately taken to one other, and were already swapping sailing stories and gossip like old friends. Kate, radiantly happy, was eagerly trying to learn as much as possible about sailing. She had begged him to allow her to crew and steer whenever possible. He had to admit she was a natural, with an intuitive feel for the wind and agility in her movements around the boat.

The morning passed without incident, the sailing perfect. Kate was hooked! – her amber eyes shone, her face glowed with exhilaration. His plan was to anchor off the lee side of Formentera to have lunch, then continue sailing in the early afternoon. At that time of day, the wind should be at its strongest, and after a good lunch washed down with wine, everybody on board would be easy and relaxed.

True to form, after the meal the wind started to blow stronger.

"Time to sail!" he called, anxious to get underway before it dropped. "We can have another swim and snorkel later in the afternoon," he explained to the Hiscocks.

They agreed, loving to take advantage of a good wind.

"The boat's all yours today, Giles," said John. "We'll leave you to show Kate her paces."

They weighed anchor with Giles at the helm, the girls raising and setting the sails. *Sirocco Sunset* leapt ahead like a thoroughbred from the starting gate.

"I'll show Kate just how fast this craft can travel," yelled Giles above the roar of the wind in the sails. He winked across at John, who returned the gesture with a broad grin of agreement and the thumbs-up sign.

"Is everything secure below, John?" he asked.

"Janet's down there, tidying up. I'll go and check."

Adroitly Giles manoeuvred the yacht until she was sailing on a reach, the sails well extended. As the noise in the rigging increased, he steered even further off the wind until it blew from the stern quarter on the port side.

He yelled to Kate to join him at the helm.

"Be careful as you move – the decks are slippery from the spray!"

The boat was heeled well over on its side, but she moved with care and agility and was soon by his side.

"This is about our fastest point of sailing, with the wind coming from an eight-o'clock position," he explained.

"What about running before," she asked. "Isn't that faster?"

"No, unless the boat actually starts to plane – goes faster than her waterline-length allows. Then she starts to plane on top of the following sea, instead of ploughing through it. It's an exhilarating experience, but rather risky – the boat can take a nose-dive down the other side of the wave, even turn turtle!"

"Sounds hairy," she grinned.

"It is, but don't worry – I won't let her do that. But I will get her running before the wind. It's a great sensation!"

He steered even further off the wind, trimming the sails until they billowed out like butterfly-wings. *Sirocco Sunset* seemed to fly in front of the wind, the huge waves chasing behind them.

He turned to look at Kate. She stood by his side radiant with excitement, obviously blissfully unaware of his intentions.

He began to feel uneasy. He'd better put his plan into operation – before he lost his nerve. Janet, the cook, and John Hiscock were still down below. Barbara and Jane were up forward, deep in conversation and well out of ear-shot. He only had to let the yacht drift slightly into wind, tighten the sails, then unobserved, steer neatly into a gybe – as if the yacht had been taken by a sudden freak gust of wind.

But first he had to get Kate in the right position. He squeezed her hand.

"Baby, would you mind going forward for me? I left my sunglasses up there, jammed on the coach-roof. I don't want to lose them in this wind."

She nodded, without a second thought.

"Go carefully!" He kissed her on the top of the nose.

She smiled up at him, her tawny eyes trusting, her bronzed skin glistening with the spray. Her pale silken hair hung lose, framing her face. She wore no trace of make-up, but he thought she'd never looked more beautiful. There was a shining mystical aura about her. He felt a wrench in his stomach, but knew he had to go ahead with his plans.

The moment she moved forward, he glanced quickly at Barbara and Jane. Still deep in conversation! With a rapid turn of the wheel, he steered across the eye of the wind, at the same time yelling to Kate.

"Kate, what the hell are you doing ...?"

As the yacht swung, the giant boom came hurtling across the deck. He saw her turn, witnessed for one frozen split-second the incredulous look of amazement on her face. Then, with a sickening crack, she was gone, the boom sweeping her forcibly over the side.

"Kate, Kate... he screamed, turning in horror to face the others. They had sprung to their feet when he yelled, their faces parchment-white, the suddenness and speed of events obviously taking them completely by surprise. He swung the wheel, yelled at John Hiscock who had appeared almost instantly on deck.

"John... quick! Take the helm. Turn the boat as fast as you can. I'm going after Kate."

"Don't be a fool," yelled John. "It'll be ages before we can get back to you ..."

He had already dived overboard, his heart pounding, his head reeling. Christ! What had he done? He'd killed Kate – Kate, who meant more to him than anything in the world. Yes! Suddenly he knew – he loved her. Before this moment he had refused to believe the strength of his emotions. Now he had realised, but it was too late! The truth came in a sickening flash – he'd killed the only thing he had ever loved. He swam frantically, his mind full of that last sight of her – her helpless look of surprise and ... something else. Yes, it was hurt – hurt that he had somehow let her down.

He moaned and screamed her name, but there was no sign of her in the foaming water. Despite the swiftness of his reactions, the boat had travelled some distance before he hit the sea. He had not even been able to spot her from the boat amongst all the waves. Now, from water level, surrounded by huge breakers, it was impossible to see anything. All he could do was strike out in what he thought was the right direction.

His swimming grew more frenzied. He began to despair. Kate had completely disappeared. If already unconscious when she hit the water, she didn't stand a chance. Her body would float face downwards. Within minutes, she would inhale enough water to sink and drown.

Just as he had given up all hope, he spotted her! A flash of pale-blonde hair trailing on the crest of a foaming wave. Kate, face down in the water! Then she was gone again – disappearing into the trough some twenty metres away.

He thrashed out towards her with all his might, his breath coming now in painful gasps. Still no sign of her. Christ! She had to be here – he must be able to see her now, even with the swell and breaking waves. Unless she'd already sunk beneath the surface! Frantic, he decided to take a gamble. Sucking in two deep breaths, he dived strong and hard into the foaming waters.

Beneath the churning surface he was suddenly in a new green and silent world where he could see quite clearly. His heart gave a lurch. Kate! – floating far below him like some exotic mermaid, her silver hair streaming above her like the fronds of a delicate sea plant, her features passive, her skin tones deathly pale.

Despite her apparently slow-motion descent, he knew she was sinking fast. He cleared his ears again. Diving was not his forte, yet without thinking, he found himself diving deeper than he had ever dived before, his chest feeling as though it would burst, the blood pounding in his head.

Somehow he managed to reach her, grasp hold of her body, halt her deadly plunge to the depths. In his elation, he choked in more water. His euphoria changed swiftly to fear and despair as he saw her face, deathly pale. Was she already dead? Could he get them both back to the surface? Every ounce of energy had drained from his body.

Summoning all his reserves, he struck out upwards, clasping her body to him. He was choking again, the seawater filling his lungs, his head starting to spin. Any second he would pass out! Christ! Would they never reach the surface!

A fierce cramping pain gripped his abdomen. He fought to stop himself doubling over....

Suddenly he broke the surface of the seething waters, thrust Kate upwards – above his own head – into the fresh clean sunlight above. Dimly he could see the white form of the yacht, hear urgent voices.

He was choking uncontrollably, sucking in yet more water. Darkness clouded his brain, but he refused to succumb to the agonising pains in his chest, the deadly cramp in his abdomen. Using every last reserve of energy, he thrust

Kate upwards once again, then released hold of her. Everything went black as he sank slowly back beneath the indigo waves...

Chapter 48

Long Island, New York. July 1985

Jimmy and Monique were sitting on the veranda discussing the arrangements for Monique's sixtieth birthday party, when the telephone rang inside.

"That will be the florists," she said, rising gracefully from the chair. "They said they would call back about the flowers for the party." With a swish of skirts, she walked into the study to take the call.

Several minutes ticked by and still no Monique. Damn it! thought Jimmy. What was taking her so long? Typical woman – spending an eternity on the telephone, just when he wanted to finish sorting out all the details of the party once and for all. Monique, nearly sixty! It didn't seem possible. She still had an enviable figure, and her good cheek bones ensured she would remain handsome, even at eighty!

He looked up, puzzled, as she walked apathetically, almost mechanically back onto the veranda, her face ashen. As if in a trance, she sank slowly into her chair and stared at him.

"So what terrible thing has happened with the flowers?" he asked, irritably.

She took a deep breath. "James, I am afraid it is bad news."

Giles! he thought furiously. It had to be Giles. God! What had the boy done this time? But seeing the ravaged expression on her face, his anger changed to fear, his heart began to thump wildly.

She continued to stare at him, then her whole face slowly crumpled up. She collapsed forward onto the table, seemed to fall apart before his eyes. Huge sobs wracked her body. She started to wail, hysterically.

He limped quickly to her side, caught hold of her shoulders, slapped her sharply across the face. Abruptly her screams died down. She looked at him in horror, then hid her face in her hands.

He found he, too, was shaking uncontrollably. Something terrible must have happened for Monique to be in such a state. He knelt by her side, gently stroked her hair. "Tell me, darling. What's happened?"

She stared at him again, her eyes strangely devoid of expression. "He is dead ... Giles is dead!" She slumped forward again, began to sob.

He felt the blood drain from his body. His head swam, he felt faint and nauseous but with a tremendous effort of will managed to keep a hold on himself. He continued stroking her hair, whispering soft assurances. When her sobbing finally ceased, he rose, moved his chair closer and sat beside her placing his hands over hers. "Tell me – as soon as you feel ready."

She clasped his hands with a strange fierceness and shuddered. "James – this will be difficult for you to understand and accept. I could scarcely believe it myself."

"Just tell me what happened," he persisted, quietly.

"He drowned.... in a yachting accident.... off an island somewhere in Spain." Tears stole down her cheeks again.

"Drowned?... Are you sure? Giles is a strong swimmer, and the last I heard he was in Barcelona!"

"He was trying to rescue a girl. She had fallen overboard from the yacht they were on ... It seems he was in love with her. Oh, James ..." She started to sob again. "The girl – her name is Kate ... it hardly seems possible, but she was the grand-daughter of Cathy Bourne – your wife, Cathy! It was she I spoke to on the telephone just now...."

His heart went cold; his stomach crawled.

Monique continued, relentlessly. "She told me she had been this girl's guardian since her parents died in a car accident. Her parents were a Peter and Samantha Radcliffe. Samantha! Your Sam!" She shouted the name. Her eyes met his in a glassy stare. "It is true! I checked with Cathy. Her daughter's name, before she married, was Samantha Proctor Bourne. Your Sam was a girl all the time – not a boy!"

He could scarcely believe what she was telling him. Sweat broke out on his forehead as the full import of her words began to sink in. "Sam?... Cathy? You mean you've just spoken to Cathy?"

She nodded, wordlessly. "She was very kind.... Not aware of the family connection. She had traced our telephone number through Giles's passport.... and the Spanish consul over there. She said she wanted to break the news to us personally, because she felt so close to us. James.... I have to tell you.... her grand-daughter and Giles were about to become engaged!"

He stared at her in horror.

She shook her head. "Don't worry. As yet, Cathy has no knowledge of your identity ... I told her I would ring back – after I had broken the news to you. She understood how shocked I was."

Again she broke into sobs. "My son, oh God! ..." With an effort, she raised her head high. The tears continued to roll unashamedly down her cheeks, but she spoke proudly, staring straight ahead. "Cathy said how brave Giles had been. He saved her grand-daughter's life."

"The girl – she's still alive?"

"Yes," she said, her tone flat. "They gave her the kiss-of-life. She was in hospital several days. Your granddaughter is alive.... but your son is dead." Her eyes fell. "And I always thought he was the survivor."

He seized her hands. "Monique.... I'm so sorry....". He waited until her sobs had died down, until she had stopped trembling. "I know how you must feel, but later ... please will you call Cathy back for me? I dare not – I'm sure she would recognise my voice."

He hesitated, not knowing how to phrase his next request. "Would you mind very much if ...? I mean I'd like to listen to the call – on the extension line in the library." His eyes pleaded with her to understand.

She nodded, numbly, then with a new determination squared her shoulders, seemed to recover her composure. "First I am going to make us both a cup of tea. Then I shall call her back."

He watched in shocked admiration as she walked sedately from the room, her head held high.

Half an hour later, he held his breath as she dialled the Spanish number. Instantly recognising Cathy's voice, he listened in distress and fascination, as his two wives talked together. He could remember Cathy's face, as if it were yesterday. He was glad he had never seen her grow old. A single tear trickled slowly down his face as he heard her soft sympathetic voice recounting the details of the accident.

Suddenly, he knew it was all over. Giles was dead! Sam had died years ago – not a son, but a daughter, whom he had never seen and never would! But there was a brighter side, he thought through the bitterness which had clutched at his heart. Cathy was still alive and well – and their grand-daughter! Kate she was called – after her grandmother. He would never see her but he hoped she was like Cathy, blessed with that same warmth and understanding. She must be a wonderful girl for Giles to have fallen in love with her – even sacrificed his life for her!

A tiny doubt niggled at the back of his mind. Giles must have been aware of Kate's relationship with himself. Had he really planned to marry her, or was he just leading her on, trying to get his hands on the fortune that would be hers. He dismissed the thought from his mind. Giles had died for the girl. He must have loved her. His son had come good in the end, thank God!

In a strange way, he felt at peace. It was all over now, in more ways than one. The pain he had felt minutes ago had begun to grow worse, but now it hardly mattered. His life had come full circle. Giles was dead, but Cathy had survived – alive and happy with their grandchild, Kate, the living witness of their love.

Another fierce pain seemed to envelope his whole body, but seeing Monique walking slowly back into the library, he tried to hide the degree of his distress.

"I don't feel so well," he said quietly and rose slowly from his chair, feeling strangely calm. "I'm going up to bed."

She rushed to his side, tried to support him, but he shrugged her gently away. "Don't worry. I'm fine, but if you don't mind, I'd like to be on my own. The shock, I suppose.... I just need some rest."

She stared at him hard, kissed him firmly – almost passionately – on the lips, then allowed him to pass her unaided.

He looked back at her from the foot of the stairs. "Monique, you're a wonderful woman. I'm sorry I could never love you as much as you deserved. But I did love you, in my way – as much as I was able."

She nodded and smiled, her emerald eyes understanding and wet with tears. "Is there anything I can bring you?" she asked, with unusual tenderness.

"No," he said, trying to smile too, despite the pain inside growing stronger all the time.

"Are you sure I should not call to the doctor?"

"No, I'll be fine."

"I love you, *mon chéri*," she said, huskily. "Sleep well!" He read the rest in her eyes. She knew they had said their final farewell.

302

Epilogue

Ibiza, Spain. August 1985

The white Renault Eleven purred quietly along the highway between Ibiza and San Antonio. It was late afternoon. Kate sat in the back, lost in a turmoil of thoughts about the events and revelations of the last few days. Coming out of her reverie, she spotted the whitewashed church of San Rafael – they must have reached the section of the road which bypassed the village. She leaned forward in her seat and spoke softly to her grandparents seated in the front of the car.

"Cathy, Leslie. I've never seen the exact spot where my parents died. Would you show me now?"

Cathy looked back at her anxiously.

"Are you sure you want to do this, Kate – after all you've been through already."

She nodded firmly. "Yes. I'm certain. It's a kind of rounding-off. I feel everything's gone full circle. Now I want to see where it all started."

She saw Leslie nod and squeeze her grandmother's hand. He slowed down, turned right onto the old road, and headed back towards the village. The car drew to a halt, just a short distance beyond the treacherous San Rafael bend.

The three of them climbed out of the Renault and stood silently by the side of the road.

"Their car went out of control back there on the bend," said Cathy quietly. "It finished up by that telegraph pole."

Kate stared silently at the spot.

"Thank you," she said eventually and hugged her grandmother. "I'd like to go now."

They set off again in silence. She heard Cathy ask Leslie if they could go for a walk instead of going straight home. The Renault turned off the main road, followed the winding road to Santa Ines.

Abruptly she found her eyes were wet with tears – the first time she had given way to weeping since that terrible day Giles had died, while saving her life.

She could remember nothing of what happened, from the moment she was hit by the heavy boom until she regained consciousness, choking and with vicious pains in her head and chest, aboard *Sirocco Sunset*. Apparently she owed her life, not only to Giles, who had saved her from the sea, but to John Hiscock and Jane Reynolds who had snatched her from the water and alternately given her the kiss-of-life, bringing her back from the dead. She still had a huge bump on the back of her head, but thank God it had only been a glancing blow from the boom. It could have fractured her skull.

Her last memory was of Giles screaming at her; a sudden awareness of the threatening boom; the strange look on his face, which had instantly changed to one of horror. She would always remember that last, split-second expression on his handsome features.

Shock followed after shock. Within hours of her own recovery, they had told her that Giles had died saving her. Only a few days later, she learned that his father in America had died, apparently from a stroke following the news of his son's tragic accident.

Then, unbelievably, came the shattering discovery that this same man was, in fact, her own grandfather. Cathy's first husband hadn't died in the war. He'd been alive all these years! Giles was a close blood relation!

She still didn't know all the details. After the terms of the will had been disclosed, Cathy gently tried to explain it all to her, but her battered mind had been unable to fully understand.

Then the greatest irony of it all – she was now a wealthy heiress. But she had lost Giles!

It was all too much for Kate. For several weeks she retreated into a state of apathy and listlessness, withdrawing in bitterness from the tragic, confusing world around her, finding no compensation in the fact that her own life had been miraculously saved. She had survived at the expense of Giles himself.

Even worse were her niggling doubts about Giles. Why had he deceived her? – He must have known who she was. Had he really intended to ignore their blood ties and marry her, without even telling her first? Or had he been leading her on?

And why had he asked her to move forward on the boat, at what she now knew to be such a dangerous point of sailing. She had instinctively not mentioned that fact to anyone, letting them assume it had been her own impromptu action. Why had he let her do something so hazardous? Had he ever really loved her? She would never know. She doubted if she had ever known the real Giles.

The tears that earlier had refused to appear now continued to slide down her cheeks, but somehow their silent flow seemed to cleanse and ease the pain and tension inside her. She knew she had to accept what had happened, for better or worse, and give up the futile soul-searching and doubts about Giles. He must have loved her – he had died for her. She had to accept the tragedy and mourn him without recrimination.

Slowly through her tears she became aware that they had reached Santa Inés. The car drew to a halt in front of the country restaurant and Cathy turned to speak to her.

Her grandmother's face fell as she saw Kate's grief-ravaged face. She caught hold of her hand, gave her a warm reassuring smile.

"Don't despair, my darling. Believe me – things will get better. I know how you feel ... I went through much the same sort of tragedy. It left me desolate, but look how things turned out for me." She smiled tenderly at Leslie, then turned back to Kate, squeezing her hand. "Always remember, Kate, that Giles loved you dearly – enough to give his life for you. Nothing can change that."

Yes, thought Kate. It was silly to doubt his love. She had been instinctively right about that. She buried her head in her hands, tried to control her sobs.

She heard Leslie's warm deep voice.

"I know it's hard, Kate dear, but try to be thankful for your own survival – we have to thank God for that. By the time they got you back on board the boat, everybody thought you must be dead. You were lucky it was only a glancing blow to the head, that both Bill and Jane were so expert in the treatment they gave you."

"If only they could have rescued Giles as well," she whispered.

"Barbara and Janet had to stay on board to keep the boat under control. It was as much as John and Jane could do to retrieve you, get you back aboard with the life-line. Naturally they grabbed you first – Giles had disappeared beneath the water. John's not a young man, and Jane's no diver. There was no way either of them could have dived for Giles, the way he had done for you."

She nodded, miserably.

"Oh, Cathy! Leslie! I loved him so much. Shall I ever be able to love and trust again?"

"Of course you will," said her grandmother, with unusual passion. "You have that marvellous gift of not only creating and inspiring love, but of returning it with interest. You'll never lose that quality, Kate. It's a part of your whole being. People feel it from the moment they meet you."

"Rather like your grandmother," added Leslie, with a sidelong smile and wink at her.

She saw Cathy blush slightly at the compliment and it brought a smile to her own lips.

"That's better," said Leslie, happily. "We've missed your smile, Kate, and your laughter. It's time for you to start living again." He opened the car door. "Now, how about some fresh air? It should do us all good."

"Yes," said Cathy. "We'll go for a walk – just as far as the coast above the islands of Margarita. Then we'll have supper – a Spanish omelette and salad in the bar over there."

"Would you mind if I had a quiet drink on my own," suggested Kate, knowing she needed some time on her own in the tranquillity of the tiny country square. "I'll sit on the terrace outside while you go for a walk. Then we'll all have supper together."

"Of course, darling," said Cathy softly, immediately understanding. "It might be better for you to be alone for a while. We shan't be very long."

They kissed her and set off along the path to the coast.

For several minutes they walked in thoughtful silence. Leslie put his arm around her shoulders.

"Don't worry too much about Kate – she's young and resilient. She'll get over it, sooner than you think. Remember, she's a wealthy young lady, with lots of decisions and responsibilities in front of her. That alone should keep her occupied for some time – give her a chance to get over Giles."

Cathy nodded and smiled wistfully. It had been a tragic and traumatic time for them all. She still found it difficult to believe Jimmy had been alive all those years. It had been Ken Griffith, his business colleague and trustee, who had telephoned her to break the news of his death, to reveal James Pritchard's true identity! She had been shocked and horrified. James Proctor – her Jimmy – had been the father of Giles. He had deserted both her and the Air Force; gone to

America and married again. Worse still, he had deceived her for nearly forty-five years. She had never felt so shattered and disillusioned!

Then the kindly Ken Griffith had forwarded her the letter Jimmy left in his will. In it, her first husband had bared his soul, tried to explain his actions, begging her forgiveness. He had always loved her, he told her. The revelation had been a balm for her soul.

Now Kate was heir to his vast fortune. It was ironic, she thought, that Jimmy's wealth had been based on advertising, the very career Sam had chosen. Talk about like father, like daughter.

The more she thought about it, the more she understood the fear which had always tormented her husband, which he'd refused to acknowledge – until his final letter to her. She had always known there was some dark Nemesis haunting Jimmy, suspected the understandable fear beneath his show of bravado. It was easy to see how a few dreadful moments of terror had led him down a road with no possible return. The worst of the tragedy had been Jimmy's, not hers – he had suffered far more than she! Eventually her bitterness and disillusionment gave way to a heartfelt sympathy. Poor Jimmy! – and poor Monique.

"You still look worried, my love," she heard Leslie say.

She turned abruptly to him.

"Would you mind if we invited Monique here for a holiday? I feel so sorry for her, losing both Giles and Jimmy within days of one another. And I'm sure she'd like to meet Kate."

He squeezed her hand.

"Of course. That's a sweet thought – especially when you've been through so much yourself."

She turned to him, smiling.

"There you go again, Leslie," she said, taking his hand. "Always thinking of me. You've had to put up with all my problems for so long, you poor thing. Yet you've had very little from me in return."

"I've had plenty in return," he said quickly. "Our relationship has been the most wonderful thing in my life."

And mine too, she thought. She stared at him, her mind suddenly clear. Tenderly she touched the face she knew so well, not knowing whether to laugh or cry.

"I've suddenly realised, Leslie, I love you more than anything in the world. I always have done, I suppose. Why has it taken me over forty years to find out? Why did I always hanker after Jimmy, as if he were the only love of my life" She threw her arms around his neck. "It only occurred to me, just now, that you're exactly what I was looking for all those years ago – unselfish, dependable, loving, completely devoted." She gazed up at him, her eyes shining.

He said nothing, but his thin aesthetic face had split into the broadest of grins. She had never seen him smile like that before!

"How have you put up with me for so long, Leslie?" she asked in wonder. "I've never expressed my feelings like this before. I know you've always been sure of my affection and trust, and we've enjoyed a wonderful marriage together. But you've never ever heard me say the words 'I love you' – until now!"

"But I always KNEW you loved me," he said, simply. "I was never in any doubt, even when you married Jimmy; even though you never said it in so many words, hadn't worked it out for yourself."

He took her in his wiry arms.

"You see Cath, I've always known you better than you know yourself. I always told you we were right together – ever since that night in the Indian restaurant when I finally plucked up enough courage to propose to you. So you see my love, nothing's been missing for me during our years together!"

She laughed with delight.

"One thing's for sure – you'll never cease to amaze me. I do love you!" Then an incredible thought hit her. "Do you realise we've been living in sin for over forty years, and we have two illegitimate children!"

He roared with laughter at the expression on her face, and she couldn't stop grinning herself.

"It's not funny, Leslie," she said, trying to keep the laughter from her eyes, her voice. "Everybody thinks we're a highly respectable married couple." She looked at him archly. "I suppose it's up to me to do it this time. I'm afraid I'm a bit too old to go down on my knees. But here goes." She stepped back and looked up into his warm brown eyes. "Leslie Bourne, will you marry me?"

He hugged her to him.

"I'd love to Mrs Bourne ... I mean Mrs Proctor."

They laughed again, and walked hand in hand up the path, to enjoy once again their favourite view over the sea and the islands.

ends